GATHER THE SHADOWMEN
(THE LORDS OF THE OCEAN)

- The Swashbuckler -

AN EPIC NOVEL BASED ON THE TRUE EXPLOITS OF
CAPTAIN LUKE RYAN
IRISH SWASHBUCKLER & AMERICAN PATRIOT
BENJAMIN FRANKLIN'S MOST DANGEROUS PRIVATEER

Mark M. McMillin

Hephaestus Publishing

GATHER THE SHADOWMEN
(THE LORDS OF THE OCEAN)
Based on the True Exploits of Captain Luke Ryan - A Trilogy
Book One: *The Swashbuckler*

Copyright © Mark M. McMillin, 1999 - 2012; Original U.S. Copyright Office Registration Number/Date: TXu000909136/1999-06-10 (originally submitted under the title *Prince of the Atlantic)*; Reform. 2018

Author's website: www.PrivateerLukeRyan.com

ISBN-13: 978-0-9838179-5-6
ISBN-10: 0-9838179-5-2

Hephaestus Publishing/www.hephaestuspublishing.com

Definition of a Privateer

"Privateers are vessels of war armed and equipped by particular merchants, and furnished with commissions from the State to cruise against and annoy the enemy by taking, sinking, or burning their shipping."

Falconer's Dictionary of the Marine (1768)

Luke Ryan's Obituary

"In the King's Bench prison, Luke Ryan, captain of the Black Prince privateer during the war, who captured more vessels belonging to Great Britain than any other single ship during the war. The various scenes he went through are astonishing. He sailed firm the port of Rush, in Ireland, early in the year 1778, in the Friendship, a smuggling cutter of 18 six-pounders, whose name he afterwards changed to the Black Prince, **and did more injury to the trade of these kingdoms than any single commander ever did.** He was taken in 1781 by one of our ships of war, tried as a pirate at the Old Bailey, condemned, and four different times ordered for execution, but reprieved; and on peace being made, obtained his pardon through the Court of France. In 1781 he had realized near 20,000.l [pound sterling] by his piracies, and lodged this sum in his bankers hands; but having trusted a woman passed her on them as his wife, they suffered her to draw the whole out on his conviction, and she defrauded him of every shilling." **[Emphasis Added.]**

> *- The Gentleman's Magazine: For June 1789 (under Obituary of considerable Persons; with Biographical Anecdotes)*

Table of Contents

Map of the British Isles 1772

Other Works by the Author:

Prince of the Atlantic
Napoleon's Gold
The Butcher's Daughter
Blood for Blood

Introduction

Gather the Shadowmen (The Lords of the Ocean) is one of three books (*Prince of the Atlantic* and *Napoleon's Gold* being the other two) based on the true, but little known exploits, of the extraordinary Captain Luke Ryan and his courageous Irishmen during the American War of Independence. While *Gather the Shadowmen (The Lords of the Ocean)* is technically the first book in the series, the books may be read in or out of sequence.

Privateers were civilian mercenaries (not pirates) who preyed on enemy commercial shipping under a letter of marque sailing on ships owned by private investors. Modern day privateering can be traced back to 17th Century England when the Earl of Warwick in 1649 sent the *Constant-Warwick* out to plunder Spanish galleons carrying New World gold. Spain (and later France) was quick to retaliate with her own privateers.

The main character in our story is a young, 25 year-old Irishman named Luke Ryan, master of the fastest ship on the water, the *Black Prince*. By all accounts, this remarkable individual was a flamboyant leader, a gifted seafarer and a bit of a swashbuckler too. For a time he and his men quietly ran a very profitable smuggling operation between France and Ireland, oblivious to the American War of Independence, until they crossed swords with the British navy one day and suddenly found themselves on the run. To escape the hangman's noose, they needed a plan, they needed sanctuary.

Another important character in our story is the great Doctor Benjamin Franklin who served as America's ambassador to France during the war. The British held thousands of captured American rebels in 'gaols' throughout England and Franklin was deeply troubled by the cruel and barbaric treatment these men were forced to endure. British soldiers routinely starved, beat and killed American prisoners. The Americans were despicable traitors, criminals, not prisoners of war, and many in Parliament intended to hang every one of them for taking up arms against the king after the rebellion was smashed. Our story is about these heroes too.

Franklin did what he could to ease the sufferings of his "unfortunate countrymen" by sending them money for food and clothing and to even finance their prisoner escapes. But money could only do so much and so Franklin tried negotiating prisoner exchanges with the British government. Unfortunately, Franklin had only a handful of British prisoners to bargain with and had no resources to snatch any more.

In walks Ryan with his fast ships, his heavy guns and a willing crew and the old, American diplomat, a preeminent scientist of world renown, and the young, Irish mariner, a common outlaw with a price on his head, forge an unlikely alliance. Franklin gives Ryan the privateering commission he needs (to avoid charges of piracy and treason) and Ryan and his men, armed for battle, waste no time setting out against the British juggernaut to capture prisoners for Franklin.

Just how bad was the plight of American prisoners? Well, the simple statistics are startling. During the war, the Americans lost roughly 4,300 killed on the battlefield compared to the 13,000 American prisoners who died in British custody. Franklin, with Ryan's help, was able to save hundreds, perhaps thousands indirectly.

Ryan's reign of terror lasted less than two years. But during this brief period Ryan and his men won a string of remarkable victories - against overwhelming odds - that truly staggers the imagination and, along the way, they made a bit of history worth perhaps a story or two...

A quick note on style, this story is more about people and the extraordinary events that changed their lives than it is about the technical aspects of sailing a warship or of military tactics. Still, the author has attempted to balance matters by sprinkling enough nautical and military terms throughout the book for the sake of authenticity (for you enthusiasts of authenticity) against adding too much technical jargon that might otherwise bog the flow of the story down (for those who find technical *stuff* tedious). There is a simple Glossary in *Napoleon's Gold* to help the reader to at least distinguish port from starboard and bow from aft and, for the purists among you, at the end of each book there is a section entitled "Separating Fact from Fiction."

Please note that you will find certain grammatical errors, or what we would consider grammatical errors today, in much of the correspondence but the material quoted is authentic (or, in the case of fictional letters, an imitation). Otherwise, any errors or mistakes in the book are mine.

By taking a few strands of historical fact and weaving them together with a bit of imagination, I hope I have spun an enjoyable yarn that all can enjoy. No less importantly, I hope I have done honor to these extraordinary heroes too.

This then, is their story...

Prologue
An Old Sailor's Tale

Amonster nor'easter, dark and menacing, swept up the east coast with an irrational, raw fury, savaging everything in its path - until it found Rhode Island. And there the ungodly storm halted and laid siege to the small safe haven called Newport, railing against its flimsy walls of wood and glass for long days like some berserk demon...

He quickly closed the heavy oak door behind him, shutting out angry winds, and paused at the top of a crude staircase to survey the dimly lit room below. The tavern was smoky, packed and uninviting. As the newcomer brushed flakes of snow off his shoulders heads turned, curious to see what fool had braved the treacherous ice in the night - but they soon looked away again, indifferent. And then he heard, as if coming from some far, distant place, the soft strains of a fiddle. Sad tunes.

He didn't much care for taverns or crowds and suddenly felt very much out of place. And so he was. Impeccably dressed in a fine tailored suit and new topcoat, he stuck out like some raw recruit. The room was filled with mariners - rough, coarse men dressed in rough, coarse clothes. This is where they liked to gather to eat and drink and gamble. And when they had had their fill of those pleasures how they loved to whittle away the hours spinning out their stories.

The newcomer did not drink, he did not gamble. He had come for the stories or, more truthfully, he had come to this particular tavern for one particular story.

He saw a familiar face in the crowd, a man wearing the dark blue jacket of the American navy, and walked down the staircase, keeping a brown leather satchel pressed closely against his chest as he moved. He squeezed through the tables, apologizing profusely to each man he bumped, until he reached the navy man.

"That old fellow over there," he asked the sailor, pointing across the room. "Is he the one you told me about before?"

The sailor casually looked up, followed the length of the newcomer's arm and removed a long-stemmed pipe from his lips. "Ah, 'tis the young Mr. Crook again I see," the sailor replied in the high-pitched accent of a New Englander, pausing to slowly exhale a cloud of gray smoke through badly stained teeth. "A good evenin' to you, young sir. Aye, the old salt sittin' in the corner over there by himself, right you are. He's the one you asked me about earlier."

Crook nodded, carefully picked his way through the crowd, towards the old man sitting in the corner, towards a man who, as the shadows played their tricks, seemed to turn more sinister with each passing step. Years at sea had etched deep lines into the old man's rugged face and a thin gray beard could not hide a jagged, white scar running down the length of his jawbone. Still it was, Crook decided, a handsome face. Despite the warmth of a nearby fire, the old man had not bothered to remove his coat, a shabby, threadbare garment, or his big fur cap. A maroon scarf wrapped around the old man's neck, a tattered piece of cloth with a curious blue crescent moon embroidered on the tip, caught Crook's eye but he knew better than to ask about such things too early on. *Patience...*

Except for its great stone fireplace, the tavern was an unremarkable place. Twin heavy stone columns - five feet high or better - supported the fireplace's massive wood mantel, cut from a ship's timber and adorned with sea themes, intricate carvings, of ships, sea monsters, myths and legends. And over the mantelpiece, mounted cross-wise like two broadswords, hung a pair of impressive 'two flue irons' liberated off some whaler.

The innkeeper walked over and tossed several fresh logs into an already generous fire. The green wood hissed and crackled at him as orange flames tickled the bottom of a black kettle, suspended in midair from a chain held in place by a circle of mermaids - three alluring, cast iron mermaids - rising seductively up from the hearthstone.

Crook could not remember having seen a more impressive or distinctive fireplace. *The great fire*, Crook then realized, *that is why the old fellow comes here.*

Out of courtesy Crook didn't extend his hand. He saw the old man's large hands with their scarred and gnarled knuckles, wrapped firmly around a pewter tankard and assumed the old man might consider shaking hands as something painful, or a nuisance. And he was right.

"Mind if I sit here with you for a spell?" Crook asked with a nervous tone. "Mr. Trevett, your name is John Trevett is it not?"

The old man slowly looked up to find a young man, with smooth skin and a pencil-thin mustache, peering down at him. He took in the younger man's fine clothes, the slicked-back hair parted neatly down the middle and the clean fingernails. He smiled. The young man was doing his best to look older, wiser. *A gentleman*, the old man thought to himself, *and a dandy one at that.* A gentleman was something not much seen down by the waterfront and would offend some in the tavern. But the old man wasn't troubled any.

"Free country mister," he shot back with an Irish brogue.

"Thank you kindly, sir. My name is Crook, ah, Charles Crook. I'm delighted to make your acquaintance, sir. I've heard about you, Mr. Trevett. I write stories, stories for the newspaper. And I've heard you may have a story or two that might be of interest to me, of interest to my paper that is."

The old man looked hard into the young man's eyes. "Can't say that I reads much anymores mister."

"Yes, indeed, well, Mr. Trevett, perhaps I could buy you a drink? Or, if you have an appetite, perhaps supper? We could - talk?"

"*Talk?*"

A runt of a man sitting nearby craned his neck around to look at Crook and burst out laughing. "Old Johnny Trevett thar mister will talk sure enough! Pour him a drink, that'll loosen his tongue. But, fair warnin', once you get him goin' you can't shut him up and who knows what foreign beach you'll wash up on!"

The runt then forced a hardier laugh and glanced around the room looking for support. "An't that so boys?"

Heads bobbed up and down in agreement. A few men even joined the runt in his laughter.

"You're in for a long cruise thar, *mista*!" added a second voice.

The crowd answered the sailor with hoots and howls.

Trevett, nostrils flaring, his gray, bushy eyebrows knotted, drilled into the men taunting him with an icy stare. "Piss off..." he told them all in a booming command voice full of threat.

The taunting instantly stopped. Men gladly returned to their own matters.

Trevett turned to look at Crook. "Pay 'em blitherin' fools no mind, Mr. Crook. 'Em heathens are just jealous because they're all young and ignorant. Young lads got no stories to tell. None of much interest anyhows to seasoned men of good character. With age, for some mind you, thar comes a privilege or two. Bein' interestin' is one of 'em."

"Indeed," Crook replied, still processing the deference given to the grizzled, old man. "Good, good. Are you up for a story?"

"A story? Well, now, the years are a heavy burden for me as you can plainly see. Even a strong man's pride and vanity must yield to the gentle ways of Father Time. Feeble tho', I an't. What kinda story? In a place like this, one hears quiet whispers in the night, hushed rumors and idle gossip - gossip of the troublin' kind. Not for me, I'll tell you plainly. I've got no stomach for fairytales."

Crook ordered a round of drinks and food from a passing tavern maid. He then stood and removed his coat, scarf and gloves, carefully laying each piece of clothing neatly across the back of an empty chair.

The old man reached over to grab a poker from the fire, red hot at the tip, and dunked it in his tankard. The liquid hissed back at him.

Crook cleared his throat. "And I have no talent for writing fiction. Facts, sir. I am interested in facts. I understand you sailed with a man of interest to me, a fellow named Ryan, Luke Ryan?"

That name brought a sudden gleam to the old man's eyes. His lips curled into a thin smile, the kind of smile brought on by some pleasant memory from long past. He drew a deep breath and whistled.

"Aye, I sailed with that rogue true enough! Haven't heard that name in ages. Now thar was a sailor by *Gawd*! Sailed with a lot of men, I did, including time with the American navy. Sailed with Dowlin, Macatter and the Kelly boys too. Sailed with all 'em lads."

"Dowlon, Macatter and who?"

"*Dowlin*, lad. Dowlin... Ha! He was a big, stout Irishman. Real lady's man. Drank like a fish too but knew his business at sea well enough. No fool that one. He and Ryan were close, like brothers they was. Macatter claimed to be from Boston. Called himself Capt'n Wilde. Ha! That man never laid eyes on Boston! He was Irish like the rest of 'em, from County Cork or so I heard. Tough, no nonsense little man. One of O'Keeffe's boys. Nearly Ryan's equal. *Nearly*. Christopher Kelly... Aye, biggest, strongest man - exceptin' for Jumbaaliyia of course - I ever laid eyes on, but greathearted too. Kelly was the kind of fella you could trust with yer life in a bad fix. No better man ever put to sea than old Chris and nary a cross word ever escaped from that good man's lips. Thar was Morgan and Hoar and, well, the whole damn crew was all first-rate. Ryan and Dowlin saw to that. Aye, I sailed with 'em alrighty. Long, long time ago that was lad."

"Truly?"

Trevett paused as if to collect his thoughts. He looked down at his curled fingers and sighed.

"I'm old now. My hands are useless and me poor old eyes aren't what they used to be. But the brain is workin' just fine, thank'ee very kindly. As if it had happened yesterday, I remember it all."

Crook nodded while absently smoothing his slick, black hair back with the palm of his hand. "Yes, excellent. That is the story I wish to hear. How grand! Would you talk to me about Luke Ryan, Mr. Trevett?"

"Luke Ryan? You wants to know about *Ryan*?"

"Yes. Indeed I do. About him and all the men who sailed with him actually. The whole story, from beginning to end."

The old man sipped his drink, smacked his lips with approval and then narrowed his eyes at Crook. "Well, now, queer that is mister. Most people want to know about famous old Commodore John Paul Jones. Sailed with him too, *Gawd* rest his soul. Jones died in Paris a pauper in

'92. Not quite a hero's death, eh? But he was a quarrelsome, boastful sort and didn't have many friends at the end. Anyway, I sailed with a lot of ships and a lot of captains. But I'll tell you the truth of it young pup. *Now listen well...*"

Trevett leaned over the table until he was nose-to-nose with Crook. "Never sailed with a braver or better man than Luke Ryan," he said in a deeper voice, a more serious tone. "He was fearless. Like a fox he was. I swear that man could've out-sailed the devil himself. Knew how to read the hearts and minds of men too. A *real* leader. Catch my drift?"

Trevett saw the blank expression on Crook's face. "See here lad. There aren't many truly good ship's masters around. Some men are good seaman, you understand, because they know thar ships and they knows the sea. Some men are good leaders because they knows how to inspire thar crew to work hard and they knows how to rouse thar fightin' spirit when needs be. Sad to say, but very few capt'ns nowadays are both good seaman and good leaders. But Ryan knew the way of it. We woulda followed him anywhere - and the money be damned. Now you see?"

Crook felt his blood stir and nodded eagerly again. He cleared his throat to try and deepen his own voice. "Those must have been heady times, Mr. Trevett."

"Aye. That's a fact, lad," Trevett answered while leaning back in his chair. "Those were excitin' times sure enough. Giants walked the Earth back then and not just the ones you read about in yer books and papers." He paused to wink at Crook. "Of course, thar were pygmies too runnnin' about. Seemed as if the whole damn world was at war with itself. This country fought old King George and beat him and all his men and ships at sea sure enough. I done my part. We won our liberty. Doubt 'em young baboons sittin' over thar understand what liberty means, exceptin' for the freedom they have for drinkin' and whorin' about town."

While Trevett nodded at his own words in satisfaction and chuckled, the young reporter reached into his waistcoat, removed a pair of wire-rimmed spectacles and carefully set them over his nose and ears. Then he reached into his satchel, removed a sheaf of blank paper, a quill pen and an ink jar and, after laying each item out on the table with meticulous care, dipped his pen into the ink and began scribbling words across the paper.

"You get that scar on your jaw sailing with Ryan?" Crook asked as he wrote.

Trevett laughed. "No son, 'fraid not. I got this beauty-mark from bein' stupid, from slippin' on some ice down the street here in town a few months back." He unbuttoned his coat, pulled up his shirt to expose his chest and, with a wide grin, pointed to a round white spot on his shoulder. "Now this here scar was made by a musket ball - a gift from the English. And this, this here slash across my gut, a Mameluke's scimitar did this to me in Egypt back in '99. I was with Ryan on both occasions."

As Crook looked up and smiled at the scars the old man tucked his shirt back inside his pants and slowly began buttoning up his coat. It was a difficult task for scarred, old fingers.

"You like writin', do you?" Trevett asked.

"Yes. Yes, I do," Crook replied as he resumed writing.

"You'll be puttin' this stuff in a book or in yer paper?"

"I'd like to write some articles about your story. Whether any of it is ever published or not I can't honestly say."

The old man slowly brought the pewter tankard to his lips with one hand, leaving the other resting on the table, its stiff fingers curled as if wrapped around some invisible object. He drained his tankard with one, long gulp.

"Hm. No matter mister young reporter. If yer buyin' the drinks I suppose I've got some time for ya. Good Lord hasn't seen fit to take me yet. Aye, I've got time. It's a long story, a handsome story and well-bred. And what I says to you about what I seen is the truth, no sailor's tall tales from me. Other things I says to you is from what different mates, mostly Kelly and Dowlin, told me 'cause I weren't thar yet. They was honest men tho'. I'll be needin' to wet me pipes now and then. I was drinkin' a rather tasty spiced punch earlier. To get the blood flowin'. You should give it a try. It's a house favorite. But with nary a drop left, now I think I'll change course here and go with Jolly Fellows with a maybe a whiskey chaser or two. And I don't cares to have my Jolly Fellows rationed out one gill at a time like aboard ship. Full tankard, hey? Hope you brought yer purse with you."

"Jolly what?"

"*Grog*, lad."

Crook again reached into his waistcoat, removed a money purse and tossed the fat bag on the center of the table with a broad smile. The coins made a pleasant clinking sound as they tumbled around. Then he took another clean sheet of paper and started writing again.

Soon half the tavern had gathered around their table to listen to Trevett spin out his tale and Crook quickly realized that the old man had a gift. Trevett recounted his adventures in such vivid detail, and with such passion, the story seemed to come alive...

Chapter One
A Man of Action

Somewhere in the Atlantic, December 1776

ow the gods who never die, and with wry humor, love to lavish good fortune, even glory, on those of us who please them - but how quick they are to snatch it back again when man, made of only dust, dares to seek his own divinity. Men, from birth, are doomed...

There on the quarterdeck, staring out across the deep and boundless sea like some immovable, bronze statue, stood - born and bred - a *soldier*. The young lieutenant ran his fingers through a tangled mass of black hair, wavy like the sea, looked up and took in the clear, blue heavens. The sun felt good against his skin. But then he saw, on the far horizon, great, billowing clouds gathering themselves in force. He sniffed the air and felt the change, the slightest shift, in the sea's ever-playful winds - and that familiar twinge along his spine. He had a nose for the weather. A storm was brewing. He removed his pocket watch, a gift to himself when he had made lieutenant, and popped open its gilt metal outer case covered in dark shagreen. *Two, maybe three hours...*

Despite his youth, Luke Roberts was now the acting first officer of His Majesty's Ship *Rose*, consumption having taken the man before him. At first, his new responsibilities had made him nervous and uncertain.

But now he wore the mantle of power with ease, as if he had been born to it. Command suited him.

And the *Rose* suited him too. She was small and swift with lovely lines - one of the successful Seaford Class frigates built in '57 at the shipyards in Hull. Her helm was remarkably forgiving and she had proven her quality to Roberts more than once in both tricky breezes and uneven seas.

Roberts was new to the frigate, having barely stepped aboard the *Rose* just before her departure from the waters off Long Island following his long, tedious journey across the North Atlantic in a cramped troop transport from Portsmouth. He hadn't even had a chance to set foot on American soil and had missed all the hot action earlier that summer too when the men of the *Rose* had covered themselves in glory supporting the British Army's invasion of Manhattan.

But he had no regrets about that. Roberts had no interest in fighting Colonial rebels and had, in fact, been sorely disappointed when he received orders sending him to the American theater.

He slipped his watch back into his waistcoat, used his sleeve to wipe away the spray of salt water on his face. It was neither a handsome nor a plain face, or so he thought. But even Roberts knew that he had been blessed with a face rich in character. His eyes were clear and intelligent, the kind that seemed to hold some mysterious wisdom from an age long past. But they were sad eyes too. He had a ready smile and a strong, square chin and liked to keep his wavy hair cut short. No braided queue for him. For the crew it was a face that exuded confidence and trust - and that was all that mattered.

Roberts looked over at the officer of the watch, gave the order to have the ship readied for foul weather. The junior officer saluted, barked out instructions to the division commanders and men jumped to.

And when the night chased down the day, the fearsome god of storm and thunder marshaled *his* towering thunderheads, tar black and menacing, into one great phalanx and unloosed an unholy power against the Earth. Savage, cold winds and sheets of rains lashed at the sea without mercy, transforming her into an untamable beast. She howled back in agony, thrashing, arching her broad back, sending huge swells - brute force to stagger the imagination - rolling across the surface.

And as the frightful gale raged on, creatures above and below the sea hid themselves away in darkness. But not the men of the *Rose*. Proud and resolute, they refused to cower before the berserk god's awesome power. They suffered stinging rains and punishing waves, one after the other, without complaint and did all that was in their power to keep their ship afloat.

For three harrowing days brave, frightened men clung desperately on to rope and wood, on to anything secure, as their ship pitched and rolled violently in the heavy seas. Sails shredded, lines snapped and, at the darkest hour, every man on deck - save one - thought they would all perish.

But not even a god's fury can last forever. On the morning of the third day, once the storm god had ceased his mindless rage, Dawn managed to pierce the gray horizon open with a sliver of silver light. The winds went slack. The heavy rains turned to drizzle. And, for reasons men born of the Earth are not given to know, the bundle of wood christened *Rose* was allowed to pass - but not without a price, a blood-price.

Unable to sleep, and anxious to know whether the gale was truly tapering-off after a young midshipman had whispered through his door that he had seen light on the horizon, Roberts buttoned-up his wool jacket, still damp from his prior watch, and left the relative comfort of his small cabin to go and stand vigil with the night watch.

He held his collar closed with one hand, gripped the rail with the other to keep his balance as he stepped on to the quarterdeck and then, through the darkness, he saw it. He saw the *Wall* and it was coming for *him*. A rogue wave - a huge, terrifying mass of water - was racing towards the *Rose*, threatening to topple her.

Roberts spun around to face the sailor at the wheel, a big, beefy Scotsman named McDunn. "Look lively there helmsman!" he cried out, loud enough to be heard over the wind. "Another monster's coming. To your starboard side! Steady, hold fast... *Brace yourself lad!*"

And then - *SWOOSH!* Tons of foaming seawater came cascading over the bulwarks, knocking the ship hard over.

Roberts found himself buried under black water. He kicked and clawed his way towards the bubbles, frantically trying to reach the surface, but his clothes were heavy and dragged him down. Something punched him in the side and he gulped down seawater. He offered up a quick prayer, dumbfounded that this was his end.

But then, his head popped up above the waves. He sucked down air so fast his lungs burned. By some miracle the ship had righted herself, had refused to capsize, and by the same miracle Roberts found himself still on board, his foot entangled in some rigging. He was astonished by his good fortune but, then again, he knew it was not his fate to die at sea.

As he leaned over the rail and coughed up salt water, he saw, out of the corner of his eye, the stout Scotsman McDunn, white-faced and shaking but still standing at the helm gripping the ship's wheel. The big man managed to give him a weak smile.

But two seamen standing on the quarterdeck with them had not been so lucky. Roberts franticly searched the ship's wake for the missing men, called out for help, but he knew it was hopeless. A hungry sea had bolted both men down whole without a trace.

Roberts spotted his hat, a black bi-corner and frayed around the edges, wedged inside a coil of rope. He retrieved his hat, used it to shield his eyes from the drizzle, and gazed up at the *Rose's* three tall masts, taking measure of the ship's trim, tack and the wind. Then he reached inside his coat to remove a chart, wrapped in oilskin, and carefully unrolled the heavy paper over the rail and began making some crude calculations. Later he would use the ship's chronometer to get a more precise fix on the ship's position but, for now, it was enough to know that they were still safely in deep water somewhere northeast of Bermuda Island.

He took in the condition of the *Rose* next. Piles of wreckage littered her decks and the petty officers were already forming their work details to begin the task of cleaning-up and making repairs. At the foremast a dozen men, pulling on rope and tackle, began hoisting a new spar into position to replace one that had been carried away by mischievous winds.

And below he could hear the bilge pumps too, churning out bubbling brine at a steady, but not hurried, pace. They had been, all-in-all, very lucky. The damage was not great.

And as the sun struggled to break through the clouds, he took in the crew, watched men stitch torn sails and splice snapped lines. Others brought stacks of new lumber up from the ship's belly for the carpenter. The main deck was soon a beehive of activity. Officers and ratings alike, hollow-eyed with empty bellies - misery has no prejudices - went about their tasks efficiently, quietly and with few complaints.

A few feet away a careless seaman dropped a precious length of planking overboard. Roberts, despite his weariness, did not lash out at the man. And that pleased him. There was discipline in that and he understood the power of discipline. Except for loyalty, and friendship, it was the one quality he cherished above all others.

And then a friend caught his eye. Patrick James Dowlin, an Irishman and recently promoted to acting second lieutenant, because of a shortage of officers and with Roberts's help, was holding a line to maintain his footing near the mainmast and bellowing out orders to the work details. Dowlin and Roberts had gone to sea together as boys and were as close as brothers.

In looks and build, the big Irishman stood apart from all others. Exquisitely handsome, tall and muscular - a match for any of the deathless gods - his dark, smoldering eyes were impossible to look away from, or all too easy to avoid, depending on the grit of the other. And like Roberts, Dowlin's eyes were filled with power, more raw, less refined perhaps, but there was no mistaking the power in his eyes. He wore his fiery, red hair long and wild like a lion's mane and wherever he went, the big Irishman drew jealous stares from men and women alike and children, unafraid, flocked to him in droves for no discernible reason. *Odysseus Reborn*, Roberts fondly liked to call him though, truly, he was far more like another. Despite his beauty, Dowlin had somehow managed to avoid the sin of vanity, which only seemed to enhance his appeal.

Dowlin caught Roberts watching him. He smiled back. "Fine day for a sail, sir!" he offered cheerfully. The man was forever cheery.

"Indeed it is, Mr. Dowlin," Roberts agreed, stretching out his arms to relieve the dull aches and taut muscles. "I take it there is nothing to report on the two men swept overboard?"

"'Fraid not, Luke. Hopefully they are in a better place."

"A better place, aye. I did not even know their names."

"Whitmore and the Swede, Jensen."

"Ah, Whitmore and Jensen..." Roberts said, repeating the names softly with as much reverence as he could muster for men he barely knew. "I'll have your damage report as soon as you can manage it, Mr. Dowlin."

"And so you shall have it straight away, sir!" the Irishman answered with a laugh and disappeared below to find the ship's carpenter.

Roberts's thoughts then turned to hot coffee. *Foolish.* He knew there would be none. Whenever the seas turn rough, the ship's cook extinguishes the galley fires. Hard biscuits and cold salt pork had been the only fare for breakfast, lunch and supper for the past three days. He reached into his pocket for a piece of hardtack, given to him earlier by the ship's kindly old steward, but found only a lump of soggy goo and sighed. At least the drizzle had finally stopped and that was something. A sailor learns to take his comforts, no matter how small, wherever he can find them.

And then - his world changed forever...

"*Sail ho!*" the ship's lookout cried down from the masthead.

"*What?*" Roberts whispered to himself doubtfully, surprised another ship had failed to make port and survived the killer gale. But he knew the sailor at the masthead; the man was a seasoned veteran with a sharp eye.

Roberts looked up at the sailor and cupped his hands. "Where away?" he shouted.

"Fine on yer port bow, Lieutenant, and headin' north by nor' east. Square rigged and, by the cut of her sail, I suspect I'm lookin' at a *warship...*"

Square-rigged meant a battle cruiser or larger. Roberts grabbed his spyglass, tried to catch a glimpse of the vessel. He instantly regretted the silly gesture. The waves were still too high. He could see nothing but rolling water. Embarrassed, he quickly collapsed his scope, hoping McDunn at the wheel behind him was not grinning. The thought of being the object of some sailor's joke at the breakfast table was loathsome to Roberts.

"Mr. Wilcox, as a precaution, I'll have the deck cleared for action."

"Aye, sir! Petty officers! To stations! Boatswain, pipe the ship to battle ready!"

The boatswains' whistle twittered loudly. A small boy, dressed in the red coat and white cross belts of a Royal Marine, suddenly appeared on deck with his drum and began tapping out a lively cadence. Petty officers barked out orders to the ratings and men scrambled.

Roberts had helped train these men - men geared for war - had spent long hours in repetitive drills with them. His heart filled with pride as he watched them spring into action.

"Mr. Wilson," Roberts called out to a midshipman, a *man* who was little more than a boy. "If you please, go forward and fetch Mr. Higginbotham, pass along my compliments. Tell him to take the masthead. I want to know what ship lies off our port bow. I want to know her type, her armament, her distance and her speed. And I want accurate information mind you well there, boy!"

Roberts thought about climbing up into the rigging himself, to get a better view of things, but quickly decided against it. Less wobbly legs than his were needed in such tricky waters and, besides, Higginbotham, a feisty, little Turk despite his English surname, had the keenest eye of any man on board the *Rose*. The Turk also possessed an amazing knowledge about a wide variety of ships. Whether it was British, French or Spanish, Higginbotham could often identify the warship, describe the quality of her crew and rattle off the number and size of her guns with eerie accuracy. Sometimes he even had an interesting tidbit or two about the ship's captain to share.

"Aye, aye, sir!" Wilson replied excitedly, honored by the lieutenant's trust in him to carry out such an important task. The boy saluted smartly and ran down the deck, eager to prove his worth.

Within minutes Higginbotham was up in the masthead and reported seeing *two* ships: a fair size sloop-of-war with white gun port bands, flying the stars and stripes of an American vessel and, sailing at her side, a larger ship, a frigate, flying the French *fleur de lys*. Higginbotham then reported seeing the smaller American ship peeling off, heading north, while the French ship pressed on, sailing east on a parallel course with the *Rose*. And then, in a dangerous show of force, a dare, he saw the French gunners opening the ship's gun ports.

Curious, thought Roberts. The French and British were not at war with one another. Or perhaps the two nations were at war and the news had not yet reached the *Rose*? War or not, incidents at sea were not uncommon between the two jealous super powers and France, neutral or not, had started openly supplying arms and money to the Americans to support their tiny rebellion against the British.

The reasons hardly mattered. Seamen risked life and limb on the king's command - with or without good reason.

On board the Continental sloop *Reprisal*, an elderly, bowlegged gentleman with long, stringy hair, resting in curls around his shoulders, gingerly picked his way across a cluttered deck with the use of a walking stick. Ambling across a pitching deck was not an easy task for old legs and the Philadelphian was no seaman. For days, the awful November gale had kept him cooped-up in his tiny, foul-smelling cabin. His good humor had disappeared with the good weather.

He had heard the ship's lookout cry out his warning, immediately left his quarters and hurried up the companionway to find the ship's master. He soon spotted Captain Lambert Wickes, found the captain on the quarterdeck looking at the sea through his spyglass.

"Trouble, Captain?" the old man asked with a hint of anxiety in his voice.

"Aye, your Excellency," replied Wickes and collapsed his telescope. "British frigate, over there. Looks to be about a sixth rater, to our starboard. Bad luck that is. They must have cut through this abominable storm same as us. We'll sheer off to the north and let the French have their fun with her. No need to be alarmed, sir. With our lead and speed, a frigate is no match for us in these seas. I'll honor my duty, sir. I've been charged by the Committee of Secret Correspondence of Congress with delivering you to France safe and sound and, by God, that's just what I shall do. Rest assured of that, your Excellency."

The older man nodded appreciatively. "I am grateful for your resolve, Captain Wickes." Satisfied that all was well, and shivering from the biting winds, he made his way back to his cabin, eager to return to his reading.

Despite his advanced age, Congress had appointed him to be one of three American commissioners to the Court of King Louis the XVI and Captain Wickes was expected to deliver him safely to France, across a hostile ocean infested with British warships.

The name Doctor Benjamin Franklin would have meant nothing to Roberts and Good Fortune would not allow their paths to cross. No, not yet...

Strong currents and contrary winds kept driving the two frigates closer. No man born of flesh and blood has the power to deny the war god his pleasure. That abomination - how he loves to straddle the world shaking his great spear, his lust for death and gore never sated.

With decks cleared for action, Roberts gave the order to load and run out the guns. No man tarried. Men flung open gun ports and smartly pushed the noses of their two-ton monsters out through the bulwarks. The deck vibrated under the rolling weight.

At 1,000 yards, the French, impatient always and forever glory-mad, cracked the peaceful sky with their heavy, bronze cannon. Muzzle flashes seared the air. Puffs of white smoke rolled across the waves, followed seconds later by the nerve-shattering sound of exploding black powder.

BOOM! BOOM! BOOM! BA-BA-BA-BOOM!

The men of the *Rose* braced themselves for pain.

But the blue-maned god of the sea, the Earthshaker, foul-tempered, unpredictable, true, but cursed with an affection in his cold heart for the island mariners, took his great trident, stirred the ocean's depths and, from nowhere, a wall of water, like the shield of a mighty warrior raised high to ward off a glancing blow, suddenly emerged between the two ships. Not one French ball found its mark in wood, flesh or sail. Shots wasted. Overzealous French gunners had fired too low and too soon. A second French volley fared no better.

As captains of men are want to do, Roberts stood in plain view, exuding confidence, showing no fear. He appeared taller, stronger to all eyes. Shots whistled overhead, but the cool tactician stood fast, calmly churning out ideas until one plan, brazen and bold, seemed best. He smiled at the lovely thoughts doing pirouettes in his mind but then shook his head in disgust when he saw French iron plunging into an empty sea. *A poor waste of precious ball and powder*, he whispered to himself.

He considered the winds and currents again. He considered the position and battle strength of the enemy. The American ship was nearly over the horizon now and Roberts decided to ignore her. The French 36 gunner was the threat. At a length of 108 feet and armed with only 20 carriage guns, nine-pounders at that, with a complement of only 160 men, the *Rose* was a small, sixth rate frigate and outclassed. He could not afford to engage the French in a slugfest head on. But he would not run either and had no intention of spending monotonous hours maneuvering for position.

BOOM! BOOM! BOOM! BA-BA-BA-BOOOOOOOM!

More shots whistled over the rails, ripped through sails and fell into the empty sea beyond causing no real damage. Still, plumes of white water kept creeping closer and closer to the *Rose*. Men looked anxiously up at Roberts, hoping for the order to return fire. But Roberts gave no such order and stood fast, showing no emotion.

He owed the men that much at least he told himself. No, he corrected himself as he kept his eye on the French. *I owe these good men much more. Wait. Wait...*

Then Roberts searched the deck for Dowlin, soon saw the big

Irishman pacing up and down the row of guns and scores of sweaty men, stopping here and there to double-check equipment, fine-tune the position of a gun or two while offering words of encouragement to each and every man. It struck Roberts that Dowlin actually seemed to be having fun.

"Mr. *Dowlin!*" he called out in a calm voice. "The Captain - has the Captain been informed of our situation?"

Only a dead man would have been oblivious to the violence swirling around them. But Roberts was not a man who asked frivolous questions.

Dowlin understood, cupped his hands to his mouth and answered Roberts back in a thick Irish brogue. "Aye, sir!" I informed him just minutes ago - with yer compliments, of course! I was about to make my way back to you to report. Capt'n's down again with the gout and some crippling stomach ailment..."

Roberts muttered a curse under his breath. Captain Bartholomew Langley Hughes was the interim master of the *Rose* while her true captain, a man named James Wallace, a hero of the invasion of Manhattan earlier in July and hated by Rhode Islanders everywhere for his ruthless attacks on their smuggling trade prior to the rebellion, had remained behind in British occupied New York to recover from a bout of severe dysentery when the *Rose* sailed. Somewhere in his past Hughes had, perhaps, been an able seaman. Roberts didn't know. But Roberts did know is that Hughes was not now, nor would he ever be, a soldier. No soldier would shrink below deck with cannon booming overhead and leave the fate of his ship, his crew, in the hands of some junior officer - no matter how grave his illness. No, Hughes, Roberts was certain, was drunk again, too drunk to leave his cabin.

Roberts mulled the matter over, his thoughts torn. Confront the coward now or let the matter lay? Dark anger, the nemesis of all men, seized him with a strong grip.

Dowlin caught the look in Roberts's eyes, could see trouble brewing, and quickly made his way back to the quarterdeck. Roberts's growing intolerance of the captain over the past few weeks had not escaped Dowlin's notice.

And then the world turned ugly.

Some Frenchman adept at gunnery had figured out the range, or was lucky. An iron ball smashed into one of *Rose's* guns, just as Dowlin passed it by, flipping both gun and carriage over. Jagged shards of wood flew through the air. Men screamed and fell to nasty, painful splinter wounds. And then a second gun suddenly broke free from its tackles. The mindless beast rolled backwards, crashed through a belaying pin rack, shattering it like some flimsy fence, and didn't stop rolling until it hit the mainmast where it pinned a seaman's leg, cutting flesh and crushing bone.

Dowlin coolly ignored the chaos swirling all around him, kept moving aft, towards the helm. *Damn Frogs*, he cursed under his breath, *are gettin' too cocky by half!*

Men rushed to help fallen comrades.

"*Belay that!*" Roberts shouted angrily at them all. "Save for that man pinned against the mast - get that damn thing off of him and take him below! I want those guns secured - NOW! The guns first! Then tend to the wounded!"

Petty officers saw to it that his commands were obeyed at once. Every sailor understood. Nothing but the guns mattered. Nothing but the guns could save them, keep them off a French prison barge.

A dozen burly sailors pounced on the two-ton man-killer and began securing it against the bulkhead with line and tackle. No easy task on a rolling deck.

Roberts watched sailors carry off the man with the crushed leg and felt pity. He knew the ship's surgeon was waiting below with his sharp blades and saws for just such a trophy. *God spare me from such a fate.* Far better, to the thinking of a young man, to die straight off than live out your days disfigured or crippled.

And then the Turk caught his eye. Higginbotham was laughing at two boys, young, pale, wide-eyed boys with bags of black powder slung around their sweaty necks. The boys had been tasked with bringing gunpowder up from the ship's magazine and distributing it among the gunners. Hard work for young legs.

"You little powder monkeys had best keep yer heads down or you'll be losin' 'em quick enough!" Higginbotham called after them in a raspy voice. But his tone was laced with kindness too. He gave them a reassuring smile. "Get along with you now. Work safe and I'll put in a good word for you two rascals later with the ship's cook for extra portions of puddin' tonight."

The boys grinned back at him, crouched lower, and cautiously picked their way across the gun deck.

Roberts nodded his approval, decided he would have the boys report below to the surgeon later if things turned really hot.

The battle grew more desperate. French sharpshooters - perched high up in the rigging - added their killing talents to the carnage. Musket balls drilled into the *Rose* now and more men fell.

The French storm was gathering strength and every heart - weak and strong – filled itself with ugly hate. Men mad to kill - pitted against men mad to live - braced themselves for the coming horror.

On board the French frigate, her captain watched the British with curiosity, perplexed by English inaction. But neither the master of the French ship nor his men had any intention of easing up against their hated rival, France's eternal foe. No, never. And though they rarely made good sailors, always the French were brave.

Eager to close with the enemy, the French captain gave the order to take in the mainsail, to slow their frigate down, allow the British to draw nearer...

Dowlin scurried up the ladder leading to the quarterdeck. He flinched when a piece of deadly debris flew past his head, barely missing him. "*Sweet Jesus!*" he said out loud to no one in particular, "*I'm goin' to kill me a Frog today...*"

The big Irishman snapped to attention in front of Roberts, saluted with a touch to the brim of his hat. "Sir," he said excitedly, the words came tumbling out, "we're closin' fast! 'Em Frogs just about got their range and timin' on us!"

Another officer might have taken exception to Dowlin's superfluous remarks, especially after leaving his post in the midst of all the hot action, and given the junior officer a good dressing-down at the end of the day. But Roberts knew Dowlin's mind. Inexperience had breathed life into the Irishman's words, not stupidity. This was Dowlin's first action wearing the insignia of an officer.

Roberts offered no reply at first. He kept his gaze fixed on the French instead, then smiled when he saw them pulling in sail.

"Mr. Roberts, the lads are anxious and ready to give it to 'em!" Can I give the order, sir? Sir? Luke, Luke - can you hear me, are you all right?"

Roberts felt the ship stray slightly, spun around and took a step towards the ship's wheel. In a low voice he admonished, but not too harshly, the sailor at the helm. "Hold the ship's course steady now, Hawkins! She requires your full attention there."

"Aye, aye, sir!" Hawkins answered crisply, taking no offense. "Steady-as-she-goes."

"Time is our friend," Roberts said softly with confidence. Not the kind of false confidence forged from crass and noisy arrogance but a quiet, confidence that comes naturally, intuitively, from within.

But like many who are blessed with keen intelligence, Roberts's poise was but a thin veneer. Underneath the façade brooded a soul perpetually filled with self-doubt. He did his best to hide it.

If he had sized up his opponent correctly, the French captain's plan was simple and straightforward. No guile, no maneuver for position. No, the Frenchman needed none of that with his advantage in heavy cannon. And the French captain's surprising decision to reduce sail - and speed - only confirmed his true intentions for Roberts. Maintain his present course and speed, bring his bigger guns to bear against the British frigate and then pound her into kindling wood. That was the Frenchman's plan, his tactic, his gambit to win new *gloire*. But Roberts intended to use French arrogance to his advantage - if only the sea's fickle winds and tricky currents would hold for just a bit longer...

He turned to face Dowlin. "Mr. Dowlin, you say the Captain is unable to take the deck, not well enough to take command?"

"Aye."

"You saw him?"

"Aye."

"Well, man," Roberts said with a hostile tone. "Don't make me drag it out of you! Has he been drinking?"

"Aye, sir, I believe so," Dowlin answered sheepishly, studying Roberts carefully. He had seen the mystery in Roberts's eyes - had seen the sadness there too - and always marveled at what he saw.

Roberts, jaw clenched, placed his hand on the hilt of his sword, a sword he had purchased new with his last guinea back in Portsmouth, and pulled the blade out an inch or so from the scabbard.

"Goddamnit," he cursed, lapsing into an *Irish* brogue, "I swear the first blood this new English steel of mine will taste will be *English!*"

Dowlin looked nervously around to see if anyone had overheard Roberts. Only Dowlin and a few of the Irish hands knew that Roberts wasn't English. He was Irish through-and-through. As a boy, Roberts had taught himself to speak and act like a proper English gentleman and had succeeded in passing himself off as the son of an impoverished English merchant, a minor nobleman and near-do-well who had lost his fortune in France. Dowlin never really understood the deception. Certainly, there were prejudices in the British Navy and advancement for officers was difficult for anyone not English. Hughes was proof enough of that. Hughes loathed *Irishmen*. No one could accuse an ambitious man of being a fool for trying to hide his Irish roots. Whatever Roberts's motives, Dowlin didn't care as Roberts was, by far, the cleverest man he knew and his best friend.

"Bloody hell! For the love of *Christ*, Luke," Dowlin pleaded. The French frigate was very close now, Hughes was in no condition to take command and Roberts was talking mutiny! He was at a loss.

And then a grizzled giant of a man straddled up next to Roberts and gently laid a large hand on Roberts's shoulder before the lieutenant could say more. "Steady now, sir," Christopher Kelly urged with a voice like rolling thunder. "Please, sir. The lads will be needin' you directly, thar an't no one else to do the job. Our lives are in yer good care."

Roberts understood Kelly's tone. The enormous Irishman towering over him meant no harm. There was no threat, no insult. Kelly was trying to protect him, nothing more.

But the odd commotion on the quarterdeck caught the eye of a royal marine, of Lieutenant Beasley Hanson, who had been forming up his men into squads when he saw Kelly's curious actions and thought them odd. Ratings didn't touch officers, ever. And Hanson didn't fancy Roberts very much. The first officer was soft and much too chummy with the crew, especially with the unsavory, uncouth Irishmen. Perhaps some treachery was afoot or maybe the smug young lieutenant was the coward Hanson had always suspected him to be. Hanson instructed his sergeant, an older man, but tough like seasoned English oak, to take command while he made his way back to the quarterdeck with two royal marines in tow.

Roberts eased the hilt of his sword back into its scabbard. "'Tis all right, Patrick," he offered calmly, then looked up at Kelly. "Steady there, lad. I know my duty and you know yours. Best return to your station now."

"Mr. *Roberts!*" Hanson called out with no charity in his voice as he bolted up the quarterdeck ladder, eyes full of threat.

Then, just below the quarterdeck, a projectile hit the water, showering them all with cold, sticky salt water.

Hanson looked at Roberts with disdain. "What the devil is going on here?" he demanded.

With a boxer's powerful arms, and a neck as thick as a tree trunk, Kelly took a step forward. "Aw now, sir, sorry, sir," he offered in his thick Irish brogue. "No problems here. I thought Mr. Roberts was about to take a spill and go over the side with that last evil roller so's I grabbed him. 'Twas close tho'."

Kelly turned to Roberts and made a knuckle. "Beggin' yer pardon, sir. Didn't mean to startle ya any. I meant no harm."

Hanson raised a sharp eyebrow at Kelly. The seaman's unsolicited remarks brought him no joy. Sailors were an undisciplined lot and could never be trusted.

"How dare you address your superior officer without first being spoken to!" he fumed. "You'll hold your tongue mister unless you enjoy the sting of the whip. I'll have you flogged!"

Kelly offered no reply, just stared down at the Lieutenant of Marines. Hanson felt fear.

"Mr. Hanson," interrupted Roberts in a level voice. "What Seaman

Kelly said is quite true. He did me the courtesy of preventing my fall over the rail. Now, if you'll *kindly* return to your station, sir, before matters get away from us..."

Dowlin winced at hearing the word *kindly*. There was never anything kind about Roberts's use of the word. It was a warning, though Dowlin figured Hanson was too thick to pick up on it.

The dislike between Roberts and Hanson had been mutual from the beginning.

Roberts had seen the joy in Hanson's eyes whenever an unruly crewman was punished. The man's heart was as cold as the steel in his sword. Even his own marines were terrified of him. Roberts disliked him for his cruelty.

Hanson had decided early on that the aloof, soft-spoken first lieutenant was not up to the task of command. And he was too chummy with the men. He didn't trust Roberts.

Hanson knew there was more going on than he understood. "Lieutenant Roberts," he began, with an air of British haughtiness, "I fail to understand how it is..."

Roberts cut him off. "Mr. Hanson! *I* am presently in command of this ship. "Did you not hear *my* orders? Return to your station, sir! Attend to your men at once - unless you would prefer charges. I am not in the habit of repeating my orders to subordinates, nor am I obliged to debate them!"

A scowl passed across Hanson's face. *This cocksure fool needs a good beating.* And it would have pleased Hanson enormously to be the one to administer the lesson. Perhaps even a duel could be arranged at the end of their cruise. *Now that would be satisfying!*

Then a voice from below interrupted them all.

"Mr. Roberts, the last I knew, *I* was in command of this ship!" growled Hughes with contempt.

The three officers spun around to see Hughes standing on the deck, half dressed in soiled britches, frayed stockings and a dirty, white linen shirt stained with blotches of red wine and what looked like vomit. Hughes stepped backwards, into the shelter of the companionway, as if some harm might come to him if he ventured out too far on deck.

"What is our situation, Mr. Roberts?" Hughes asked.

Roberts heard the malice in the captain's tone and considered Hughes carefully. *God, the insufferable arrogance.*

Gray stubble covered the captain's receding chin. A crescent-shaped slice of fat protruded from a half unbuttoned shirt. The ship's frugal rations hadn't harmed Hughes any. The wind toyed with the loose strands of his thin, disheveled hair, making him appear far older than his age.

Hughes's appearance was comical. But no one laughed.

Roberts swallowed hard. "Sir, I sent Mr. Dowlin earlier to you to report. We sighted a French frigate, a thirty-six gunner. She was providing escort to a smaller, American vessel but the Americans have slipped away, heading due north. I gave the order to clear the decks for action. The French fired first. The lads are ready for a fight, sir and, with your permission, Captain, I intend to engage the enemy forthwith. That is unless, of course, you feel fit enough to assume command yourself..."

Hughes shifted his cold stare away from Roberts and took in the gray clouds swirling above their heads. He squinted from the glare, frowned at what he saw.

"Awful weather this, not very suitable for action," he snorted while absently scratching his exposed belly. "The French you say? Firing on us? Queer that is. We must finally be at war with the bastards. Good. The French. Humph! Gluttonous, lazy miscreants. The whole country stinks of rot. Very well then, about time we gave them another decent drubbing."

"Your orders, Captain?"

"Mr. Roberts, understand this," Hughes grumbled in carefully measured tones, still taking in the heavens and avoiding eye contact with Roberts. "It is with the king's pleasure that I command this ship and I shall remain in command until either Captain Wallace recovers or the Lords of the King's Admiralty, in their wisdom, decide otherwise. Aye, *my* orders. Well, sir, you will do your utmost to maneuver us away from the enemy and not engage. Return fire if you must to defend the ship certainly but you are to withdraw at the first opportunity. Keep the good

Rose away from all perils. We're a small frigate, no ship-of-the-line fat with men and arms. And you say there is a second foe lurking about out there somewhere, the Americans. I respect American seamanship far more than French. Take no risks. The old girl has already taken a terrible beating from the elements during the past few days. Aye, a terrible beating."

"But Captain," Roberts answered evenly, "like it or not, we are already engaged, sir."

"Then disengage us, Lieutenant. We sail carrying sealed dispatches for the governor at Fort Charles in Port Royal under strict orders for secrecy - that is our mission, our sacred duty. Why, this little voyage of ours is not even to be recorded in the ship's log."

"Seems most irregular, sir."

"Irregular or not, those are our orders. No dishonor in refusing to fight under these conditions, I'd say. Now, retire below I must. The surgeon has ordered it, has urged me to keep to my bed. He has so far been unable to diagnosis, let alone treat, the severe abdominal pains that torment me. Do keep me informed, however. Wake me if you must. Now you have *my* orders. Carry on..."

And with that, the captain turned on his heels and disappeared below.

Hanson did an about face and marched back to his marines on the main deck - but not before Dowlin caught a hint of satisfaction on the marine's lips. Dowlin disliked the arrogant Englishman as much as Roberts, even more so, and would gladly have picked Hanson up right then and broken his puny body in two over his knee. He had the strength.

"Mr. Roberts, beggin' yer pardon, sir," Kelly asked softly with a sly grin, "but hasn't the Capt'n put you in a fine pickle now?"

Dowlin nodded in agreement. "Mr. Kelly here is right, Luke. You've never commanded a ship in battle before. If the French take us, you'll be the one blamed, yer career ruined. And even if we beat the French - well, now, you know as well as I do..." he paused to raise an accusing finger at the spot where Hughes had just stood, "that man will claim all the glory for himself. And, I'll wager all I have, his report to the Admiralty won't even mention yer name when the time comes. Thar's the rub."

Then - no warning - a ball smashed into a lanyard only a few feet away. The three men flinched.

A ship's standing rigging, the shrouds and stays, made from heavy cordage and coated with black tar for weatherproofing, are part of a vessel's superstructure used to hold her masts a spars in place. One cut cable too many and a mast will give way. Disaster.

The lanyard's deadeyes suddenly gave way. Shrouds began snapping with a *pop, pop, pop*. And heavy, black cables went coiling into the air like so many snakes.

A man standing next to the helmsman dropped to his knees, eyes wide with fear, gagging, as he frantically grabbed at a splinter lodged obscenely in his throat. Another man was tossed on his back. Blood started oozing from a puncture wound to his chest, pooling into a thick puddle on the deck. Nasty, painful wounds.

And then, a horrendous *CRACK*! Every man heard the evil sound and anxiously looked up, fearing the worst - a shattered mast.

But British luck held fast. Only a short length of the main yardarm had split away. The severed piece of wood tumbled towards the deck until entangling itself in a web of rigging. The beam swayed back and forth ominously in mid-air like some giant broken arm, banging against the mainmast, threatening to do more damage with each pass. The severed wood had taken a section of mainsail with it too. Part of the heavy canvass draped itself around the deadeyes, the rest flipped over the side. The helmsman reported a sluggishness in the steering.

With men falling, the double-headed twins Death and Destruction, those two horrors born to ruin men, saw an opportunity now and swooped down from the skies, wings outstretched, eager to wet their talons in blood and gruesome gore. Only those poor, wretched souls doomed to die can see their dark shadows looming overhead. With a surgeon's skill, the twins set about cutting spirit away from flesh - and discarded the corpses for comrades left behind.

Men rushed to stack the dead around the masts and out of the way until there was time later to wrap the bodies inside their hammocks for burial at sea. And so the grisly work of war went on...

Roberts smiled confidently, to ease any lingering concerns. "Lads! Mr. Dowlin! If you please gentlemen, we have no time for this now. Every man to his station! On my signal, we make the French regret this day..." He turned to face the men below on the main deck. "You men there - standby the sheets and braces! Be ready now for a hard turn to *port!*"

"The order to fire, sir - do I have it?" Dowlin again asked anxiously.

"No, Mr. Dowlin. Hold your fire until I give the word."

Dowlin did not care for that answer, not one bit. But knew better than to question Roberts about it. He turned on his heels and started to make his way back amidships until Roberts stopped him.

"Wait, Mr. Dowlin. On second thought - pick out six guns and a few swivels. Let the men fire at will. Send the rest of your gunners below and out of sight."

Dowlin looked at Roberts with a blank expression. "I'm not sure I understand, sir."

"Patrick... Place yourself on board the French ship for a minute. If you saw our pathetic return fire, what would you make of it?"

Dowlin pushed his hat back off his forehead. "Well, now. Half-dead crew, sick crew, mutinous crew? Don't know for sure..." And then he understood and grinned. "Ah! The reason hardly matters. We make the French think we're shorthanded. That's yer ploy!"

Roberts smiled, patted Dowlin on the shoulder. "See to it now, Mr. Dowlin. Let's give those cocky Frenchmen every reason to keep feeling smug. I want that ship to stay right where she is. Let them think they can pound us into sawdust..."

Dowlin rushed back to the main deck barking out orders and soon a half-dozen of *Rose's* great guns were blasting away. The rest of the gun crews were rounded up, sent below, and ordered to keep out of sight.

On board the French frigate, the French captain, unimpressed by *Rose's* feeble efforts, decided to maintain his ship's present course and speed and urged his gunners, already hot and sweaty, to keep up their deadly fire. Let the English come.

Roberts cocked his head back, considered the trim of *Rose's* sails one more time. The air was hazy with white smoke. The roar of battle was all around him. It was time to put his plan into motion. It seemed so simple. The prospects both thrilled and unnerved him. He was staking a great deal, the lives of his men, his reputation and career, on one bold stroke. His empty stomach growled.

"You there, Mr. Wilcox!" Roberts called out. "I'll have the reefs shaken out of the tops'ls, topgallants too. I intend for this ship to spring into motion like a cheetah when I give the order!"

"Aye, aye, sir! Like a cheetah!" Wilcox shrieked, barely able to contain his excitement. "All hands to tops'ls!"

Wilcox never had to be told twice what to do. His father had sailed for the king before him, as had his father's father before both of them.

Within minutes, the ship's rigging swarmed with petty officers and ratings. Topmen worked their way out along the yards carrying the fore, main and mizzen sails. And standing precariously on swaying rope stirrups, hanging on to spars by armpits with a boiling sea far below and musket balls whizzing by them, the topmen struggled with the reef points. One-by-one the sails shook themselves out with a loud flap. The ship heeled over sharply as the canvas caught the wind. The *Rose* lunged forward with terrific speed.

Roberts turned to the helmsman and nodded. The man understood the signal: be ready to turn the big ship around on a moment's notice. Hard work even for the powerful Scotsmen. Less than 200 yards of water separated the two vessels now. Roberts watched, waited. *What did Hughes say? Take no risks?*

Roberts took a deep breath, held it for a moment. "Mr. Hawkins! Hold... Wait... Wait for it... Almost, get ready - NOW! Now, bring her about hard to port - four points! Mark your helm well! Good! Good! Now hold her steady!"

Roberts turned, shouted to a group of hands working the rigging, pointed to the mainmast. "See to those braces lads! To port! To port! Mr. Thornton - the main yardarm there - get some axes and have that mess cleared away! And that torn canvas dragging in the water, it's slowing us down! Cut it loose. Cut it loose this instant! And get the rest of your party aloft - we need every square inch of sail, royals too!"

Men scrambled in every direction to carry out his orders. But Roberts wanted more and raised a challenge for them all: "Mr. Thornton, your lads seem sluggish today! Are they not the pride of the Royal Navy? That's the boast I always hear! I want speed! We win or lose this day by how well your men do!"

The chief petty officer froze in place like a deer in the woods surprised by a sudden intruder and blinked. He should have thought to give the order to cut away the wreckage before Roberts had time to think of it. Thornton was a man who took pride in his work and was not accustomed to having an officer, even if it was Roberts, doing his thinking for him. Red-faced, he made a knuckle and turned to his men. *That's one to you, Mr. Roberts...*

"You heard the Lieutenant, me lads. Grab them axes! Up into the trees you go my fine, little monkeys. Let's show them land lovin' Frogs how real seamen work a ship! Shake a leg now! I don't fancy sleeping in chains tonight eating French slop - do you?"

Thornton's division scrambled up the ratlines and into the ship's rigging, ignoring the hungry sea below, ignoring the blood-lusting French sharpshooters above. Axes bit into wood and chopped at tangled lines to free *Rose* from her own wreckage.

Roberts looked for Dowlin next and found him with his gunners. "Mr. Dowlin! It's time. Get your men ready. Man the starboard batteries. On my signal, I'll have you give our *full* response to the French! A raking fire!"

He raised his arm and pointed at the starboard guns so there would be no mistaking his orders. *Now things will get hot!*

And his winning words filled every heart with courage. Gunners poured back on deck, scrambled to load the starboard guns.

Roberts's command made little sense to Dowlin at first. The French were on their portside. But he knew better than to question the order. "*Move!*" he shouted to his gunners. "Hurry lads! One minute! One minute to have yer guns primed and loaded... Not a second more - and I'll skin the hide of any man I catch slacking!"

Their lust for blood and glory at a fever pitch, eyes burning with wild fire, Dowlin's gun crews readied their guns for action, readied guns that faced an empty sea. They had their fill of the French - had their fill of patience too - it was time to pay the French back, pay them back in kind.

Roberts, no fool, understood the prudent course of action was to steer *Rose* away from the French, to play a game of cat and mouse, to bide their time, to maneuver for some advantage, or to turn tail and run. This was the time-honored tactic of the sea. This was the sailor's way. But Roberts had weighed the risks and saw an opportunity. His thoughts turned to Hughes, caught himself wondering what the man was doing. The captain would have felt the ship's hard turn over. *He should be the one on deck. The ship is his responsibility. Damn Hughes to hell! Then again. No. This is what I wanted. This is my moment. What will be, will be.* He closed his eyes and prayed: *please Lord, win or lose, let there at least be honor...*

Under full sail, with every man working as one, the *Rose* turned sharply towards her attacker and, into the turn, her speed increased even more as a confluence of favorable winds and strong currents propelled her forward. Roberts considered the ship's new course and speed and calmly instructed the Scotsman at the helm to adjust his course slightly.

"*Sweet Jesus!*" Kelly cursed, standing behind Roberts, his hands resting on a swivel gun. He understood Roberts's plan clearly, *enlightenment.* 'Tis goin' to be a near thing thar, Mr. Roberts!"

Roberts turned to smile at the giant. *Right you are Mr. Kelly*, he mused to himself, *right you are.*

Roberts removed a tattered handkerchief from his breast pocket, wiped away the droplets of rain from the lens of his spyglass and put it to his eye. He could see the French captain's face plainly now, could see how elegantly dressed the man was in a fine, blue coat with a red sash. A fancy gold scabbard hung from his belt. Roberts looked down at his own soiled coat, with its threadbare silver piping and tarnished brass buttons. The condition of his britches and stockings were no better. He had paid a handsome sum for his uniform in Portsmouth. An image of himself surrendering the *Rose* in his shabby clothes, defeated and humiliated, suddenly flashed before his eyes, sent a shiver down his spine. *Must not think like that*, he scolded himself, *not now; keep your nerve man…*

As the tawny lion, proud and strong but mad with hunger, will take on a black bull, sleek, alert, pawing at the earth beneath its hooves - until the lion discovers the bull's fearsome strength and flees when the monster finally lowers its horns and charges at it - the French struggled desperately to turn their great frigate around to escape when the English charged at them. The French captain raised a cane or a baton, Roberts wasn't sure which, and pointed it at the *Rose*, frantically shouting out new orders. His men did their best to turn their ship in towards the *Rose*, to protect their ship's vulnerable stern. It was a feeble, wasted effort.

Blustery south winds and the sea's sweeping currents prevented the cumbersome vessel from turning to starboard with any ease. Like a wagon with its wheels mired deep in the ruts of a muddy road, the horses cannot turn right or left no matter how much they labor - the French could not turn, could not maneuver their ship out of the way in time.

Roberts smiled. Events were unfolding before his eyes exactly as he had foreseen moments earlier. The better maneuver for the French, the cleverer tactic, would have been to turn to port, away from the *Rose*. But even so, Roberts simply would have countered that move by turning the more nimble *Rose* to starboard, resuming their original course and speed. The outcome would have been the same.

Roberts had positioned the *Rose* with flawless precision. She could cut across the French frigate's wake no matter which way the French tried to turn.

Oblivious to Roberts's plan, French gunners and sharpshooters, with no charity in their hard hearts, kept up their barrage of deadly iron. *Rose* shuddered from each direct hit. More men fell.

One sailor up in the rigging lost his grip and hit the deck with a sickening, dull thud at Roberts's feet. Roberts had to turn away from the grotesque heap of broken bones sprawled across the hard wood. Another man plunge headfirst into the water, flapping his arms like a bird on his way down. The sea swallowed him raw, no shame, no guilt. The House of Death welcomed two new tenants.

But like some seasoned prizefighter, dogged, determination never lacking, the *Rose* kept coming, top speed, plowing straight for the French frigate. And except for the blood yet to be spilled - for honor's sake - the battle was all but over. Every man, English and French alike, soon understood this simple truth.

"Mr. Dowlin, Mr. Wilcox!" Roberts called out with a gleam in his eye, now certain, beyond any doubt, that his plan would succeed. "Gentlemen. Her rudder! Target her rudder! A gold ducat and keg of rum to the gun crew that sheers off that prime wood!"

Dowlin and Wilcox, nearly giddy, seized the moment and issued orders smartly. The gunners aimed their lethal bronze with care, waited for the command to fire, and used the time to savor their shining moment. Anticipation electrified the air. Now the French would learn first-hand what it meant to be caught in a *murderous fire...*

Rose came in close behind the French frigate, turned abruptly to cut across her stern, a stern ornately decorated by skilled master craftsman with intricate gold carvings and scrollwork. French shipwrights knew how to build fine vessels. The frigate was a beauty. But ornate decorations, no matter how lovely, are no match against heavy iron, kissed with deadly gunpowder. To the delight of his gunners, Roberts had brought them in close, very close. Their work was child's play.

Dowlin needed no prodding, needed no words of encouragement either, and bellowed out commands like some raging madman. "Give 'em a belly full, lads! I want her rudder! Take yer aim. Steady! Watch yer linstocks. Steady lads. As yer guns bare now... When yer ready... *FIRE!*"

Wilcox followed Dowlin's lead and issued the same order to his division. And, one-by-one, as the target passed across their sites, *Rose's* gunners brushed their slow matches against the touchholes and British guns erupted in a series of thunderous booms in rapid succession, followed by shooting red flames and thick, gray smoke. From her waterline to the masthead, the French ship disappeared in a cloud of smoke, obscuring any damage...

English gunners would not rejoice, not yet. They hustled to haul in their great guns, swab them down and reloaded muzzles with lightning speed. They moved as one, like a precision machine, like the *Rose* herself.

Dowlin, who liked to boast that he was the best marksman in the British Navy, took command of the Number Three Gun and, with a boyish gleam in his eye, personally aimed and fired off a nine-pound round. No wasted shot either - every sailor heard his iron shot splinter wood, followed instantly by French screams and curses.

On the quarterdeck acrid smoke filled Roberts's lungs. Some men never get used to the smell, always choking on the fumes. But Roberts had always found the smell somehow pleasing.

Through the noisy chaos, his ears ringing from the explosions, he heard cries of *suave qui peut* and when the wind shredded the veil of smoke swirling around the French frigate, he saw what havoc his gunners had wrecked and struggled to keep his poise. A tingling, a sense of ecstasy, rose in him like some great bubble threatening to burst. With all his mite, he wanted to shout triumphantly up to the heavens but, no, he allowed himself only the pleasure of a light slap on the ship's handrail with the palm of his hand.

The French frigate's rudder was gone, completely shot away. And her sturdy mizzenmast, like some great tree felled by the mighty blow of a lumberjack's whetted axe, had snapped at the base and tumbled into the sea, taking a dozen sailors with it along with the French colors. A tangled mass of rigging held the whole mess in tow. A few heads, bobbing in the water, managed to cling to the wreckage but strong currents swept the weaker souls away and there was nothing to be done for them. The Fates decide such things.

The ship's magnificent stern had been pulverized into a smoking jumble of twisted, broken wood. Small fires had erupted in inside the captain's great cabin and the pitiful cries of frightened, dying men filled the air.

"*Glorious!*" Dowlin cried out jubilantly, intoxicated with excitement. "Glorious! Damn my eyes! Damn my soul! Look at her lads! *Whoa!*" He removed his hat and slapped his thigh. He looked for Roberts and caught the first lieutenant smacking the ship's rail. He shouted over to him, his voice brimming with emotion. "Look at her, Mr. Roberts! Well done, sir, bloody well done!"

Roberts smiled back and nodded. Despite his youth, he knew how fickle Fortune could be. He knew as well that and such a moment might never come again. Still, this was his shining triumph and no one could ever take it away from him. He savored his victory quietly.

The whole crew joined Dowlin in his elation, cheered wildly. And then, with hearts freed from fear, but beaten down by emotion, a calm settled over the ship. Some men found a quiet spot to sit and cry. Others bowed their heads in silent prayer, offered up thanks to the Father who rules us all, thankful to still be alive.

Across the blue waters, the French heard the rousing British victory cheer. They summoned up their pride, took stock of their predicament. But pride could not save them. Without a rudder their vessel was nothing more than a floating gun platform, an easy, helpless target. The British could sail circles around them for hours, picking off French guns and Frenchmen at their leisure. And so the French, in shock, and with no more fight left in them, stood back away from all their heavy cannon and the sounds of war fell silent.

As men who ride across the sea's ruling waves know all too well, she is a temperamental mistress. And any man who takes her erratic mercy for granted does so to his sorrow, always. British mercy, as the French well knew, was no different and so now every Frenchman, so far from home, defenseless, naked, waited anxiously, pondering what the Fates would soon hand him.

Chapter Two
A Frigate Won

rom seemingly nowhere, soothing, mystical powers had tamed the angry sea, had transformed her from a cauldron of black, boiling rage into a lake of shimmering, green tranquility. And where the sun had managed to poke her long fingers through the steel-gray clouds, patches of water sparkled in her shafts of golden light like so many dazzling jewels - God's own signature written across the waves for all to see. Pure magic.

Captain Hughes, having made a sudden and miraculous recovery from his illness, had managed to wash, shave and dress and now stood on his quarterdeck surveying the world around him with Olympian aloofness. Less than 100 yards off, with sails furled and gun ports closed, the French frigate rolled over the sea's gentle swells with a lazy indifference. Off her mainmast boom fluttered a large, white flag, the international signal for parlay. The shattered ship appeared to be in no immediate danger of sinking and Hughes ordered two boats lowered away with a boarding party, led by Lieutenants Roberts, Wilcox and Hanson, to accept the French surrender.

Roberts was the first to make his way up a rope ladder draped over the frigate's side, refusing the hand of a French sailor to help him aboard. A small detachment of French Royal Marines, smartly dressed in spotless dark blue coats and freshly whitened cross-belts, snapped to and presented arms as Roberts stepped on deck. Hanson and his marines, smartly dressed in their bright red coats and cross-belts, formed up behind Roberts in two neat rows with crisp military precision. The marines held their muskets at the ready with fixed bayonets. The polished steel glittered in the golden sunlight.

Roberts ignored the pageantry, made a quick look around. The deck had been freshly scrubbed down. A nice gesture he thought. The mizzenmast had been shot away of course and the mainmast showed the scars of battle but, all-in-all, the ship appeared to be in remarkably good condition. He saw a great number of splices to the rigging and made a mental note to check the quality and condition of ship's supply of hemp. Small work. The real damage, he knew, would be below. He felt a perceptible list to starboard. The ship's wells were filling with seawater and shoring up the damage under the ship's waterline would be the first priority. Then he wondered: why had the French not tried to scuttle their vessel? That is what he would have done.

A young lieutenant, wearing a fresh, exquisitely tailored uniform, stepped forward with a small squad of junior officers in tow. The Frenchman came to an abrupt halt in front of Roberts, removed his cocked hat, cradled it in an arm wrapped in bloodstained, white linen, and snapped to attention. Though a bit short, the lieutenant was, with soft brown eyes, a pencil-thin moustache and flawless olive skin, an exceedingly handsome man. He had an aristocrat's delicate nose and kept his glossy, black hair pulled back in a fashionable ponytail.

Roberts couldn't help but smile. *No one*, he mused, *should be that damn good looking, well, except perhaps for Dowlin - Ireland's own gift to women.*

The Frenchman made a slight bow. "*Monsieur*, may I inquire, to whom do I have the honor of addressing?"

The Frenchman's English was polished. He spoke with only the hint of an accent.

The French crew, conspicuously unarmed, stared defiantly at the curious English officer, dressed in a torn and dirty uniform with several days' worth of stubble on his chin. They waited anxiously for him to speak. Only an hour before, they had been launching deadly missiles of lead and iron at the Englishman and his ship, supremely confident that victory was theirs. How, Frenchmen had asked one another, with just a simple puff of English smoke, had it come to this?

"I am, sir," Roberts began in a stiff, formal tone wishing to make the correct impression, "Lieutenant Luke Roberts of His Britannic Majesty's ship *Rose*."

"*Monsieur* Lieutenant Roberts, if you will permit me, I am Lieutenant David Antoine Henry Robard de Sartine, First Officer of His

Most Christian Majesty's ship *Le Toulon* and now your obedient servant, sir. I am honored to make your acquaintance. May I present *Toulon's* surviving officers to you?"

"Please," replied Roberts. And as Sartine formally introduced his officers in the order of their rank, Roberts acknowledged each man with a slight bow of his head.

"And your captain?" Roberts asked, after Sartine had introduced the last officer.

"I regret to report, sir, he succumbed to his wounds only moments before you boarded."

"I see," replied Roberts awkwardly. "I am sorry."

"Ours is a hazardous profession, no? He died a soldier's death. He died in battle with sword in hand and with honor. Permit me to observe, if I may, *Monsieur* Roberts - a most brilliant piece of seamanship. My compliments to your captain, to you and to your crew. If it is not too bold of me to say, the men of the *Rose* have distinguished themselves with gallantry and bestowed great glory upon your prince."

The compliment brought a smile to his lips, Roberts could not hide it, and he bowed. The French word *suave*, Roberts thought to himself, fit this man perfectly.

"Your hard turn to port at the last moment, at the critical moment, *Monsieur le Lieutenant* - your captain, he had anticipated we would be unable to counter this maneuver in these tricky seas by turning to starboard?"

Roberts managed to stifle the laugh rising from his gut with a cough. "What my captain knew or did not know I cannot say Lieutenant de Sartine. He was, I regret, incapacitated... I fear a mysterious affliction forced him to keep to his quarters throughout the entire engagement. As for our tactics, we were lucky. I credit the winds and currents."

Hanson bristled at Roberts's candor about Hughes and his eyes betrayed his loathing for Roberts. A loyal subordinate would never have been so honest with the enemy. But Roberts, Hanson was certain, felt no loyalty to Hughes.

"Ah. I understand," Sartine replied with more truth than Roberts realized. Sartine had caught the look Hanson's eyes. "That explains your captain's absence here now. And your crew, I must say, they appear to have all recovered?"

"Beg pardon, *Monsieur* de Sartine?" Roberts asked, perplexed.

"I speak of the malady that infects your crew. At first, you engaged *Toulon* with so few guns and we saw only a pitiful number of men on deck. We thought perhaps the plague or a mutiny? And then your ship made the turn, cut across our stern. Your gunners appeared and unleashed a withering fire, a taste of hell. I thought that... *curious.*"

"Ah..." Roberts began awkwardly, uncertain how he could answer the Frenchman's question without seeming haughty or offensive. And he was unclear whether the Frenchman had just rebuked him subtly for fighting unfairly or just handed him an indirect compliment? "Aye, we did have a problem there for a bit," he offered evasively and narrowed his eyes, "perhaps we can exchange our thoughts on tactics with one another later over a glass of port?"

Sartine smiled cautiously. "I would welcome such a discussion at your pleasure, sir, though I think we might be able to find something better than port on board. With your permission, let us proceed with the business at hand then. *Monsieur*, duty compels me to ask - what terms does His Britannic Majesty propose to offer *Toulon's* company of officers and men?"

"Aye, of course, *Monsieur le Lieutenant.* First things first."

It hardly mattered what terms Roberts offered, as the French ship was completely helpless and would sink if repairs were delayed too long. Roberts knew the French would accept any terms he offered. They had no choice. But before he could reply, he caught himself wishing, praying, that he would never suffer the humiliation of surrendering a ship under his command. Such a thing, or so he imagined, would be too painful, too disgraceful. He was surprised by how relaxed, even cheery, Sartine appeared. *The French*, he thought, *do not treat war seriously enough.*

Roberts cleared his throat. "*Monsieur* de Sartine, you, your officers and the crew of the *Toulon* have done everything men of honor can be expected to do for king and country and therefore I ask you, in the name of His Britannic Majesty King George III, to surrender your ship. If you agree, I am at liberty to offer the following terms: the officers of the *Toulon* shall be permitted to retain their arms and their property and shall be transferred, together with their baggage, over to the *Rose* as guests of His Britannic Majesty. Every French officer shall be accorded all the privileges due his rank. As soon as it is practical, you and your officers shall be provided safe conduct back to France, or if you prefer, *Rose* shall deliver you to the nearest French territory in these waters. As for your crew, they must surrender all arms and shall remain on board *Toulon*. They shall be taken to England where they shall be incarcerated until satisfactory prisoner exchanges can be arranged with your government. The *Toulon*, her armament and supplies, of course, are forfeit and shall become the property of His Britannic Majesty. I trust you will appreciate the generosity of our king? Would you, *Monsieur*, like a moment to confer with your officers before responding to these terms?"

Sartine shook his head. "No, no. That shall not be necessary. Your prince is gracious. On my authority, we accept these terms. If you would indulge me on one matter though?"

"Oh?"

"The men of *Toulon* are disciplined, a good crew. The best I have ever served with. If certain assurances can be given, I beg you to consider: do not lock these men up below in shackles. It is a long voyage back to England and men die easily in blistering heat."

"What assurances can you give?"

"You have my word, so long as my men are treated humanely, there will be no trouble, no attempt to escape. And I agree to remain on board *Le Toulon* as your hostage to guarantee this pledge."

Sartine's concern for his men struck a chord with Roberts. He was beginning to like the Frenchman. He considered the request for a moment, decided to accept and nodded in agreement.

Sartine and his officers snapped to attention and saluted in unison. And with that simple formality completed, *Toulon* became the property of the King of England.

"Oh, I nearly forgot," Roberts said. "One last matter, *Monsieur* de

Sartine. Our two countries, how long have we been at war? I assume this is about the Americans? And who declared first, your king or ours?"

Sartine raised an eyebrow. "It is true we happened upon an American vessel in these waters. And it is true that France is sympathetic to America's desire for independence from England. But war between our two countries? I am aware of no state of war between France and England."

"But, sir, you fired on our ship! What other reason would you have to attack a British warship if England and France are not at war?"

"But I would not know *Mon Lieutenant*," Sartine said and shook his head. "Whatever the reason, or whatever orders we had, were known only to my captain."

"You were escorting an American vessel, correct?"

"*Oui*," said Sartine with a sheepish grin and shrugged his shoulders. "I deny it not. But kings do not make lowly lieutenants privy to their royal designs, eh?"

Satisfied the French were in no position to renege on their promise of surrender, Roberts made his way back to the *Rose* in one of the long boats, leaving Wilcox behind to assess the full extent of *Toulon's* damages along with Hanson and his spit-and-polish marines to keep him company. With a sudden shift in the winds, a blast of hot, humid, air came rolling up from the Caribbean, turning November back into August. As sailors pulled gently at their oars, Roberts closed his eyes and began to doze until he was startled by a splash. He opened his eyes to see a great sailfish suddenly leap out of the water with a small treat wriggling helplessly in its mouth. Was this, he wondered, an omen of some sort? If it was, what could the omen mean?

He let his mind wander. *The mighty swallowing the weak?* Silly, superstitious thoughts he mused to himself. And then again, sailors, stretching back in time to ancient mariners like Jason and his Argonauts or even to the mighty Odysseus, his favorite hero, had always been a superstitious lot. Ah, wily Odysseus, the man of twists and turns, famous tactician and dear to the gods - when Roberts was a boy an Irish priest had captured his imagination with Homer's poetry. The kindly priest told him the story too of how the god-like King of Ithaca had devised a rouse to end the ten-year stalemate between Greek and Trojans. The Greeks abandoned their ramparts along the beach, sailed away, and left the great wooden horse, a death gift, before shinning Troy's impregnable gates. And after Troy fell, after all the spoils or war had been divided, Odysseus and his men crossed the storm-tossed sea in their long, curved ships for home. But Poseidon turned on the hapless Greeks. Odysseus's men would all die and Odysseus, shipwrecked, would be forced to endure pain on pain before he saw lovely Ithaca and his family again.

Now there was a man, Roberts smiled to himself. He considered the sailfish again, finally decided it was indeed an omen and that it was good.

His thoughts turned to Hughes next. Hughes would be waiting for him he knew, eager to dress him down for one concocted offense or another. His empty stomach turned sour.

The rowers smartly shipped oars. The boat coasted smoothly up alongside *Rose* where a midshipman was waiting for Roberts with a ladle of cool water and orders for him to report immediately to the captain. Roberts acknowledged the command, felt the anxiety beginning to build in the pit of his stomach.

During the past few months Roberts had done his best to avoid Hughes and had enjoyed a fair bit of success at it too - no simple feat on board a small ship. He did not care for Hughes very much and the thought of seeing Hughes now, no matter his victory, brought him no joy. The uneasy strain between the two officers had been obvious to all.

Roberts took a deep breath before knocking forcefully on the captain's door.

"Enter!" Hughes ordered gruffly.

Roberts found the captain sitting behind his desk with pen in hand, writing, and despite the heat, Hughes was wearing his wool jacket, buttoned up to the collar. Hughes continued scratching his words onto paper and did not trouble himself to look up.

Roberts removed his hat, cleared his throat and stood uneasily at attention. "Sir, you asked for me?"

Hughes insisted that his officers observe strict military protocol at all times. No informality or familiarity was tolerated. No one was ever offered a refreshment or asked to sit. And, unlike most ships' captains who dined and drank with their subordinate officers, Hughes always ate his meals in private. There was no fellowship, no polite conversation, no after dinner card games. Nothing. Hughes seemed to disdain all men equally.

"Aye, Mr. Roberts," Hughes replied, still writing, leaving smudges on the paper from too much ink on his quill. "You have successfully arranged for the surrender of the French?"

"Indeed, sir. I am pleased to report the French have agreed to His Majesty's terms, all of them. I regret to say, however, the French captain, a man named Aspheim, was killed during the battle. The ship was assigned to Vice Admiral Comte D'Estaing's squadron. Captain Aspheim's orders were to escort the American sloop *Reprisal* to France, presumably to L'Orient. Beyond this the first officer had little to say and claimed he was not privy to any other orders his captain may have been given. He also denied knowing what or who was on board the *Reprisal*. Certainly, the American ship is carrying someone or something of importance to warrant a frigate escort. In any case, the ship's log and papers, and any written orders Captain Aspheim may have had, were destroyed by the fire in the captain's great cabin."

Hughes grunted. "That's what you were told by the first officer?"

"Aye," answered Roberts, anticipating Hughes's frame of mind. "What I was told may be true or not, Captain. There is no way to know with any certainty. I personally inspected Aspheim's quarters and the damage was severe. We did manage to find the captain's iron lock box and pried it open but found only ashes inside."

"Continue, Lieutenant..."

"Well, sir, we secured the crew below deck and I left Mr. Hanson and Wilcox on board with ten marines and twenty armed seamen. Mr. Wilcox is presently surveying the full extent of damages. I have also charged him with the responsibility of compiling a complete inventory of all equipment, arms, supplies, spare parts, tools and the like. With your permission Captain, priority shall be given to affect repairs to *Toulon* as I have satisfied myself that the *Rose* is seaworthy and ready for immediate action. I am most pleased to report that *Toulon*, I believe, is salvageable and, pending Mr. Wilcox's concurrence of course, my impression is that basic repairs can be made at sea. Even so, she is presently taking on too much water and, should the weather unexpectedly turn foul again, there is some danger of her sinking if we don't work with haste to plug her holes. She has a five degree or so list to port..."

"Well, dammit man," Hughes interrupted and finally looked up at Roberts, "is it five or is it six degrees? Or do you fancy it to be some other number? Precision is an indispensable quality I demand from all my officers, sir!"

"Indeed. My apologies, Captain Hughes. I will verify the exact degree of list together with the precise volume of water pouring into her wells and report the proper calculations to you straight away."

"As this ship's *de facto* first officer, I had hoped for more from you Roberts. No need to mince my words with you either. Your predecessor was a better man, had far more promise. And as any competent officer in His Majesty's service knows full well, apologies have no worth Lieutenant, none whatsoever. Let us hope there is no need to remind you of this simple, obvious truth again."

Roberts could feel the blood pumping to his temples, could feel the flush in his cheeks. He swallowed hard and used his last bit of energy to keep his temper in check.

"I shall reflect upon my failings, sir, and redouble my efforts to do better."

He had hoped his report that *Toulon* could be saved would have pleased Hughes, would have improved the man's mood. As captain, Hughes after all would receive the lion's share of the prize money fetched at auction for the frigate. Enough money to make him a modestly wealthy man. And his prestige in the navy would rise too. It was not every day, after all, that a captain of the Royal Navy brought in a fine, enemy frigate.

If the good news about *Toulon* brought Hughes any pleasure, he showed no signs of it. Hughes returned to his writing and ignored Roberts for what seemed like an eternity to Roberts. Roberts stood uncomfortably at attention, watching Hughes scribble with only the sounds of creaking planks and the rudder's pintles rubbing against the gudgeons to keep him company.

Hughes finally set aside his pen and looked up at Roberts. "You... You, Mr. *Roberts*," he snapped, pronouncing Roberts's name as if it were somehow distasteful, "shall begin to redouble your efforts by seeing to the *Rose's* needs first - why the most junior of midshipmen possesses the good sense enough to give his own ship priority over all else! And only when the *Rose* is fit shall you insure the safety of *my* prize! Is that understood?"

"*My prize?*" Roberts thought to himself, turning the phrase over in his head. But he was too tired to dwell on it much. The adrenaline rush was long gone. And hadn't he already assured Hughes that the *Rose* was seaworthy and battle ready? Saving the *Toulon* was the priority now, but he knew better than to argue the point with Hughes.

"As you wish, Captain."

"See to it then. That is all. You are dismissed, Lieutenant."

But as Roberts turned on his heels and began reaching for the door, Hughes stopped him.

"No, wait," Hughes commanded, and then added in a condescending tone, "there is another matter we must discuss."

Roberts smartly did an about face. "Sir?"

"You are to select a prize crew, prepare a list for my review. I am entrusting you with the, ahem, what name did you call her? Ah yes, *Toulon*. I am entrusting you with the *Toulon*. I am making you prize master. I am placing the responsibility of getting her safely back to England in your hands and I will hold you personally accountable. Are we clear?"

"Aye, of course, Captain. Perfectly clear." Roberts had to suppress a grin. Hughes had just, no doubt unwittingly, answered his prayers. He was getting off the *Rose* and away from Hughes, at least for brief respite.

Hughes turned his head to look out at the sea through his cabin's open windows. "Before it slips my mind, there is actually a one last matter... That hand, his name? What is his damn name? Wait, yes, I have it now, that *Irishman*, Kelly. I understand he was insolent. What have you done about it Roberts?"

"Done, sir? Why, nothing."

"Aye, I suspected as much."

"But, Captain, Mr. Kelly was hardly insolent. To the contrary, he displayed great bravery during the battle."

"Do not question me, sir! He was insolent I say! There are witnesses. No, sir. Not on board my ship. I'll not tolerate such behavior lest it spreads like some filthy disease and infects the whole crew. Tomorrow before breakfast, you shall call all hands to witness punishment. A dozen lashes, a baker's dozen, should suffice. That, I should think, will improve the man's demeanor for the duration of the cruise. On second thought, let's make it a round twenty, hey?"

"But, sir-" Roberts tried to protest until Hughes cut him off.

"That shall be all, *sir*! The matter is closed, Lieutenant."

"But, Captain, with all respect, I beg you to reconsider. I think -"

Hughes's cheeks turned crimson. The veins in his neck began to bulge.

"*Enough!*" Hughes roared and slammed his fist down hard on his desk. He looked up at Roberts with undisguised disdain in his eyes. "You forget yourself! I'll not debate ship's policy with a junior officer! Understand that I don't bloody well care what you think, Mr. Roberts. I'll not give *Irish* trash any more thought than I would give to a piece of dung stuck to the heel of my boot! I have noted your chumminess with certain crew members since your arrival to the *Rose*. Oh indeed I have. And I tell you plainly, sir, your judgment here is unsound and ill-advised and reveals a weak nature! If you desire - in your naïveté - to encourage their slovenly and impertinent ways you may do so if and when you should be so fortunate to be given command of your own ship someday. But mark my words: your only reward will be to have your throat slit as you lay asleep in your bed. Now see to your duties. Not another word from you *Mister*! Not *a-n-o-t-h-e-r* WORD!"

Roberts, seething, but helpless, did a quick about face for the second time and left Hughes's great cabin. The tremendous rush excitement he had felt when Hughes made him *Toulon's* prize master had all but evaporated. His thoughts turned to Kelly. Poor Kelly, Roberts was certain this was some of Hanson's fine work.

Hughes's dislike of him, his intense dislike of him, baffled him. Since coming aboard *Rose*, Roberts had strived to do his best, to be a competent and loyal officer. But from the very moment he had assumed the duties of first officer, Hughes began to belittle, insult and ignore him. Mercifully, Hughes was careful to save the worst of it when there were no witnesses. Roberts had at first tried to understand, had agonized over how best to correct his 'flaws'. But as the weeks wore on and his introspection gave him no answers - only added to his confusion - he found himself giving the matter less and less thought. He was determined to make the best of things until he could submit his papers requesting a transfer. Some things in life, he had come to realize, simply cannot be explained or understood.

Roberts made his way topside, to fill his lungs and head with fresh air, and then went looking for Dowlin. He soon found the big Irishman near the ship's forecastle, busy overseeing the work of several riggers.

"Mr. Dowlin, a moment of your time if you please."

Dowlin gave Roberts a wide, friendly grin. The Irishman always had a ready smile for Roberts.

"Turnin' into a lovely mornin' Mr. Roberts isn't it?" he asked casually, looking out over the horizon. Tropical, white clouds were beginning to beat a hasty retreat against the rising sun.

Roberts stood at Dowlin's side, looked out over the same waters. "Aye, I suppose so Patrick if you like heat," he answered wearily. The day was already uncomfortably warm and sticky and he could feel the humidity, at oppressive levels, building. "Are you prepared to give me your report on the ship's readiness?"

Dowlin turned to look at his friend, took a moment to study Roberts's face before he answered. Roberts looked pale and drawn and his chin was covered in stubble. His usually bright, clear eyes were surrounded by dark, half-moons and bloodshot.

"My *Gawd*, Mr. Roberts, but you look terrible, sir. You really better catch a few winks and put on some fresh clothes, sir."

"The report if you please, Patrick."

"Aye, sir, straight away if that's yer pleasure. We suffered fourteen dead, includin' the two hands who went over the rail during the fight who are presumed dead, and twenty-three wounded. Of the twenty-three wounded, eight are pretty bad, sir. Five won't last the day, accordin' to Smythe anyhows, if you can believe anythin' that rum-soaked dimwit of a surgeon 'as to say. We've plugged up all *Rosie's* leaks and just a few minutes ago, I rotated the lads at the pumps. The carpenter and his apprentice are up and about mendin' things. And if you look over thar, we are hoistin' up a spar to brace the main yardarm. Splices to the riggin' already been seen to. Exceptin' for a fresh coat of paint p'haps, she'll be as good as new by this evenin'. If I may say, sir, not a bad job of it. Not a bad job at all. Other ships I know would have simply limped back into the nearest friendly port. Not the *Rose!*"

Roberts absently scratched at the stubble on his chin. "Very good, Patrick. Very good indeed. I want you to continue with your repairs to *Rose* and when you've finished here, lend a hand to Mr. Wilcox over on *Toulon*. I need her seaworthy, Patrick. And there is no time to waste so, as weary as the men are, you'll need to push them a bit. The captain has instructed me to select a prize crew and has made me prize master. Draw up a list of names for the prize crew for me, the *dependable lads*. You get my meaning?"

Dowlin nodded. He understood. Roberts wanted the Irishmen.

"Good. Add your name to the top of list. I'm going below now to see to the wounded, then I intend to take your advice and retire to my quarters. Send a midshipman to wake me at around at four bells if you please."

"Aye, aye, Mr. Roberts."

"Patrick, I'm sorry to say there is one last, unpleasant, matter. The captain has ordered all hands to witness punishment and cannot be persuaded otherwise. Mr. Kelly is the victim this time around. He is to be flogged for the incident on the quarterdeck this morning. Punishment will be carried out before breakfast on the morrow."

Dowlin raised his eyebrows, leaned close to Roberts. "What," he whispered, "will you do, Luke?"

Roberts stared down at the deck. "Don't know, don't know. I will tell Kelly myself, after supper. One last thing, Patrick..."

"Sir?"

Roberts smiled, reached out to clasp Dowlin's shoulder and shook it gently. "Though I fear the Admiralty shall never learn of it, your skill and bravery this morning was exemplary. Well done, lad. Well done indeed! I am very proud of all the lads certainly, but I am especially proud of you! You fight with the heart of a lion! Please pass my compliments on to the men. They did their duty and fought exceedingly well and, if we can save *Toulon*, they will all profit handsomely from their efforts."

Dowlin blushed and smiled, an extraordinary smile, like that of a bashful schoolboy.

Roberts returned Dowlin's smile, glad to have given the compliment, and then realized that Dowlin had somehow found the time to shave, wash and put on a clean uniform. Dowlin had labored as long and as hard as any man on board and yet looked fresh and rested. Roberts could only marvel at his friend's stamina.

In all the years they had known each other Dowlin had never, not once, disappointed him. Roberts found Dowlin's unwavering cheerfulness and boyish energy a source of strength for himself and Dowlin's playfulness gave balance to his own, more sober, nature. And where elation and melancholy were constantly pulling at Roberts in different directions - he did not find life as carefree or as simple as others - Dowlin took life's trials in stride and laughed at everything, even adversity. And how Roberts, and the whole crew, loved listening to Dowlin as he spun out the most outrageous stories about his romantic escapades. Dowlin never wearied of telling a good tale and, except for the ship, women were his favorite topic. Vanity had no part in it though. The good-natured Irishman's stories were filled with humor, often at his own expense. Dowlin simply enjoyed living.

Dowlin took Roberts's hand and shook it warmly. He had no

family, thought of Roberts as his brother and now felt a brother's pride.

"'Twas you who did it, sir," he answered, still grinning. "All the hands know that Mr. Roberts, no matter what the Capt'n puts in his bloody report. A damn magnificent piece of work to be sure! "'Twas splendid to watch - somethin' for the navy's battle books, I'd say..."

"Hm... High praise indeed, Pat. Can't say I deserve it. Luck played some part in the outcome. But thank you. Well, allow me four bells and then send someone around to fetch me. Carry on, Mr. Dowlin."

Dowlin touched the brim of his hat with two fingers and Roberts, having satisfied himself that things on board both ships were well under control, disappeared below. But before returning to his small quarters, he made his way to the wardroom, which had been temporarily converted into the ship's hospital.

The air was stifling and filled with the putrid smells of sweat, urine and vomit. He passed by the rows of dead, already wrapped inside their hammocks for burial and lined-up against the bulwarks. They needed no comfort. And then he saw the bloody rags littering the deck and an amputated arm protruding over the rim of a barrel stowed away in a corner. A shiver ran down his spine. He quickly turned away from the ghastly sight. He began to feel queasy too but knew, for the sake of the wounded, he needed to collect himself and see it through. Someone of authority had to give these poor lads a few words of comfort. They deserved that much at least for their sacrifices. Lord knew, they would not receive much else from the Crown.

Roberts spoke briefly to the surgeon, found the smell of rum on his breath, and quickly excused himself to go and speak with the wounded. He offered words of praise and hope to each man as best he could. And after he had finished speaking to the last man, he sent word to the carpenter to have a vent installed in the wardroom to increase the flow of fresh air, adding that the carpenter was to make the task his priority. Roberts then returned to his cabin and tumbled into his bunk, still wearing his damp and dirty clothes, and slipped into a deep, sound sleep.

Chapter Three
A Frigate Lost

Young midshipman Clarke tapped him gingerly on the shoulder until the first officer began to stir. "Mr. Roberts. Mr. Roberts, sir. Beg pardon. Mr. Dowlin sends his compliments, sir. He asked me to wake you. 'Tis four bells. Sorry, sir."

Roberts struggled to focus. It took him a moment before he understood where he was. Seconds before, he had been lying on a beach in North Africa, half-naked and coughing up brine. Odd, he thought. He had never been to Africa. He swung his legs down from his bunk and rubbed the sleep out of his eyes as he sat up.

"That's fine, Mr. Clarke. No need to ever apologize for doing your duty, leastwise not to me."

"Aye, sir. Sorry sir."

"How's the weather?"

"'Tis a lovely autumn day, sir! Blue skies and light breezes blowing up from the West Indies. A bit sticky, hot for some I should think. A few of the lads are missing England and home."

"But not you?"

"No, sir! I love the sea and don't miss English weather one bit."

Roberts stood and patted the young midshipman on the shoulder. "Mr. Clarke, should fortune ever find you a castaway, I have little doubt you would be no worse off for it. I suspect you would feel right at home living out your days on one of those island paradises we hear so much about."

"Wouldn't that be something now, sir!"

"Indeed, indeed it would. Very well, be along with you now and see to your duties. There's a good lad."

Relieved that he had survived the ordeal of having to wake the ship's first officer, Clarke smiled, did an about face and walked straight into the door, smacking his nose. The boy blushed and hurried on his way.

That made Roberts smile. It had been not so long ago when he had been just as awkward and clumsy.

Roberts went to the forward pump to wash and shave in the cold seawater. After putting on a fresh uniform, he made his way to the crew's quarters. There is not much living space on board a British warship. Rows of hammocks had been crammed into a very small area. Some sailors were resting in their hammocks. Others sat around barrels, using them as makeshift tables and passed the time playing cards or dice. A few men were still eating their suppers at the galley tables, salt pork and potatoes again, but at least the galley fires had been relit and the cook had made fresh bread with the last of the flour. Fresh bread was a luxury and far better than eating weevilly, hard biscuits. And someone had given the order to issue an extra gill of rum to each man too and rum was far better than watered down ale or brackish water taken from a barrel infested with small critters.

The soft sounds of a fiddle floated down from the top deck to the galley and Roberts was pleased to find the men in a mellow, easy mood. They deserved the precious few pleasures that life aboard a warship could provide. He always tried to keep a fix on morale. When the crew was in a surly frame of mind, not an infrequent occurrence when a cruise dragged on into long, monotonous months and supplies dwindled, Roberts could be stern and aloof. Tough discipline was needed under such circumstances to insure the general welfare of all on board. But when the crew was relaxed, he relaxed as well and the men found him friendly and talkative. Woe to the unfortunate sailor who misconstrued his pleasant manner for weakness though. Roberts treated the men with fairness and respect and demanded the same in return and, except for a small handful of malcontents, they gladly gave it to him.

Through a haze of tobacco and cooking smoke, thick enough to make his eyes water, he saw Kelly resting in his hammock. The hammock sagged so much against his huge frame that it looked as if his weight might rip the coarse material in two at any moment. And as Roberts stepped into the galley, a sailor abruptly called all hands to attention. Every man stopped whatever he was doing and jumped to.

Kelly swung his legs around and eased himself down from his

hammock. Unlike most large men, Kelly's size didn't interfere with his agility and the big man's quickness never ceased to amaze Roberts. Sometimes for entertainment, the men organized wrestling matches and, even in middle age, Kelly, with both strength and quickness, was the ship's undisputed champion.

Roberts's lips curled into slight smile. "Easy there lads. Just popping in to see how the victors of the South Atlantic are faring. You all gave a fine account of yourselves this mornin'. I thought you should know."

"Three cheers for the Lieutenant!" Higginbotham cried out.

But before any man could raise his voice, Roberts held up his hands to stop them. "Avast there lads. No. No. Capt'n's orders. There'll be none of that now."

An awkward silence fell over the galley.

Roberts looked around, took in the face of each man, and smiled. "There now lads, return to your own matters. Important doings, I'm sure. Don't want to interrupt any of that. And thank you for your good intentions. Mr. Kelly, a moment of your time if you please."

The men returned to their own affairs and Kelly, hunched over to avoid hitting his head on the overhead beams, followed Roberts a few paces over to a stack of barrels where they could have a little privacy.

Roberts looked into the big man's eyes, tried to take stock of the Irishman's inner strength. He leaned forward, placed a hand on Kelly's shoulder and, in the voice of his youth, whispered in an even tone, "Brace yourself lad. Tomorrow after breakfast, Capt'n's orders, twenty lashes."

Kelly's broad shoulders stiffened and he grimaced at the news. "A flogging?" he asked in his own thick, Irish brogue. "Aye, sir. I heard a rumor about it already. Amazing how few secrets there are aboard ship. A gift from Lieutenant Hanson, no doubt. He thinks anyone on this end of the ship is scum. Won't be the first time, suspect it won't be the last either. I'm most grateful to you, sir, to come and tell me yerself. Most grateful."

"That's not why I'm here man!" Roberts protested, continuing in his own Irish brogue. "You were trying to protect me, I know that. I can't allow an innocent man to suffer for my transgressions."

Kelly gave Roberts a reassuring smile. "No worries thar, sir. I can handle the cat."

Roberts stared hard at the big Irishman in the dim light of an oil lantern, swinging gently back and forth overhead. The shadows played their tricks, deepened the creases in Kelly's craggy face, giving him a sinister look. An ugly scar running down the side of his left temple did nothing to improve his appearance. Kelly was not a man to bump into in a dark alley. And yet he had kind eyes, betraying a kind and gentle nature.

The big Irishman looked down on Roberts with an almost paternal expression, like that of a loving father taking measure of his own son. Roberts's heart warmed to the man. Kelly possessed a simple peasant's pride, the pride of quiet dignity that comes from surviving life's trials, from being armed at birth with nothing more one's own wits.

His weather-beaten face told his story, the story of a sailor's life and it had been the only life he had ever known. It was a hard life that made hard men. Like most of the other Irishmen on board, Kelly was from a small, prosperous sea-town north of Dublin named Rush, or *Ros Eo* in the Gaelic, meaning *Headland of Yew Trees*, and, like Dowlin, over the years had followed Roberts to each new assignment, to every new ship.

"Very noble of you, Mr. Kelly. But I intend to take this matter up with the Capt'n again directly."

"Now look here, sir. Why go and do somethin' foolish - beggin' yer pardon, Lieutenant - like that? No good will come of it for you or for me. I'll be flogged either way and you might just get yerself court-martialed. For that matter, no good will come of it for any man on board this here ship. You want the navy to go and hang you, sir, leavin' the rest of us to the tender mercies of Capt'n Hughes? I see no good, clear sense in that, Mr. Roberts..."

Roberts considered Kelly's words carefully and sighed. He knew Kelly was right.

"Besides," Kelly said with grin and a wink. "Me and some of the lads have a bit of a wager goin'. A month's sea pay says that I'll neither cry out nor faint. A grunt or two is allowed. Ya don't want to spoil me chances of makin' a tidy little profit here on the side do ya, sir? Now if our good Capt'n had ordered himself a keel-haulin', well, then be *Jesus*, old Kelly here might go weak in the knees. But the cat an't nothin'. No worries. Let it be. That's the best you can do for this old sea dog."

Roberts shook his head slowly, weighing each possibility over in his mind. If he did confront Hughes with the truth it would do nothing to save Kelly from a lashing - of that much he was certain - and would most likely bring about his own arrest for conspiring to commit treason, or mutiny. He doubted Hughes would have the good sense to overlook the matter, even in the interest of his own self-preservation.

If charges were preferred against Roberts, a board of inquiry would be convened and he would stand trial. But Hughes would be taking a risk too as the board might also agree to hear evidence against him, about his own possible dereliction of duty, or cowardice, in the face of the enemy - though the Admiralty was historically squeamish about putting its captains on public display. Hughes's reputation would suffer even if he were exonerated of any wrongdoing. Small comfort for Roberts as his own career, even with his acquittal, would be unsalvageable, his reputation forever tarnished after such an investigation. And if the board found him guilty, maybe the navy would forgo hanging him, simply discharge him in disgrace, but he would forfeit his pension and few ships' masters would touch him after such an untidy mess.

Kelly was no fool. The man had thought things through.

Grim-faced, Roberts nodded and patted Kelly on the shoulder. "What you say may all be true, Mr. Kelly..." he said and paused, lost in thought for a moment. "So be it. We'll leave matters as they are then. I am in your debt and won't soon forget what you have done, Mr. Kelly. Now go and try to get some rest. You'll need your strength in the morning."

Kelly made a faint, but brave, smile. "'Til the mornin' then, sir. And I'll be smilin' in Lieutenant Hanson's general direction each step of the way. Rest assur'd of that, Mr. Roberts."

"Glad to hear of it, Mr. Kelly."

Roberts left Kelly to his thoughts, made his way to the forward companionway ladder. It was his custom to start at the ship's forward section and work his way back to the stern when conducting inspections. This route also allowed him to avoid Captain Hughes, if by chance the captain happened to be on deck, because Hughes rarely strayed off of the quarterdeck when he wasn't in his great cabin.

As was also his custom when first stepping on deck, Roberts paused to take stock of the world around him. The sun was low in the water and huge, filling half the western sky. Except for a few stragglers on the far horizon, the clouds had all but vanished. The winds had shifted yet again and now a cool breeze, flowing down from the north, caressed the warm, night air, teased the senses. And then he spotted lovely Venus, the Moon's faithful handmaiden and stalwart friend to men who roam the sea's broad back. She was beginning her long traverse across the evening sky.

He heard the splashing of oars and glanced over the rail to see a long boat ferrying more men and lumber over to *Toulon*. The French frigate, hundred yards or so away, made a handsome sight with all her lanterns lit. And then he heard the sounds of carpenters laboring with their saws, axes and hammers. He could hear laughter too, and a few choice curse words carrying across the still waters.

By comparison, the *Rose* was quiet. Except for the Second Dog Watch, and a few marines standing silently at their posts, the deck was deserted.

Roberts scanned the full length of the *Rose*. The smell of tar, paint and freshly sawed wood hung heavy in the air. The deck had been cleared of all debris, meticulously scrubbed and sanded down. The main royal yardarm had been repaired nicely and any frayed or spliced line had been replaced. Every gun, after having been cleaned and polished, was secured properly in place.

Roberts nodded his approval. It was first-rate work. Then he saw Dowlin standing amidships, leaning over the ship's rail and watching the sun sink beneath the waves with a long-stem pipe hanging from his mouth.

As Dowlin turned to watch Roberts strolling towards him, he tapped the bowl of his pipe against the rail, emptied the tobacco. He knew Roberts didn't care for the smell of it.

"Mr. Roberts, "lovely evenin', sir. Yer lookin' a tad better if I may say so."

"Thank you kindly, Mr. Dowlin," Roberts replied, casually slipping into his Irish brogue again. He stood next to Dowlin and leaned against the rail with his back to the sea. "'Tis indeed a fine evenin'. It would appear compliments are in order, Mr. Dowlin. She's looking very trim and fit, very trim and fit indeed. No slackers, no shirkers on your watch, I'd say."

Dowlin grinned. "As promised, Luke. The Capt'n's Sunday inspection will be easy-breezy, will be of no concern."

Weekly inspections were an old navy tradition. Every Sunday morning British captains everywhere conducted a full readiness inspection of his warship followed by mandatory religious services. The men worked hard on Saturdays to get their stations in good order. Some captains took their inspections more seriously than others. Hughes lived for them and it really didn't matter how much spit and polish the men applied. He was a master at discovering the most minute deficiency, or at least what in his mind was a deficiency, and doled out punishment with unrestrained generosity. Extra duty or reduced rations of spirits and tobacco was the usual penalty for any seaman who had, in his words, *slacked-off*.

Before *Rose*, Roberts had taken great pleasure in preparing his station for Sunday inspection and thrived on any compliments. But Hughes did not hand out compliments to anyone, ever. Frustrated with the captain's impossible standards, Roberts eventually gave up and delegated the task to Dowlin. The big, easy-going Irishman accepted the responsibility with zeal and his eye for detail served him well. If Hughes castigated one of his men unfairly for some minor infraction, Dowlin, with a nod from Roberts, saw to it that the punishment was never enforced. A man put on half rations would mysterious find a portion of pork or bread wrapped inside a handkerchief laying inside his hammock. A man restricted below would find a book or whittling tools and wood to the pass the time away.

Roberts smiled. "Today is only Thursday, Patrick. You're just a wee bit early, hey?"

Dowlin tried to look serious, but couldn't suppress his boyish grin. "Aye. Me and the lads might have overdone things just a bit. You know how I get. But the ship was lookin' a bit ragged. Besides, doin' the work now will mean less to do come Saturday. Took the liberty of askin' the Capt'n for permission to send some of our lads over to Frenchy thar to give Wilcox a hand with his repairs. Thought it wise, Luke, to add a few marines to the watch too - just in case 'em tricky Frogs try somethin' foolish."

"Has the Captain been about?"

"An hour ago, aye. He took in some air, checked the log and retired for the evenin'. Not a word out of his mouth. Oh, I almost forgot." Dowlin paused to reach into the inside of his coat to retrieve a sheet of paper. "Can't read it in this light too good, Luke. But here's the prize crew list you asked for."

Roberts read the names. Dowlin had selected well, choosing the good, dependable Irishmen. He had also included the names of twelve marines to provide security.

"Very well. You've done enough for one day. I'll assume this watch. Get yourself some rest."

Dowlin nodded and saluted. He wanted to ask about Kelly, but then thought better of it.

As South Wind blew her hot breath across the green waters to greet the new day, a rising sun, blood red and menacing, peaked above the horizon. Roberts pulled at his collar, already damp with sweat from the warm, sticky air.

The ship's full company of officers and men were assembled. With a grim nod from Roberts, Dowlin gave the order for all hands to witness punishment. At the twitter of the boatswains' mate whistle, the crew hustled to form ranks. Division heads counted their men and reported the number to Dowlin - and God help the unfortunate petty officer who couldn't account for one of his own during roll call. After the division heads had completed their reports, Dowlin turned to Roberts, saluted and informed him that all officers and men were present or accounted for.

Standing at the mainmast the ship's master-at-arms, a beefy Irishman named Thompson, a brutish looking man, held a black cat-of-nine-tails in his hands. It was his duty was to enforce the captain's discipline and Thompson had always gone about his work with relish. Even his fellow Irishmen despised him.

Stripped to the waist and flanked by two burly marines, Kelly was led up to the deck and forced to lean against a grating set up against the mast, face first, exposing his back to the master-at-arms. As the marines bound his hands to the grating with strips of rawhide, Thompson rolled his whip up into a coil and dunked it into a bucket of seawater sitting at his feet. Then he stretched the leather taut, could sense that all eyes were on him as he went through his curious ritual, and savored the moment.

As *Rose* rolled peacefully over the gentle swells, the ship's company waited quietly in the sweltering heat for the captain to appear. They listened to voices and sounds drifting across the water from *Toulon*. The carpenters were still at it. Long minutes passed.

Roberts nervously tapped his foot against the deck and was just about to send a midshipman down to invite the captain on deck when he heard Hughes's short stubby legs pounding against the companionway's steps. The captain strutted onto the quarterdeck in his full dress uniform, like some peacock wishing to impress all the other birds with its fine plumage.

Roberts touched his hat but conspicuously neglected to wish Hughes a good morning.

"All hands present and accounted for to witness punishment, sir," Roberts reported dryly.

Hughes nodded and walked over to the quarterdeck's forward rail.

He looked down on the crew with smug disdain and cleared his throat.

"Men of the *Rose*, the Articles of War are well known to you - I review them with you each and every Sunday. Raising a hand to one's superior makes that man liable for, and I quote: "death or such less penalty under the Articles as a master of a ship sees fit." Impertinence, disobedience, insubordination - these crimes cannot and shall not be tolerated aboard any of His Majesty's warships. Certainly, such acts shall never be tolerated aboard this ship! I thought I had made myself clear."

He paused and then with a dramatic sweep of his arm, pointed to Kelly. "It would seem that there are some among you who think my authority aboard this ship can be challenged. I assure you that you are wrong. That *man* has insulted one of his Majesty's Royal officers. A serious transgression. Punishment must be exacted, discipline maintained. A hard lesson for all to be sure. It gives me no pleasure to do what now must be done."

He turned to look at Roberts. His eyes were cold, narrow slits.

"Lieutenant Roberts, you may carry out punishment. Twenty is the number, sir, I believe *we* discussed and agreed was appropriate."

Roberts obediently looked over to the sergeant of marines and nodded. The sergeant in turn nodded to a glum-faced drummer boy and the boy proceeded to tap out a steady cadence. The sergeant offered Kelly a strip of leather and he accepted, biting down hard. And then, the cat-of-nine-tails lashed out, cracked the still morning air and men flinched.

Many did their best to look away as Thompson laid into Kelly. The drumbeat rolled on.

With each stoke of the whip, Kelly bit down harder on his leather gag. Droplets of sweat rolled down his rough face, followed by tears as the lash cut deeper slices into his soft flesh. But he did not faint and, good to his word, he did not cry out, no, not once. Not that proud man.

After the twentieth stroke, Thompson took the bucket of seawater at his feet and doused Kelly's lacerated and bloody back. Then several sailors cut the giant free and helped him below.

Roberts fought down his nausea.

"You may," commanded Hughes with a faint smile on his lips, "call

all hands to breakfast now, Mr. Roberts. I believe that we have made *our* point."

"Aye," Roberts replied simply, without any emotion.

"Oh, Mr. Roberts," Hughes added as he turned to leave the quarterdeck, "I'll have that report of yours on the French ship together with your list for a prize crew without delay. I assume your preparations are completed. You will be able to set off today I trust?"

Roberts nodded affirmatively. "Aye, Captain. At your pleasure."

Hughes removed a silver watch from his pocket, checked the hour.

"Very well," he snapped. "I have a quarter past eight. You may report to me in my cabin in fifteen minutes."

A faint smile touched Roberts's lips as he watched Hughes disappear below. His thoughts turned to a curious encounter earlier, during the night. An encounter with one of the Irishmen, an encounter he knew would forever change things, would forever change his life...

A seaman named Morgan, while securing the ship's stern guns in the captain's cabin after the battle, happened upon a crumpled ball of paper lying underneath the captain's desk. Michael Morgan, an illiterate man but hardly dull-witted, and never slow, for no particular reason took the paper and stuffed it down his trousers. Morgan understood his actions could be construed as a treasonous offense, but something moved him to take the risk anyway.

Morgan brought the document to Roberts, who, at first, wanted to unleash the full fury of his displeasure at Morgan. But Morgan was a first rate seaman - and loyal - so Roberts simply took the paper and dismissed Morgan without any rebuke.

Roberts had almost tossed the ball of paper over the side but then thought better of it. He took a stroll around the deck and when he was alone, he smoothed the paper out over the ship's rail and then held it up to a lantern. The contents of the document stunned him.

It was a rough draft of the captain's report to the Admiralty describing *Rose's* engagement with the *Toulon* and Hughes was taking all the credit for the victory. Hughes exaggerated *Rose's* damages from the storm, accused several unnamed seamen of cowardice and, to Roberts's astonishment, accused Roberts himself of a dereliction of duty in the face of the enemy. A great victory in a crippled ship against the hated French - in spite of an unwilling crew and an inept first officer - was the captain's boast!

Roberts read and reread the captain's words to make certain he hadn't misunderstood or misconstrued their meaning. But Hughes's report was clear. Hughes, for reasons beyond Roberts's comprehension, was not merely content with seizing all the glory for himself. Roberts could have accepted Hughes's exaggerations about his own part in the battle; Roberts had even expected it. But Hughes's blatant determination to destroy him shocked and baffled him.

Roberts neatly folded the paper in four and slipped it back inside his pocket. For a long while, he could do little more than stare down into the sea's inky black waters - and brood. The same words kept popping into his head over and over again: *the bold man comes off best... the bold man comes off best...* He couldn't shake the phrase off. And then an idea, a solution to his dilemma really, struck him square in the face. He hurried below to find Dowlin.

"What the f-, Luke?"

"Wake up Pat," Roberts said whispering and shook him. "Read this."

Dowlin rubbed the sleep out of his eyes and took the paper from Roberts, mumbling something under his breath. And then his jaw dropped.

"Bugger me, Luke, this bastard," he said with disgust, "has had you in his sights from the very first. Never could put my finger on the *why* of it. Where the shit did you get this?"

"Morgan. Morgan found it discarded in the Captain's great cabin."

"*Jesus.* Morgan can't even read. He takes this from the Capt'n's cabin and gives it to you?"

"That about sums it up."

"What the fook was he thinkin'? Well, 'tis bad enough Hughes takes credit were none is due. But I say, if that was all thar was to it, so be it, Capt'n's prerogative and all that horseshit. But to go to all this trouble to try and ruinin' yer good name - and on such a bald-faced lie - I must be daft, I don't get it. Most vexing isn't it? Well, I warned ya, didn't I? You just wouldn't kiss his arse. Now whatcha goin' to do, eh?"

"I have considered the matter," Roberts responded vaguely with a confident smirk. "I have an idea and I'll discuss it with you later, at a better time. Oh, by the way, Pat, I have modified your list for the prize crew. I trust you will have no objection."

Dowlin either didn't hear Roberts's last comment about the prize crew or chose to ignore it. "Considered the matter have you? Bloody hell, Luke! Oh sweet *Jesus*, fine and well. I've just considered the matter too - I say we just slit the son-of-a-bitch's throat and toss his worthless carcass overboard on the next new moon. We'd be doin' the Empire a good deed if you ask me. The navy has far too many fools runnin' around with rank!"

Roberts shook his head. "And get us all hanged? Rest easy there, Pat. There will be no killing. I think I've stumbled on a better way. A way that will see us through this. Let's speak no more of it for now. Later, with clearer heads, we can discuss the matter through and through."

"Well, if I could find any spirits around here, I'd gladly raise my glass to clearer heads..."

It had returned. He could feel the repulsive thing, always lurking inside his head, wrapping its strong tentacles around his brain, squeezing ever harder. His head began throbbing. Roberts massaged his temples. But there was no stopping it now. The beast would come and bring excruciating pain. And he knew the ugly thing would not yield, not until it had laid its victim low - not until it had forced him to pray for death. Only then would the beast release its painful grip and vanish.

His watch showed 8:20. He stopped by the galley and helped

himself to some rum, draining the tin cup with one gulp, and then took another. The cook said nothing. Fortified, he made his way to his quarters to replace his sweat-soaked shirt with a fresh one and then made his way to the captain's cabin.

As Hughes sat at his desk reviewing Roberts's report, gold-tipped rays of sunlight filtered in through the cabin's open windows behind him. The light did little to improve the cabin's usual gloominess. Roberts remained standing rigidly at attention, his hat cradled in his arm, while Hughes considered the young officer out of the corner of his eye.

Roberts appeared relaxed, had even addressed him with a cordial tone for once. *Odd*, thought Hughes. Content with the report, he tossed the paper aside with his usual smug indifference and reached for the prize crew list. As he went down the list, slowly reading the names out loud, he caught Roberts looking beyond him, with his eyes fixed on the sea.

Hughes tapped the list with his index finger and sighed. "Bless me, Mr. Roberts, but your sense of humor is lost on me. This list of yours is an odd assortment of riff-raff. I swear, sometimes you actually seem to be partial to these Irish misfits. Come now, you can't be serious asking for some of the men listed here."

"Beggin' your pardon, Captain. All good seamen, sir. *Rose's* complement of officers and men is already seriously deficient. The ship's company is down by nearly a third. I propose to take as few men as possible so as not to jeopardize your command. But I'll need stout, dependable lads for the prize crew to make up for my own lack of numbers. And, like it or not, sir, the Irishmen are good sailors."

Hughes found that explanation perplexing. Except for Morgan, every man on Roberts's list was an Irishman and, as far as he was concerned, every one of them was a troublemaker. And Roberts hadn't asked for any marines, not a one. Well, Hughes thought to himself, he would be glad to be rid of the whole damnable lot of them! Still, there was something not quite right...

"Well, sir, I shall be blunt with you. I must question your own good judgment - or clear lack of it. I see the names of shirkers and slackers on this list. I see the names of men who cannot be trusted. Why look here, you've even included the names of several insubordinate swine. Dregs - the lot of them. I must say, most curious."

Roberts said nothing.

A thin smile touched Hughes's lips. "Why bless me, Mr. Roberts, here is the name I see of Seaman Christopher Kelly. I missed it earlier. Ah, I'll wager he'll give us no more difficulties for a month or two! Well, I shall speak plainly to you, Mr. Roberts. I find this list amusing. Ordinarily I would call you a fool for requesting such men. But what you say is true. We are in a bit of a fix here. I'll grant you that much at least. Our orders have not changed. After we complete our mission at Port Royal, *Rose* is to keep to her present station, scouting the South Atlantic. Potential hostilities with the French and Spanish to worry about, hunting down American warships and chasing enemy merchantmen - a most difficult mission the Admiralty has entrusted me with. Aye... This ship is woefully undermanned as you say. And, despite the lateness of the year, it would seem we may not have seen our last hurricane yet. I dare not risk reducing the ship's complement beyond what prudence will allow. But, you want no marines to accompany you?"

"You unquestionably have the more perilous mission, sir. I will only be ferrying a ship back to England across the wide-open sea while you patrol hostile waters around the islands."

"True, very true, but I neither care for, or trust, the French. I'll not lose my prize to any of their skullduggery. You'll have your prize crew here, Mr. Roberts, but you'll also take Lieutenant Hanson and a dozen marines with you with orders to shoot any disobedient French sailor - humph - or any insubordinate Irishman for that matter, on the spot. Perhaps I can't replace able-bodied seamen out here, but I can put in at St. Lucia at least to take on supplies and perhaps borrow a few marines."

Roberts realized that Hughes had made up his mind. But he offered a mild objection anyway fearing that, if he did not, Hughes might grow even more suspicious.

"Sir, with your indulgence. Your approach is most prudent, of course, but, if I may, the marines will just be in the way. More mouths to feed. I will keep strict control over the ship's armory and I have the binding oath of *Le Toulon's* first officer that there will be no treachery, no attempt to retake the ship. He has in fact even agreed to remain on board *Toulon* as a hostage to guarantee that promise."

Hughes actually started laughing at Roberts. "A Frenchman's word you say?" he scoffed. "By God, Mr. Roberts, I see that you are serious! You would put your trust in that? *You* gamble on the word of a French officer when it is *your* prize that is at risk if it pleases you to do so, sir. I'll have you take no such risks with my prize, Mr. Roberts. You shall take the marines with you and proceed directly to Portsmouth and that is that. Understood?"

"Clearly understood, sir."

"Good. The matter is closed then. Now, Luke, I have written out instructions for you on how and where to make the necessary arrangements to deposit my share of the prize money once the frigate is sold at auction. I have no wife and I have no family in Portsmouth I can trust with such a sensitive transaction, so I must impose upon you."

Roberts raised an eyebrow. Hughes's had never called him by his given name before. "I would be most happy to attend to it for you, sir."

"Excellent. I also have sealed, official dispatches here for the Admiralty. You shall personally see to their delivery. God willing, I shall see you in Portsmouth sometime in the spring. That is all, you are dismissed..."

Roberts said no more. There was nothing more to be said. He saluted smartly, turned on his heels and left. Hanson and his marines would complicate matters. He would need to think on that. But he was not concerned. Something would come to him. It always did.

Roberts made his way amidships to the crew's galley to check on Kelly and found the big Irishman lying face down on a table, wrapped in bloodstained linen gauze. The surgeon had washed Kelly's face in spirits of hartshorne and had given him a dose of laudanum, a mixture of opium and cider, his supplies of anodyne having been exhausted.

"Is there anything I can do for you Mr. Kelly?" Roberts asked in a whisper, slipping into his Irish brogue.

"No, sir," Kelly replied weakly. He looked up at Roberts with a pale, sweaty face. "Just let the lads know. The wager's mine."

Roberts forced a smile. "Aye, so it is," he said and lightly touched

Kelly's bare shoulder. "I'm taking a prize crew to sail *Toulon* back to England. I've taken the liberty of adding your name to the crew - if you think you can manage the transfer over in the ship's longboat. We sail this very morning. Are you up to it lad?"

"Bless you, sir. Take old Kelly here with you and damn this ship and damn her capt'n too."

Roberts nodded. "Excellent. So be it. Rest easy now, Chris. Later today then, I'll see you on the other side, on board *Toulon*."

"On the other side?" Kelly asked, intrigued by Roberts's curious choice of words and managed a weak smile.

"On the other side."

"Aye, sir. On the other side it is then, sir."

Chapter Four
Their Scheming Ways

ulling gently at their oars under a blazing, noonday sun, a dozen sailors rowed Roberts and his sea chest over to the *Toulon*. He was the last man to be transferred over to the frigate. No omens crossed his path this time. He removed a soiled handkerchief from his coat pocket and blotted away the beads of sweat popping up along his brow. As the long boat drew closer to the frigate, he instructed the boat's master to circle around *Toulon* so he could have a closer look at the repairs to her hull. Her handsome stern decorations had not been restored of course, but the carpenter had done his work well. Every hole had been skillfully patched and a new rudder, crude but functional, swayed lazily back and forth in the gentle currents.

Satisfied, Roberts climbed aboard and was greeted on deck with the military honors reserved for ship captains. The boatswains' mate blew his whistle. His prize crew, and the French officers assembled on deck, snapped to. The gesture warmed his heart. The idea must have been Sartine's. None of the British officers would have ordered it, certainly not with Hughes only 100 yards off. Then the marines presented arms. That was some of the sergeant's handiwork. Hanson never would have approved it and, in fact, Roberts caught Hanson cast a disapproving eye at his sergeant.

Roberts counted, including himself, four British officers, five petty officers, thirty British seamen and eleven marines, including one sergeant. Nearly 400 French sailors were locked below in the ship's dark, stuffy holds. Most of the small arms and swords had been removed from *Toulon's* arms' lockers and transferred over to the *Rose*. The British sailors, except for their rigging knives, were unarmed. That left ten British marine muskets to consider. *Only ten...*

Roberts folded his arms behind his back, paused to take in the condition of the ship. Everything appeared to be in good order. The missing mizzen had been replaced with a short stump. It wasn't pretty but seemed sturdy enough. *Toulon's* decks had been scrubbed clean and the list to port was gone. The rigging had all been neatly repaired. Wilcox, a feisty, humorless man from York, and often difficult to deal with, was nevertheless a proud professional and had done his job well.

Roberts turned to Sartine. "*Monsieur* de Sartine, you have inspected this ship, sir?"

"*Oui, Monsieur* Roberts."

"And?"

"The work of your men is exceptional. I can find no fault. *Le Toulon* is ready to sail at your command."

"Very well."

"The ship, *mon Capitaine*," Sartine added, pausing to make a grand sweep of his arm and an exaggerated bow that was a bit too theatrical for Roberts, "is yours." And then, with grand flourish, Sartine saluted smartly.

Roberts ignored Sartine's promotion of him to *captain*.

"How many of your officers wish to be transferred over to the *Rose, Monsieur* Sartine?"

"Transferred? Why, none, *Mon Capitaine*."

"I see," replied Roberts, though he really didn't see and absently started tapping the deck with his shoe. The French officers would have stood a better chance of reaching French soil sooner on board the *Rose* than with him.

"Mr. Wilcox, sir, do you concur with *Monsieur* de Sartine? Is this ship ready to sail?"

"Aye, Lieutenant Roberts, all is in good order, sir. She'll wear nicely from here to England, at your pleasure..."

"Very well then. My compliments to you and to your men, Mr. Wilcox. The ship appears fit, very fit indeed. Mr. Dowlin, if you please, make ready to sail at once. I'll have the reefs shaken out of the topgallants. If she handles well enough with that then, at your discretion, Mr. Dowlin, you may lay on more canvas - as much as she'll bear in this light wind. Proceed due east for the present. I'll mark us a more precise course in the ship's log directly. The charts are in my trunk. Mr. Dowlin, you may signal *Rose*. We are under way and departing her company. No need to add *my compliments...*"

"Aye, aye, sir!" grinned the ship's new second in command and, mimicking Sartine, offered his own grand salute. Dowlin did an about face, barked out orders to get under way and then dismissed the ship's company.

Roberts turned to Sartine as men dispersed and went about their duties. "Lieutenant Sartine, would you and your officers favor me and my fellow officers with your company at supper tonight?"

Sartine bowed his head. "It would be a distinct honor."

Roberts nodded. He noted, with just a touch of envy, that Sartine carried himself with a certain style. There was, with no sign of being pompous so far, a subtle or polished arrogance about Sartine, or at least the good-natured Frenchman was very self-assured.

"Mr. Dowlin, you shall assume the first watch. As we are shorthanded, I shall work out watch rotations to include Lieutenant de Sartine and his officers." He turned to Sartine again, "if, of course, that is acceptable to you, Lieutenant Sartine."

Sartine bowed again. "I am flattered by your trust, *Monsieur* Roberts."

"Excellent, Lieutenant Sartine," Roberts replied and turned to Dowlin. "Lieutenant Dowlin, the ship is yours," he said and excused himself to go below to the captain's great cabin.

The room was pitch-dark, Wilcox's men having planked over the blown out windows. But the quarters were spacious, even luxurious by British standards. He opened his sea chest and unpacked his things and, when he felt the ship get underway, he grabbed his charts, British charts usually being superior to anything the French used. And then he made his way back up the companionway and to the quarterdeck.

He saw Dowlin standing next to the helmsman at the ship's wheel and walked towards the wheel to stand quietly by Dowlin's side. He looked up at the masts and saw the British Union Jack fluttering haphazardly in the wind above their heads. Above the Royal Navy's colors, the sky was a pretty blue with puffy, white clouds speeding past the ship.

The large frigate was handling surprisingly well in the light breezes. *An auspicious beginning*, thought Roberts.

Then he felt a slight shift in the winds from the north. The change was nearly imperceptible at first. That meant a flow of less humid air moving down towards them, something, happily, to look forward to. Such weather refreshes men's spirits. A good omen Roberts mused to himself, a man not accustomed to seeing, much less reading, omens.

Sartine then came up on deck, spotted Roberts and Dowlin reviewing the ship's log and joined them. "All meets with your approval, sir?" he asked.

"All is in good order, *Monsieur* de Sartine. Thank you. *Le Toulon* is as fine a vessel as I have ever sailed on."

Sartine nodded. "The weather is changing. By this evening it will be delightful, no?"

"Quite so. I had the same thought just a moment ago. You have a good nose for the weather. Perhaps we can arrange to have your crew enjoy some liberty on deck. Small numbers could be rotated back and forth. Their present accommodations, I imagine, are not so agreeable."

"Most generous," Sartine answered with a smile. "The gesture will be greatly appreciated by my men, I can assure you."

"Mr. Dowlin, will you see to it?"

"Aye, sir, straight away," Dowlin replied reluctantly and threw his friend a suspicious glance. He did not like the French, had no interest in their comfort and did not care to become too chummy with them. Roberts's order was clear enough though and he saw no point in debating the point. He disappeared below to pass the orders on to the marines guarding the French prisoners. Still, he saw one plus. Hanson, at least, would have a fit and that could be fun.

"Hm, *de Sartine...*" Roberts said, allowing the name to roll off his tongue slowly. "You are of noble birth?"

"My adopted family is of modest nobility, *oui*. I am just a seaman. My mother and father died when I was very young and there was no title or estate to inherit. Perhaps you know the name Count Antoine Raymond Jean Gaulbert Gabriel de Sartine? No? Well, no matter. He is the king's Minister of Marine. He was a dear friend of my father and took me in after my parents died. I call him uncle."

"I see. You come from a family of mariners then?"

Sartine laughed. "No, no. I am the first. I am, how do you English say? Um... The black sheep, I am the black sheep of my family. The Sartines are landowners and landlords, not mariners."

"Oh."

"My uncle, I am certain," Sartine added with a shrug, "has never even seen the ocean let alone sailed across it. And you, Lieutenant Roberts?"

"Humble beginnings, I'm afraid," Roberts offered evasively. "My parents died when I was very young as well. I was raised by my father's brother. Your English, I must say, is excellent."

"Yes, *merci*. I had the pleasure of living in London for nearly two years."

Roberts instinctively liked the Frenchman. "I cannot say that I am much acquainted with London. Well, I must return to my duties. We shall have plenty of time to talk later. Until this evening then?"

"*Oui, Mon Capitaine*," Sartine answered.

The two officers exchanged salutes and Sartine left Roberts on the quarterdeck with only the helmsman and one armed marine standing watch to keep him company.

Roberts remained on deck, mostly by himself, throughout the afternoon and into the early evening. He took pleasure in watching the sun majestically sink beneath the waves as night closed in around the ship. He had spent the day letting his mind wander, but had not squandered his time on idle daydreaming. No. He used his time, his bit of solitude, to plot and scheme. Different ideas swirled around in his head, flimsy thoughts of no substance at first, until one thought took root and flourished into a plan...

Supper was an awkward affair. Only Roberts and Sartine really enjoyed themselves. The two men spoke freely, appreciated the other's humor, and quickly developed an easy rapport. The rest of the officers ate their meal of salted beef, potatoes and fresh bread quietly and with little pleasure. When they had all finished, and after a steward had cleared the plates from the table, Dowlin, Hanson and Wilcox offered their apologies and excused themselves. The French officers quickly did the same, except for Sartine who remained behind after Roberts had motioned him to stay.

Roberts had the steward leave three remaining bottles of Madeira on the table and dismissed him for the evening. He and Sartine continued drinking liberally, in an unspoken contest to see who could hold his liquor best. Sartine matched Roberts's glass for glass. Too much liquor made Roberts drowsy and clumsy but he never lost his wits, no matter how much he drank, and Sartine seemed to have the same gift.

After talking about small matters for a time, Roberts paused, held his crystal goblet up to the candlelight to study the cut glass's intricate designs. "Your hand, *Monsieur* de Sartine, how does it heal? Do you require any medication? We brought some medical supplies on board with us as I have found English medicines to be superior to French."

"It is nothing, sir. Truly. A minor splinter wound and there is no infection. I am flattered by your concern. I was near the stern when your broadside, the *coup de grace*, struck us."

"You were then very lucky."

"*Oui*, indeed. I was very lucky. Two men standing next to me were not so fortunate."

Roberts eyed Sartine carefully in the dim light. "Ah, the hand of fate, I suppose. For each of us, our time on this earth is marked from birth. Life is, at best, precarious. On a different subject, sir, you strike me as a man of honor and, I would ask you directly: is my assumption correct? Are you a man of honor?"

The Frenchman thought the question odd, was caught off-guard, and took a few moments to consider his answer. He had to struggle to keep his thoughts focused. The Englishmen was up to something.

"Yes. Without honor, what does a gentleman have really? Nothing..."

Roberts nodded with satisfaction. "Just so. May I speak plainly?"

Now it was Sartine who took a moment to study Roberts with care. He tried to get a fix on what the look in Roberts's eyes might mean. But the Englishman showed him little. *A gambler's face*, Sartine told himself.

"I usually find the direct approach best," Sartine said with a wry smile, his speech beginning to slur. "Although, this way is not always well understood by my countrymen. We French can often be, well, oblique."

Roberts carefully sat his glass down on the table. "The rules of such a dialogue would require... an oath, an oath of fidelity and of secrecy... a promise from me to you and from you to me that what is said now, at this table, tonight, will never be repeated. Agreed?"

Now Sartine was truly baffled and again took time to consider Roberts's proposal before answering. He suddenly realized how low he had slouched down in his chair and tried sitting up straight to correct his posture, did his best to reclaim some measure of sobriety.

"I must say, I find this all most intriguing. You have my word, *Monsieur* Lieutenant Roberts. What is said between us now goes no further."

"Good. I believe in honor as well, though I have seldom found it among the *English*..."

Sartine bolted upright in his chair, wondering if he had heard the Englishman correctly. "What? I beg your pardon?"

But before Sartine had even uttered his question, Roberts had seen the confusion in Sartine's face.

"You heard me correctly. And I am not drunk, if that is your thought. I assure you, I am quite sober."

"Well, in truth," Sartine said with a smile, using a hand to cover his mouth to hide a small burp. "I may not be able to make the same boast. But I am not too drunk. Not yet. What is it precisely, I wonder, my new friend is trying to say to me? The English can be so difficult to understand at times. You island people can be, well, confounding."

"True, how true, but the hour is late," Roberts offered vaguely. "Perhaps we can talk later? I may have a - proposition - for you. Would you be willing to discuss the matter further, at a later time with clearer heads? Once again, you must agree to secrecy. You must, on your honor, agree to forget the whole affair should I ask you to do just that. But before you answer, know this: I will assure you, here and now, that what I have to say would involve no wrongful act against your king, would compromise your obligations as a French officer... Your integrity would not be jeopardized in any fashion. What I have in mind could benefit us both."

Sartine drained his glass. He did not yet understand what kind of man he was dealing with, except, he was certain, Roberts was unusually shrewd. He was curious, saw no harm in pursuing the matter later. Sartine gingerly set his glass down on the table, stood up unsteadily, and used his hands to smooth out the creases in his uniform.

"Is this ship rocking or am I?"

Roberts laughed. "A bit of both I fear."

"Hm, indeed. I take it you are not English? Scottish, Irish perhaps, or American?"

Roberts stood and firmly shook Sartine's good hand. "Irish, aye, but that is a fact not known by many."

Sartine tried to see the man behind the mask but could not. "I am beginning to understand one thing at least, *Monsieur*; wine or no, you are a clever, careful man. I will do my best to remain careful and clever in your company."

"I respect that."

Sartine bowed his head and, as an afterthought, said, "I am, sir, your humble servant."

Roberts smiled as he watched Sartine run his hand along the table's edge to steady himself and left the great cabin to make his way back to his own quarters. Roberts was confident he could safely confide his plan to Sartine at a better time. What the Frenchman was prepared to do, or not do, remained an open question. Roberts had planted the seed and that was enough for now.

For the next few weeks, *Toulon* made good progress under fair skies and a driving wind - West Wind's good gift to the seafarers to speed them along their way. The delightful weather made hearts light. Even the tyrannical Lieutenant Hanson, for just a bit, eased his harsh grip over his spit and polish marines.

Roberts and Sartine spent most of their time together on the quarterdeck and grew to know each other well. Sartine was a mediocre seaman and knew it. The deep, blue waters held no power over his soul. He missed the firm earth under his feet. He missed the sights and smells of land. But Roberts found his judgment balanced and thought him exceptionally astute and, with each passing day, he grew more confident that Sartine was the right man to help him see his plan through. The two men formed an easy friendship.

Regarding matters concerning the ship, Roberts was always sensitive and careful to consult with Sartine first, treating him as an equal and not as a prisoner. They routinely took their meals together and talked of many things, from navigation and naval tactics, to God and politics, Roberts often speaking to Sartine in French to practice his rusty skills. Even Dowlin, a simple man with an innate dislike for anything elitist, and never fond of anything French, came to like the sophisticated, but affable Frenchman. Sartine and Dowlin shared a love for pursuing life's simple pleasures and enjoyed trading stories of their escapades.

While *Toulon* continued to plow the waves towards England, the schemer bided his time until one fine morning he decided he was ready. He had conceived his plan back on board the *Rose*, on the very night Morgan had given him Captain Hughes's discarded paper, but had used his time on *Toulon* to polish each facet of his plan until it gleamed with perfection in his mind's eye.

Roberts was sitting at the captain's desk, writing, when he heard a rapping at his door.

"Enter," he commanded.

"You called for us, sir?" Dowlin asked as he and Kelly stepped inside and removed their hats. Except for the beams of sunlight poking through the seams between the planks covering the cabin's blown-out windows, and a few candles, the room was dark. The beams of sunlight had settled on Roberts's shoulders.

Roberts rose from his chair and handed each man a glass of Madeira. Kelly, all healed up now, turned to Dowlin with a befuddled look, unable to remember the last time an officer had offered him, a lowly seaman, a drink! The Irish giant awkwardly accepted the small, delicate glass, trying not to crush it with his huge paw. He had never held crystal before.

"Gentlemen," Roberts started off, reverting to his Irish brogue. "Thank you for coming. The three of us have sailed together for a long time. We've been through a number of scrapes together, through thick and thin, and we have formed a bond between us. I know I can trust both of you. I won't waste your time on pleasantries. Unless either of you has an objection, I intend to speak bluntly. Fair enough?"

Dowlin and Kelly exchanged perplexed looks and then Dowlin drained his glass, reached for the bottle and poured himself another. "I'm all ears Luke. What's on yer mind?"

Roberts cleared his throat. "Lads, I am resigning my commission as an officer in the king's navy, effective immediately."

Dowlin burst out laughing, swallowed his wine down the wrong pipe and started choking. Kelly gave him a hardy pat on the back until he stopped.

"What the devil are you talkin' about, Luke?" Dowlin asked, red-faced. "I don't get the joke."

"No joke."

"Have you gone mad? You've always been a man of such uncommon, good sense before. You can't resign. The king will have yer head stuck on a pike outside London Tower he will."

Kelly tossed his glass back, swallowed his wine with one long gulp. He said nothing.

Roberts smiled. "Aye, well, be that as it may, I've served in the king's navy long enough, lads. I've had a belly full and now I have thought of a way to leave the service behind - nice and tidy."

"Ha! You best lay down and rest yerself now, lad," replied Dowlin with a smile. "Do you want me to fetch the surgeon? I think you've gone and caught the fever and are delirious!"

Roberts ignored Dowlin's sarcasm.

"I'll be damned if I'm going to deliver Hughes's report to the Admiralty, a report, Mr. Kelly, that falsely accuses me of misdeeds. And your punishment, Chris - spiteful, sheer meanness, that's all it was. You did no wrong, Chris. It was me who lost his temper tho' you're the one who paid dearly for it. I never planned to stay in the king's navy forever anyway. Thought you two lads might just be interested in joining me, seeing how we've always sailed together."

Dowlin cocked his head to one side. "Good *Gawd!* Yer serious aren't you? Weeeell go on, Luke. You've piqued my interest now. I'll give you that much. Tell us what foolishness has diseased yer mind this time around."

Kelly nodded. "Aye, sir, I'd like to hear yer plan. I might be needin' a wee bit more of that juice you got thar, sir, if you don't mind."

Roberts handed the bottle over to Kelly. "'Tis all very simple, lads. We let the French retake the ship. They take us to France, throw us into prison and then -"

Dowlin shook his head in disbelief and cut Roberts off. "What nonsense is this slippin' through yer teeth thar, hey? Yer brains have been touched by the sun! You think a stinkin' French prison is better than bein' in the king's navy?"

Roberts held up his hand. "Easy there Patrick, let me finish?"

Dowlin shut his mouth and grunted, annoyed with himself for having lashed out at Roberts so harshly. He knew he was a hothead. He set his glass down, grabbed the bottle out of Kelly's hand and took a long swig.

"Now," Roberts pressed on, "this plan is just between the three of us. No one else is to know, not even the Irish lads on board. We'll need Sartine's assistance though. Hear me out. That is all I ask. We cut a deal with Sartine. We allow his men to retake the ship and Sartine becomes a hero. We wouldn't be the first prize crew to be overwhelmed by our own prisoners. There are less than fifty of us and nearly four-hundred Frenchmen on board. After we're in prison, Sartine will arrange our *escape*. We'll take any of the Irish lads willing to go along with us and then vanish, with no one the wiser. The British will never come looking for us. They will have no cause to."

"Beggin' yer pardon, sir," Kelly interrupted. "But what about the English lads?"

"Ah," Roberts replied with a sly smile. "Unlucky souls I'm afraid.

Pity they won't be able to escape with us. We'll have our French friends hold them in a separate jail. All the Irish lads will be incarcerated with us. If Hanson or Wilcox asks about you and me, Pat, their French jailers will tell them we were sent on to Paris to be tried for crimes, or maybe told that we died from the fever - or told nothing at all. Whatever seems best at the time. It won't matter much to them what happens to us after they're returned to England a month or two later in a prisoner exchange. We'll be forgotten soon enough."

Dowlin stared down at his shoes. "I see you've given this a lot of thought and care, Luke."

Roberts rocked back and forth on the heels of his feet, a proud smile on his face. "I have. Aye, I have indeed."

Dowlin looked up at Kelly and then back at Roberts. "Ought to just leave the English bastards to rot in jail," he offered dryly. "I trust you, Luke. I trust you with my life. I trust Mr. Kelly here too, good man he is. Not ashamed to say so out loud. He's pulled my bottom out of the fire more than once. I suppose I trust most of the other Irish lads too - but I'm not sure I trust all of 'em, if you get my drift. Not sayin' I have any cause not to trust them, just not sure with something this dangerous hanging over our heads."

"Agreed, Pat. But that's the beauty of the plan, none of the lads will need to know. They don't need to know anything about it for it to work. When the French retake *Toulon*, it will seem real enough to all and when we break out of jail, no one will have any reason to think it was staged. Once we're free, we just won't quite be able to make our way back to merry, old England. That's it. The British won't catch us because they won't be lookin' for us. Who in London will trouble themselves over a few missing Irishmen and one derelict English officer? And, if for some reason we do ever need to explain ourselves to British authorities, we'll have some story handy about how it took us time to plan and execute our escape from France. The French will have no reason not to confirm the lie."

Kelly scratched the top of his head. "If you don't mind me askin', sir, what'll we do once we're all out of a French prison? I don't speak no French. Don't have no landlubber skills either and I wouldn't care to sign-up with the French navy."

"Aye," answered Roberts with a glint in his eye, "what'll we do indeed, hey? Now there's the first intelligent question either of you blockheads have asked me. *Toulon* is worth a small fortune; I wasn't intending to part with her for *free*. Sartine comes from a rich and influential family. We get him to stake us enough money to hire out a small lugger, something a dozen or so men can handle easy enough, then we try our hand at the honorable profession of *smuggling* and seek our fortunes running contraband."

"*Smugglin'?*" Dowlin asked, astonished.

"Aye," Kelly offered softly with a smile on his lips. He understood Roberts's plan straight off. "Fancy that, smugglers..." he added, pronouncing the word *smugglers* with slow satisfaction.

"Aye," replied Roberts with a wink, "smugglers."

"Well, damn if I don't feel the shade of old Jack the Bachelor standin' here with us this very moment," Dowlin offered with a grin. "Sends a cold shiver down my spine."

"Aye," Kelly agreed with a laugh. Jack the Bachelor indeed! Jack Field: rascal, thief, smuggler, friend to the poor, a *bête noire* to the English, a Robin Hood to the Irish and Rush's most notorious son. They say before he died in '72 he stashed away a fortune in loot inside a cave along the shore not far from his home in Rush. A huge green serpent guards it still - or so the story goes - devouring any treasure hunter fool enough to enter."

Dowlin dismissed the part about the serpent with a wave his hand. "Auck, a Dutchman's tale to spook youngsters and simpletons. But do you remember the rhyme, Chris?"

Kelly nodded with a chuckle, wrapped his great arm around Dowlin's shoulder and joined Dowlin in reciting the poem:

> "*The lover may sigh*
> *The courtier may lie*
> *And Croesus his treasure amass,*
> *All these joys are but vain*

They are blended with pain
I'll stand behind Field with my glass..."

The two native Rushmen shook with laughter and then took turns taking long swigs from the bottle of Madeira.

Dowlin began to appreciate the simple beauty of Roberts's plan and started to feel better about things. "Yeah, ole Jack, a good fellow and an honorable thief to be sure. And when next I am at the Royal Oak in Rush, I'll raise my glass high to his memory. But do ya think," he asked with more enthusiasm in his voice now, "Sartine will go along with it?"

Roberts shook his head. "Dunno, but why shouldn't he?"

Dowlin shrugged. "What prisoner wouldn't agree to be set free?"

Kelly grunted. "Ahem, excuse me, Lieutenant. A fine plan you've got thar. Grand it is indeed. But, beggin' yer pardon, sir, just how do the French retake the ship? Thar's Lieutenant Hanson and his marines to consider..."

"Aye," Dowlin interjected and took a deep breath. "'Em pretty red coats could spoil yer little dance sure enough."

"A complication to be sure - but you leave that to me, Christopher Kelly," Roberts answered, still smiling. "Are you in or out lads? No hard feelin's if you're not with me. Take your time; think it through. Not the kind of a decision a man should make in haste."

Dowlin broke out into a wide grin. "I'm in Luke. Lord help us all but I'm with you. No need to be thinkin' on it any longer for me. My brain muddles things up that way. It's simpler to just follow yer lead. Always has been."

"Aye," added Kelly, beaming, "for better or worse, I'm in too, Mr. Roberts. I've followed you to every new ship, to every new assignment. Too old to be changin' my ways now. I say, sir, you musta been inspired by the Almighty himself to concoct such a wicked plan as this." He paused to sigh, a pensive sigh, then added, "Well, God bless and look over us Irish, 'cause no one else ever has or ever will!"

Roberts patted both men affectionately on the shoulders. He was elated and could have hoped for no better response from his friends.

"Excellent! Shall we shake on it then? Pat, Chris, no one is to know about this scheme but the three of us. I'll discuss the matter with Sartine this very night. If he's in, our journey is about to take an interesting twist. If he's not, well, then, no harm done but we'll need a different plan..."

"Oh," offered Dowlin, "I have a strong hunch, as I chew on the beauty of this little adventure of yers, Luke, that Sartine will be most receptive."

"Why so confident, Mr. Dowlin?" asked Roberts.

"'Cause, Sartine and me, *Jesus*, I hate to confess this, but Sartine and me are cut from the same cloth and if I'm in, he'll be in. Yep, I'm certain of it..."

Days of fair skies and calm seas, uneventful days, followed after the meeting of the co-conspirators in the captain's great cabin, the place where secret plots were hatched and pacts were made. Steady winds pushed *Toulon* along smoothly and men, English and French alike, fell into an easy routine. But when mischievous North Wind caught word of a certain Irishman's scheming ways, she was all too eager to lend a helping hand, and *Toulon's* good luck came to an abrupt - and dicey - end.

The ship's barometer dropped precipitously when ominous, towering thunderheads gathered themselves in force behind the stern. A squall line formed, obliterated the sun, and unloosed devilish winds over the ship, followed by sheets of stinging rain.

From the quarterdeck, Roberts watched in awe as the storm swooped down on them. But there was also a gleam in his eye - the weather was perfect. This was the moment he had been patiently waiting for. Dressed in his tarpaulin and sou'wester, he grasped the ship's rail firmly to brace himself against the buffeting winds. Then Dowlin and Wilcox joined him there and the three men watched as dreadful darkness closed in all around them.

"I'll have all but the tops'ls taken in, Mr. Wilcox," Roberts shouted loud enough to be heard over the wind. "Best to have the storm jib set too if you please."

Roberts had waited too long to give the order to take up sails. A better seaman would have sent his men up into the rigging well-before the heart of the monster storm had overtaken them. But Roberts knew what he was doing. His error in judgment escaped the notice of the dependable, but unimaginative Wilcox.

"Aye, sir!" he answered. "It don't look none too good, sir. Nasty squall for this late in the year."

"Aye, Mr. Wilcox. You best have your men shake a leg. Mr. Dowlin, send for *Monsieur* Sartine. I need him, now! Make sure the galley fires and all the lanterns have been put out too. And you there helmsman, keep her steady, watch your course and steer small! There's land less than twenty leagues off our starboard. The storm will try to push us towards it. I don't fancy running aground in these seas!"

The helmsman nodded back.

Dowlin went to find Sartine while Wilcox and his men climbed into the rigging, up into the blackness, and out along the treacherous yardarms where they struggled to pull in the sails. The topmen labored frantically as merciless winds assaulted them from all sides and the rain turned hard.

Brilliant flashes of light crisscrossed the dark skies and then, a clap of thunder, terrifying in its intensity, put fear into every heart. North Wind whipped the waves into a terrible frenzy, sending mountainous rollers against the ship. Walls of foaming seawater poured over her rails and at times half the ship was submerged under water. But *Toulon* plowed stubbornly on, pitching and rolling violently against the raging sea.

Wilcox hurried back to the quarterdeck with only half the job done. "Mr. Roberts, trouble, sir. I need more lads in this weather, before these winds tear us apart!"

And then, as if to confirm Wilcox's prudence, a ferocious gust whipped around the ship and ripped the royal main sail in two.

Roberts nodded grimly.

Sartine and Dowlin stepped on deck and joined Wilcox and

Hanson at the wheel. The four men huddled together, shoulder-to-shoulder, bracing themselves, and waited for their orders.

Roberts pointed up to the masts and shouted. "Lieutenant Sartine, this is a most wicked gale. Out situation I fear is desperate. I need more hands to haul in her canvas or we'll all perish. We haven't enough English lads to manage things. Your men, I need them, now. But their release is temporary, only until this ship is out of danger. After the task is finished, your men must again surrender. Agreed?"

Sartine looked up into the masts, squinted his eyes against the pelting rains. A flash of lightening briefly illuminated the dark figures lined up along the yardarms, struggling to pull in the reef points. Roberts had not exaggerated matters.

He looked back at Roberts and nodded. "*Oui*, as you command."

"Sir," interjected Wilcox, "No question I need more lads. But do you think it wise to be settin' all those Frenchies free?"

Roberts looked over at Hanson, waiting for him to protest as he knew he would. The lieutenant of marines did not disappoint him.

"Ahem, not a particularly satisfying proposal, Mr. Roberts," Hanson offered blandly. "I cannot guarantee the ship's security with so many Frogs running amuck. Certainly there is a better way?"

And then a great bolt of lightning, more fearsome than any of the others, split the sky in two directly overhead, followed an instant later by a tremendous clap of thunder. Spirits quaked, knees buckled and not one man could say - with any truth - that he had not felt the hand of Death resting on his shoulder that day.

Roberts tilted his head against the rain, pulled his collar up tight around his neck. The winds were now driving the rain sideways. He looked into the grim faces of Sartine and his three officers. The storm was far more than he had bargained for and for a moment, he considered putting off his plan. But the gambler in him drove him on, there was no turning back.

"Your concerns are duly noted, gentlemen. But the alternative is not very appealing. We risk losing this ship and all souls on board if we procrastinate much longer. On my responsibility, Mr. Hanson, I need more muscle on deck. Unless," he asked gamely, "you want to send your marines up into the rigging? No? I thought not. Release fifty Frenchmen, Mr. Hanson. That number should suffice. Keep the rest secured below. See to it, now!"

As Hanson left to carry out his orders, Roberts turned to Sartine. "Lieutenant Sartine, I leave it to you and to your officers to issue the necessary commands to your men."

Sartine nodded and followed Hanson below to assemble French volunteers. Soon 50 French sailors were swarming on deck - obeying the orders of their French officers. They scurried up into the ship's rigging and worked the sails side-by-side with Wilcox's men.

Roberts and his officers stayed huddled on the quarterdeck, where they watched and waited. Once all the sails had been hauled in, Sartine returned to the quarterdeck to join them.

Then, while Hanson was too busy keeping his head down low, and shivering against the winds, Dowlin slipped below deck unnoticed, went to look for the sergeant-of-marines. It did not take him long to find the man in the galley, with five of his marines, all hunched together, trying to keep warm and dry.

"Sergeant, Mr. Roberts has orders for you and yer men," Dowlin told him, relishing the moment. "Yer to send one of your lads below, to help guard the French prisoners. Post two men next to the arms' locker and have the other two standby in the capt'n's cabin, as a reserve for any trouble. Understood?"

The sergeant blinked and stared at Dowlin, dumbfounded. "But, Lieutenant," he protested. "If I do that, it'll leave only two men topside with Lieutenant Hanson with me and the other marines scattered below over three decks. With all 'em Frenchies runnin' about free as you please, that seems a tad foolhardy. We're already spread out awful thin, Lieutenant Dowlin."

Dowlin gave the sergeant a bleak but sympathetic nod. "No doubt, Sergeant, no doubt. A fine pickle we find ourselves in. We could sure use more of our own trusty lads right about now - but old Captain Hughes saw fit not to lend us any more. But it's a nasty storm ragin' above all our heads. Near as bad as what hit *Rose* four weeks ago. Without more lads to work this ship, it's sink or swim. I don't fancy either of them choices.

You?"

The sergeant shook his head. He knew very little about seamanship and he caught himself, once again, wishing he had signed up with the army. It wasn't the first time some sailor had given him an inept order and he figured it wouldn't be the last. *Damn fool officers*, he muttered under his breath as he watched Dowlin bolt up the companionway and back out into the storm.

Dowlin next found the Irishmen, ten strong, and sent them below to work the pumps, along with Kelly to keep them there and then headed topside. That left less than twenty English seamen and two marines on deck - and the marines were far more interested in keeping themselves from being swept overboard than in keeping an eye on the French.

Hanson, his arm wrapped around the mizzenmast shrouds and hanging on for dear life, was totally unaware that his marines had been scattered piecemeal about the ship. And, in all the confusion and haste to save the ship, no one had thought to arm the English seamen.

Roberts rubbed the bridge of his nose. That was the signal.

The French moved smartly, without hesitation. Sartine had chosen his men well. Armed only with knives and belaying pins, they moved swiftly first against the two marines carrying soaked and useless muskets, easily overpowering them. Then they quickly surrounded Wilcox's men and herded them all against the mainmast. Unarmed and outnumbered, Wilcox and his men offered no resistance. The angry French mob turned on the four British officers trapped on the quarterdeck next. Without firing a shot, the ship was theirs!

Hanson drew his sword.

"*Stand fast there, Hanson! Put that steel away!*" Roberts commanded sternly. "Do you want to get us all butchered?"

Hanson's eyes darted around at the menacing faces glaring at him and sheathed his sword. He leaned over the rail to spit, then turned to face Roberts with an evil look.

"*Merde...*"

Roberts wasn't sure if Hanson was commenting on their predicament or insulting him. It hardly mattered now and he ignored

Hanson.

He turned to face Sartine. "Lieutenant Sartine," he said through clenched teeth. "You gave your word, sir! I demand you order your men to stand down! Now! I'll hold you to your honor, sir!"

Sartine played the role assigned to him with dramatic flourish. Roberts had to suppress a smile. Sartine could have been an actor.

Sartine solemnly nodded to Roberts, then turned to face his men. He stretched his arms out, motioning them to quiet down and listen.

"Brave sons of France," he declared in French. "I gave my binding oath as a French officer. I promised we would not try to escape. You are fearless. Good lads all. And today you make me proud to be a Frenchman, but - I implore you - stop this madness now! The ship is still in difficulty."

A small, burly Frenchman, armed with a musket he had taken from one of the marines, spoke first, using the very words he and Sartine had rehearsed earlier that day.

"Sir, maybe you gave your word. I mean no disrespect, but none of us gave ours!"

The French sailor glanced at his shipmates, seeking their approval, and they answered him with enthusiastic nods and cheers all around. More thunder rumbled ominously above all their heads.

"We'll not surrender ourselves! I'd rather take my chances in this storm than rot aboard some British prison barge. No! We have taken our ship back as our king would command us! That is our sworn duty!"

The unruly Frenchmen, 50 strong, erupted into one joyful, mighty cheer.

The burly ringleader looked over at Roberts, shook his musket menacingly at him and said in broken English, "Lieutenant, we control the deck. You are a prisoner. Order your men below to surrender. The ship will be ours - with or without your blood!"

Sartine looked at Roberts meekly and shrugged. "*Mon Capitaine*, I have honored my word to you. But I am powerless to do more. These men are obedient to our king and would obey him before they would obey me. What is done is done. I urge you to surrender, avoid any needless bloodshed."

Roberts considered the forces arrayed against them. "Allow me a moment to consult with my officers, *Monsieur* de Sartine?"

"But of course, *Monsieur*."

Roberts, Dowlin, Wilcox and Hanson retreated back to the ship's stern rail and the four officers huddled together against the wind and stinging rain. More bolts of lightning flashed across the sky. The brunt of the storm had overtaken them.

"This is," Roberts offered solemnly, "our counsel of war, gentlemen. I shall be brief. Unless you can slip below somehow and marshal the rest of your marines to retake the ship, Mr. Hanson, and I don't see how you can possibly manage that, it would appear we have no choice. We must surrender before this ugly gale kills us all. I see no other good options for to us."

Even Hanson, still in a bit of a daze over how quickly their good fortune had deserted them, and numb with fear from the storm's fury, realized the hopelessness of their position. Not one word of protest slipped through his teeth this time.

Wilcox leaned his head towards Roberts. "Sir, our lads still control the lower decks, along with the arms' locker and -"

But Dowlin cut him off. "Are you daft man? The French control the upper deck and the helm. They hold twenty of our lads and the four of us and could slaughter us on a whim. What good does it do us anyway, Wilcox, to control the lower decks with only a few lads and no one to lead 'em? Who knows if they can even reach the arms' locker? And even if they do, muskets with wet powder won't give us any advantage in firepower."

It did not take even the unimaginative Wilcox long to realize Dowlin was right. In good, old fashion common sense, Dowlin surpassed most others.

"Aye. You're right I suppose, Mr. Dowlin. Goddamn French. If only we'd thought to arm our own lads and keep more of 'em on deck with us, we might of 'ad a fightin' chance."

"Wish I'd thought of that..." agreed Dowlin with an odd smile on his lips. Stashed inside his belt and hidden away, just in case something went awry, were two loaded pistols wrapped in oilskin to keep them dry, a pair of brass knuckles and a handful of good throwing knives.

"Perhaps," replied Roberts reflectively. "Let's not start blaming ourselves now for any of this. This killer storm overtook us so quickly, and with so little warning, there was no time to react. Remember too, we had the word of the French officers. It might have made no difference anyway. There are too few of us. No one could have foreseen the intensity of this storm. And this ship will certainly capsize before either side wins the battle. Well, we best do what needs to be done before we all drown. Are we all agreed then?"

His three lieutenants solemnly nodded their assent with no further discussion. Roberts struggled to maintain his balance, carefully made his way forward, towards Sartine and his French warriors. He saw they had bound all of his men together with rope and two Frenchmen, arms knotted with thick muscle, now had the ship's wheel in their hands.

Roberts took the back of his hand to wipe the water out of his eyes and shouted into the wind at Sartine. "Lieutenant Sartine, do you extend to us the same terms as were offered to you and your men by His Britannic Majesty King George?"

"But of course, Lieutenant Roberts. After all, we are Frenchmen - not barbarians."

"Then..." Roberts began to say, pausing to search the faces of his three officers one last time, "the ship is yours, sir."

The French cheered wildly. Roberts sent Wilcox below to inform the rest of the marines and Kelly's men of the surrender while elated Frenchmen hauled the British Union Jack down, threw it into the sea and raised the French royal *fleur de lys* in its place. The Frenchmen with weapons hustled the English officers below and locked them inside a small berth used to quarter midshipmen. Sartine then gave the order to turn the wheel hard to starboard, bringing *Toulon* on a new course, a course for the coast of France.

Chapter Five
Trading Names

oberts and his two cellmates ate their supper quietly together at a small table. A friendly guard with orders to see to their every comfort had brought them generous portions of roasted lamb with gravy, boiled carrots, fresh bread and butter along with several bottles of a decent Bordeaux to wash it all down with. The Irishmen heaped their plates high and enjoyed the sumptuous feast. Inside one basket, they even found fresh strawberries and delicate pastry tarts for dessert. The Irishmen had never eaten better. The king's less fortunate prisoners residing at Dunkirk's jail hardly fared as well.

Dowlin raised his glass high. "A toast," he offered, "to Luke Roberts, the grandest schemer to ever sail from the shores of lovely, green Ireland!"

"Aye!" added Kelly and tossed his glass back, draining his wine with one swallow. "To the man of twists and turns."

Roberts was in extraordinary good humor and accepted the compliments gladly. Their plan could not have turned out better. After he and his officers surrendered, the French managed to disarm the remaining British marines without incident. *Le Toulon* weathered the storm without much damage and safely made her way back to the great French naval base at L'Orient. Roberts, Dowlin and Kelly, and the ten Irish seamen, were taken north to Dunkirk and incarcerated in the king's jail there. Wilcox and Hanson, along with the English seamen and marines, remained imprisoned at L'Orient where they waited until arrangements could be made for their return to England.

The Irishmen were treated like princes. Not only were they well fed, each man had a cot to sleep on, books and newspapers to read and clean clothes to wear. Cell doors were never locked and they were allowed to stretch outside in the prison yard as often and for as long as they cared to.

"Lads, we escape," Roberts announced nonchalantly as he sipped his wine, "by week's end. Sartine informed me of this during his visit this morning. He also told me that he has a surprise waiting for us too and intends to return tomorrow to show it to us."

"Hope the surprise isn't the scaffolds and a hangman's noose," offered Dowlin.

"Do you trust him, sir?" Kelly asked suspiciously.

Roberts burst out laughing and slapped his hand on the table. "Well, it's a bit late not to, don't you think Chris?"

"What I mean to say, sir, is that he's, well, French."

"Aye, he's French through-and-through. That's a fact. And to the English, we're *Irish*. So? Sartine's a good man. Aye, I trust him. What reason would he have to double-cross us? All will be fine. On another matter, as of today, I go back to the name of my birth. Luke Roberts shall hopefully quietly fade away from the world's memory and be forgotten."

"Never liked the name anyhows," Dowlin commented absently as he attacked the food on his plate. "Too English."

"And just what is yer real name might I inquire, sir?" asked Kelly.

Roberts smiled. "I was born in France but later brought to Kenure, close to your old village, Chris, Rush, when I was just a wee, young lad. Luke has always been my given name but Ryan is my true surname. My father, Joseph Ryan, was a lieutenant in the Irish Dillon Brigade in service to King Louis. He died when I was just a babe and my mother, with little money and no family in France, was forced to return to Ireland where we lived with my father's brother, my Uncle John. When I left Ireland to join the English navy, I took the name Roberts, after Sir Robert Echlin, the Bart of Kenure, who was kind to me as a boy."

"Well, 'tis an honor to make your acquaintance, Lieutenant Ryan!" offered the Irish giant enthusiastically.

"Mr., Mr. Luke Ryan," Dowlin corrected him.

"Aye, Mr. Luke Ryan it is then!" Kelly answered with a wide grin.

Chapter Six
In the Name of Friendship

It was well past midnight when the jailer shook Ryan on the shoulder to wake him, and then did the same to Dowlin. He led the Irishmen outside the jail where they found Sartine waiting for them, standing next to a carriage. Sartine, looking rather silly in an oversized straw hat and wearing a false beard, waved both men into his carriage and handed the jailer the proper warrants. The jailer released his two prisoners into Sartine's custody without a word - years of managing the jail had taught the man to ask no questions.

"No smirking, Patrick, now, put these on..." Sartine said and handed Ryan and Dowlin their own disguises to wear. "You never know who might be watching. Even the English have spies lurking about in Dunkirk, *n'est-ce pas?*"

The two Irishmen chuckled at the large, floppy hats but did as Sartine asked.

The ride down to the waterfront was short and uneventful. And, except for the sound of the hooves of horses clapping against cobblestone, the world was dull and quiet.

Sartine leaned forward to look out the front window. When he found what he was looking for he knocked on the carriage's roof with the tip of his cane. The driver obediently pulled back on his reins and halted his team.

Sartine opened the carriage door and stepped onto a pier, rotting from age and neglect. "I shall warn you, Luke," Sartine whispered as he waved both men out of the carriage, "she is old and has seen better days. But the harbormaster has given me his utmost assurance that she has a few good years left in her still and the man would not dare mislead me. It is a good start, until we can arrange for something, shall we say, more suitable for a man of your particular talents? I thought it best not to move too quickly, not draw attention to ourselves - yes?"

The two Irishmen stepped out into the raw, night air, saturated with a damp chill, and found themselves staring at a small vessel tied against a deserted pier. Someone had already lit two torches and lashed to the gangplank.

Ryan took a deep breath, savored the pungent smells of brine and fish for a bit and listened to the small waves splashing up against the pilings. Off in the distance, hidden in the mist, he heard the lonely ring of a buoy bell.

Sartine removed his beard and pointed at the ship. "This vessel," he said, smiling, "is without a captain or crew. May I present you, *mon cher ami*, with your first command, with your own ship."

Ryan turned and looked at Sartine perplexed. "I do not understand, David."

"Her papers are all in order," Sartine replied. "She is yours. I give her to you free and clear. You are sole owner and may do with her as you please."

Like a child considering some special gift in its hands, something wrapped in festive paper with ribbons tied in bows, Ryan's eyes filled with wonder. He stood, frozen, and marveled at the sight.

"But, David, this is not what we discussed. I don't..."

"Shhhh..." Sartine said, putting a finger to his mouth. "Speak no more of it. Accept what is offered to you graciously, in the name of our friendship. Go now, *mon Capitaine*, inspect your ship. I shall wait for you and Patrick here. You know how susceptible I am to *mal de mer*. And then back to jail you must go until all can be made ready."

After their return to France, Ryan had thought better of asking Sartine for any money in exchange for *Toulon* and so Sartine's gift took him by complete surprise. He grabbed one of the torches and stepped aboard the vessel. Dowlin followed close behind.

The two Irishmen stood quietly on the deck and took stock of the ship's condition. Even in the darkness, there was no hiding the obvious. The vessel was squat, fat and ugly. She was a two-masted lugger measuring little better than sixty feet in length from stem to stern. Litter and discarded materials of all sorts covered her deck. Her paint was chipped and badly weathered. Her rigging was in a sad state of disrepair.

A number of lines were frayed or cut or simply missing altogether and the spars carried no sails.

Ryan ignored these defects. He pictured the ship as she would have looked new, rolling down the ways and into the water for the first time. He could almost smell the newly cut wood and fresh paint. *By God*, he thought, he was the master of a ship! His ship. He could hardly believe his good fortune. Fate was fulfilling the dream of a young boy from years long past. Giddy with excitement, he took a deep breath and relished the moment.

Dowlin, far less impressed, shook his head in disgust. As Ryan dreamed, Dowlin started mentally compiling a list of every deficiency he could find and then gave thoughtful care to how much sweat and money it would take to make the old bucket seaworthy again.

The usually unflappable Irishman picked up a long piece of broken wood and tossed it over the side with a frown. "Saints preserve us, Luke. This be a sad wreck. Must be someone's idea of a joke. Sartine has no eye for ships, that's for sure. This one's ready for the scrap heap - should anybody be askin' me that is..."

Ryan shrugged. He wasn't about to let anything, not even Dowlin, spoil his fine mood. "Come now, Pat, let's have a closer look. I have a good feeling about her."

"Oh, a good feelin'?" Dowlin asked with a smirk and grunted. "Well, I often get a good feelin' when I'm with a pretty woman but it fades quick after the second or third tryst between the sheets. After we satisfy our hearts' desires, I come to my senses, always..."

But when Ryan began strolling around the deck, ignoring him, Dowlin dutifully fell in behind him and said no more.

Ryan stopped over a partially caved-in grate covering the main hatch and peered inside. Dowlin pulled the grate back and they descended down a rickety ladder to inspect the decks below.

Considering the vessel's small size, her holds were surprisingly large. There was ample space to haul a good size cargo. Dowlin poked his nose around every nook and cranny, ran his fingers along the overhead and then against the bulkhead planks, feeling the wood and seams. He carefully checked the oakum - made of tarred hemp and cotton and driven into the strakes between the planking as caulking to make the hull waterproof - and grimaced. Much of it needed replacing, a long and tedious task. He took an iron bar and pried open several loose planks, grabbed the torch out of Ryan's hand and laid himself flat down. He lowered the torch through the opening between the planks and saw the standing water in her wells, which did nothing to improve his mood.

Dowlin finally stood, made one last sweep of the lower deck in the dim, flickering torch light, and faced Ryan. "Luke, I don't know. I just don't know..."

"Pat, we can do this! Think of it man, our own ship! Beholdin' to no one! We'll be the masters of our own fate!"

Dowlin laughed, and not a friendly laugh either. "*Auck!* Listen to ya, always dreamin' you are! You've got yer head up yer arse again. This here an't no ship. It's a bundle of rotted wood held together by frayed rope and rusty old nails. And Lord only knows what the sea worms have done to her bottom. She's probably got more holes in her than a cook's colander. And we both know damn well - it's me who'll be tryin' to fix this stinkin' French wreck. I've emptied my bowels inside shitters in better repair than this. Am I the only soul aboard this here piece of worm wood who's still got his wits about him?"

Ryan broke into a wide grin. He knew his man. Dowlin was more talk and bluster than anything else. You just had to know how to read Dowlin's moods, which Ryan did.

"Would you prefer, Mr. Patrick James Dowlin, we return to the king's service? It's not too late you know. No one would be the wiser if you were to change your mind and sail back to England..."

Dowlin slowly shook his head. "You make a fine point thar, Luke. No. No more English ships for me." He took one last look at the bulkheads, clenched his jaw and nodded. "Alrighty then. So be it. I'll be gatherin' the lads together straight away. This old pig will sail sweet *Jesus* or I an't Patrick James Dowlin. I'll be needin' materials and tools. I suppose you and his high and mighty lordship outside have already thought about that and will be procuring, or should I say purloining, what I need soon enough, eh?"

Ryan gave Dowlin an impish smile and nodded. He knew Sartine was enough of a seaman to know what the Irishmen would need to fix the old lugger up.

"You shall have whatever you need, I promise."

"Humph, we'll see about that," Dowlin said, and then asked with mock disdain, "I suppose you'll be too busy to lend a hand around here?"

Dowlin knew his man well too. Ryan was not the best at using tools or fixing things.

"Why thank'ee kindly, Patrick," Ryan answered in his Irish brogue. "Glad to leave it all in yer capable hands. Knew I could count on you, lad. Much obliged. I do indeed have some errands to attend to before we sail."

"By *Gawd*, Luke, you think yer too good to get yer hands dirtied anymore! Yer startin' to believe you really are some English lord or somethin'..."

But Dowlin was hardly serious. He never liked any one, not even Ryan, looking over his shoulder, meddling in his work. It was an unnecessary intrusion, a nuisance.

Ryan laughed and gave his friend a firm pat on the back. He knew Dowlin would come around.

How the sometimes stormy, red-haired Irishman liked to curse and complain for all to hear about some daunting task confronting him at first, but, in truth, he was always itching to get at it. He reveled in the challenge of bending something to suit his will and was already determined to make this ship a good sailor again. Once Dowlin had the tools and materials in hand, he would work side-by-side with the men, night and day, like a man possessed, until the work was finished. Complaining about it was part of the fun and a ploy to get his ego stroked. Ryan knew that one solid compliment from him would lift Dowlin's spirits for a week. He decided then that he would give Dowlin a half interest in their new venture, but thought it best to hold off telling him.

"Pat, as long as we keep her near the coast, we should be fine. She appears seaworthy enough to me. We'll make most of the repairs at sea. Too many idle eyes on these docks, I'm sure. If we find anything major, we'll put into Boulogne or Cherbourg. You and Kelly just worry about getting everything stowed aboard. Hire some of the locals to help you. I want to keep our lads out of sight, just in case someone recognizes one of them, as unlikely as that might be. Still, I've heard there are a fair number of us Irish in Dunkirk. You and Chris keep your heads low too. I'll handle the rest."

"Rest? What rest? Looks to me like I've got all the heavy work to do!"

"Don't you think it would be good to have a cargo before we sail and have somewhere to sail it to?"

Dowlin took a deep breath and slowly exhaled. "More schemes I see swirlin' around in that head of yers, hey? Well, in for a penny, in for a pound. Whatever wine or ale Chris hasn't managed to pour down that gullet of his tonight when we get back is *mine*."

After they made their way topside, Dowlin walked around the deck one more time pulling, kicking or poking at things while Ryan stood quietly at the helm, resting an arm on the ship's wheel and let his mind wander a bit. He took a moment to look out across the black water and considered his good fortune.

Ryan was not a man given to prayer, did not think about God much. He found religion, confusing. But it seemed only fit and proper to acknowledge his newfound fortune. There was so much promise in the air, he wondered whether there was some divine inspiration at work. Some say that all good things come from above. He didn't know. But he vowed, if this opportunity was some divine gift, he would do his best and see the matter through to wherever it might lead him. Twelve souls had entrusted their welfare into his care. Twelve souls depended on him. With all his heart he hoped, he prayed, he would not falter, or fail to honor the Father's trust.

Sartine returned the Irishmen to the jail but before departing, he turned and called out after Ryan. "Luke, you need a name. What name will you give her? Do you know?"

Ryan ambled back to the carriage, took Sartine by the hand and shook it warmly. "*Friendship*," he replied with a broad smile.

Sartine smiled back, bowed his head and then his coach

disappeared.

A few days later, the master schemer, lean in years but not in wisdom, set the last piece of his plan into motion. A small group of Irishmen, 13 in number and of no particular importance to anyone, made good their *escape* from the French king's prison in the coastal town of Dunkirk. The local Admiralty officer, claiming the Irishmen would have been released eventually anyway in a prisoner exchange, instructed the local militia commander to not trouble himself looking for the escapees. The matter was then officially closed and the paperwork on the Irishmen was lost.

Ryan led his Irishmen to an old, abandoned army barracks on the outskirts of town where they laid low and waited anxiously. Only Dowlin and Kelly knew of Ryan's plans for future mischief.

While his men stayed in hiding, Sartine introduced Ryan to a prosperous and reputable Dunkirk businessman named John Torris who, from time to time, liked to dabble in smuggling on the side. Torris was Flemish by birth, but worked and lived in Dunkirk, along with a silent partner, Charles Torris, his brother. The Torris brothers were members of France's burgeoning upper middle class, neither aristocrats nor *nouveau riche*, but financially very comfortable.

Torris agreed to deliver, on consignment, everything the Irishmen needed to get started: labor, tools, materials, supplies and a cargo of beef, tea, indigo and spices. Ordinarily such an arrangement with a smuggler with no reputation, or credit, would have been impossible considering the risks involved. But Sartine agreed to act as guarantor and that proved good enough for the Torris brothers.

Once French shipwrights had completed basic repairs to the lugger to make her seaworthy, all under Dowlin's watchful eye, laborers brought on board, and stowed away, hundreds of crates and barrels and boxes of gear, equipment, supplies and cargo. Ryan then moved his men from the Army barracks to a quiet, little redbrick warehouse overlooking the waterfront. Still ignorant of Ryan's plan, the Irishmen assumed that Ryan had found them all a way back to England. But when Dowlin and Kelly produced bottles of rum and glasses, and began pouring out drinks for each man, more than one face looked around, confused.

"Lads, it has been my privilege," Ryan said with a smile as he accepted a glass of rum from Kelly, "to serve with each of you. You're all good men. No point in mincing words with you. I see the confusion in your faces. I will soon make clear to each of you the reason we are here. You each have a choice to make. I have decided not to return to England. Mr. Dowlin and Mr. Kelly have chosen to stay with me. Each man here is invited to join us, or return to England if you wish."

The Irishmen turned to look at one another. There were whispers and murmurs.

"Well, there, I've said it. You are free to do whatever suits your fancy. Join me or return to England to finish out your enlistments with the Royal Navy. If any man here chooses to go back to England, I only ask that you keep this little conversation private."

Doubt settled over a face or two.

Bartholomew Mulvany was the first to speak out. "Deserters, sir?"

"Retirees..." Dowlin interrupted.

Mulvany nodded at Dowlin, then turned to Ryan again. "Beg pardon, sir. I know all the lads will agree with me that thar's not much love here for the English or their navy. But what do we do? Where would we go?"

"Why, Mr. Mulvany," Ryan answered, "we stay put right here in France and we try our hand at smuggling of course."

"Smuggling? But how is that, sir? Ah, what I mean to say is, sir, won't British red coats be lookin' for us on one side of the ocean and French blue coats on the other, so to speak? With respect, sir, one country's navy or the other is bound to nab us sooner or later..."

"Ah, an excellent point," Ryan replied gamely. Mulvany could always be counted on to speak with good, clear sense. "Think it through for yourself, lad. I've seen to it that no word will go out about our escape. The British won't be looking for you. You're rotting away in some French jail as far as any one knows. As for the French, I shouldn't worry about them. Wonderful system the French have here. You pay the right people and bloody nobody bothers you after that. Everyone's happy. Rest assured, the right people have already been paid off and paid off nicely. No French men-at-arms will come looking for you. Not today. Not tomorrow. Not next week. We are most welcome here. So that leaves the British navy and, in particular, the king's revenue ships and those we must avoid. If any one of us is caught, we agree tonight - a blood oath among us all - to tell the British the same story. We tell them about how we escaped from a French jail. No lie there and in point-of-fact, that is exactly what all you lads have just done. Then you can say that you were separated from your mates and jumped from ship-to-ship trying to make your way back home. So, we are about to disappear into France and nobody will care."

Doubts soon gave way to confident smiles. Nods were exchanged all around.

Michael Morgan, the illiterate thief of crumpled-up captain's papers, spoke next. He removed a knitted green and blue striped cap from his head and nervously rubbed the bridge of his nose. "'Tis a beauty of a plan, sir. Truly. But how do we get ourselves a ship? An't goin' to make the French none too happy if we steal ourselves one of theirs."

A broad grin stretched across Ryan's face. He was having fun. "Lads," he replied, "it's already done. A ship, your ship if you decide to sail with me, sits in the harbor right now waiting for you. She needs a little work..."

Dowlin pretended to choke. "Never. Never have I heard you tell the lads a lie before, Luke," he interrupted playfully. "Lads - she needs a bit more than a little work. But she's sound enough until we can spruce her up some. Nothin' you women can't handle, hey?"

"She's old, true enough," continued Ryan. "But for now she'll do and soon I will have legal title to her. Don't ask me how. It's a long story. An Italian from Genoa owns her, but he is willing to sell her to me for a share of the future profits we make. She's ours for the taking and we can come and go as we please. She sits, not far from here, low in the water with a heavy cargo and she's ready to sail."

It did not take long for every man to warm to Ryan's plan. Each man saw his opportunity for a new life and no one had any desire to return to the navy. And no one had any good prospects waiting for him back in Ireland. After the bottles were emptied, each man gladly agreed to sail with Ryan and gave his pledge of secrecy.

Ryan did not share everything with them. There was no need. As far as his men knew, Sartine and the French had retaken the *Toulon* by force and their escape from jail was real and now, Ryan had somehow succeeded in paying off the French authorities. The fewer details anyone knew, the safer they would all be if something went wrong later. If any man was caught, or left the ship, there wasn't much information of any interest he could give up. Ryan thought it was a good plan and was well pleased at how eagerly his men had accepted it.

He began seeing the world as his playground. And, for now at least, he saw the world as a place of endless possibilities.

Chapter Seven
The Smugglers take an Oath

 small army of Irishmen waited patiently inside the Torris warehouse for the cover of darkness. And when it came, Kelly led the men out to a lonely, dilapidated part of Dunkirk's old waterfront where Ryan and Dowlin stood waiting at the rail of an old lugger. The men were well armed and moved along the docks quietly, quickly, like shadows in the night.

With everyone on board, and with the tide beginning to ebb, the ship's new master wasted no time. Without fanfare, he issued his first order: cast-off lines and head for open sea. And as Ageless Dawn - matchless in her beauty - rode across the morning sky in her golden chariot, piercing steel-gray clouds with her shafts of saffron light to chase the night away, the crew, anxious about the unknown, but excited too, slipped the mooring lines and silently raised the sails. The old lugger moved out clumsily into the harbor's murky waters at first but once she reached deep water, once she touched the Atlantic, she picked up surprising speed. The helmsman marked his course for Ireland, their destination, and spirits soared.

After breakfast, Dowlin set the men to work with unrelenting zeal. Stacks of freshly cut planks and seasoned timber, sail cloth, tools, sturdy rope, chain, paint, varnish, blocks, tackles and tar covered the deck. Had a storm hit them just then ship and crew would have been in serious jeopardy. But Good Fortune, endless in her bounty, chose to watch over the small band of bold Irishmen as they scudded across the barren sea while gracious Spring, with her soft caresses, kept the waters calm.

The crew's first priority was to pump the water out of the wells and this proved to be an easy task. A good sign. As every man knew though, the real test would come later when rough weather hit them. With the wells drained, Dowlin went about replacing the ship's rigging, all of it, line by line, and once this task was done he had the men replace any cracked or damaged planks.

For the next few days, the smuggler hugged the French coast while the Irishmen practically rebuilt her. Tacking against light zephyrs, she barely made four knots. In choppy seas, her blunt nose made her cumbersome to handle but she managed well enough for Ryan's purposes. And then, when her master had satisfied himself that she was seaworthy, he had his helmsmen turn into shore. The Irishmen put in at the small harbor of Berck and dropped anchor.

Ryan had all his men assemble on deck. He had jotted down some notes, but tossed the paper over the side. To speak from the heart, this was the way that seemed best to him now. The men gathered around under a flawless royal blue sky. Present, of course, was the congenial Patrick James Dowlin from Dublin, a match in strength and looks for any of the deathless gods. And standing next to him was a man sired by giants, Christopher Kelly from Rush. They had sailed with Ryan from the beginning. The rest, all stouthearted Irishmen with the salt of the sea in their blood, came mostly from Rush or Dublin. Every man was a veteran of at least a dozen battles, accustomed to hardship and a few could even boast of having some experience at smuggling.

Ryan paused to look into the face of each man and smiled. There in the front rank stood William Knight, master and pilot. Knight was a tall, quiet man who loved to play the fiddle. Standing next to him was Andrew McCloud, gunner's mate, who, after Kelly, was the oldest of the lot, but still as strong as an ox and liked to boast, with good cause, that he had the foulest mouth in all the king's navy. Next to McCloud stood one of Ryan's favorites, Michael Morgan, helmsman and petty thief of discarded papers. He wore a long, red beard, to hide the scars left by chicken pox on an otherwise handsome face. His skills at guiding a ship across the boundless waves were nearly supernatural and, despite being illiterate, he had brains enough to do many things in life but was content, for his own reasons, to remain a simple sailor. Standing next to him was Bartholomew Mulvany, seaman, a man who loved to drink and brawl in port but, when on board ship, was a disciplined first-rate hand. And in the second rank, standing behind Mulvany was Bryan Rooney, gunner's mate. Short in stature and a bundle of nervous energy, he could work and shoot any cannon as well as any man. He was the first among the Irishmen to sport an earring. Then there was Thomas Smith, seaman, the youngest man on board. He looked and talked like a preacher but in a fight or bad weather the man had no fear. Standing next to Smith was Brian Dixon, boatswains' mate, a man who rarely drank or swore and liked to quote the Scriptures whenever possible. And next to him, always with a smile on his face, was Christopher Hoar, gunner's mate, a man nearly as big as the Irish giant himself but with more fat wrapped around his large frame than muscle. He was a bit of a dandy too, liked to wear his long hair in a ponytail and meticulously combed and braided it each morning. He also owned the heartiest laugh of any man on board. Connelly Steward, seaman, standing near the back, was a bald, quiet fellow who sometimes could be moody and difficult and often like keeping to himself but, remarkably, was well liked by everybody. Ryan had thought that if anyone would have decided not to join him, it would have been Steward. But there he was grinning up at Ryan with one of his rare smiles. And the last man, Thomas Connor, master's mate, a man of mediocre nautical skills who probably would have done better in life on land, was staunchly loyal and loved by all his mates for his playfulness, outrageous humor and for his good stories of which there seemed no end. On every ship he had served, he had been the keeper of the ship's good morale.

Including himself, 13 good souls in all. *Thirteen*, Ryan thought, *a good number.*

Only a few months earlier they had all been professional sailors serving in the world's mightiest navy where life was often cheerless and discipline was always hard. But the men standing in front of him now were no longer an English crew. They looked more like a collection of carefree misfits. Any one of them could have strolled into a pirate's cove unnoticed. Uniforms had been discarded and now there were earrings, bandanas and new mustaches and beards. Cutlasses were tucked into belts and knives were hidden inside boots. The mood was relaxed, but there were no slackers here. Every man tackled his labors with little instruction or supervision.

Dowlin, always striving for perfection in an imperfect world, and never afraid to get his hands dirty, excelled all others at hard work and inspired the rest to try and match him. And Kelly, well, he was like a father to them all. The Irishmen were experiencing a freedom they had never known before and, like children roaming free for the first time, they were thriving on it.

It warmed Ryan's heart to see his men happy. They had served England well and in exchange for risking life and limb, they had been paid small wages, fed meager, often-rotting rations and had suffered beatings from brutish men for the slightest of infractions.

Somewhere out on these very same waters, Ryan mused, was the *Rose* sailing with a less fortunate crew. And poor, old Hughes would still be unaware of the loss of his grand prize. It would be another month or two before news of the *Toulon* would finally reach him.

Ryan cleared his throat and placed his hands on his hips. "Lads," he began a bit nervously in his Irish brogue, always his custom now when speaking to the men, "dear God but you certainly do look like smugglers! I dare say you looked and moved liked ghosts coming aboard this ship the way you did seven days ago. The *Shadowmen*, that's what I'll call you! If, that is, we move in and out of Ireland just as smartly. Good to have each of you aboard!"

His winning words brought an easy smile on the face of each man. Here, at last, they now served a master who would treat them fairly and with respect and, like themselves, he was Irish.

"Hear me now, lads. Listen to what my heart has to say. I'm not much for making speeches but I thought we should have ourselves a chat, a chat about who we are and what we are doing out here in the middle of the ocean. I, of course, am the master of this good ship."

That brought on a rousing cheer.

"We know who you are!" Dowlin bellowed out laughing. "I'm waitin' for you to tell us who we are!"

The whole crew joined Dowlin in his laughter.

Ryan held up his hands, calling for silence. "Patrick Dowlin here - God's very own gift to Ireland's women - or so he likes to boast - is the ship's first officer. Christopher Kelly, the Goliath of Ireland and a man who has gotten each one of us out of a nasty spot or two at one time or another, is hereby promoted to the ship's second officer. As for the rest of you knuckleheads - you'll have to fight amongst yourselves for whatever position suits your fancy..."

The men laughed and applauded.

"Lads," Ryan continued, "we're smugglers now and, in the eyes of the king, petty outlaws. I don't yet know how much money we can make at this new business of ours so I cannot say what your wages will be. I propose that one-third, of whatever we take on each haul, be put aside for keeping this ship properly maintained and well stocked. We'll need another one-third to pay-off our benefactors in both France and Ireland. That leaves one-third to be divided amongst ourselves in proportion to each man's rank. As captain, I'll take eight shares. First lieutenants, second lieutenants and masters shall receive four shares apiece. Carpenters, gunners, boatswains, master's mates, stewards, sail makers and armorers shall receive two shares apiece. Gunner's mates, boatswains' mates, carpenter's mates, coopers or any lad under sixteen - should we ever take such a lad on - shall be paid a one and a half share each. That is, I believe, the custom."

Men looked at one another and nodded their approval.

But then Ryan's smile vanished; his expression turned serious.

"Good. That's settled then. Now, about the terms of your service and discipline. You all know me, have served with me for some time now. And, I trust you will agree, you know that I am a just and fair man. When we served the king, we were all subject to the Articles of War, subject to the whims of the ship's captain too, a man who held the absolute power to take away a man's life, or maim him, with little accountability."

Ryan paused and looked at Kelly. "Mr. Kelly, do you suppose there's a cat-o-nine tails on board somewhere?"

"Dunno for sure, sir," he answered uneasily. "I'll wager I could muster one up. You be needin' it now, Capt'n?"

"Aye, I shall indeed. If you please, Mr. Kelly, be a good fellow and fetch it for me, now."

The men looked nervously all around, wondering who among them had committed an offense punishable by a lashing. As Kelly disappeared below Ryan, with his arms folded behind his back, quietly rocked back and forth on his heels and waited until Kelly returned with a coiled lash in his hands and handed it over to Ryan.

"Thank you, Mr. Kelly. Mr. Dowlin. If you please, sir, I'll have all hands stand to, to witness punishment."

Having no idea what Ryan was up to, Dowlin gave Ryan a puzzled look but asked no questions. The ship's master had given him his orders and that was all he needed.

He ordered all hands to fall into close order formation and then called the crew to attention. He knew how Ryan felt about floggings though. Ryan would never use the hated lash.

With the men standing in rank-and-file formation, Dowlin approached Ryan, snapped to attention and saluted. "All hands present to witness punishment as ordered, sir."

"Thank you, Mr. Dowlin," Ryan answered soberly as he ran the length of black leather through his fingers and took in the twelve faces staring at him. "All right lads, here are the rules. They're simple so nobody will soon be forgetting them. There'll be no piracy, no rape, no killing, no pillaging or plundering against anybody. You might look like pirates - but you're not. *Never* forget that. As long as you serve this ship, you obey my orders and you obey without question. We're smugglers, simple smugglers. We're businessmen trying to make a pound or two. If any one of us is caught, it's a minor prison term at worst. We're all Irishmen here and, I say, we be men of honor too. I won't risk the hangman's noose for any crimes against good folk no matter how profitable it might be. These then, are *my* Articles of War: if any man violates these rules, he'll be banished, put ashore at the first landfall no matter where that landfall might be. As I am not the Almighty, this is the only punishment I feel fit to meet out. Are we all agreed?"

Every man nodded his consent.

"Very well then. Now, another point. Everyone here is a volunteer. You are free men and as free men, you can take whatever is due you at any time you wish and quit this ship. But - any man who leaves this ship owes the rest of us a vow of secrecy. We don't discuss this ship, its business or her crew with any outsiders, ever. That's our binding oath, our blood oath - one to the other - until we go our separate ways or death finds us."

Ryan paused for a moment to let his words sink in, searching for any reaction, but he could not read them. "Well, if any one of you has any different thoughts on these matters, you should speak up now..."

No one spoke, not a sound. Ryan nodded his approval.

"Excellent," he said and smiled once again. "I take it we're all agreed then. So be it. It makes my heart swell with pride to serve with such a fine lot of scoundrels as yourselves."

Ryan then took the whip and tossed it over the side. Connor called out for a cheer for their new captain and the crew answered him with a hearty a *hip, hip, hurray*! Dowlin took Ryan's hand first and shook it. Then Kelly did the same and both men gave Ryan his solemn pledge that he would honor the oath. The crew formed a line and, one by one, stood in front of Ryan and gave the same pledge.

Ryan was confident that every man would give his full devotion to his mates and to the ship. They were, after all, his countrymen and bound by a common cause.

"Enough talk lads! What say you? Shall weigh anchor, raise her canvas and go make some money?"

The men answered him with another rousing cheer.

"Very well. Mr. Dowlin, you may have the lads stand down. Is it your judgment that this ship is fit for sea?"

Dowlin grinned, felt a tingle race up his spine. "Thar's some work that can only be done in the docks, nothin' that can't wait tho'. She will," he said boldly with a wink, "take you anywhere you want to go Capt'n, at least on this side of the Atlantic. I'd hold off on sailin' around the world just yet if I was you..."

"I shall heed your good advice, Mr. Dowlin. Set your course west by southwest. We sail for Ireland. Dublin is our destination!"

"Aye, sir! Dublin it is," Dowlin responded enthusiastically. He gave Ryan a brisk salute and spun on his heels to face the crew. "As you were lads. You heard the Capt'n. You've all been allowed to dawdle far too long. This ship is our mother. She puts food in our bellies and clothes on our backs - we show her our love and tender care so she'll show us her love and tender care in return." Then, raising his voice high for all the world to hear, he commanded: "now, get yer lazy carcasses back to work thar - and someone best get word to Ireland's fair daughters that Patrick James Dowlin is comin' home!"

With hearts filled with high hopes and a yearning for new adventure, the men returned to their duties. As the topmen climbed up the ratlines, Connor led them all in lively song:

> *"A sailor on the topsail yard*
> *While reefin' softly sings,*
> *I'd rather pick some cherries here*
> *Than be pullin' these here strings.*
>
> *I'd rather of a kicking mule*
> *Be the undisputed boss,*
> *Than pull this weather earring out*
> *On this here Flemish hoss."*

Dowlin looked over at Ryan as the men sang. "Fine speech thar, Luke. Didn't know you had it in you. Got worried tho' for a bit with that damn lash in yer hands. Thought for a moment you were goin' to use it on me!"

Ryan patted Dowlin's shoulder. "And scar that flawless flesh of yours? Disfigure the man most craved by women? Why fine lassies everywhere would put a price on my head for committing such a sin!"

Dowlin pursed his lips, slowly nodded in agreement. He saw no need to be modest. "Aye, Luke," he said with a boyish grin. "Truer words were never spoken!"

Chapter Eight
The Dublin Connection

t was an Irishman's night, dreary, dark and moonless. The air was still and the sea was at peace with the world. *Friendship* sliced through the calm waters of St. George's Channel like a ghost. On her port side stood ancient Ireland, land of Druids, Celts and mystery. Long ago the Druids, full of magic, had come to tame the island. After the Druids came the Celts, full of dreams and brawn, to settle it. And now the English had come, with their guns and their laws, full of arrogance and hungry for power, to rule it.

Ryan checked his pocket watch. "This looks to be just about right Patrick," he whispered.

The two men looked out over a patch of empty water. A thin mist was rolling in towards the shore. Ryan kept his eyes fixed on Ireland's rugged coast.

"I'll have the launch hoisted and lowered over the side if you please."

Dowlin raised an eyebrow and looked at Ryan suspiciously. "Here, Capt'n?" he asked in a hushed voice.

"Aye," replied Ryan without hesitation, still staring at the coast a quarter a mile away. Dowlin struggled to see whatever it was Ryan was looking at and saw nothing, no signals, no lights, no fires or landmarks of any sort.

"Are ya sure, Luke?" Dowlin asked again with a puzzled look. "Well I know your skills at navigation. But a magician, you are not..."

With a sly smile, Ryan turned to Dowlin and pointed at the water below them. "Look down over there Pat, in the water, there, over there, lad..."

Dowlin bent his head over the rail, looked down and saw a dozen small, wooden casks, painted in bright colors, yellows, reds and greens, bobbing up and down on the water's black surface.

"Some floating barrels? You want me to put you ashore here

because of this here cluster of flotsam?"

Ryan, still smiling at Dowlin, now had a mischievous twinkle in his eye. He waited.

Dowlin knew the look and started smiling too. The significance of the casks finally clicked.

"Ah, sweet *Jesus*! I must be goin' feeble. It's a bloody marker! You had someone row out here to dump this rubbish and anchor it to the bottom for us."

He patted Dowlin on the shoulder. "Very good, Patrick, you're learning."

"Maybe."

"Oh but you are tho' a bit slow to my way of thinking," Ryan added playfully. "You've got to start thinking devious thoughts. But don't you worry none, with time we'll turn that kind nature of yours into a pirate's black heart!"

Dowlin grunted. "Clever bastard you are, Luke. I'll give you that much! But how did you know the currents wouldn't sweep yer precious markers away before we got here, hey?"

Ryan shrugged. "An Irishman's luck? Well, p'haps not. Truth be told, if we had missed the buoys, we would've just sailed past Dublin's lighthouse on the south side of the harbor, turned the ship about, and continued sailing three leagues or so due south. I would have had you put me ashore then. That would have been close enough for our purposes. These buoys saved us a bit of time, that's all. It was a bit of an experiment too I suppose as I was curious to see if we could even find them. They might come in handy someday for some other purpose."

"Oh, and what other purpose might that be, Luke?"

"I have no clue. Now, Mr. Dowlin, the boat if you please. Smell that air? Mmmmm. I smell money in it and there's some to be made by us on this fine night."

"Glad to hear it," Dowlin replied with a grin.

With no ships in sight, and with no one lingering on shore, Dowlin passed the order on in a soft voice, nearly a whisper, to shorten sail and hoist the long boat over the rail. Sound carries a long distance across still water so he gave the crew strict orders to make no noise. Ryan, he knew, was a cautious man with a suspicious nature and those qualities had earned him the trust and admiration of the men.

Kelly formed a small landing party of four and had the men wrap pieces of cloth around the sweeps and grease the oarlocks too to muffle any sound. Then they rowed Ryan to the shore, to a place known as Dun Laoghaire, a few miles south of Dublin. Dublin is where Ryan's business would take him but he thought it best to enter the city by land, not sea, to avoid the curious and the meddlers who inhabited Dublin's waterfront in droves.

Dowlin was to sail the ship north and rendezvous with a shore party at a prearranged landing site to deliver their first cargo. Ryan had carefully made all the necessary arrangements back in France while sitting in a Dunkirk jail. The smugglers only had to avoid the king's revenue ships, forever patrolling the Irish Sea, and handsome profits would be waiting for them in Rush. Easy work Ryan and Dowlin had both agreed - if they kept their wits about them and their luck held fast.

A few yards from shore Ryan jumped from the ship's launch into knee-deep water and waved Kelly off. Kelly touched his hat, had his oarsmen reverse seats and silently disappeared back into the blackness.

The landing site was a desolate place, nothing but sand dunes and tall grass with marshes stretching out beyond the dunes. Ryan took a deep breath of air, inhaled the smells of the marsh. It felt good to stand on Irish soil again, after being away for so long.

He looked up and down the beach until his eye caught the silhouette of a man standing next to a horse about 100 yards off. The man was old and poorly dressed and gave Ryan a toothless grin as he approached him.

Ryan removed five silver coins from his purse and handed them to the old man, one more than had been agreed to. The old man touched the brim of his skullcap, left the horse with Ryan and disappeared over the dunes on foot without a word.

Ryan entered the city at about midnight. He was surprised by how many Dubliners were still out and about at that late hour. No matter, it made him less conspicuous. He headed for the waterfront, not a place for the faint of heart, down cobblestone streets, made slick by a thin sea mist, with only the pale glow from scattered street lamps to light his way. Twelve years had passed since his last visit to the city and then he had been no more than a boy. He did not know Dublin very well and had not liked the city then and he did not like it now. Dublin, like any other large city Ryan had ever visited, was a gloomy, dirty, suffocating place. At least the directions given to him were good and soon he found what he was looking for.

He tethered his horse to a hitching post outside an old, brick building with a sign over the door that said *Red Dragon* and stepped inside onto a dried mud floor. The tavern was a noisy place, filled with rowdy men playing cards, trading stories, some with more truth than others, and drinking. Ryan made his way through the crowd, over to the tavern's fireplace, and started to warm his hands when an older gentleman, using the brass handle on his cane, tapped him lightly on the shoulder.

"Mr. Ryan is it not? Mr. Luke Ryan?"

Ryan spun around and recognized the man smiling up at him at once. Patrick Daniel O'Keeffe was a short, plump man - a bit shorter and balder now than how Ryan had remembered him, but still the same man Ryan had known as a boy. Ryan returned the older man's warm smile and found himself admiring O'Keeffe's stylish clothing. Ryan had a weakness for fine tailoring, though he could find no use for such extravagance on board ship. O'Keeffe was wearing an expensive dark gray coat and red waistcoat with intricate embroidering around the cuffs and buttonholes. A flashy diamond stud pinned to a silk cravat caught Ryan's eye in particular. O'Keeffe looked like money; he looked like power. And so he was.

Though he cherished his anonymity too much to ever step inside Dublin's halls of power, or lend his name to the papers, O'Keeffe wielded real power. His extensive business interests, some legal, some not, stretched across Ireland and even far beyond her shores. Over the years he had diversified his holdings into more legitimate enterprises as he prospered but still, from time to time, he liked to dabble in other things and had a particular fondness for smuggling.

O'Keeffe embraced Ryan with sincere affection and then stood back to look at him. "How are you lad? It's been what, ten years?"

"Closer to twelve, Mr. O'Keeffe."

"Twelve years! Bless me!" O'Keeffe said chuckling and rested his hands on Ryan's shoulders. "My, my. Look at you. A man, all grown up, stands in front of me. You've turned out grand, just grand, my dear boy. Yer poor dad, the saints keep him, would be so proud of you now. Come along lad, I've saved us a quiet table over there in the corner. Let's fill yer belly with some wholesome food and maybe treat ourselves to a wee bit of strong drink too - enough to knock the chill out of yer bones, hey?"

"Thank'ee, sir. You're most kind."

"Kind? Nonsense. Come along now, lad."

As they walked past crowded tables, O'Keeffe stopped to hook his arm around the waist of a young girl passing by. She was pretty and smiled brightly at O'Keeffe. "Sweet Sarah, my dearest, when you have a moment, I need drinks and food brought to my table for me and my honored dinner guest here."

The young girl curtsied and quickly disappeared into the kitchen. O'Keeffe eyed her appreciatively with each step as she walked away.

"Isn't she a lovely, little thing?" O'Keeffe asked with a wink but then looked up at the low ceiling. "Oh, Mrs. O'Keeffe, don't you be mindin' nothin' now. I know I am too old, just a cantankerous, old goat now. I like to look a bit, nothin' more. Where's the harm in that my dear heart?"

He chuckled to himself and patted his round paunch before resuming his way across the room.

"Mrs. O'Keeffe has passed on I gather?" Ryan asked.

"Aye, four years ago it is now I'm afraid," O'Keeffe replied and added, with a slight quiver in his voice, "married over forty years. Every one of 'em a blessing too. Lord knows she was a fine, fine woman. Anything is possible for a man who has a good, loving woman standing by his side."

"Aye, she was very fine indeed. She was always kind to me and the Kenure lads. Always had a molasses cookie or some other treat handy for us. Sorry for your loss, sir."

"Auck!" O'Keeffe bellowed and stabbed the air with his cane. "We'll have no more depressin' talk tonight. We're here to celebrate yer safe return to the flock, my boy - and to God's own country! Well, whether we Irish are among *His* chosen flock or not is perhaps a discussion for another day..."

At O'Keeffe's table sat a young woman waiting for them. O'Keeffe could see that Ryan didn't recognize her.

"Mr. Ryan, permit me to introduce my daughter to you: Miss Shannon O'Keeffe."

"Shannon?" Ryan asked with surprise. He reached back through the dusty corridors of boyhood memories, frantically trying to reconcile the stunning beauty staring up at him with the scrawny, young girl he had known so long ago.

"Luke, it is so good to see you again," she replied softly, looking up at him with eyes, large eyes, the color of emeralds. She smiled sweetly at him.

O'Keeffe leaned close to Ryan's ear and whispered, "you can close yer mouth now son."

Ryan felt the burning on his checks, suddenly felt very foolish.

Shannon caught the blush and found it endearing. Growing up she had been one of the Kenure *boys*, a pack of rascals with an eye for mischief. She had played with Ryan and the other boys in their games and had taken part in their silly pranks. She could run, swim and fish and had been as tough and as fast as any of them.

Ryan kept his eyes on her as he took his seat. The girl was now a woman and she had flowered into a remarkable beauty. She had her curly, blonde hair pulled up in a bun and off her shoulders, giving her a slight boyish look. She was still the rebel Ryan thought and smiled approvingly.

As he took his chair, she studied his face, rugged and tan, and found it pleasing. His long, straight nose, high cheekbones and square chin were well proportioned and dignified. But it was his eyes, deep blue like the sea, which stood out most. They were kind and alert and not afraid to probe. She liked that. Most men couldn't hold her gaze for very long. She had almost, but not quite, forgotten the power in his eyes. Then she remembered the sadness in them too. He had, she decided, a serious but handsome face.

"Why, Luke Ryan, look at you now," she said in a confident voice with a refined accent that was more English than Irish, but not *quite* English. "All grown up I see." Then in a softer, more demure voice she asked, "It's been a long time hasn't it Luke?"

"A very long time, indeed, Shannon."

"I took the liberty," interjected O'Keeffe, "of bringin' Shannon with me because she oversees the books and records to all my business affairs now that I've started goin' senseless in my old age."

"Father!" Shannon scolded, throwing him a sharp look. She turned to Ryan, her eyes softened and she smiled. "If you're a shrewd man, Mr. Ryan, you'll watch this one. He's like a sheep in wolf's clothing - sharp as he ever was."

"Look there now, my sweet Shannon," chuckled O'Keeffe. "You've said too much by half. Armed with such knowledge this brigand will swindle us in our sleep."

The pretty, young tavern maid named Sarah interrupted the light conversation with a platter of cheese and bread and three tankards of ale.

Ryan raised his drink and proposed a toast: "To fair Ireland, to friends reunited and to your continued good health, sir."

"Aye, well said, lad," replied O'Keeffe and added in a whisper, "And to prosperous business - may we all be here tomorrow to take a generous cut of it!"

Ryan sipped his drink, a rich, dark ale that was far better than the watered-down mixture measured out by stingy cooks in a ship's galley. He savored the taste of home for a bit.

"Like it?" O'Keeffe asked, grinning.

Ryan nodded.

"Somethin' new, made by man named Guinness. He has a small brewery down on Crane Street on the banks of the Liffey. I lent him some money a while back to get started. I'd say the man knows his trade-craft well enough."

"'Tis very good, sir," Ryan answered approvingly. He turned to Shannon. "It is good to see you again, Shannon," he offered in a neutral tone. "I must confess though, I don't think I would have recognized you in the crowd..."

Shannon studied him carefully over the top of her tankard. "Oh? N matter, I would have recognized you, Luke."

Ryan felt his cheeks blush again. "So Shannon, you lend your father a hand with the business? John has other interests to attend to I take it?"

A dark shadow suddenly passed across her bright face. She exchanged a sad look with her father. John was Shannon's older brother and O'Keeffe's only son. He had been one of the Kenure ruffians when they had all been children.

"John's gone, Luke," O'Keeffe said bitterly. "A fine son he was too. Couldn't have asked for any better. Thievin' British press gang snatched him up not too far from here not but six years ago for serve in the king's ships. I had sent him here to Dublin on a business errand. British bastards. They had no right takin' him. He was just a boy. But what could I do? Among the lords of the British Admiralty, I count no friends. He was killed at sea in some insignificant, forgotten battle somewhere. And against what enemy, I could not say - but those are the king's enemies, not mine. Happened not long after my Mary passed away. At least the good Lord chose to spare her from that grievous, wicked hurt."

Ryan saw the old man starting to choke back tears, looked down into his ale and drew a deep breath. "I've seen the face of war myself and it is not a pretty face. No. Seen many a good lad killed or maimed in action. I'm truly sorry for you both. John was a good friend to me and a good lad to be sure."

O'Keeffe reached into his pocket for a handkerchief and blew his nose. "Well, death is never very far off for any of us is it?" he asked rhetorically, teary-eyed. "It's the way of things. It is God's plan for us poor mortals. We live. We try to build somethin' in this world with the time the good Lord sees fit to give us and then He takes us when it pleases Him to do so. The livin' are left to go on. But there now, enough of this morbid talk. Let's not spoil a fine Irish reunion. Share yer tale with us young Luke. Tell Shannon and me what happened to you when you left this lovely green island for the cold, black sea all those years ago. And I'll have you tell us the proper way too: the whole story from start to finish leavin' no point unsaid. That's the way *we* Irish like our stories told!"

Ryan obliged his host. Father and daughter listened to him tell his story, from beginning to end, and both were completely absorbed.

Ryan began with his leaving Ireland at the tender age of eleven to serve in the king's navy. British warships were full of young boys performing menial tasks. Most eventually went on to become career seamen. Something inside of him drove him on though - he wanted more. He taught himself how to be *English*. He even learned to speak like an English gentleman. He discovered he had a good ear for languages and refined the French his mother had taught him as a very young boy. He picked-up some Spanish and Italian from sailors and prisoners as well. He worked tirelessly at mastering every position on a ship. And when others relaxed or went ashore on liberty, he spent his time mostly reading. He studied sailing techniques, navigation and battle tactics from every book he could get his hands on. He particularly liked books on military history and loved to read about war's greatest commanders. He was eventually rewarded for his efforts with a promotion to midshipman. And then, after he had proven his mettle, an old ship's captain on the verge of retirement, a man who had taken a liking to him, helped him obtain the officer's commission he so craved.

Ryan finished his story with the *Toulon*, Hughes's double-cross, and his secret arrangement with Sartine.

O'Keeffe and Shannon barely touched a morsel of food while they listened to Ryan's tale. Not only did they find Ryan's story compelling, he had a gift for telling it well.

The old man, never easily impressed, was impressed now. O'Keeffe was known as a man who not only made money for himself but made money for his partners too and over the years many a young firebrand had tried to gain his favor - with little success. But more than the story, O'Keeffe found himself impressed by the man.

"My God, dear boy, what a wonderful tale and told in such grand style! Aye, told the Irish way. You have accomplished much. Yes, quite an achievement by any measure, I'd say. But tell me now, the truth too, are you on the run? British soldiers huntin' you down? Not that such a circumstance would offend me but it might complicate matters for us just a wee bit."

Ryan gave O'Keeffe a smug smile. "No need to be worrin' yourself there," he replied in his Irish brogue and with a twinkle in his eye, "I believe I've covered my tracks well enough. As far as the British navy is concerned, I'm rottin' away in some French prison under the name of Lieutenant Luke Roberts from Bristol. A man of no particular importance to anybody. After the Admiralty gets Hughes's report on my, ahem, incompetence, I doubt any priority will be given to obtain my release. Should the British make inquiries to the French about me, they'll be told I escaped from a Dunkirk jail and disappeared. My trail should end there. If I am recognized, I am Roberts, an escaped prisoner from a French prison making my *long* way back home. To anyone else, I am Luke Ryan, born in France, in Gravelines outside of Dunkirk, and the son of a lieutenant attached to the Dillon Brigade who died in service to the King of France. I have good contacts in France who will confirm either story if challenged."

"Bless me, lad! But I must keep a close eye on you. Yer a man of many talents I see. Wily like a fox too. You remind me of your father. I remember him well. He wore the white cockade, was a staunch Jacobite and a patriot. He fought with Bonnie Prince Charlie in Scotland durin' the third Jacobite uprising of '45."

"I fear you flatter me too much, Mr. O'Keeffe. I am no patriot, no Jacobite. In fact, I have no politics. I have no religion. I am just a simple man, a petty smuggler."

"Hm. As you say. Still, ever since you were a young lad full of mischief and gettin' into all sorts of trouble with my John and young Shannon here, I had you marked for a clever boy. Aye, even back then, I did. A boy with a good road ahead of him, if he chose to take advantage of it. Always a ringleader you were - and as smart as the good Lord makes 'em."

"Tell us, Luke," Shannon asked, "after your mother passed away, why did you go to sea with the British in their warships? When you left Ireland, we thought you had fallen in with pirates or sailed off to the American Colonies."

"To learn," Ryan answered simply, without hesitation or emotion.

"The few times my Uncle John took me sailing with him up and down the coast were grand. I loved the sea from the very first. I had no use for the farm my uncle had. As you know, I was young when my mother died and then my uncle was tossed into jail for a time for smuggling muskets into Ireland. He wasn't able to teach me much. The British navy is the finest navy in the world. None better. I wanted to learn all I could. I wanted to be the best. Not like those men sitting over there drinkin' and gamblin' away their money with no real future ahead for any of them. They're just struggling to get by, from voyage to passage, from drink to drink, until the day comes, and it usually does for their lot, when they wreck their ships near shore or get themselves caught."

"You see, Shannon," interjected O'Keeffe softly, eying Ryan carefully, "more shrewdness at work here. Ambition too I dare say. We are in the company of a man who intends to distinguish himself and make his mark in the world. Nothin' wrong with that in my book. Not a thing."

"In the end," offered Ryan, "that is all any man, or any woman, can do really. We all strive to distinguish ourselves in some good way."

"Why did you leave the navy?" Shannon asked with more suspicion than curiosity, prying, probing his thoughts as if searching for some flaw in his story.

O'Keeffe threw his daughter a stern glance, a warning, but she ignored her father and persisted.

"Well?" she asked.

Ryan rocked back in his chair and gave her a broad smile. "Well now, Shannon, I learned what I needed to learn. School was over. And, I had... *difficulties*... difficulties with British justice."

O'Keeffe burst out laughing and slapped his hand on the table. "Difficulties with British justice! Ha! Ha! Ha! By God, doesn't all of Ireland, lad! Damn my soul! Doesn't the whole world! Let us drink to British justice, wherever it might be found someday!"

Shannon couldn't help herself, started laughing too. All three lifted their tankards high, clanked them together and drank to O'Keeffe's toast.

"Shannon, dear daughter of mine, always lookin' out for my

welfare. Some things we must take on faith child. You knew Luke as a young lad. He hasn't changed. Not his heart anyways. He was a fine boy then. He's a fine man now. Bury yer doubts girl, at least for a time. Let the man prove himself. The risk to us is small enough. I didn't get to where I am today by not bein' a fair judge of character and takin' a risk or two. Luke here is the genuine article. And I know you think so too. Trust yer instincts daughter."

O'Keeffe shifted in his chair, turned to face Ryan. "Now Luke, down to business, lad. I think of you as my own son. Yer uncle spent three years in a British jail because of his work for me. To most in these parts, he was a simple farmer working a plot of land. That good man was more than that, quite a bit more. He should have served no more than six months in jail accordin' to the local magistrate who sentenced him. But the British held him unlawfully after that, tryin' to force him to disclose names and places pertaining to my interests. They knew he was a smuggler and a ringleader and runnin' guns and liquor into Ireland. They suspected he was involved in treasonous acts but couldn't prove a thing. Yer uncle never said a contrary word about his fellows and died in prison of a broken heart. He was a good man and a patriot like his brother, your father. He did some fine smugglin' for old Jack Field and me until he was caught. And then off you went, running away to sea. Against my wishes as I recall. Now you've returned from purgatory, after twelve years of servin' in British ships, and with yer own ship and a rich cargo. My, my, my. And you speak like an English gentleman to boot! I don't believe I've ever known a young man who accomplished more than this! Not all on his own anyways..."

"Thank you, Mr. O'Keeffe," Ryan replied, returning to his English accent once again. "Of course, I thought of you when I put this plan together. The title to my ship, *Friendship*, is perfectly legal. She's properly registered and she can carry whatever you think will sell. She's a small lugger to be sure and not pretty to look at mind you - but she'll haul a heavy load. You remember Patrick Dowlin? He's my first officer. A fine seaman and a first rate officer. Each member of the crew has served with me in the king's navy and I know the quality of each man well. Every one of them is a solid Dubliner or Rushman and I can vouch for every man.

And, as I wrote you, I have good contacts on the Continent, including the Torris brothers."

"Aye. I know John Torris by reputation," O'Keeffe acknowledged. "He is well-connected at Versailles, or so they say. Torris is a reliable businessman. Always been trustworthy accordin' to some folks I've asked here who have had dealin's with him. Bit of an unusual combination for a man from the Continent, I must say. Heard of his brother Charles but I don't know him. Flemish aren't they?"

Ryan nodded silently.

"Dunkirk is a good place to call home port, Luke. Lot of good Irish stock living over there. This ship of yers, *Friendship*, she'll reach the agreed upon rendezvous point north of Rush in the mornin'?"

"Aye, sir. God willing."

O'Keeffe nodded in satisfaction. "Indeed, God willing. All the necessary arrangements have been made on this end. I have men and wagons at Rush waiting and I expect everything to go as planned without so much as a hiccup. Come now, let's finish our supper and then you'll ride back to Kenure with Shannon and me."

"Sir, you're most kind, but I can stay here at the inn. No need to trouble yourself."

O'Keeffe raised a disapproving eyebrow. "Troublin' myself? Is that what I'd be doin', lad? And you've spoken with such good, clear sense this evenin' up 'til now! Well, I'll not leave one of my own stranded here and that's the end of the matter. It's a fine inn, mind you. I should know. I own it! But you'll be our guest in my house under my roof. The hour is late and we best be off soon. Let's finish our supper. And don't insult yer new partner - yer senior partner at that mind you - by arguin' with him. Makes for bad business and bad digestion."

Ryan yielded to the old man's wishes. And once their desire for food and drink was satiated, the small party rose from the table to leave and as they did a young boy, who had been keeping an eye on O'Keeffe from a corner, jumped to his feet and raced outside ahead of them to find and wake O'Keeffe's driver.

After O'Keeffe slipped back inside the tavern to fetch his hat, and then stopped at a table to exchange pleasantries with an acquaintance,

Ryan and Shannon waited outside for the carriage to be brought around and stood awkwardly next to each other in silence. She was nearly as tall as he was.

She turned to look at him, curious what she might find when their eyes met in the dark. She was not disappointed.

"If I may inquire, what is your ship's cargo?" she finally asked, trying to ease the awkwardness between them.

"On this run we are bringing in several hundred hogsheads of salted beef, Dutch teas and a fair quantity of indigo and spices from the Orient."

"My, my. That does sound exotic."

"It is all rather routine I'm afraid, dear lady. But routine I suspect is good in this business."

"So," quipped O'Keeffe as he rejoined the couple and patted Ryan on the shoulder, "are profits! And we ought to be able to sell these goods quickly and fetch a handsome price for you!"

"Indeed, sir."

O'Keeffe smiled and rubbed his round stomach approvingly. "The price for Dutch tea has gone through the roof recently. Ten shillings and a six pence per pound! But liquor and guns still sells best, lad. Most likely always will. We'll have to work on that, hey?"

"Whatever brings us the best price, certainly, Mr. O'Keeffe."

"Just so me lad, just so."

Brilliant shafts of golden light peeked through a gap between the heavy maroon drapes, and settled on the mariner's face. Ryan stirred. He was usually an early riser but had slept well under O'Keeffe's roof. He pushed back the drapes, threw the bedroom windows open and filled his lungs with country air. The sun was just rising over the treetops. He muttered a soft curse to himself for sleeping in so late. He quickly washed, shaved and slipped on a set of fresh clothes that had been laid out for him over a chair and then ventured down stairs. Not hearing any one about yet, he decided to step outside for a walk.

O'Keeffe's house was an attractive, white clapboard structure, two stories high, with pale blue shutters and trim. Four modest Grecian columns stood at the front entrance guarding a spacious front porch enclosed by an intricate white lattice fence. A gravel driveway looped around the yard and ran down a soft hill, ending at a black, wrought iron gate that opened out onto the main road.

It was a handsome, but unpretentious home. From the main road, the house looked like any one of the many other modest country farmhouses dotting the Irish countryside and made little impression. But the house's exterior was deceptive. A large extension, hidden from the road by tall, swaying maples, poplars and thick hedges, had been added to the rear of the house. Acres of open field surrounded the house.

O'Keeffe liked to nurture his reputation as the simple owner of several Dublin shops and a landlord over a few small farms. Neighbors though thought it odd that a guard, with musket in hand, often stood at the front gate but O'Keeffe was known to be a bit eccentric and the local authorities didn't seem troubled any. Politicians and the law, well acquainted with O'Keeffe's generosity, quietly ignored him.

When Ryan returned to the house, he found O'Keeffe and Shannon in the dining room eating breakfast together. O'Keeffe greeted him with a warm smile.

"Well, well, look who's up! Day's half over lad. You men of the sea certainly enjoy some casual ways. I'd of thought yer kind was made of iron."

Ryan returned O'Keeffe's smile with a boyish grin. "Beggin' your pardon, sir, a fine feather bed you gave me to sleep on and no officer of the watch to wake me. This is indeed rather late for me. I'm usually up and about before the morning sun. I didn't hear you good folks so went outside for a quick stroll. A good mornin' to you both."

Shannon reached for a sterling silver pot and poured steaming coffee into a fine china cup, decorated with delicate, hand-painted roses. "Good morning to you too," she said, keeping her eyes fixed mostly on him as she poured. "You slept well then, Luke?"

"Aye, that I did, like the dead," he answered, gingerly accepting the delicate cup from Shannon using both his hands, trying not to spill its contents on the fine linen tablecloth.

Shannon considered his outfit for a moment. She had picked it out herself and had guessed his size well. The clothes were perfect. The knee-high riding boots were new, but the coarse blue shirt with brown suspenders and heavy, black trousers were worn and rugged, the kind favored by common laborers.

"I must say, you look like a farmer in that outfit, Luke," she told him teasingly. "Clothes suit you fine. Is the fit to your liking?"

"Aye, not used to wearing boots tho'," he answered and realized, as he took his chair, that Shannon was dressed in the same rugged clothing. "I suppose I'll manage well enough. We off to plant some crops today? Can't say I remember how."

O'Keeffe laid his newspaper down over his lap and smiled. "No planting today, dear boy. Wouldn't seem right to let a ship's capt'n get his hands soiled - even if it is good Irish dirt and manure mind you."

O'Keeffe chuckled at himself but then his expression and tone turned businesslike. "After breakfast Luke, I'm off to Belfast on business for several days. I thought I'd make a short detour through Rush to check on our mutual arrangements there. Any word you want delivered to yer ship?"

"Aye, sir. Thank you. Dowlin is the man to see and talk too. He's a big fellow with long, red hair. If you see him, I'd be grateful if you told him that the plan is the same and I'll join him in a week or so. He knows what to do with the ship and crew."

"Delighted to, very good. I thought it might be good for Shannon to accompany you on yer little jaunt along the coast. That way I'll have someone on this side of the world who'll have first-hand knowledge of the different landin' sites you might take a fancy to."

"Oh?" Ryan asked with surprise. "I, well, I, ahem -"

"Shannon is the one who suggested it. I have the utmost confidence that you will see to her welfare. Lord knows that had I said no she would have ignored me anyway."

"Father!"

"I will," Ryan interrupted, "return her safely to you, Mr. O'Keeffe."

"I know you will. Traveling with a woman might be less conspicuous than traveling by yerself anyway. We're a land occupied by a foreign army mind you. Strangers are frequently stopped and questioned. Shannon knows what to say if you are stopped and where to find comfortable lodgings. She is traveling to check on some of my properties and you are to play the part of the hired hand. Provisions and horses are ready for you whenever you have a mind to set off."

"Most kind of you, sir," Ryan said and turned to face Shannon. "Can you ride?"

O'Keeffe started chuckling and proudly answered for his daughter. "Ha! Can she ride? She rides better than most men, lad!"

Shannon, her green eyes flashing, threw her head back and let out a hardy laugh. "Certainly, I can ride better than *you*, Captain Luke Ryan!"

Ryan and O'Keeffe answered Shannon's feisty words with wide grins. Ryan knew better than to directly respond to her challenge. He had seen the stables behind the house during his walk earlier, had supposed she rode often, and had almost no experience with horses himself.

"'Tis all settled then," said O'Keeffe warmly. "After breakfast, I'll be headin' north and you two young folks will be headin' south. Let's see, today is Tuesday. We'll meet back here, say, by next late next week sometime?"

"So be it, sir."

After breakfast, Ryan packed a few items and followed O'Keeffe's daughter through the kitchen and out the back door over to the stables. The horses were saddled and ready for them. A young boy led a good-natured mare with a dappled gray and white coat over to Ryan and handed him the reins. Shannon went over to a reddish-brown stallion, a magnificent animal, and took a moment to caress its long neck before pulling herself up on the saddle, without help, and nudged her horse outside. She handled the great beast, clearly a more spirited animal than the mare, with an easy confidence. At the end of the drive, the gatekeeper let the riders through and they took the road south.

By pre-arrangement with O'Keeffe, Ryan had sent his ship and crew north, to Rush, to deliver their first cargo. The small seaport town, with its windmills and clapboard cottages built along windswept dunes, was home to a large pool of talented, experienced seamen who didn't mind breaking a law or two. And with its rugged coastlands and caves, Rush had long been a favorite port-of-entry for smugglers operating along Ireland's east coast. But Rush also attracted the attention of British revenue cutters, forever patrolling the Irish Sea, and of pirates too.

When he was still a young boy, Ryan's uncle had taken him on several short runs in and out of Rush, always landing at the same place, until his uncle's luck ran out one day. The British ran his ship aground and tossed him into jail. Ryan had not forgotten.

Using multiple landing sites chosen at random meant more coordination between himself and O'Keeffe. But Ryan thought it a small price to pay to keep the British revenue service guessing.

The two travelers made good time across the green countryside and chatted about mundane matters. After exhausting all small talk, they rode quietly together for a while until Earth's eternal torch began fading behind the western hills and night settled over the land. The temperature started to cool and the savory smoke from cooking fires filled the air. Civilization was not far off.

As they cut through a purple moor, blanketed in swirling ground mist, Shannon was the first to break their silence. "About a mile or so down this road, Luke, is an inn. My father has already made arrangements for us there for the night. In the morning we can make our way to the coast and continue south."

Ryan lifted his head, caught a glimpse of her face from under his hat's wide brim. Her cheeks were flushed from the day's heat and a few freckles covered her sunburned nose. The color only enhanced her beauty.

He looked away and stood up in his stirrups. "Aye, that is welcome news," he said with a weary voice. "I will confess that I'll be grateful to get off this damned beast, Miss O'Keeffe."

She giggled and swung her head around to look at him. "My... But you do look like a farmer in that hat! Getting a wee bit sore in the saddle are we? Come now, Luke! Let's see what you're made of - I'll race you to the edge of town! The loser buys the winner supper..."

But before Ryan could utter one word of protest, the girl with the long, blond braids kicked her heels into her horse's flesh and spurred her stallion on with a wild yell. Her horse tore down the narrow dirt road at a full gallop, leaving Ryan sitting in a cloud of dust. The wind took her hat but she did not stop and continued to ride hard down the road with, what seemed to Ryan, an almost reckless abandon.

Ryan tightened his grip around the reins and charged after her, uttering a curse under his breath. But the spirited stallion with its spirited mistress easily outpaced him and reached the town first. When Ryan finally caught up, he found Shannon standing in the road stroking her horse's sweaty neck with a triumphant look in her eyes.

She smiled at him as the mariner brought his horse to a clumsy stop. "I trust that even an Irish rogue such as yourself, sir, is good for honoring his wager?"

Ryan laughed. "That might be a bit presumptuous on your part my lady, but aye," he answered, bowing his head in a gesture of mock defeat, "you won, certainly. I dare not incur your father's wrath by welching on a wager with his daughter. So, I confess freely, for all the world to hear, that you won. Both my backside and my purse will soon be broke tho' if we race anymore today."

He reached behind his back and produced her hat. "But, I should at least be given some credit for chivalry. This, I believe, is yours ma'am."

Shannon laughed at his easy humor and took her hat.

Ryan removed his own hat and used his forearm to wipe the sweat off his brow, watching her out of the corner of his eye. The last flickering rays of light, muted tones of yellow and orange, settled on her shoulders, setting her golden braids on fire. He had never seen anything more exquisite. He saw a trickle of sweat running down her temple, took a handkerchief, and slowly reached over to gently dab her forehead.

"There now, that's better," he told her. "A proper Irish lass shouldn't be seen in public sweating."

And as if he had fallen victim to some spell, he could not bring himself to look away. He could feel his pulse begin to race, breathing seemed difficult, and an odd sense of anxiety and joy, mixed, seized him.

She held his gaze firmly and smiled at him. A coy smile, yes. "My good sir, what, may I ask, are you staring at?"

"Why madam," he replied boldly, in the crisp accent of an English gentleman, without hesitation - surprising himself as he had always been shy around women, "I am staring at *you*."

She looked away, stared down at the road, and, for an awkward moment, neither spoke. She already knew, from the moment he had swaggered into the *Red Dragon* the night before, that she loved him. She had always loved him. Yes, this man, whom she had only known as a boy years ago, she loved still.

He came from humble beginnings, true. He was not rich. He had no family name to parley into money. He was not the tallest or the strongest man. And, though she could not quite put her finger on it, in a curious way, he was no longer even Irish. Such things mattered not at all to her. She found his rugged face, with his intelligent eyes and coal black hair, with waves like the sea, exceptionally handsome. And he carried himself with a confidence, a quiet dignity, she found appealing, even sensuous. He was a proud and a gentle man. Not even his plain clothes could hide these qualities. She could still remember his natural grace and charm as a boy. He had something, a power, which even back then had drawn others to him. He had always been the leader, the scrapper - and her protector.

She knew other men who were just as handsome, just as charming and confident. But the man sitting uncomfortable on his horse next to her had other intangible qualities, the kind the eye cannot always see. So now she struggled to understand her longings for him, longings she had every intention of suppressing and keeping secret.

Over the years she assumed that, with time, she would eventually grow out of her young girl's silly infatuation and, for a brief time, she thought she had. But now there she was, a full-grown woman with a full-grown woman's maturity and good sense, with sweaty palms and a fluttering heart. Love's first blush.

She had been uncertain about her feelings when her father first told her that Ryan was returning to Ireland. Over thirteen years had passed. A long time. The news had made her heart flutter. She had felt that. But beyond this she was unsure of what she might feel or what, if anything, might happen.

Her father was always encouraging her to meet young men and had been prepared to accept as a son-in-law any man she fancied. Many a dinner party had been arranged on her behalf towards that purpose. But the young beauty accepted calls from only a handful of men and then only to appease her father. She found her suitors all lacking.

Ryan did not quite know what to make of her silence and instantly regretted his boldness. "Well," he finally said softly, "forgive me if I've offended you Shannon. That was not my intention and I apologize for my brazenness. Shall we go find this inn of yours?"

Her head spinning, she could only nod, tugged at her horse's reins and continued down the village's main road on foot.

Ryan dismounted and followed. He felt a bit ashamed.

In the center of a small village outside of Wicklow, they came to a quaint two-story inn, a building of whitewashed stone and a thatched roof with black shutters and window boxes. Someone's loving hands had crowned each window box with a colorful array of fresh flowers.

The inn's proprietor, a congenial and gregarious little man, recognized Shannon instantly and gave her a wide and friendly smile.

"Good to have you back, Miss Shannon! Was told to be expectin' you sometime soon. Been a while hasn't it? And if I may say so, yer as pretty as yer dear mum and she was a true beauty! Follow me now. Got a nice table for you and the gentleman right over here, Miss Shannon, next to the fire. How's yer papa? As ornery as ever I'll wager?"

"He's well, thank you, Mr. O'Donnell," Shannon answered, smiling. "And how are both you and Mrs. O'Donnell?"

"God is good. Life is good."

"And your boys?"

"Both turning into strapping young lads and full of the devil as always thank you for askin'. Now anythin' you be needin' - anythin' at all - you just give us a holler, hey? I'll be seein' to yer supper. You know my reputation for fine cookin'. Haven't lost my touch. Not yet anyways. The misses will vouch for that. Horses will be seen to and there are two clean rooms with comfortable beds waitin' for ya upstairs when yer ready. The boy over there will bring yer bags up to the rooms straight away."

"Thank you kindly, Mr. O'Donnell. I'll be sure to give my father yer best regards."

"Ha! Ha! That I do, that I do," O'Donnell replied chuckling as he wiped his hands on his apron. Then excused himself.

Ryan and Shannon took their seats and enjoyed the fire quietly until O'Donnell returned with two large tankards of ale and plates heaped high with slices of fresh ham, boiled carrots and baked potatoes.

The weary couple ate casually and talked little. For dessert, Mrs. O'Donnell brought them fresh fruit tarts and served them tea and after supper, they retired to their rooms and agreed to an early start in the morning.

Standing alone on a rocky shore, Ryan looked out across the broad ocean and witnessed the birth of a new day. Ageless Dawn, matchless in her beauty and wearing a halo of golden light around her regal brow, rose above the blue-green waters of a still and quiet sea to join her lordly lover, the Sun. Wrapped in glittering saffron robes, she set the sky on fire, leaving a trail of pink and turquoise hues behind her. And then radiant Dawn, fond of men who roam the Earth, called upon her favorite handmaiden, Spring, and beseeched her to bestow her gift of magic. Spring obeyed her mistress gladly and blew her warm breath across the land to ease the heavy labors of mortal men...

Ryan never tired of watching the sun's rising. He stared in awe, felt the magic of it renew his spirit.

He was sitting at the table, drinking hot tea and reading a newspaper when she came downstairs. She smiled brightly at him.

"Good morning, Luke."

Ryan returned her smile, set his tea and paper down and stood to pull a chair out for here. He was not well versed in the ways of etiquette, but knew to do that much at least.

"Good morning, Miss Shannon."

"All dressed and ready to set out I see," she replied and suppressed a yawn with her hand. "Looks like the day will be warm and bright. What time do you suppose it is?"

"About seven, I should think."

"And when did you awake?"

"Four o'clock, *of course*."

She looked at him in disbelief. "Four?" she asked and assumed he was joking at first. But she saw by his expression that he was serious.

"Aye. I took a nice stroll down to the shore. It's turning into a fine Irish mornin' indeed. You've missed one of the loveliest sunrises, I am afraid. A rare gift. Not to worry, there will be others no doubt in the days to come. Breakfast is ready for you, if you have a mind to eat. O'Donnell sets quite a breakfast table. No poor man's fare here I'll tell you plainly. Never seen anything quite like it. An admiral in King George's navy doesn't eat as well."

Shannon rubbed the sleep from her eyes. "Some good strong, hot coffee for me first I think."

They ate their breakfast quietly together. Afterwards, they gathered their things, mounted their horses and headed east until they reached the sea. They then turned south and rode along the coast. By midmorning, the wind was up and white-capped waves dotted a dark blue ocean.

Ryan pointed to a pair of white sails off on the far horizon and that brought a smile to Shannon's lips. They rode to the edge of a small cliff, rested for a bit and watched the breakers crash against the rocks below them. Ryan stood up in his saddle and removed his hat to let the wind rustle through his thick, wavy hair.

"Lovely isn't it?" he asked.

"Yes," Shannon replied, keeping her eyes fixed on the breakers. "'Tis truly lovely. You already miss the sea don't you, Luke?"

Ryan, sensing her uneasiness, turned to look at her. "Aye. I never tire of it. Have you ever been at sea, out on a ship or boat I mean?"

"No," she replied, stifling a small giggle. "Never."

"Well now, we shall need to remedy that omission in your education won't we?"

Shannon turned to look at him, to see whether he was serious or just teasing her. "Luke, do you mean it?" she asked excitedly.

"I do."

"Oh, that would be splendid! On your honor, sir, I shall hold you to your word!"

Ryan pointed down the coast. "See that tower way yonder?"

Shannon followed the length of his arm and nodded.

"By my reckoning, just a little ways beyond that tower is Arklow and the River Avondale. If your father was able to make the arrangements for me, there should be a small vessel waiting for us there. You game? I'll give you fair warning, it's a tad rough out there today."

She tossed her head back, smiled at him defiantly - another challenge. "Let's ride!"

Ryan nodded, returned her smile with his own. "Unless you have a mind to see man and horse tumble down this cliff together and on into the jaws of a hungry sea, no more races tho'…"

"No more races," she agreed, keeping her eyes fixed on the horizon. But then she couldn't help herself and stole a glance of him out of the corner of her eye, watching him as he stretched his back and arms before settling back in his saddle. She felt a twinge of guilty pleasure.

Ryan took the lead and they rode along the rugged coast towards the small town standing off in the distance. At noon they stopped along the beach and unpacked a basket of roasted chicken, boiled potatoes, biscuits and cheese prepared for them by Mrs. O'Donnell. Ryan produced a bottle of wine from his saddlebag, a gift from Mr. O'Donnell, and offered the bottle to Shannon. She took a sip and handed the bottle back. Ryan didn't favor wine much, but he took a long swallow and was pleasantly surprised. It was a respectable claret. O'Donnell, he gathered, was trying to keep in someone's good graces.

Late afternoon found the couple in the small seaside town of Arklow, named after the Viking warlord Arknell. Shannon led them to another inn where, once again, arrangements had already been made for them. The couple agreed to stay the night, it being too late in the day to venture out on the water, and took their supper at the inn.

As the evening wore on the inn became quite busy. The locals were a merry and friendly group and sang and danced to lively, old Irish folk tunes. A blind man, sitting on a stool next to a roaring fire, worked his fiddle with skill while his partner, a plump, rosy-cheeked woman, tapped out a lively beat on a drum. And for a time, however briefly, people forgot their cares.

As a tavern maid cleared their plates, Ryan called over to the innkeeper and asked for pen and ink and removed a clean sheet of paper from his jacket. Using crisp, neat strokes, he started drawing ragged lines across the paper and then moved the table's oil lamp closer, pausing to study his handiwork in the dim light.

Shannon watched him work, a touch annoyed that he was plainly going to make her ask what he was up to. "Is this some secret doings or do you intend to someday tell me what it is you are doodling?"

Ryan grinned, turned the paper around and pushed it over to her. "Is this about right?"

She studied his artwork and nodded. He had drawn a detailed map of the ground they had covered over the past two days with the names of roads, hamlets and distances. Each significant bay, cove, stream, the flat beaches and the marshes, were all clearly depicted and drawn close to scale.

"You have a gift, Luke. Why, this is remarkable. The rendering is so precise."

"No, no, not really," he said nonchalantly and shrugged. "Any fair seaman can do this but I thank you for the compliment. I can teach you if you like. You probably were beginning to think that we were on holiday. Not so. Well, shall we retire? Tomorrow we'll see what manner of sea legs you have. We'll sail south down along the coast. There's more work to do. Fair warning tho', we should depart early."

She looked at him wide-eyed. "Not four in the mornin'?" she asked with feigned alarm in her voice, her full lips curling into a pout.

"Ah, 'tis an excellent suggestion you make, my lady!" he roared and slapped his hand on the table, beaming at his own bit of sarcasm. "Agreed! Four it is. I'll be sure to rap loudly on your door and wake you should you oversleep..."

She arched her eyebrows. "Why sir, I do believe there's a bit of a mean streak in you."

Ryan smiled, leaned back in his chair, folded his arms and said nothing. Never had he felt as happy as he did now. A curious, indescribable joy filled his heart.

Bright, glorious stars dotted a pitch-black sky. And as it has been since the beginning, and as it shall be until the end, magnificent Orion, mighty hunter, with bow in hand, led the triumphant procession of celestial giants in their great wheeling turn across the heavens.

Shannon stared down at the small boat gently being rocked back and forth by the river's inky black waters. She looked down with trepidation at the ripples of water slapping against the boat's hull or pilings, leaving behind a gurgling sound before vanishing in a swirl. The boat was rigged as a ketch, with a mainmast amidships and a small mizzenmast set just behind the tiller.

A man on the wharf held the bowline for Ryan as he carefully stepped down into the boat. He took a torch, inspected the 25 footer for leaks first, and then checked her masts and rigging. The boat maker had been a bit ambitious with two masts on such a small vessel thought Ryan but found the boat sound enough for his purposes.

He took Shannon's hand, helped her step down. She seated herself on the thwart behind the mainmast, clenching the wood firmly in her hands. The man on the wharf then handed Ryan their ditty bags and a small wooden locker packed with food and drink. After stowing their things underneath the bow, Ryan handed the man several coins, then took a seat at the tiller.

The man let the bowline go and pushed the boat off with his leg into the River Avondale's dark waters. Ryan stood to raise the mainsail, making the boat rock unevenly, and Shannon looked up at him apprehensively.

"All is well," he told her with a reassuring smile and gingerly sat back down after he had set the mainsail.

The canvas caught a light breeze and held it. Ryan trimmed the sail and swung the boat around. The river's currents did the rest. The ketch picked up speed and floated smoothly over the surface towards the open sea.

"You all right?" he asked.

Shannon watched him work the tiller back and forth with an easy confidence and put on a brave face. "Yes. I think so. Aye, actually, I am fine. I was a trifle jittery at first. I admit it. But now I am, remarkably, feeling very much at ease. This could actually be most exciting, even amusing. I am enjoying this."

Ryan smiled at her, pleased at her willingness to try something adventurous and a bit risky. "It shall at the very least be amusing, good lady. I give you my word on it. If you will pardon a bit of immodesty, you are in good hands. And we'll keep the shore very close to us, I promise. Should we capsize, a highly unlikely possibility, I remember you being a strong swimmer. So, relax..."

With the first hint of light rising above the water, the two mariners left the sanctuary of the estuary, cut across a small bay, and were soon out playing in the sea's vast realm. And once out on the ocean a brisk wind overtook the light breeze and Ryan took full advantage of their good luck. He raised the jib and mizzen sails. The small ketch responded well to nature's invisible hand and picked up more speed.

Shannon removed her hat and let her golden hair blow freely in the wind.

"Even the most experienced sailor sometimes succumbs to seasickness, Shannon. Should you start to feel ill, just say so and we'll head in for shore. No shame in that."

"Do you ever get seasick, Luke?"

Ryan grinned again. "No. Never..."

She looked at him with an air of defiance. By sheer force of will she simply would not allow herself to get sick. And then she saw it: Dawn, matchless in her beauty, with golden crown and trailing purple robes, majestically rising above the sea's dark waters. And in her presence the Moon, and all the stars that never die, obedient to their laws, faded back into the heavens.

"Oh, Luke, this is exhilarating! Truly, lovely. Never have I seen a sunrise more beautiful. Why, it takes your breath away. Thank you, Luke. Thank you for this, for this extraordinary gift."

Ryan touched his hat, as if saluting a fellow officer. "Your delight is my delight, my lady."

They continued sailing south. Ryan found the ketch sturdy and easy to control. They hugged the shore, leisurely tacking back and forth against a contrary south wind through the early morning. And when he saw something of interest, usually a cove or a cave, he turned in towards shore to survey the terrain more closely and check the water's depth.

When one particularly interesting spot caught Ryan's eye, he beached their boat and the two explorers set out on foot to reconnoiter. After Ryan had seen enough, Shannon served them breakfast before they set out again while he worked on his crude map using one of the boat's benches as a makeshift table.

As the day wore on the winds shifted yet again and the ketch picked up terrific speed. To their starboard stood green Ireland with cliffs, like the walls of an impregnable citadel, that could never be beaten down. Not even by the relentless breakers of a greedy sea. And to their port, stretching out as far as the eye could see, was the Irish Sea - and just beyond those waters, not far out of sight, lay great, powerful England, mistress over all the world's oceans.

The sun was warm but the sea's cool breezes kept her full powers in check and the day was delightful. By noon, white puffy clouds began to appear, drifting lazily across an azure blue sky. And when, on the far horizon, the two mariners saw the sails of different ships, they took turns making up stories about where each vessel was from, her destination, and what cargo she carried. The couple laughed and giggled at each other's stories like children. Their mood was carefree.

"My uncle used to call a day like this *a gift from God*," Ryan commented absently.

"A lovely description, Luke. Indeed, it is a beautiful day, a gift. Do you suppose, Captain Ryan, a woman could be taught how to sail?"

"Why of course, *Mademoiselle!*" Ryan answered without hesitation. "That was my plan. Truly, you read my mind. I would be delighted to serve as your tutor. The ship is yours, Shannon."

"What? Now? Here? But, I meant -"

"What better time than now? What better day than today, eh? Come now. Let's get you your sea legs."

He lashed the tiller down with a leather strap and grabbed both her hands to help her stand and then carefully moved her around, as if they were dancing, to exchange positions. He felt his knees quiver as her body brushed up against his. The sensation was unexpected and he quickly tried to suppress the feeling. As she took her seat, he reached back, released the tiller from the strap and took her hand, placing it over the long smooth wood, keeping his hand over hers until she had a feel for the tiller's motion and control. Once she seemed at ease, he released his grip, set her free, and sat against the mainmast facing her.

He watched her work the tiller and felt pride's warm rush touch his heart. But then, he sensed her aloofness too and reminded himself of his promise to O'Keeffe. He was out on business, nothing more.

"Man has been yoking the wind to serve his purpose for thousands of years, Shannon. There's really not much to it. You are doing fine. How about that now? You're a sailor! We've made a bit of history today. Capt'n Shannon O'Keeffe, first woman officer of the new Free Irish Navy!"

She tossed her head back and laughed, then looked directly at him, her eyes shining, her cheeks flushed by the wind, and smiled. "This is glorious, Luke!"

"Watch her trim now. Keep one eye on the wind by watching the curve of the sail; try to keep the wind from spilling out of the canvas. Watch your course too and keep her steady. Don't fight her now, guide her. She'll do most of the work for you if you let her. There! There! You have it now! Well done. Not much different than riding a horse now is it?"

She quietly savored the moment and did not answer him. She couldn't remember being any happier. A touch of Heaven. *But would it last forever* she thought to herself. She stayed at the tiller until late afternoon, until Ryan spotted Wexford and then they swapped positions again. Wexford was one of Ireland's major port cities with a busy, congested harbor.

A favorable wind had brought them farther south than Ryan had originally planned and they would need to find lodging on their own as O'Keeffe had made no arrangements for them in Wexford. Using only the mainsail, Ryan skillfully maneuvered the ketch through the harbor, passing many ships and smaller fishing trawlers, and brought her expertly up alongside an empty section of wharf within easy walking distance into Wexford proper.

A young British sentry patrolling the wharf eyed the couple suspiciously as Ryan secured the ketch. But the sentry saw nothing of interest and continued on his way after Ryan bid him a friendly good evening.

Ryan found and paid the harbormaster for the privilege of docking their boat, grabbed their ditty bags and the couple made their way on foot along Commercial Quay that ran, as the name implies, parallel to the water. They walked into the heart of town and stopped at half dozen different hotels without success and so returned to Commercial Quay where they tried their luck at several taverns and inns along Wexford's waterfront district and kept walking well into the evening until they eventually found an establishment with two available rooms. But Ryan wasn't pleased as every waterfront of every port town is, without exception, seedy and rough. He paid for their accommodations in advance and then the couple walked down a dark stairwell and into a cellar where the inn had a tavern. They found a small, empty booth off in a corner and took it.

The tavern was dingy, unattractive and noisy. Hard working women with hard looking faces flirted with the customers. The air was thick with smoke and no fiddler played his soft tunes to entertain friendly, wholesome guests here.

Ryan picked at the food on his plate, found it not very appealing, and set his fork aside. He looked up at Shannon and saw that she too had barely touched her meal. Even in the tavern's dim light she was beautiful. He suddenly wanted to reach over and touch her face. Her sun kissed skin, her bleached and windblown hair, only enhanced her beauty. He looked away instead, struggled to focus on other matters but found his will power lacking. That displeased him. The inability to control one's emotions was, *undisciplined.*

After a time, he thought of something safe to say, summoned up the courage to look at her again. "Tomorrow we can sail back to Arklow," he said in even, measured tones. "Or at least we can make Gory if the winds are against us, and then sail on to Arklow the day after. Once in Arklow we'll pick up the horses and get you home or, if you prefer, if you are weary, we can leave the ketch in Gory and hire a carriage to take us back to Dublin."

He couldn't help himself and smiled warmly at her. "If it would please you, Shannon," he continued, trying to suppress any emotion in his voice but had trouble hiding his affection. "I'll teach you some of the finer aspects of sailing on the journey back. P'haps you might even enjoy learning the basics of navigation. I would be pleased to teach you."

Shannon nodded enthusiastically and returned his smile. She leaned over the table and kissed him on the cheek. "Thank you for today."

A tingle shot down his spine. He could feel himself blushing. Her kiss had caught him off guard and the master tactician, a man who always kept a ready plan tucked away for some unexpected contingency, found himself lost in uncharted waters. He fumbled to find the right words.

But as he fumbled, a man, a great bear of a man, suddenly stood up from the table next to them and started hurtling crude curses at his companions.

His chair tipped over as he staggered to his feet and struck Shannon in the back. She calmly ignored it.

The big man slowly raised an arm and pointed an accusing finger at one of his companions. "I'll cut yer thievin' heart out for cheatin'," he said slowly, slurring his words. "Sa, Sa, Sam, Samuel, no, no foolin' I swear by all the saints above I, I, I'll do it. Now... put... the... bloody... money... ba, bab, back and then cut them goddamn cards again!"

The big man's companions all simply laughed at him.

"Sit yerself back down Josh before somebody cuts *YOU*," one of them scoffed. "Yer makin' a damn fool of yerself."

The big man reached back to take a swing at the other man and clipped the back of Shannon's head with an elbow as he brought his long arm around.

She winced and turned to confront the big man. She wasn't about to ignore two acts of rude behavior in one night.

But before Shannon could say a word, Ryan called out to the drunken sailor, certain that Shannon did not fully understand how dangerous the situation was becoming. "Steady there now lad. You just bumped the lady here. No doubt it was an accident. No harm done. Why not take your disagreement with your friends outside?"

The big man pivoted around and focused his blood-shot eyes on Ryan. He cocked his head to one side and narrowed his eyes, as if perplexed by this new and more interesting target.

"Yer talkin' to me mister?"

"Aye, I'm talking to you," replied Ryan carefully.

"Weeeeell, look'ee here," said the big man, noticing Shannon for the first time. He looked her up and down with appreciation until his gaze settled on her cleavage. "Look'ee lads, a fine fig... figure of a lass sittin' right next to us all this time and we didn't even knows it. Looks like a de, de, delicious fresh tart to me. Strawberry maybe? Mmmmmmm. Oh and she looks like she could use some lovin', lovin' by a real man, hey?"

The big man's generous gut quivered as he howled at his own humor.

A quiet settled over the tavern as heads turned to watch the trouble brewing.

Shannon looked away from the lout, stared down at her plate.

"No need to be sh... sh... shy lassie. That thar shr... shr... shrimp of a man sittin' with you can't give you what I can. Come now love. Let's see what you taste like. Give us a kiss, gives us a long slop, sloppy kiss."

Ryan had already coolly sized-up the threat. In a fair fight the big man would have crushed him. Despite his gut the man had a powerful boxer's build. But there is no such thing as a fair fight in any tavern along the waterfront of any town.

Ryan could almost feel the heat rising off of Shannon. *Her blood must be boiling.*

Somehow she managed to keep her poise though, said nothing, and Ryan was grateful for that. *Smart girl.* If there was going to be a fight, he wanted it, he needed it, to happen on his terms.

The big man's companions laughed and clamored for more. They began taunting him, exhorting him to press on with his vulgar advances towards the woman, a real beauty. They were all eager for some entertainment.

One of the barmaids, her unlaced blouse barely able to contain her ample breasts, joined the fun. "Give her a kiss Josh and if she's any good then let's pass her around so's we can all have a taste! I love strawberry tart!"

The whole tavern erupted with hoots and howls.

Ryan remained in his seat, eyeing the big man with contempt. "*Now* that shall be enough, sir! Why not return to your game with your mates. No need for any trouble here."

The big man belched and glared at Ryan. Ryan's refined English accent had not escaped his notice.

"Ooooh, beggin' yer pardon yer lor, lord, lordy, lordship," he said mockingly, then made a grand sweep of his arm and bowed. He turned to his companions. "Look'ee here now lads, we got ourselves a *fine* English gentleman. Sooooooooos proper and all. Can't say I care much for his arrogant ways tho'. Can't say I care much for Englishmen."

"P'haps," a voice in the crowd called out, "he could use a lesson in Irish manners Josh, hey?"

"Aye," snarled the big man. He spun around to face Ryan again. His eyes were filled with sheer meanness. "You an't in England now, friend. Here we does things different. We shares and shares alike pretty, little trinkets like this... An't that right lads?"

The big man's friends answered him with whistles and more hoots, goading him, taunting him, daring him. They wanted blood.

The big man, towering over Shannon, placed his large, grimy hands on her shoulders, eased his fingers underneath her blouse and began massaging her soft flesh.

She gritted her teeth, reached for her fork and gripped it tightly. She began to tremble but vowed she would die before this pig raped her.

Ryan did not stand, remained seated, and took a deep breath. "You forget yourself sir!" he said, managing to keep a level voice. But there was no mistaking his threatening tone. "You're drunk... You've lost all sense of decency and have gone much too far. If you know what's good for you - you'll know your place and take your filthy hands off the lady. Now, back off - *NOW!*"

Shannon, now pale and shaking, locked her eyes on Ryan and froze.

Ugly indignation suddenly melted away the big man's playful mood. No one, certainly no stranger, gave him orders.

"Me what?" he asked, snarling. "*Me place?* Is that what you said? Why you arrogant, little British shit! I'm a proud son of the *Whiteboys* - you know who they are? Me and my friends are protected. I can do whatever I want to you and to your little wh, whore bitch here with no worries. And I want to bleed you! I'm goin' to bleed you real slow. And when I'm finished carving you up, mmmmm, strawberry tart..."

The man's glassy, blood-shot eyes turned wild. Ryan knew the look, had seen it a dozen times before. He knew a little bit about the Whiteboys too, the *Buachailli Bána*, a lawless, violent gang of thugs who belonged to a secret, agrarian society.

The big man then pulled a long double-bladed knife from the top of his boot with his left hand and smiled down on Ryan with evil in his heart. Rage oozed from every pore.

All eyes were fixed on him as he fondled the knife with something like affection. His friends, their lust for blood at a fever pitch now, stood and wildly cheered him on.

"Aye, cut him, Josh, cut him!"

"Cut him good, Josh! Teach this fookin' English tallywhacker a lesson!"

"Go ahead, Josh! Bleed the bloody bugger! Fresh, English dog meat for the fishes..."

The big man had no choice in the matter now, couldn't lose face in front of his friends. He suddenly lunged at Ryan with his knife, like some wild beast without a care in his murderous heart. The Englishman's soft throat was his target.

Men jeered. Shannon gasped.

Even drunk, the big man was quick once he made his move.

But Ryan was quicker still. He grabbed his attacker's left wrist, just before the big man's knife reached his throat, and wrapped his left leg around the man's left knee - behind the joint, a weak spot - and yanked down hard.

The big man's leg buckled under his own great weight and he lost his balance. He tumbled forward until his skull hit the table's sharp edge with a wicked crack. The hardwood gouged his soft flesh. A stream of blood spurted through the air. And then, a split second later, with all his strength, Ryan smashed the big man's wrist against the table. The deadly blade flew from the big man's hand, spun across the table and landed on the floor, barely missing Shannon.

The sailor landed on his knees with a great thud. Ryan thought he heard the big man's knee pop. Blood trickled down from a nasty gash over the big man's left eye.

It had all happened so quickly that no one had even seen Ryan remove a small, double-barreled pistol tucked inside his shirt. Ryan put the pistol against the man's bleeding forehead and cocked one hammer back. The big man, dazed and gasping for air, remained on his knees. His wild eyes turned scared.

The man named Josh was finished. Ryan looked over at the big man's companions - standing, hesitating, each man silently debating what to do next. Ryan knew this was the critical moment for himself and Shannon. He had no chance against all the big man's friends at once and was certain no one in the tavern would offer any help to an *English* gentleman.

The mariner summoned up his most compelling, command voice.

"*No one dare move!*" he boomed out confidently across the room for all to hear. But he could feel the pit of his stomach churning too. He could feel the sweat trickling down his armpits.

"Shannon!" he called out sternly.

She jumped, startled.

"Pick up the knife!" he ordered through clenched teeth as he kept a wary eye fixed on the big man's companions.

Still dazed, she hesitated for a moment but then gathered her wits and picked up the knife.

Ryan turned his attention to the big man.

"Now laddie..." he said with a scowl on his face, exchanging his English accent for an Irish brogue just as casually as if he had changed his shirt. "I can put a musket ball into that empty skull of yers or not. It makes not a whit of difference to me. Then I'll be dealin' with yer friends. What happens next will be of no concern to you because, well, you'll be stone *dead* you poor fool. Now, what's yer pleasure? Life - or death? Think it through for a bit..."

The big man took a deep gulp of air, felt woozy and tried not to vomit.

"Well? Speak up lad! Yer bleedin' on me. What's it goin' to be?"

The big man understood his choices. He had sobered up enough for that much.

"Nothin' worth dyin' for here," he answered softly and shook his large head in capitulation.

"No more trouble then?"

The big man nodded back. He had had enough. There was no more fight left in him.

Ryan looked over to the big man's companions. "There you have it lads. We can all go on living to see a new day. I say the matter's closed and not too much harm has been done. All agreed?"

There were nods all around the tavern. No man wanted to get hurt or killed over a friend's drunken stupidity.

"Excellent. Have a care then lads and see to your friend here. He'll be needin' a few stitches but I suspect he'll mend soon enough."

Ryan released the big man's arm and carefully laid his pistol on the table - within easy reach - as two of the big man's friends came over to help him to his feet. They propped his arms over their shoulders and carried him out of the tavern while others drifted back to their own matters.

Before Ryan could ask Shannon if she was all right, the tavern's proprietor, a twig of a man dressed in a dirty white apron, walked over to their table carrying a musket, an old blunderbuss covered in a fine coat of rust, and held it tightly against his chest.

"Don't know who you are mister," he said nervously and lowered the blunderbuss at Ryan's chest. "Don't care. You're trouble and I think it's best you and the lass here leaves this place straight away."

Ryan had to suppress a laugh. The musket was in such disrepair he was certain the weapon would blow up in the proprietor's face if he tried to use it. But even if he was wrong, Ryan felt no fear. In his haste the proprietor, Ryan saw, had forgotten to install the flint.

"No, sir. I don't believe we can do that," Ryan replied calmly, switching back to his refined English accent. "Inasmuch as it is late and we've already paid for our rooms my good man, we shall not be leaving your fine establishment on this lovely evening. And besides, the lady and I have done no wrong this night."

The proprietor pondered his next move and hesitated. He hadn't expected to be told no.

Shannon stood, leaned close to the innkeeper's ear and whispered a few words. The innkeeper looked at her with surprise, considered her for a moment and lowered his musket. He gave Ryan one last look, then turned and walked away in silence.

Ryan stood. "What in the world Shannon did you say to him?"

"I gave him my name, that's all," she replied with a smile. "That is my only weapon in a place like this."

"Ah, clever girl."

"I am indebted to you for the second time in one day, Luke. I didn't even know you carried a pistol. Just as my father observed: you're resourceful and shrewd. You're a man of many talents I see. Thank you, Luke. Thank you again for protecting me."

"Well, perhaps I am a wee bit lucky too," he replied truthfully. "I regret bringing you here, exposing you to such an offensive place. We should not have sailed this far south. I am truly sorry for my poor judgment."

"Please, Luke, you need not regret a thing. I've been in the presence of vulgar men before. And I would not trade this day for anything. I shall have fond memories of it, always."

"Hm, well, shall we?" he asked and took her hand.

He led her up the stairs and to their rooms.

"Here's your key," he told her after unlocking the door to her room. "And you'll keep this door bolted from the inside now and pound on the wall if you need me. I'm in the adjacent room. I don't expect we'll have any more trouble tonight though. After they stich him up, that fool's head is going to be pounding mighty hard for a day or two."

She studied his face. Her green eyes were wide and moist, as if she might suddenly start to cry.

As a butterfly will elude a child trying to catch it - only to be caught effortlessly by another when it lands haphazardly on a shoulder - so it can be with love. Look for it, chase it, and too often you will not find it. Love must find you.

She wrapped her arms around his neck and pulled him into her. She could resist him no longer. Her body ached with desire. She pressed her herself against him, could feel his own excitement building.

She pressed her open mouth against his lips and tasted him with her tongue. Her passion for him, like the raging waters of some great river cascading over the towering falls, was unstoppable.

Hot with lust, Ryan seized her in his arms and showered her with hard, fast kisses. But then he found the strength to pull away.

"Shannon, I am a plain seaman, a smuggler - nothin' but a petty thief, I..."

She put her fingers to his mouth, cut him off. "Hush my dear Luke."

She searched his eyes and wanted to hold on to this moment for as long as she could, that most precious, exquisite of moments when love first blooms between two willing hearts. It was the moment she had dreamt about as a child years before and now she wanted to savor the pure ecstasy filling her whole being. Then again, despite the yearning in her heart beyond telling, she felt the faintest hesitation too, her joy restrained, reserved. She understood such bliss is fleeting, that it is snatched away from mortals, always.

She ran her fingers through his thick, wavy hair.

"It is time. It is time I declared my love for you, Luke. You're so much more than the man you have described. And, I have noticed, sometimes you say too little and sometimes you say too much. Now you would say too much. Shhh..."

She kissed him again, caressed the taut muscles of his arms. His strength surprised her. His lose fitting shirt had hidden his fine, muscular build from her. She opened the door to her room and drew him inside.

Ryan hesitated. "What about your father, Shannon? He has entrusted me with your welfare."

His concern brought a warm smile to her lips. "Always the gentleman. And so you have honored that trust. I love you, Luke. I have loved you since we were children. When I heard you were returning to Ireland my heart filled with joy. I did not want this moment - not unless I was certain you wanted it too. And here we are. I am a grown woman. My father's reach is long, true, but it does not extend into my bedroom. Tell me you do not want me. Tell me now Luke Ryan that you do not love me and I'll pursue this no further. Otherwise, this is good and right. How could something so exquisite not be?"

Ryan reached for the door and locked it as the floodgates of his heart opened wide. A joy filled his soul that he had never experienced before and, somehow, he knew at that very moment, he would never experience again.

"I... I guess I have known for a while that I loved you too, Shannon. I wasn't certain what to make of it at first, what to do about it. I didn't know if you would feel the same way."

"Foolish man..." she admonished softly. "Hush now - and take what is already yours."

She began to unbutton her blouse but he grabbed her, held her close for a moment afraid that, like some dream, she might vanish if he dared ease his grip. Then he yielded to her irresistible sensuality, to his own irrepressible urgings, and his mouth again met hers. He undid the rest of her buttons, kissed her neck, her breasts, her stomach. His fingers began to probe and explore her soft skin. She moaned with delight and eagerly surrendered herself to him, no hesitation, no guilt, relishing the spasms of pleasure washing over her body as they tumbled onto the bed.

And as the two young hearts reached out, longing to become one, a cool breeze, fresh and clean, poured in through an open window to caress their glistening flesh while the Moon, full and radiant, watched over them with a jealous eye. And through the rest of the night, the man and the woman, two souls, one heart, took delight in pleasing the other.

Chapter Nine
Of English Stone & Iron Men

With a vibrant population of over 13,000 and its excellent deep-water harbor, impressive naval yards and abundant victualing facilities, Plymouth was one of England's major commercial seaports, a crown jewel, and served as headquarters for the Royal Navy's Grand Fleet - the invincible guardian of the empire's home islands. Just west of the city, atop a desolate, windswept headland overlooking the sea, stood a fort-like structure known as Old Mill, so named because of the quaint windmills that had once dotted the heights many ages ago. Unlike England's other great naval prison, Forton Prison in Portsmouth, which had originally been built as a hospital, Old Mill had been specifically designed and built to be a prison. Construction of Old Mill had been completed in 1695 but, with no war and no prisoners, the facility was soon closed and abandoned in the early 1700's. Now, in the spring of 1777 and flush with victories on land and at sea - and with an influx of thousands of fresh American prisoners - the British Admiralty ordered Old Mill restored and reopened for business.

Prisoners destined for Old Mill usually arrived in Plymouth by ship where they were paraded down the city's narrow streets, past its handsome ivory stone buildings with their blue tiled roofs, in chains to the jeers and taunts of its angry inhabitants. Plymouth was a navy town and its people had no sympathy or pity for Colonial rebels, for men who had murdered, kidnapped or wounded their loved ones.

After leaving Plymouth behind, the prisoners continued their trek down a winding, country road and through the picturesque farmlands and orchards of Devon. The walk was pleasant enough until their journey came to an abrupt end at a pair of spiked, wrought-iron gates and an imposing 20-foot high wall of whitewashed stone, frieze-topped with broken glass.

There at the iron gates the prisoners were greeted by snarling dogs and armed guards, mean-spirited brutes, eager to introduce the new men to their new hell. But before entering the prison, the American prisoners were lined-up against the wall, forced to strip, and searched one last time with British redcoats gladly helping themselves to anything of value missed earlier by their Royal Navy brothers. The prisoners then dressed and were prodded at bayonet point through the gates and into a modest courtyard with small buildings for administration, cooking and quarters for the guards. Once past the courtyard the prisoners were led in single file through a second gate, through a second interior wall several feet higher than the outside wall, and into the heart of the facility. Before entering inside, each man noted the 20 to 40 feet of open space between the two perimeter walls and hearts sank. The ground between the double walls was patrolled regularly by two and three man squads with dogs and seemed an impenetrable barrier to the new prisoners. Even if a clever man could somehow find a way to scale over the first wall he would be seen and caught in the open spaces before he ever reached the outer wall. Escape seemed impossible.

Once inside the facility the prisoners faced not one large building as many might have expected but saw a number of two-story buildings, made of whitewashed clapboard, built in rows around a rectangular field measuring 250 by 158 feet. The grassy prison yard was a barren patch of earth except for a single lamppost planted in its center and, off to one corner, stood a very small brick house, which served as the prison hospital.

Prisoners were then segregated by nationality. The Americans were hustled over to the largest of the buildings, over to "Long Prison." Long Prison, so named because of its length, was a windowless, poorly constructed barracks with only a handful of working fireplaces. Perpetually cold and damp inside, Long Prison made for a dark and depressing home.

Old Mill had been designed to hold a maximum of 1,200 men. But the current population, mostly Americans, far exceeded that limit and overcrowding was becoming a serious problem with conditions at Long Prison being the worst.

Even without overcrowding, the environment at Long Prison was harsh. Only a handful Americans had hammocks or cots to sleep on.

Most men had to make do with straw mats infested with bloodsuckers, stingers, biters and tormentors of every kind. And there was precious little water for cleaning or cooking and none for bathing. The few fireplaces that worked were too small to provide any real heat and the Americans, stripped of any warm clothing by the guards, were ill-clad against the bone-chilling dampness of Southern England and sickness and disease was rampant.

While the new men were able to overcome the stench and filth of their new surroundings in time - gnawing hunger is a relentless and unforgiving pain. According to the rules, each prisoner was to receive a minimum of three quarters of a pound of beef per day. But rules rarely applied to the Americans and after the meat had been boiled down, each man's portion was closer to six ounces and served in a tasteless, watery broth. Every prisoner was also supposed to be issued six ounces of bread per day and some cheese but, when there was bread it was stale, sometimes moldy, and the cheese handed out was rancid more often than not. Fresh fruits and vegetables were nearly nonexistent and the beer was watered down. The guards pilfered anything edible.

Prisoners from other nations, mostly Frenchmen and Spaniards, fared much better. These were soldiers, honorable prisoners of war, not rebellious thugs and criminals destined to be hanged.

The "Keeper" of Old Mill, the prison's head administrator, was a man by the name of William Cowdry. Cowdry was universally reviled and despised by the Americans. They called him "the great tyrant" behind his back, along with other, less charitable names. Cowdry was arrogant, indifferent to prisoner hardships and arbitrarily cruel. For reasons known only to himself, Cowdry took perverse pleasure in randomly selecting certain American prisoners from time to time for punishment, men who had committed no infraction. Some men were placed on half rations, some were placed in the stockades and, the truly unlucky ones ,were tossed into the *black hole* where they were forced to lie in filth and cold water for days on end until such time as Cowdry decided, on a whim, no rhyme or reason, to end their misery. Not every man survived the ordeal. No one, not even the guards, understood the logic behind these haphazard, malicious acts.

And Cowdry's interest in inflicting pain went beyond the physical. Breaking a man's body is easy, breaking his spirit is often far more challenging. A number of American prisoners had family and friends in England but Cowdry denied any visitations. Letters between prisoners and family were intercepted and frequently lost and any petitions addressed to Parliament complaining about prison conditions or Cowdry were forbidden. With no end to the war in sight more than one man, unable to cope with his loneliness, unable to overcome the feeling of hopelessness savaging his sense of worth, took his own life.

For the Americans, Old Mill was just about the foulest place on earth.

In the center of the prison yard, next to the lamppost, stood a short, stocky man with short, gray hair, broad shoulders and an unremarkable face - except for its toughness with a fixed expression, like chiseled granite, that said *don't mess with me*. Jeremiah Simmons dropped his ditty bag in the dirt and took in his new surroundings. He was not pleased. Prospects could hardly have been more depressing.

Still, he took in a deep breath and managed a thin smile. He was, he knew, a survivor and he would, he promised himself, make the best of it. He would endure to fight again...

Chapter Ten
"'Tis a Good Business Lads!"

small boat ferried him out to the old lugger riding anchor peacefully in the middle of the harbor. He saw Dowlin standing at the rail, watching patiently, as the boat made its slow turn to pull up alongside the ship.

"Well, sweet *Jesus, Mary n' Joseph!*" Dowlin called down to Ryan with a hearty laugh, then waved the men over. "Look'ee what we have comin' aboard, lads. What the devil are you all dressed up for Luke? Been to either a wake or a weddin' in them handsome clothes, I'd say!"

Ryan removed his French cocked hat, trimmed in gold, and made his way up the rope ladder dressed in a blue, double-breasted coat with silver buttons and a richly embroidered, bright red waistcoat. He had tucked his doeskin breeches into his black riding boots at the knee. He made a dashing sight.

He was particularly fond of the boots Shannon had given to him. He had purchased the rest of his clothing at one of Dublin's upscale clothier shops, after the haberdasher there had assured him the style was the latest in men's fashion.

His men rushed to the rail, whistled and shouted out catcalls to him. Ryan simply smiled back and ignored them all as Dowlin extended his hand to help him aboard.

"Had I known you were goin' to dress for the occasion," Dowlin offered with a grin, "I'd have gone and hired us a proper boatswains' mate to pipe yer grace aboard! *Gawd,* don't you look dandy!"

The crew closed in around Ryan, chuckling at Dowlin's bit of theater. Dowlin then playfully snapped to attention and saluted.

Ryan returned Dowlin's salute with feigned smugness. "Appearances *are* important, Mr. Dowlin," he answered with the tone of an arrogant English lord. "Something a heathen such as yourself will never understand I am altogether certain, coming out of the caves as you did off that desolate rock you call Ireland."

That inspired laughter among the crew and there were easy smiles all around.

"That's not what some of the fair lassies of Rush have been tellin' me for the past several nights..." Dowlin replied with a droll smile and winked at the men.

Kelly leaned close to Dowlin, said softly, "I'll wager it weren't yer fine appearances 'em pretty lassies took a fancy to lieutenant!"

"Aye," beamed Dowlin, adding boastfully, "you do make an excellent point thar, Chris. *Stamina*, now thar is a worthy quality to win over a fair heart. If only the number of lassies a man bedded down was the measure of his wealth instead of the number of coins in his purse. Bless me, I dare say, I'd be as rich as the bloody King of England! Ha! Ha! Ha! No, richer!"

Men howled and stamped their feet. Hearts were light.

"Speakin' of fair lassies," asked Dowlin, "ah now Capt'n, could that fine new set of clothes of yers be for the benefit of a pretty set of ankles? Let me see now," Dowlin paused using his fingers to count, "funerals, weddin's and courtin' young lassies. Well how 'bout that, thar be three reasons to wear such fine clothes as these!"

He reached over and rubbed the lapel of Ryan's coat appreciatively through his fingers, feeling the fine texture of the material.

Ryan grinned back sheepishly. "By God, lads," he said, determined to avoid giving a direct answer, "at least we know Mr. Dowlin here can count up to three!"

Kelly took a step towards Dowlin and, as tall as Dowlin was, Kelly was a head taller. Like everyone else, Dowlin was forced to look up at the big man.

"Ah now thar, sir," Kelly interrupted. "Beg pardon, Mr. Dowlin, but we should let him be now."

Dowlin shook his head, was about to say something to the giant but then thought better of it. Kelly was Ryan's guardian. It had always been so. It would always be so. No need, thought Dowlin, to put Kelly's nose out of joint.

Kelly turned to Ryan with a proud smile. "Luke, we've taken on a few new hands. John, Timmy lad, come on over here. Capt'n Ryan, may

I present to you me brother John and my eldest, my son, Timothy Kelly."

The great bear affectionately wrapped a huge arm around his son's shoulder and hugged him. The boy, tall and lean, with freckled cheeks, blushed and, having a shy nature, looked awkwardly down at his feet. There was no mistaking him for anything but an Irishman.

Ryan nodded. The boy had a sweet, angelic face and Ryan liked him straight off.

"They signed on board a few days ago. John here is a first rate seaman and was a gunner's mate for good ole King Georgie - he knows and has lived by the warrior's code. He even did some sailin' before that for a bit with old Jack the Bachelor too. Timmy here aren't nothin' but a silly boy of course. Like havin' teats on a bull, useless but," Kelly paused to rub his large paw of a hand affectionately over the boy's curly, reddish-blonde hair, "he's a good lad tho' and I figures he'll make a good seaman someday, once we knock all that sod out of his ears."

"Excellent," replied Ryan. He gave John Kelly, who was not as tall as his brother but had the same massive build, a nod and smiled at the younger Kelly. "'Tis a good business lads! We may have use of a gunner's mate before we're through. Good to have you aboard, Mr. John Kelly. And you son, can you read and write?"

"Oh, absolutely, sir," Tim answered enthusiastically, looking up at Ryan for the first time. "I finished all my schoolin' and can read and write better than any of my schoolmates back home."

"Very well, then! You're probably the only one on board who can read and write! But you're hardly finished with your schooling yet I'm afraid. Lots to learn for a young pup with any ambition, I'd say. Sails, lines, spars, weather, navigation, trigonometry... Well, we'll talk about those things later. Good to have you aboard too, Mr. Timothy Kelly. If you learn half of what your papa knows about the sea, you'll make a most excellent seaman indeed. Work is hard on board a ship but the pay is good and we eat pretty well. I trust you'll pull your own weight. Mr. Kelly, I place this child in your care - see to his schooling and teach him the ropes. Make me a first rate sailor out of this boy of yours."

Kelly grinned, a proud smile, touched the brim of his hat and grabbed Tim by the shoulder. "Aye, aye, sir! We'll start straight away.

Come along Tim. Let's see if you remembers anything yer old pap taught you about makin' knots."

As the men began dispersing Ryan turned to Dowlin. "No troubles, Patrick?"

"Nope," Dowlin replied. "Smooth as silk, not a hitch. I had her, ahem, I mean had the *ship* that is, tucked away in a lovely secluded spot just a bit north of here. Nothin' but a bird flyin' overhead could have spied her. Boarded by some revenue agents two days ago when we put in here at Rush. But they had no complaints as the holds was empty and all her papers were in order. Told them we were here hopin' to secure some of the good king's business. Goods went ashore a week ago while you were out frolickin' about. We took care of the paperwork at St. Maurus Chapel and it's waitin' for you in yer cabin when you have a mind to look at it. Monies all been accounted for. Larger sum than I figured on. O'Keeffe did his part. This could be big doin's, Luke. Wish we could haul somethin' back to France and play it on both sides of the water."

"Aye," offered Ryan, "we'll have to think on that. Don't want to ruffle the feathers of our French hosts any tho'.

"You make a fair point thar, Luke. Always thinkin' ahead of the rest of us you are."

"By the way Patrick, we'll be picking up two new hands. A fellow named Edward Macatter and his number two man, Alexander Weldin."

Dowlin paused for a moment considering the names and then recognized the second name. "I remember Weldin now. Had to think on it a bit. A Dubliner as I recall?"

"Aye," answered Ryan. "They're both O'Keeffe men and are temporarily out of a ship. I agreed to take them on with us, as a favor to the old man. Macatter is from County Cork, I'm told, tho' I hear he likes to tell folks he's from America. Can't blame an otherwise honest man for a bit of deceit, eh? He used to go by the name Captain Wilde when he was the master of his own ship. Weldin was his first officer. Don't know the particulars of how he lost his ship. Captured, I suppose. Here's the hard part: to avoid rufflin' any feathers, I intend make Macatter first officer and reduce your rank to second."

Ryan's last words brought Dowlin no joy. He looked at Ryan with disappointment on his face but offered no argument.

Ryan winked and touched his arm. "Pat, this is no reflection on you. None at all. This arrangement is only temporary, only until Macatter gets command of his own ship again. And Macatter's title is little more than a facade. *You* are my *de facto* first officer. If we run into any trouble, I shall always trust and count on you first and on your balanced judgment, good friend, even if I must tell Macatter to step aside. And your share of the profits stays the same in any case!"

Dowlin removed his pipe from his pocket and chewed on the stem, thought things through for a minute. "I suppose I can sit back for a bit and kick up my heels. Let someone else do all the heavy liftin' for a change. These newcomers best know their business tho'. I'll not sit idly by and let some idiot run this ship aground, not after all the hard work we've put into her."

"Agreed..."

Ryan looked around the ship, taking in her condition, and smiled. Dowlin had been busy. *My ship by God!* That thought warmed his heart. Dowlin, always a perfectionist, had every piece of gear properly stowed and every rope and line properly coiled, tied-off or stored. The deck had been sanded down white with holystones, named so because the size of sandstone blocks used to smooth the wood was about the size of a bible. The bulkheads had been given a fresh coat of paint and the handrails freshly varnished. Dowlin had the ship ready for a captain's Sunday inspection. A lesser man with little to do in port would have slacked-off or worse. Not Dowlin. Never.

"Yer orders, Luke?"

"Mr. Dowlin, at your earliest convenience, I'll have the hands weigh anchor. Let's get us under way."

"Aye, Capt'n. Dunkirk?"

"Aye. Dunkirk. We'll make a swing by Bray. Take her in on the windward side and pick up the two new men first. Then on to Dunkirk. I have a mind to fatten our purses even more."

Dowlin smiled broadly and turned to look at the Irish giant. "Mr. Kelly, if you please, call all hands to weigh anchor. We'll be leavin' *Gawd's* lovely country behind us now."

Kelly touched his hat, acknowledging the order, and bellowed out his master's command to the crew like some great bull. The ship's small company sprang to life. Mulvany, Dixon, McCloud, Morgan, Steward, Hoar and young Tim, six stout men and one boy, manned the capstan and strained to turn it.

"Heave thar, lads! Heave! My mother can put more muscle to wood than that! Put yer backs into it. Heave hard, I say!" Kelly called out to his swarthy, sweaty men pushing with all their might.

Then Steward began singing an old English sea shanty:

"old stormy he was a bully old man..."

The others chimed in and answered him in chorus:

"to me way you storm along..."

And then Steward continued singing solo again:

"Old stormy he was a bully old man..."

And the crew replied:

"Fi - I - I, massa, storm along."

With a clank, clank, clank of the capstan, the men slowly raised the anchor. And after the anchor was secured to the cathead, just as he had done a 1,000 times before in the king's navy, Kelly turned to the officer of the watch, saluted and reported that the ship was ready to sail.

Dowlin gave Kelly a nod, the silent order to unfurl the square sails and raise the fore gaff boom. Some men scurried up into the masts while others manned the braces. A lookout climbed up the mainmast to take his post at the masthead and had a bird's eye view of the world. Morgan took the tiller. No one had to be told where to go or what to do. Like the well-matched gears of a precision machine, *Friendship's* crew worked in perfect unison with single-minded purpose.

Ryan watched in admiration, was pleased by what he saw. His men moved with skill and purpose, impressive by even rigorous British naval standards.

Dowlin began singing his own shanty and the men smiled. He rarely sang but when he did, the crew knew they were in for a treat.

"A Yankee from Maine," he said, "taught me this gem:

I once knew this fetching, young lass from Nantucket..."

And as they labored, the men sang back in cadence:

"Heave, heave, heave away!"

"Who kept my bed cozy and warm for a single gold ducat..."

"Heave, heave, heave away!"

"After only one night 'twas love at first sight but then in the mornin' when I showed her me ship the miserable old wench declared with hardly a stare: 'why yer ship, sir, an't nothin' but an old bucket!'"

"Heave, heave, heave away!"

"With a coldhearted glare I reached into her pair, took back my gold ducat and said with unabashed flair: 'well my delectable dove, my portside love, you've insulted me pride; so I will bid you ado as you haven't a clue and you can go fook it!'"

"Heave, heave, heave away!"

"And the moral of this story my hardy, good lads? You might come to know some bewitchin' young lass, p'haps one with talent who can polish yer spar, polish it like glass. But never forget: a ship is yer protectress, yer one and only

true mistress as we ride across the rolling waves and it would hardly be right to suffer any insult, no matter how slight, even when uttered by the fairest of Nantucket..."

"Heave, heave, heave away!"

The men sang and chuckled and saw to their duties with no supervision. Dowlin had seen to the crew's efficiency. He had drilled them regularly in between their liberties on shore. He was determined that ship and crew would rival any of the best-disciplined warships in King George's great navy.

And along the water's edge a small army of old men, with fishing poles in hand, watched the crew of a small, fat vessel weigh anchor and unfurl dirty, maroon sails, patched in places with pieces of square, gray cloth. She wasn't pretty, but the old men on shore could see that her master knew his business well enough as she moved out smartly. They kept to their leisurely fishing and listened to the crew singing. A few knew the tune and could not resist humming along as they watched the old lugger disappear into the gray mist.

Morgan, an Englishman by birth, but raised in Ireland, held *Friendship* steady on a course for Bray, south of Dublin, and saw young Tim standing awkwardly around with nothing to do.

"Tim! Come here boy."

"Sir?"

"Take this here tiller and I'll teach you the finer points of handlin' a ship."

Their 10 to 14 day voyage to France was a simple trek across the ocean Morgan explained as Tim eagerly took the tiller. They would sail to Carnsore Point and then head south until they saw the English Isles of Sicily where they would make a left turn, head due east, and sail around the southern tip of England. After that, it was a straight run to France with the prevailing westerly winds at their backs. Once they were in French waters off the port of Brest they would hug the French coast and head north until they reached their homeport, the *Church of the*

Dunes, Dunkirk. Easy work.

Pacing along the deck and lost in thought, Ryan noticed a slight luff in the sails and turned to check the helm. He saw Tim at the tiller. *Well, time to break the lad in a bit.*

"Ahem. Mr. Kelly. Steady as she goes there!" Ryan demanded with a hint of feigned annoyance. "The wind will catch her and do the work but then you have to hold it. You're spilling wind and wind is precious. Learn to keep a firm grip - but not too firm - don't want to dampen her spirit any. You'll soon learn how to get the most out of her. Pay close mind to Mr. Morgan. There's none better at coaxing speed out of a ship."

"Just like handlin' a woman!" Morgan said, smiling.

"Oh, yes, Luke!" the boy replied enthusiastically and grabbed the tiller with a firmer hand. He corrected their course slightly until the wind filled out the ship's sails again.

Morgan gave him a stern look though, waited patiently and said nothing. Time to see if the boy had any wits.

Tim looked back at Morgan, confused, but then soon realized his error and corrected himself. "I mean aye, sir," he said in a high-pitched voice. "Aye, aye, Capt'n! Beg pardon, sir."

Morgan nodded approvingly.

Ryan looked away to hide a smile. It had not been all that long ago when he had been the awkward boy standing on a pitching deck looking foolish. And then his thoughts began to wander. The image of Shannon's lovely face smiling at him warmed his heart. He caught himself thinking about her more and more and the sea, for years his home, suddenly seemed an empty place.

As the war between Great Britain and the Colonies dragged on, Good Fortune continued smiling on the Irishmen. Life was good for all. Not one shipment was lost or confiscated and profits exceeded all expectations. War makes for good business and Torris, Sartine and

O'Keeffe were all happy men. To each went a share of the profits after every run and though Sartine had never asked for any money, Ryan always saw to it that he got his share. Ryan thought of it as more than just a show of appreciation, it was an investment in good will to be redeemed at some future time.

The Irishmen smuggled mostly French brandy and Dutch tea into Ireland, but they also brought in exotic goods like silks and spices from the Orient. These were the goods that fetched the highest prices. And then there were the firearms; more than a few in Ireland wanted their countrymen to join the Americans in the rebellion, to end English tyranny in Ireland, and began arming themselves.

O'Keeffe's men, Macatter and Weldin, were roundly accepted after they proved themselves to be good fellows and capable sailors. Macatter, a barrel-chested, serious little man in his mid-forties looked like a ship's captain with his round face and neatly trimmed beard. He liked to tell everyone that he was from Boston. But the men knew better. He spoke with an accent that said County Cork. In good looks, humor and his knowledge about the sea, Alexander Weldin was nearly a match for Dowlin, strength for strength. He was tall and lean and liked to wear his dirty-blond hair pulled back in a ponytail. Ryan found him easygoing and highly competent.

The whole crew worked well together, not an unexpected situation when money flows freely. But Ryan had noticed early on that there was something different about this crew. Bickering was rare, each man helped the other gladly and no one ever picked a fight. The men had what the French call *esprit de corps*. Dowlin and Kelly noticed too, but neither one could quite put his finger on why this was so. Even while in port, when men from other ships went their separate ways, and with plenty of time for trouble, Ryan's men spent most of their time together and any insult to one was an insult to all.

Ryan stood alone at the bow and buttoned up his coat against an early morning chill. He could smell the faint aroma of fresh bread baking in the ship's oven. His thoughts turned to Shannon, warm, pleasurable thoughts. He smiled. Despite the week they had just stolen together, he was already longing to see her again, to feel her skin, her breath, against his own. But his ship was sailing along the French coast and Shannon was an ocean away.

Seagulls, swooping down through the thin mist, a flock strong, came to greet the mariners just as the Tower of Dunkirk slowly came into view. Ryan watched the gray and white gulls circle overhead, squawking at each, vying to see which champion among them would hazard the first dive. And then, feeling restless, he made his way back towards the stern and found the giant Kelly standing at the helm. With his feet planted firmly on deck, his powerful hands wrapped tightly around the tiller, Kelly looked like some royal sentry, faithful and immovable. Or, no, thought Ryan. Not like just any sentry. Kelly could have been Heimdall with his great horn Gjall at his side guarding the wondrous rainbow bridge, the Bifrost, to Asgard. Yes, Ryan smiled to himself, like Heimdall. Ten ordinary men could not have dislodged Kelly from his post by force. But with one simple nod from Ryan. the giant yielded and surrendered the tiller. Ryan carefully maneuvered the ship into Dunkirk Harbor, past a maze of vessels standing peacefully, and found a quiet spot of water to drop anchor.

Life was good and he was pleased. Their first run had made them easy money, and a lot of it. But in the back of his mind, tugging at him always, he couldn't help but wonder: *how long, how long can it last?*

Chapter Eleven
"Our Unfortunate Countrymen"

s he removed his heavy, green coat and fur hat, Franklin reflected on his first 100 days in Paris. He laid his coat and hat, along with his walking stick, over an empty chair in the corner of his tiny study while his grandson, Temple William Franklin, pulled back the long window drapes to let in the sun's warm shafts of light. Temple, an eager, handsome young man of nearly 20, had accompanied Franklin to France on board the *Reprisal* back in December and over the last few months had become an indispensable asset to the old man.

Franklin sat down at his *escritoire* and began sifting through a pile of letters and reports from America, hoping to find some kernel of good news. But in the spring of 1777, he and his seditious co-conspirators could find precious little to cheer about. The revolution was one last setback away from total collapse. 1776, a year that had started off with so much hope and promise, had been disastrous for the rebels.

While news from the Colonies could be sporadic and confusing at times, and take a month or longer to reach Paris, Franklin knew that General George Washington, the commander-in-chief of the Continental Army, was in a desperate situation, struggling just to hold his tiny, rag-tag forces together. Washington's men, though tough-hearted and willing to fight, had suffered one crushing blow after another during the summer and fall of 1776. And then his battle-weary troops had to endure enormous hardships throughout an unusually harsh winter. Half-starved boys with little military training marched and counter-marched across snow-covered hills in threadbare clothing, sometimes barefoot, and had been in no condition to form ranks for any kind of major pitched battle. And while Washington's sensational crossing over the icy Delaware and surprise raid against Trenton on Christmas Day was an impressive tactical victory against sleeping Hessian mercenaries, and a terrific boost to morale, the battle had little strategic impact.

The British commander-in-chief, General Sir William Howe, merely shrugged Trenton off as an inconvenience and continued to fine tune his grand design to end the war once good weather returned in the summer. Howe's plan, intercepted by General Washington's spies, was brutally simple and a good one on paper. After the spring rains ended, Howe intended to march his army out of New York City, heading north along the Hudson Valley, to link up with a second British army marching south down from Quebec under the command of General John Burgoyne. Howe's plan was to cut the rebellious colonies in two. He also had in mind to seize the rebel capital of Philadelphia later in the year which, by happenstance, was where Franklin kept his home.

Washington forwarded his intelligence bonanza on to Congress but grimly informed its members that he didn't have enough men or arms to stop Howe. Despair soon settled over Philadelphia.

News about the war at sea was little better. The life blood of the Colonies was commerce and in commerce the Colonies were as much an island as England. The American economy was heavily dependent on maritime trade with Continental Europe and the Caribbean Islands. The British high command understood this, had committed large numbers of ships and men early on in the conflict to cut the Colonies off from the sea. And the strategy was working. The British navy had successfully swept America's fledgling navy from the oceans and had seized or blockaded all her major ports. Britain had a lethal chokehold on the Colonies.

As American regulars and militia on land and sea lost battle after battle, retreating on all fronts, the lines of prisoners heading into English jails grew longer. This was when Franklin and his two co-commissioners to the Court of Versailles, Arthur Lee, an aristocrat from Virginia, and Silas Deane, a lawyer and former Congressman from Connecticut, first started receiving disturbing reports about the mistreatment of captured Americans.

Franklin sent word of this back to America of course. But General Washington had his hands full with more urgent matters and Congress showed little interest so, by default, the task of trying to protect the welfare of American prisoners fell on Franklin's shoulders.

Franklin's French secretary, an unassuming, dependable young man named Lair De Lamotte, stuck his head in the doorway to Franklin's study. "*Bonjour*, Doctor Franklin, I trust your walk has refreshed you," Lamotte offered with a friendly smile and handed Temple a thick bundle of letters. "Today's correspondence, *Excellency*."

Franklin looked up at Lamotte and returned his smile. He had liked the pleasant, young Frenchman from the first, even though Lamotte's translations were not always perfect.

"*Merci*, Lair," Franklin answered and grabbed the bundle of mail from Temple by the string. He fumbled around inside his vest pocket to retrieve his wire rimmed bifocals, put them on and then cut the string with a pocketknife. He quickly scanned the various envelopes, began separating them methodically into different stacks according to each letter's order of urgency, when one letter in particular caught his eye. He opened it immediately. It was a letter from his principle adversary in Paris, Lord David Murray Mansfield Stormont, Great Britain's Ambassador to the Royal French Court.

"Well, well, well, what do we have here?" Franklin asked rhetorically as he sliced through the Ambassador's wax seal. "Bless me, perhaps the third time is a charm, eh Temple?"

But Franklin angrily tossed the Stormont's letter aside after reading it. He had never had much patience for British arrogance. He turned and stared out the window, considered what his next move might be.

When he had first learned just how harshly "our poor unfortunate countrymen" were being treated by the British, the good-natured doctor lost his composure and wasted no time launching a publicity campaign to educate the British public about the barbaric mistreatment of American prisoners in hopes of raising public outcry. He also petitioned members of Parliament, vigorously protesting the conditions at the British prisoner-of-war camps, including letters to David Hartley. Hartley, statesman, inventor and passionate slave abolitionist, was the son of the famous philosopher David Hartley and still a close friend of Franklin despite the war.

Franklin informed Hartley that American prisoners were "*... fed scantily on bad provisions, without warm lodging, Clothes or Fire; and not* *suffered to write or receive visits from their friends, or even from the humane and charitable among their enemies. I can assure you, from my certain knowledge, that your People, Prisoners in America, have been treated with great kindness.*" Franklin closed his letter with this personal appeal: "*Your King will not reward you for taking this trouble, but God will, I shall not mention the good will of America; you have what is better, the applause of your own conscience.*"

In a separate letter to the English newspapers, Franklin, knowing his letter would be published, had accused Britain of numerous "*barbarities*" including bribing slaves in America's southern states to murder their masters, inflaming Indians to massacre American families, debauching seamen and mistreating prisoners. "*You are*," Franklin declared, "*no longer the magnanimous and enlightened Nation we once esteemed...*"

In another letter to Parliament, he asked for permission to send American representatives into British jails to inspect conditions and offered to provide 600 pounds sterling to buy food and clothing for the prisoners - but only if Parliament would first give assurances that the relief money would actually be distributed to American prisoners. And as a gesture of good will, Franklin ordered, without condition, the immediate release of 200 English seamen being held in French jails along with this dire warning to Parliament: Americans would not tolerate British atrocities much longer and would retaliate against helpless British prisoners if the British government failed to act. Franklin knew that some in Congress were already publicly demanding an eye-for-an-eye.

But all of Franklin's pleas and threats had come to naught. And then he had an idea, an inspiration really - prisoner of war exchanges. And that is why he had written, with the consent of his two fellow Commissioners, to Stormont, to discuss his proposal. His letter to Stormont was short and to the point:

"*My Lord*
Captain Wickes, of the Reprisal frigate, belonging to the United States Of America, has now in his hands near 100 British seamen, prisoners. He desires to know whether an

exchange may be made with him for any equal number of American seamen, now prisoners in England? We take the liberty of proposing this matter to your lordship and of requesting your opinion, if there is no impropriety in your giving it, whether such an exchange will probably be agreed by your Court. If your people cannot soon be exchanged here, they will be sent to America.

We have the honour to be, with great Respect, My Lord, Your Lordship's most obedient, and most humble Servants."

Franklin had sent this same letter to Stormont twice before and Stormont had ignored Franklin on both occasions.

Franklin reached for Stormont's reply and reread it, out loud for Temple and Lair's benefit. "Well boys, Stormont has returned my letter without opening it, scribbling across the envelope: '*the King's Ambassador receives no applications from Rebels, unless they come to implore His Majesty's Mercy.*'"

He shook his head in disgust. *Stormont was an idiot.* He then reread his own letter to Stormont, to see whether he had inadvertently given some offense. But he saw no insult.

"Stormont is a pompous ass and witless too. Lord only knows how a man can negotiate through life burdened by two such enormous handicaps."

"He is indeed a pompous ass, Grandfather!" Temple readily agreed, smiling at his grandfather's use of coarse language.

After the war, Franklin would learn that Stormont had actually opened and read his letter, made a copy of it, and sent it on to Lord Weymouth in London together with the following brief note:

"My Lord
I send your Lordship a Copy of a very Extraordinary and Insolent Letter, that has just been left at my house by a Person who called himself an English Gentlemen; I thought it by no means proper to appear to have received and kept such

a Letter, and, therefore, My Lord, instantly sent it back, by a Savoyard, seemingly unopened, under cover to Mr. Carmichael, who, I discovered to be the person that had brought the letter. I added the following short, unsigned noted: 'The King's Ambassador receives no letters from Rebels, unless they come to implore His Majesty's Mercy.'"

Franklin stood away from his chair and walked into the drawing room and thought back on a dinner party where he had been asked about Lord Stormont's exaggerated reports of British victories in America, to which he had replied: "*la verite et le stormont sont deuxl*" or *truth is one thing, Stormont another.* Parisians, always eager to embrace the latest droll remark, instantly adopted the phrase and converted the name Stormont to a verb, *stormonter,* meaning to distort or lie, *mentir.* Stormont was hardly amused when he first learned about Franklin's bit of wit at his own expense.

Franklin stood next to the fireplace and warmed his hands, lost in thought for a time. Then he called for Temple and Lair, told them to bring him pen and paper.

"Temple, be a good fellow and take down this reply to Lord Stormont:

'*In answer to a letter which concerns some of the most material interests of humanity, and of the two nations, Great Britain and the United States of America, now at war, we received the enclosed indecent paper, as coming from your Lordship, which we return for your Lordship's more mature consideration.*'"

Temple quickly scribbled down his grandfather's words, rewrote the letter in a neater hand and gave it to his grandfather to review, along with a candle for the sealing wax. Franklin signed it, peppered sand over the wet ink, trying not to smudge the words, and then turned back to the fire and rubbed his hands against the flames. The warmth felt good against his skin.

"Lair, I want copies of my original letter, together with Stormont's reply and this note to be provided to the London newspapers. You know which ones. That ought to stir up the bee hive on the other side of the Channel."

"I shall attend to it your Excellency straight away."

"Good. My dear, young friends, I've often found English lords to be boorish and condescending with little actual substance to justify their arrogance. With rare exception, I have found these folk to be an insufferable breed of men and my opinion has not much changed with Lords North, Sandwich or Stormont. If the King refuses to entertain our applications concerning basic human decency, then we must wait for an American victory or two to help mellow His Majesty's mercy. Yes. That is precisely what is required, an American victory, a decisive American victory, a miracle of sorts. So easy to say, but so elusive to obtain. Who, I wonder, and how, to accomplish the task?"

Chapter Twelve
A French Gift

Throughout the summer of 1777 and well into the fall, Good Fortune openly, shamelessly, doted on the Irishmen. The Irishmen had completed a dozen successful runs with ease. But then, in late October, the weather turned foul and Ryan decided to put the old lugger in dry dock for a much-needed overhaul and gave the crew extended liberty. Back at his hotel room in Dunkirk, which he rented throughout the year to keep his few possessions, Ryan found an invitation from his friend, and benefactor, Sartine waiting for him. He caught the next coach to Paris.

After Sartine's triumphant, though quiet, return to France with the *Toulon*, the man he called uncle, the Count Antoine Raymond Jean Gaulbert Gabriel de Sartine and France's Minister of Marine, had the promising young man promoted to captain and reassigned to Paris to serve as his aide-de-camp. Parisians excelled all others in the time-honored practice of nepotism. And good to his word, the younger Sartine told no one the truth about how he and his men had retaken *Toulon*.

Ryan met Sartine at his family's large estate north of Paris and the two men spent a lazy morning riding and hunting. Despite winter's approach, the day was warm and pleasant. After a time riding quietly through woods, covered with a thick carpet of fallen leaves, and with no game to shoot at, Sartine pulled on the reins of his horse and moved up alongside Ryan.

"You are looking fit!" Ryan offered jovially. Sartine looked lean, tan and well-rested. If his new post in Paris included any stress, the young Frenchman showed no signs of it.

"As are you, *mon ami!*"

"Aye. Life at sea and the good salt air keeps a man fit."

Sartine smiled, nudged his horse around to cut across a shallow stream. Ryan followed him across the stream and up a steep embankment. Once over the rise, the two riders entered a green meadow with a carriage parked in the middle of the field. Next to the carriage was a table, draped in white linen, with two attendants standing by in formal dress. The servants had already meticulously set out sterling silver bowls, china plates and crystal glasses.

"A delightful spot, no?" asked Sartine. "I am famished. Let us take our lunch in the manner of French gentlemen!"

Ryan laughed and took a moment to admire the table in the wilderness. "I'm flattered David and quite unaccustomed to such elegance. This is remarkable. Do you always take your noon meal so?"

Sartine grinned and shook his head no.

"Well, you live like a king!"

"No, no, Luke. I live in the officer's barracks. I come to this place only one or two times a year to hunt. These lands belong to my uncle."

The two men tethered their horses to the carriage and sat down to a sumptuous feast.

"Life in Paris must agree with you, David," Ryan said.

Sartine helped himself to a baguette and some cheese and smiled broadly. "Indeed! What is not to like? Parisian women are the most beautiful in all the world. And the most passionate! Delectable, little doves each one. I have spent time in London, Rome, Moscow and Vienna. Paris has it all, my friend - food, art, fashion, commerce, science, politics and opportunity! She is the world's crown jewel. She has no equal! At sea, I was a minor officer of no importance. A nobody, a bore. Here, in the capital of the world, I am important! People seek my favor. Life is fun again! And I owe much of my good fortune to you, Luke."

The servant offered a platter of roasted meats and boiled vegetables to Ryan. He helped himself to a full plate.

"I am glad for you, David. But I cannot take much credit for your success. The count is your uncle after all. I fancy you would be where you are today without me. Had our paths never crossed, it might have taken a wee bit longer for your star to rise, that's all. In any event, we have helped each other."

Sartine laughed. "Luke, you can be so self-deprecating at times. *Too Irish*! Not the French way let me tell you... No, no, not at all. A man should not be afraid to boast when he has earned the right to do so. But that we have helped each other, yes, I do agree." Sartine paused to take a slice of cheese and a handful of grapes and washed it all down with a generous swallow of wine. "Every month Torris faithfully forwards the financial statements pertaining to your enterprise to me, tallies up my share and deposits monies into my account. I see you are making a handsome *profite* from your business, no?"

"Indeed," Ryan replied happily, unable to conceal his pride.

"You have been most generous to me, Luke. And I am grateful. Most men are swine. Few trouble themselves to repay their debts these days and no one, no one but you, would repay a debt and then add to it a bonus, a gratuity, without any legal requirement to do so. Unheard of! You are an exceptional individual and generous. With time, God only knows what monumental achievements await you. Forgive me; I talk like a philosopher. Voltaire perhaps? Ha! Then again, perhaps not. My point is simply this: generosity should be met in kind with generosity."

Ryan wiped his mouth with a napkin. "We have been generous to each other. I expect nothing from you but your continued friendship."

Sartine laughed again and raised his glass. "As you say, *mon Capitaine*! We must drink a toast to generosity, to friendship!"

"To good friends, to generous friends!" Ryan replied.

"Indeed! Now, you say *Friendship* is in dry dock?"

"Aye, routine repairs. Two or three weeks, then we'll set out again."

"Set out again? But winter is nearly on us! Do you not fear winter's rage out on the open sea, *mon ami*?"

"Fear winter's rage?" Ryan asked laughing. He could feel the wine's mellow magic at work.

"My dear Captain David de Sartine of His Most Christian Majesty's Royal Navy - I fear that all this good Parisian living has made you soft! That is my only concern on this fine day! Your countrymen, I have always thought, love the land too much. That's why you do not make particularly good seamen. There's money to be had my friend, even at this time of year! A little discomfort, a little risk perhaps, but it is worth it for the profits we can make. Indeed, I'll wager prices go up nicely again this winter. And that's money in both our purses."

Sartine refilled their glasses with a new bottle of wine and then smoothed down the corners of his mustache, using his thumb and index finger - always a sign he had something on his mind. "Very well, Luke. As you wish. Excellent in fact. But I fear you are the master of *Friendship* no more. France has need of your vessel and she has been confiscated."

"What?" Ryan asked, alarmed.

"Luke, Luke. Where is your trust? I assure you - you will be well compensated. No need to sulk. Are we not friends? Are we not *good* friends?"

"Aye."

"Then you accept the trade, wonderful!"

"Trade?"

Sartine started to chuckle, pleased that he had startled Ryan. "But of course! The glory of France is not built on theft. Oh, did I fail to mention the new ship to you? Ah, sorry. I picked her out myself. With ships and women, you can always trust my extraordinary judgment! I have an uncommon eye for *qualité*! Her previous owner displeased the king for one silly reason or another a while back and the navy soon thereafter confiscated the vessel. His loss, your gain."

"But David, I am pleased with the ship I have," Ryan insisted. "And we are spending a handsome sum refitting her even as we speak."

Ryan's thoughts turned to Dowlin and all his hard work, but even as he was offering his mild protest, he could see his words falling on deaf ears. There would be no debate. Sartine's decision was final. Dowlin would be difficult to deal with once he learned the news.

"Rubbish," replied Sartine as he leaned over to poke Ryan playfully in the ribs. He leaned back in his chair, propped his feet up on the table and popped several more grapes into his mouth. "Trust me, Luke. You are getting the better end of the bargain by far. You'll be thanking me within the week! She is a very fine cutter and when I first saw her, I knew she had to be yours. You will see... Enough talk of business for now. I find it tedious. Let us finish this most excellent wine and after it is gone, we shall return to the house and rest. Later this evening you shall accompany me to a dinner engagement that requires my presence. There are rumors that the Queen herself may attend! In Paris, there is always a party worth considering. And because of my uncle, I am invited to all the better social events. Tonight's extravaganza will be fun, I promise. And by tomorrow, you can be in Calais where all the necessary arrangements have been made to transfer title of this new ship over to you. Well I know how you ambitious fellows are always in a hurry!"

Ryan, still unsure, could only sigh, said no more and drank his wine.

Ryan was the only passenger on a coach that was always full. Some of Sartine's handiwork.

As the coach, with its team of four horses, bounced along a stretch of badly rutted road, his head began to pound. He had drunk far too much the night before and already the driver had stopped twice for him so he could empty a sour stomach. Sartine was never shy about reaching out for the good things in life. Ryan managed a smile despite the pain in his head as his thoughts turned to the Queen. Sartine had introduced them. It was all a blur now, but he remembered chatting with her for longer than a brief moment. She was lovely and laughed easily.

The party had been well-attended by beautiful women. Too bad, he thought, Dowlin hadn't been with him. *Now there was a man who could give Sartine a run for his money.* Yes, he would bring Dowlin with him to Paris next time. Sartine and Dowlin in Paris together would make a dangerous pair. He smiled at that mischievous thought - until it brought on a fresh wave of pain. He rubbed his temples and slouched low in his seat, hoping to die.

On the afternoon of the second day, Ryan was jolted from a long and peaceful nap when the driver brought the coach to an abrupt stop and informed Ryan that they had reached their destination. Ryan grabbed his ditty bag and stepped out onto a street, lined with attractive three-story townhouses. Something tickled his nose and he looked up to see the season's first flurries. Winter had arrived early and uninvited.

The driver pointed to the house in front of him, cracked his whip and drove off without a word, without even asking for money.

After knocking several times a servant finally answered the door, let him in and showed him to a large, lavishly furnished office where an older man, sitting behind a great desk piled high with papers, absently caressed a shiny, bald head. The older man waved Ryan in.

"Ah! *Monsieur* Ryan, I see you found your way," he said in broken English and rose to offer his hand. "Permit me to introduce myself, Henri Dupery, *a votre service, Monsieur.* I am an *advocate* here in Calais and have been instructed to prepare certain legal papers for you. Uneventful trip I trust?"

"Indeed."

"A drink first perhaps?"

"No. No thank you, *Monsieur.* I fear that I had a bit too much in Paris and I am still suffering from the ill-effects of my indiscretions."

"*Oui*, I understand, *Monsieur* Ryan. That is Paris, a most decadent place! She can seduce the most pious man to overindulge! You shall find Calais far more *agreable*. Well, I do not wish to detain you, shall we complete the necessary formalities?"

Dupery rummaged through the mess on his desk looking for something. He was a fidgety, little man and Ryan wondered if all attorneys were like Dupery. Nervous men made him nervous.

"Let me see, ah yes. The papers are here in this folder. All is in order. You will sign triplicate copies of each document, here, here and here if you please."

Ryan could see that the man was in a hurry and that suited him just fine. "Is there anything here I should read before signing?"

"I think not. I certainly can answer any questions you may have but, this transaction is very simple, very straightforward and routine. Title to one cutter, described in more detail in the attached copy of her registry, is being transferred from the French government to you. The bill of sale has already been executed by Captain de Sartine showing that payment has been received in full and I shall hold this document in escrow until you sign title of one vessel, registered as *Friendship*, over to the French government. All transfer taxes, the costs of registration and harbor fees have been duly paid. Once you accept title of course, the French government is relieved of any further obligation to you and you bear the full liability for any costs and expenses associated with the cutter from today on. This, I trust, meets with your approval?"

"It meets my approval," Ryan said and began scratching out his name were Dupery had indicated without reading the documents.

"Excellent, *mon Capitaine. Merci.* This folder now contains your set of documents. You shall take your papers, along with these instructions, and deliver them to the Calais harbormaster. He is expecting you. You shall find everything is in order. My driver and carriage are at your disposal. My driver knows where to go. My congratulations on your purchase. It has been a delight meeting you and, may I add, *bon voyage!*"

"The pleasure is mine. Your fee, sir?"

Dupery waved him off. "No, no. That has been already been seen to. Good day to you, *Monsieur...*"

A squat, burly man, nearly dwarfish in size and gnawing on a fat blood-sausage, set his lunch aside and wiped his greasy fingers on his shirt before gruffly snatching Dupery's folder out of Ryan's hands. He rolled up his sleeves, exposing a pair of thick, hairy forearms covered with tattoos of sea serpents, and quickly reviewed each piece of paper. Satisfied, the harbormaster grunted, put his seal next to Ryan's signature and then walked Ryan outside his office and pointed to a ship lazily riding anchor in the middle of the bay. Ryan turned and looked at the harbormaster quizzically, uncertain whether he was looking at the right vessel.

The harbormaster nodded. "*Oui*, she is magnificent is she not?"

Ryan whistled softly and agreed.

"My man there on the wharf, huddled over the fire basket, he will row you out for a quick inspection if you like."

Ryan eagerly accepted the harbormaster's offer and was soon being ferried over to his new ship by a sad looking boatman, toothless and bent with age.

She was elegance on water. Long and sleek, she had the lines of a thoroughbred. Her two enormous masts, debarked and hewn from giant Norwegian spruces, and raked in the French style, rose majestically into the sky like two great towers. Lashed to her foremast were three massive spars to hang the square sails and a long fore-gaff for a generous foresail. Extending well over her stern rail from the mainmast was a truly impressive driver boom for the mainsail and fitted to her nose was a sturdy bowsprit, made from two spars lashed together in the middle for additional strength, to carry the jibs.

She was rigged to carry an impressive amount of canvas to catch the wind and, with her curved deck and a razor sharp bow to slice through the waves, she looked fast, very fast. This was a ship built for speed. But there was nothing flimsy about her. Even from a distance, Ryan could see that her construction appeared uncommonly solid.

According to the papers Dupery had given him, she had been built in the shipyards at Boulogne and completed only a few months earlier. At a length between perpendiculars of just under 100 feet and a burden of 140 tons and with a beam of 20 feet, she was not a huge ship, but was large enough - and she was armed. Ryan took in the four medium-sized cannons lashed to her deck, keeping quiet vigil like sentries on duty. Not a lot of armament perhaps but it was enough to fight off a British revenue cutter or small pirate ship and, with a war going on, finding any serious weaponry for a civilian ship had become nearly impossible.

Sartine had been true to his word. The cutter was magnificent.

As the toothless boatman brought his vessel gently up alongside the cutter, Ryan reached for the Jacob's ladder hanging over the side and tied off the boat. Seeing the boatman shivering against a fresh wind, Ryan handed the man a gold crown to warm his spirits, an extravagant tip, and promised to be quick.

She was like nothing he had ever seen before. Her design was something new and bold, something revolutionary. Her builders had been exceptionally gifted craftsman - and ambitious. No ornate scrolls or flourishes or gold gild adorned her stern. No grand figurehead had been mounted to her sharp prow. But her construction was sturdy and true. She possessed a distinct ruggedness. Clearly, she was not meant for some silly nobleman's pleasuring and comfort. No. The architect who had designed this ship had a single purpose in mind: *speed.*

Only the highest quality oak, teak and mahogany had been used in her construction. Her decks had been reinforced and her bulwarks double-planked as if she had originally been intended for military service.

Ryan took a few minutes to stroll up and down her curved deck, admiring his new ship. He had never laid eyes on a finer vessel. And then he noticed a bit of sawdust around the gun ports. The cuts into the bulwarks were fresh. And then he saw the blue tampions stopped into the gun muzzles, each one emblazoned with a brass *fleur de lys*. He chuckled to himself. Sartine had pilfered the guns from one of the king's armories!

He drew a deep breath and smiled broadly. It was a good day. But he was anxious too. More than most, an Irishman grows wary when Good Fortune wraps her golden countenance around him for any length of time. The wily Irishman takes what is offered to him gladly, true, but, always, he bides his time, bracing himself for the day he knows will surely come when Good Fortune - fickled always - deserts his side for no good earthly reason.

Ryan looked out over the sea and bowed his head. Well he remembered the tale of King Agamemnon, greatest of the Argive Kings, who neglected, there on the shores of Troy, to offer splendid sacrifices to the Earth Shaker. Agamemnon's long-haired Achaeans had erected a massive parapet in a desperate attempt to protect their well-benched ships from man-killing Hector's fire. But in their haste, they had forgotten the sacred rites owed to the gods. They slew no sleek black bull with ruthless bronze. They poured no wine, sprinkled no barley over the land to honor the gods. And so, after Troy fell, Poseidon, in a fit of rage against the thoughtless Greeks, swept their massive fortifications away with one sweep of his huge hand. And so now the Irish mariner, sage, thoughtful, bowed his head and offered up his prayers, with heartfelt thanks, to the Father who rules us all.

Chapter Thirteen
A Lover's Gift at Christmas

yan set aside his dislike of horses, purchased a good mount in Calais and rode hard on to Dunkirk, arriving in the old seaport just before midnight. He found Dowlin at the crew's favorite watering hole, sitting between two attractive women, both giggling at something Dowlin had just said.

Dowlin saw Ryan walking towards him, panting and sweating from the long ride. He started laughing.

"Luke! What the devil are you runnin' from? You seen a ghost or is some Parisian tart chasin' yer sorry bones down lookin' for more?"

"Ladies, please, could you excuse us for a bit?" Ryan asked in between gulps air to catch his breath.

Neither woman budged so Ryan repeated his request in French. Still they didn't move and simply continued staring dumbly up at him.

Dowlin let out a deep sigh. He knew Ryan's moods. Ryan meant business. He rose from his chair, waving his arms through the air and growling like some fearsome bear. The women started giggling again and scattered.

"Yer here to ruin me fun is that it?"

"Patrick, a word if you please. I have news, tremendous news!"

"Oh, that so?" asked Dowlin and rubbed his chin. "Let me guess. King George is goin' to pardon the lot of us and make you and me admirals? No? Hm. Wait now, you found some buried gold somewhere out in the country left behind by the Romans? Better - you won some Arab's harem in a game of chance? No. No. Of course not... Well now bless me, let me think now. Bugger me if I know. But whatever it is, couldn't it have waited 'til mornin', Capt'n? I had those fine French lassies in the palm of my hands. And I accept news, good or bad, much better after a pleasurable night's lovin'."

Ryan sat down and took a swig of ale from Dowlin's mug, then turned Irish on Dowlin. "Thar'll be plenty of time for romancin' later, you big oaf. Stow away your randy thoughts for a bit. Now, about our good fortune! We have a new ship!"

"We have a what?" Dowlin asked playfully. "Ha! Ha! You sayin' our own little piglet sank in the dry docks? Never heard of that happin' before! By *Gawd*, this is tremendous news! Wait 'til all 'em French science men try to figure out this peculiarity!"

Ryan ignored Dowlin's sarcasm, his words started tumbling out. "Are you drunk, Pat? Did you not hear me, lad? We have a new ship! We've traded up you might say. She's the loveliest craft you've ever laid eyes on my friend."

Dowlin arched his eyebrows and laughed. "Loveliest craft you say? Why Luke, what you just chased away, 'em two buxom lassies are the loveliest craft I've laid eyes on this dreary night. And they was both eager to *sail...*"

"*Auck!* Be serious for a moment will ya? I'm tellin' you lady fortune has smiled down on us once again."

Dowlin could see that Ryan was serious. "All right, all right, Luke. Settle yerself down and keep yer powder dry. I'm listenin'. Never knew you to lose yer head before over a bit of fun." He paused and took a long drink. "Well, now that I have nothin' better to do tonight than listen to yer banter, so go on and tell me what this is all about."

Dowlin listened patiently as Ryan recounted his time with Sartine in Paris, his trip to Calais, and then described the new ship.

"You met the Queen?" Dowlin asked. "My, my, haven't we climbed up a rung or two? A large cutter you say? That Sartine's a corker to be sure. This is all fine and well I suppose. But we've got our own ship laid up in the docks being refitted. The dock men finished gravin' her bottom just this mornin'. She's nearly ready. All that work will cost us a pretty penny. And now you want to take on a second ship? Doesn't sound much like good business to me but then what does a man like me know about business, hey?"

"Pat, this cutter is straight out of the shipyards - she's newly built! She's nearly one hundred feet long and she'll carry twice *Friendship's* load or more at, I'll wager, three times the speed! We'll make more money and we'll make it faster! God, when you see her Patrick, well, I'll let you be your own judge. She's by far the finest ship I've ever seen. And that's the truth of it lad... and she's ours!"

"Ha! She's yers you mean to say."

"No Pat, I said what I meant clear enough. She's *ours.*"

"How do you figure?"

"Patrick, that night Sartine took us to the lugger, tho' I may not have said so then, you became a half owner of *Friendship* - my gift with Sartine's blessing - and now you're a half owner of this new cutter. We are partners, fifty-fifty."

"I don't have the money..."

"Fool. You don't need to invest any money. The French are selling her to us for a trifle, in exchange for the lugger, and I paid the lugger off for us some time ago. We are clear of any debt and don't need to put up one *sou* for the cutter. We are free men and masters of our own fate, Pat. How many Irishmen have ever been able to say that?"

Ryan sat back in his chair with a wide grin after he had finished. But Dowlin could only manage a frown and stared down at his mug. His lack of enthusiasm confused Ryan. He studied the big Irishman for a moment, then reached out and grabbed Dowlin's shoulder.

"Very, well. Out with it. You're not happy with this? Don't you see? This is our chance at something big! It's the beginning of something truly good. Someday, God willing, we'll own a whole fleet of smugglers. I swear it!"

Dowlin looked up at Ryan with a hard look in his eyes - his playful mood was all but gone. "Luke. Durin' all our days together, I've never known you to do anythin' foolish before. Never. But, I'll tell you straight to yer face - yer a damn fool now. *Jesus, Mary 'n Joseph,* yer good senses have gone and deserted you!"

"What the devil are you talking about? What's wrong with a larger, faster ship?"

"Not the ship, Luke. To give me a stake in any of this, to be makin' me a half owner, that's what I'm talkin' about. Yer a thinker and a fine one at that. Yer clever ways have improved yer lot in life and you've been greathearted enough to drag me along with you. 'Cause of you always kickin' me in the arse, I did some fine work on the king's ships and got myself promoted all the way up to acting lieutenant. Patrick James Dowlin, an officer in the king's royal navy! Imagine that now... An orphan with no money, no schoolin', no future, doin' all that. Without you, I'd be some lowly seaman now livin' a poor seaman's life aboard some stinkin' harbor barge or p'haps I'd be dead or, most likely, I'd be rottin' away in some prison somewheres like me dad and me granddad before him. I like sailin' and I like whorin' and drinkin' and gamblin' and not necessarily in that order. No bloody ownin' anything for me. Pay me a fair wage, that's all I ask. Better, make me a master of one of 'em grand fleet ships you have plans for. That would suit me just fine. I'd make a first rate ship's capt'n. The truth of it is Luke - had I known I was a part owner of *Friendship*, I'd of lost my stake in her gamblin' in some crooked game and you would be sittin' right thar where you are now holdin' a knife at my throat."

Ryan listened quietly, lost in thought, unsure of what to say.

Dowlin could see Ryan's frustration. "Luke. Listen to me now. By far, by far, yer the best man I've ever known. We're as good as brothers. Best damn sailor I ever sailed with too. Keep on dreamin' up 'em grandiose schemes of yers. While you've been dreamin' and savin' yer money, I've been spendin' mine. Spendin' it on the things that give me pleasure. And what of it, I says? I got no regrets. By *Gawd*, I'm a happy man, Luke! I owe you for that. But I'm a simple man too. A man's got to know his limits. Life is good right now. And I don't want to spoil it none. I don't want no more responsibility than what's been apportioned to me already."

Ryan thought hard on Dowlin's words, knew he had no choice but to yield to Dowlin's wishes. Dowlin was not too drunk and was never, ever, a fool. There was truth, even wisdom, in his words. And Ryan understood too that, in his own way, Dowlin was now repaying him for all his past kindnesses by this one simple, unselfish act of friendship. He was protecting Ryan and himself from his own weaknesses.

Ryan had helped him rise above some of those weaknesses, but not all. He had, with patience and kindness, helped Dowlin find his strengths and build on them. And Dowlin was grateful for that and proud of the man he had become.

Ryan looked hard into Dowlin's eyes. He drained his mug with one long swallow, wiped his mouth with the back of his hand, and nodded.

"So be it then. Captain Dowlin it shall be. But when you grow up some day, when you learn some maturity, then we'll talk about these matters again."

That brought a smile to Dowlin's lips. "Excellent!" he bellowed feeling relieved, feeling as if some crisis had just passed him by. "Now where the devil is this new ship of yers?"

"Calais. We'll sail *Friendship* down to Calais as soon as she's out of the docks and make the trade."

"Aye, Capt'n. That lugger was so damned slow. I'm amazed we haven't been nabbed by the English by now. Be good to have a faster ship."

"Quite so. Oh, did I mention, Pat, she's got firepower - four heavy guns."

Dowlin's eyes lit up. *Cannon.* "And what, may I ask, is the name of this fine ship we now serve?"

Ryan considered it a flaw in his character. He was superstitious. During his hard ride from Calais to Dunkirk, he had thought about a new name and had toyed with *Lady Luck*, *Pride of Ireland*, *Celtic Angel* and the *Adventurous* but none seemed right.

"Why tempt fate?" he answered cheerfully. "The name *Friendship* has served us well enough. We'll keep it."

"*Friendship* it is then, Luke! Let's have a drink, tip our glasses to old Dionysus and then make a toast to *Friendship*. Might as well have more than one come to think of it, celebrate things proper! Looks like my two fine French prizes have moved on to warmer waters, over to 'em Frogs sittin' in the corner. Well, if I can't get my spar dipped tonight, I'll get drunk instead - a small taste of paradise either way..."

The *Shadowmen*, as the crew liked to call themselves now, took their old lugger and made the easy sail down to Calais in ballast. As they slipped into the harbor, the Irishmen lined themselves up against the rail to get a better look at their new ship.

"Oh she's grand, Luke!" Dowlin exclaimed enthusiastically, genuinely impressed.

Kelly whistled. "She's a vision to be sure! Just as lovely as you described her, Capt'n."

"She's definitely bigger," Dowlin added. "We'll be needin' more lads to sail her, Luke."

Even Macatter cracked a smile, a rare event for the solemn first officer. "She's a beauty all right Luke and she looks fast, mighty fast indeed. Never saw anything quite like her. At first glance she almost looks too fragile for the sea."

"Fine she is indeed, lads!" Ryan exclaimed proudly. "And Ed, well, you'll see when we get aboard her. She's solid through and through. Waters calm enough. Let's ease up alongside, lash the ships together and make things easy on ourselves."

After the crew transferred all their gear, equipment and supplies, cleaned the old lugger out, Ryan gave the order to weigh anchor and sail. He was eager to put the cutter through her paces, to see what she could do. But Dowlin stopped him. When it came to ships, he was never rash. Not his way. Even covered in a dusting of snow Dowlin could see that the cutter had been allowed to sit idle in the harbor too long without any general maintenance.

"Luke," he said with a twinkle in his eye, "not yet. She needs a bit of lovin' first and I'm just the man to give it to her."

Ryan nodded and smiled. He knew Dowlin was right to curb his zeal.

The proud-hearted Dowlin could not resist replacing a frayed line or two and inspecting every nook and cranny. For three days, the Irishmen pampered the neglected cutter, spruced her up. Top to bottom she was scrubbed clean and given fresh coats of paint and varnish, her decks were sanded down white. And then, under some spell or inspiration, Dowlin decided to paint the exterior of *his* new ship black.

Hull, masts and spars, everything was painted black except for the thick coat of pale yellow tallow, made from one part tallow, one part brimstone and three parts resin, applied below the waterline to keep away wood hungry sea worms. After the Irishmen had set down their brushes, the new ship was black as night.

Following Dowlin's example, Kelly had all the ship's white canvas sails taken down and dyed in splotches and streaks of dark and medium grays. It was a messy task but the camouflage scheme would make the cutter even more difficult to see on the ocean's dark waves - and make a more fearsome sight. Kelly then constructed four false crates, one to fit over each gun, to hide them away from view. In addition to the ship's four-pounders, the Irishmen found muskets, pistols, swords and a dozen swivels stored below, still packed in grease and resting in their original shipping crates from the foundry. If any trouble found them, the swivels could quickly be carried topside and mounted on the handrails for additional firepower. The cutter had teeth.

Ryan gave Dowlin and Kelly a free hand. Never wise to interfere with a master artisan as he labored feverishly over some consuming inspiration, over his next masterpiece.

When all their work was finished, the Irishmen stood back to admire their handiwork and no man had ever set foot on a finer vessel. The whole crew shared the same sense that, somehow, the ship had found *them*. For what purpose, no man could say. But each man felt the hand of destiny resting on his shoulder and marveled at it.

Morgan, returning from Calais, pulled at the oars of the lugger's small launch, loaded down with covered baskets, and came up alongside the cutter. Ryan had sent Morgan into town earlier to purchase the best food and liquor that money could buy. And under a canopy of bright stars, the Irishmen relaxed and enjoyed their feast and after every man had slaked any desire for food and drink, Knight grabbed his fiddle, entertained them all with wistful, Irish melodies.

And in the morning, when the sun rose above the rail, Ryan called all hands on deck. It was Sunday, the day for prayer and for captains' inspections. Ryan decided to honor his men for all their hard work by conducting a proper inspection of their ship. This was something new for Macatter and Weldin as neither man had ever served in the navy but the rest of the crew knew the drill, knew it well, and fell into neat rank and file formation. The men understood that their captain was paying them all a compliment, showing them his respect, and, for a time, the Irishmen were all back in the British navy again, back on board a disciplined man-o-war. Ryan couldn't have been more proud.

Grace on water, that's what she was. The sleek black cutter glided through the calm waters of the English Channel with little effort. And there was nothing flimsy about her either - she moved with power and balance even with her holds crammed full with Dutch tea, Chinese silk, French brandy, sugar from the French West Indies and - German 1740 Potsdam muskets and French flintlock pistols. These were the things that fetched the best profits and only the best smugglers could get their hands on them. To the delight of the Irishmen, their new speedster was as fast as she looked, faster even. Under full sail with the right breeze, she skimmed across the water like some angel, riding the wind with wings outstretched.

Most ships' captains are cautious souls who rarely, if ever, push their ships hard. These men fear losing a spar or a rudder or dread running aground because of some faulty chart or mistake in navigation. Their ships do no more than plod along. Other captains are known as *hard drivers*. These are men of grit and daring, men who take pride in extracting every knot of speed out of their vessels. And when the sea and wind converge in perfect balance, like two lovers, intertwined and tumbling in passion's grip, hard drivers are in their glory because they can *crack on*. These men crowd every spar with sail and set their ships free to fly across the waves.

But fearlessness can only carry a man so far. Among the hard drivers the best are never careless with their daring and they know how and when to temper their prideful ways. They must possess exceptional navigational skills too, know how to pick their way - day or night -

around islands, rocks, sandbanks and through the unpredictable currents of an ill-charted sea. They must be indifferent to hardship, blessed with a keen intuitive sense and their courage can never waiver.

Yes, the master shipwrights who had cut the timber from good live oak, bending the planks to match their will with skilled, loving hands, had built themselves a thoroughbred. But, like any racehorse bred for speed, *Friendship* needed just the right kind of driver to realize her true potential. She needed a master of steel nerve balanced by a sober respect for a temperamental sea who would never slink away from mounting trouble. And yet, she needed a master with a sensitive touch too who understood her subtle ways, who could patiently coax the best out of her.

Ryan was such a man. He knew it and his Irishmen knew it and, together, they were determined to learn how to charm the most out of their extraordinary ship in fair weather or foul. And there was something else, something intangible, no one understood it but every man sensed it. It was if they had all served together before, long ago in a different life, in a different age. This was, they understood, a gathering of the faithful for a voyage that would take them all far beyond Ireland.

Standing near the helm, Ryan decided it was time to shake her down, to see what she could do, and so he ordered every inch of canvas spread out across the cutter's long, black spars. Then he made his way forward to the bow, removed his hat to let the wind caress his hair and took pleasure in feeling the sea spray against his skin. His heart pounded with excitement.

Only Shannon made him feel more alive than the thrill of the sea. *How good it would be to have her here by my side to experience this*, he thought, savoring one of those rare, sublime moments when the spirit manages, if only for a breath, to peek beyond the horizon of the material world. And then a tingle shot down his spine, jolting him back into the foggy realm of mortal men. His thoughts turned to more familiar matters. He longed to see her, to caress her face with his fingers, to hold her close in his arms, to feel her skin next to his. She had cast a spell over him. Standing at the prow, he smiled broadly and decided that perhaps he and his *Shadowmen* could all afford to spend a little additional time in Ireland at the end of this run...

Under pleasant skies the days came and went with a lazy indifference as the cutter continued sailing west, tacking against the prevailing westerly winds. Other ships her size would have bucked and struggled against such unfavorable blows, making slow headway. But *Friendship* paid the contrary breezes no heed and scudded across the sea's blue waves, eager to please her new master.

And armed with speed, Ryan ordered his men to cut straight across St. George's Channel. He and his officers all agreed: there was no need to hug the coast to hide from British patrols as they used to do with their old lugger. Ryan and his men were confident they could out-sail any trouble and so the brazen *Shadowmen* pointed their ship straight for Rush, straight across the open sea. After reaching the shores of Ireland several days later, and without incident, they quietly unloaded their treasure and went into town to recruit new men. Ryan's reputation for skill and audacity and for the good treatment of his crew had spread up and down Ireland's east coast and finding new men to crew his new ship proved an easy task.

But before the Irishmen could set off again for France - for one last run before Christmas - North Wind, always eager to cause some mischief on unsuspecting mortals, blew her cold breath across the water and whipped up a gale fierce enough to lord it over the sea. And so Ryan, a hard driver maybe, but no fool, paid his men their wages - handing out fat bonuses too - and gave liberty to all until the New Year.

He borrowed a horse and hurried on to Kenure some 20 miles away through a thick, gentle snow turning everything it touched white. And when he reached the wrought iron gate to O'Keeffe's property, the old guard waved him through after recognizing him. As he approached the house, he saw the light of one lone candle in the upstairs window, the window that faced the sea, Shannon's bedroom window, and he smiled. The candle, he knew, had been lit for him.

He let himself inside, dusted the snow off his shoulders, and found

Shannon sitting by the fire in the front room scribbling notes in a book. She let the book slip from her fingers when she saw him and ran into his outstretched arms.

"*Luke*! *Luke*! Oh you've come home to me safe and sound!" she cried out joyfully. She wrapped her arms around him, pressed her long, lithe body into his and the two hungry lovers showered each other with fast, tender kisses.

Then Ryan pushed her gently away to look at her. She was even lovelier than he had remembered.

"Did you doubt me woman?" he asked, slipping into his Irish brogue.

"Doubt you? No, never, my dear heart. Doubt the weather - yes. But never you..."

His heart began to pound. He still had difficulty accepting that this beautiful woman was his.

"You think a bit of snow could keep me from you? Not a chance of that my lovely lass. You look like a gift from God above Miss Shannon Grace O'Keeffe. How I have missed you and I love you so..."

He pulled her against him, held her close.

She kissed him on the cheek and brushed the snow off his hair. Beyond his physical touch, a warmth, comforting and alluring, embraced her whole body. He completed her and she hoped, with all her heart, that she completed him.

"And I love you, Luke. More and more each day."

"Speakin' of gifts," he said and reached down to the floor to pick up a plain white box tied with string, "this is for you, Merry Christmas."

She giggled, took the box and blushed. "Christmas isn't for two days yet, Luke."

"Beggin' your pardon, ma'am! Far be it from me to argue with a lady. But Christmas is today for me... Please, open it; let's have a look inside. If it's not to your liking I'll need time to go into town to find you something more suitable."

She undid the string and removed the lid. Her eyes sparkled.

"Oh, Luke! 'Tis the loveliest dress I've ever seen! And the color, beautiful, it matches the sea. You are a rascal!"

"You sure you like it?" Ryan asked doubtfully.

She took the silk dress with its intricate embroidery from the box, held it up against herself to admire its beauty and twirled around in a circle. "I love it! Do you?"

"Aye."

She ran her fingers over the dress's delicate stitching. "The workmanship is so fine, Luke. Truly, it is lovely! A treasure. Where did you ever find such an exquisite dress?"

Ryan smiled at her warmly, was relieved he had chosen well. "Comes from Paris. I'm pleased you like it. I was assured the style and color is all the rage among the high society in Paris this season. Oh, I brought this back with me too, a new magazine about the latest in ladies' fashion: *Souvenir a l'Anglaise et Recueil de Coiffures*. If you see anything that strikes your fancy, I will do my best to purchase the article when I am back in France. Well, never bought a lady's dress before. Almost didn't take the risk. Picking your way through treacherous shoals in a driving gale at night is a tad easier to my way of thinking. You're certain you like it?"

"Oh yes! It is gorgeous! I'll wear it for *you* proudly on Christmas Day. I'll be the envy of all the women in Dublin. I have a gift for you as well my young man. Not quite as extravagant as yours, but, well, I hope you like it."

She kissed him lightly on the cheek, disappeared into a back room and soon returned with what looked like a big ball of yarn. She stretched the ivory colored material out and held it up for him. It was a fine, heavy jumper, cable-knitted with intricate patterns.

"With some help a woman from Aran, I made this for you. It is made with **báinín** yarn and they say the oils in the wool help keep water from soaking through the material. Took me several months to finish it. I thought it would help keep you warm and dry at sea."

Ryan smiled, removed his coat and tried the thick Irish wool on. He was delighted by the gift. "'Tis lovely and I'll wear it proudly ma'am and think of you when I do."

"I am glad and I have one more gift," she said and took his hand. She slipped a ring, made of gold and shaped like two hands holding a heart in its center, over his small finger. "'Tis called a Claddah ring. They say a poor fisherman designed this for his lover while he was a lowly slave. My heart is in your hands..."

Ryan grabbed her around the waist, pulled her into him again and the lovers traded long, soft kisses. His hands moved down to her hips, pressed them against his own and she responded cooing, rubbing against him, taking pleasure in her own power to excite him.

"You are such a pirate!" she giggled.

"Aye - and I've come to plunder your hidden treasures..."

"*Reeeally?* Ohhh, my!"

"What," a cranky voice cried out from upstairs, "is all the commotion goin' on down there?"

Shannon looked up at the ceiling. "It's Luke, Papa," she called up to her father. "He's come home."

"Well, just don't stand down there dawdlin'. Come on up here young Luke and let's have a look at you lad!"

Shannon locked her arm in his and led Ryan towards the front stair case. "He's not well, Luke. Pretty much bedridden now. I'm overseeing as much of his business interests as I am able. He asks about you often. I do believe you've become his favorite." As she led him up the stairs, she slipped her hand down his trousers and said in a sultry voice, "you certainly have become my favorite..."

"You mean there are others?" he asked playfully.

"Hm, there could be," she offered, smiling coyly. "A girl can get frightfully lonely when her man is at sea for so long. But, with gifts like yours, well, I think you need not worry - too much."

"Such a tease. But I am curious, which gifts, pray-tell, in particular give you the most pleasure?"

She answered him by pressing her lips against his, tasted him, letting him know just how much she missed him. They both giggled as they turned the corner into O'Keeffe's room.

The once robust man lay weak and helpless in his bed. Doctors had come and gone administering their potions and their treatments to him. But no cure for his ailing body could be found and each doctor in turn had tried to prepare Shannon for the worst, giving the old man only a month or two. But six months had passed since his last examination and O'Keeffe took a wicked pleasure in confounding them all.

"Yer a sight for sore eyes, lad!" O'Keeffe said warmly, struggling to raise an arm up to extend his hand.

"Thank'ee kindly, sir," Ryan replied, taking O'Keeffe's hand. "Good to see you. Sorry you're feeling poorly."

"I feel grand! I'm dyin' is all. There's a difference. My body's failin' me but the mind is as sharp as it ever was and there is no pain, thank the Lord for that. Another good run? Macatter and Weldin aren't gettin' in yer way any I trust?"

"Naw, they're good lads, the both of them," Ryan replied honestly. "Glad to have them. And aye, on this last run we brought over twice the cargo as before. Not a bad piece of work, hey?"

O'Keeffe managed a weak smile. "Aye, indeed Luke, not a bad piece of work. I received yer letter about this new ship a few days ago. She sounds like a dandy. Sit down lad and tell me all about it. Tell me the whole tale now, start to finish. And don't be skippin' any details... That's not how we Irish like our stories told!"

Ryan looked over at Shannon and smiled as he pulled up a chair next to the bed. Shannon, with adoration for him sparkling in her eyes, returned his smile and, when her father looked away briefly, she blew him an alluring kiss.

"Aye, sir," Ryan began as Shannon excused herself. "I'm not one prone to exaggeration, as you know well, but this ship - I'll wager all I own - is the fastest ship in the whole Atlantic! She's cutter rigged and close to a hundred feet in length. I've never seen another design quite like her. Her bow is sharp, her hull is lean and her masts are stepped well forward but raked to carry an impressive amount of canvas. These different aspects in her design all combine to give her great speed and good balance. And she's armed, only four-pounders and swivels but..." he paused to wink at the old man, "enough to manage any small trouble..."

O'Keeffe smiled approvingly. "Go on with ya, lad. Don't stop, yer doin' a fine job of it."

"Well, sir, most her crew are stout Irishmen and many have seen service on one British warship or another. Thirty-six souls all told now. There's an English fellow, a Scot or two and one American on board as well. Good, reliable lads all. Last haul should fetch us a pretty penny. Mostly liquor, silk, and some crates of muskets of course."

A keen sense of pride for the young mariner filled the old man's heart. "Luke, you remind me so much of me own boy. I had hoped to see him grow up one day to become the man that you are now."

"Don't think on that now, sir," Ryan replied with a soft voice and patted O'Keeffe gently on the shoulder.

"Any trouble with Torris?"

"Why no, sir. Should we expect any?"

"Always expect it, lad. Trouble will always find you, especially when you are raking in money. 'Tis only a matter of when. You know, there's a fair amount of talk about you goin' around."

"Talk, what talk?" Ryan asked anxiously, genuinely surprised.

A slight smile touched O'Keeffe's lips. Bedridden and out of touch with much of the outside world, it gave the old man pleasure to know some piece of news or gossip that others didn't know yet.

"Don't be alarmed lad, no one knows *you*. There's talk about some darin' young captain of a phantom ship that's as slippery as a water snake. Capt'n of the *Shadowmen* is the name given to this young scrapper by some."

"Fairytales for children, Mr. O'Keeffe. Too much talk tho' and I'll speak to the lads on it. Rather say too little and look silly than say too much and prove my stupidity for all the world to see. Can't be too careful."

"Well said lad and well I know," answered O'Keeffe with a sly grin. "But you say you have the fastest ship on the high seas, that's yer claim? Bold talk there I must say, young Luke - even for an Irishman!"

O'Keeffe laughed at his own words until he started coughing. He reached for a bottle of medicine sitting on the nightstand with a shaky hand and winced at the brown liquid's bitter taste when he took a spoonful.

Ryan patted him lightly on the shoulder again. "Easy there now, sir. When you're well enough and regain your strength, I'll take you out so you can get a good look at her. You'll see, I haven't exaggerated nary a word to you."

"Ah," replied O'Keeffe, "I don't doubt you there, Luke. Just givin' you a hard time. That's about all I can do these days. Give folks a hard time. Poor Shannon takes the brunt of my ornery ways. She's a wonderful lass. Don't you think? I don't know where I'd be now without her."

"Aye, she is a wonder indeed," Ryan answered.

O'Keeffe threw Ryan a suspicious stare. "Aye, true enough. Now see here lad. I don't know who the two of you think yer foolin'. Certainly not me. I see the look in yer eyes. I see the look in her eyes. The disappearin' for hours on end out in the fields together every time yer in town and not a soul knows where either of you are. The giggling in the hallways followed by long bouts of quiet... Ha! I'm ailing, Capt'n Luke Ryan, but I'm neither blind nor deaf son. Be off with you now, let an old man sleep. If you can handle that Shannon of mine as well as you can handle that precious ship of yers, well, yer a better man than me and I say God bless the both of you!"

Ryan felt his cheeks blush. There was no sense in denying the old man's words. He nodded as O'Keeffe paused to catch his breath.

"I'll give you fair warnin' though," O'Keeffe resumed with a smile. "As an honest business partner, I owe you that much. I'll wager you'll find that lass of mine a good bit faster than that ship of yers - and a wee bit more difficult to handle."

"I will take your words to heart."

O'Keeffe winked and let out a long sigh. "Be off with you now! Far be it from me to interfere with two young hearts toyin' with love. Risky business in that. More dangerous than smugglin', I'd say. Well, now you've done it; you've worn me out. We'll talk more later."

As Ryan stood, the old man reached out and grabbed Ryan's wrist. "Oh, and Luke, just so you know, I'm proud to call you partner..."

He found her in the front room curled up in a chair next to the fireplace waiting patiently for him. The room was dark except for the orange glow from the embers of a dying fire. He tossed in a fresh log into the fireplace and walked to the window, then pulled the curtain back to look outside. The snow was coming down furiously now in big, thick flakes. The glass panes rattled against a lively wind. Then he went to her.

She stirred and looked up at him with a smile that said: *I love you.* Her eyes sparkled in the flickering light and then she took his hand.

"Thank you, Luke."

"For what?"

"For spending time with a poor, old man. It pains me to see him waste away like this. Not so long ago he was strong, like a bull. He stood tall and folks listened when he spoke. So full of life he was, even after the loss of mother and then John. Their deaths tried to grind him down but his strength saw him through those dark times. Now he is almost spent, helpless. That is the source of his greatest pain. God forbid I live so long."

Ryan kissed her softly on the forehead and sat down on the floor next to her feet. "Hush," he whispered to her. "No more of such talk. Your father knows about us, about our feelings for one another."

She stroked the waves of his long, black hair. "Not much ever escaped that man; no doubt he does know about us." She giggled. "We've been rather obvious."

For a time the two young lovers sat together in silence, watching the flames slowly devour the wood. And when the last log had been reduced to smoldering ash, she took his hand and led him quietly upstairs, to the room with the window that faces the sea.

For Christmas Eve, Shannon decided to feature her new silk dress from Paris along with a modest, but elegant, pearl necklace and matching earrings that had belonged to her mother. Her father had made a gift of them to her that morning.

Bubbling with pride, Ryan watched his lovely lass, with the long, blond braids, gracefully descend the staircase. In all his life, he had never seen a more stunning woman. Not even the glowing and sashed Parisian ladies could compare to Shannon.

"Truly, you look like royalty tonight, Shannon. You take my very breath away."

A soft smile touched her lips and she curtseyed. "And you my good fellow, how fine you look in your formal, new coat! What a handsome figure of a man you are."

"You are my heart's treasure, Shannon. A delight to the eye and mind. You stir my spirit in ways I never thought possible."

She longed to seize him, to feel his flesh pressed against her own, but resisted the urge. "There is this quiet, this understated dignity about you my sweet, gentle man. Why anyone in London's high society would take you for a gallant English lord or a prince."

"Yes, well, tonight my dear lady I'm nothing more than a boring Frenchman of no particular merit here on business should anyone ask. *Parlez-voux français, Mademoiselle?*"

"No!" she replied giggling. "Beyond a modest few phrases, I speak little French."

Ryan smiled mischievously at her, placed her hands inside his own and spoke to her in French again. "Ah, pity *mademoiselle*, then you will not understand when I say: you are like an angel, most excellent. You have become the light that inspires me, my North Star to guide me. With each passing day you are the reason for my being. Your kindness, your strength, your passion for life that I will never fully grasp - your extraordinary gifts overwhelm me. In my eyes, you have no equal in all the world exquisite lady. Truly, I love you more than life. I pray, I pray that I am worthy. I shall love you with all that I am until death overtakes me. I swear it..."

"Tell me you rascal," she threatened him mockingly, "tell me what you just said - or I shall assume that you have insulted me and demand satisfaction!"

"No need for that good daughter of mine!" O'Keeffe bellowed from the top of the stairs dressed only in his nightshirt and cap, startling the young couple. "If he doesn't, I'll translate the young poet's French for you later if you like my darlin' girl. He has a gift for sweet words, I'll give this brigand that much at least. Well, well. Dear Lord, what a lovely pair you both make. The riff-raff who calls itself the high and mighty in pretentious, old Dublin doesn't deserve the likes of either of you!"

Shannon threw her father a stern look. "Papa! Get yourself back to bed this instant!"

"Ah, shush darlin'. 'Tis wrong for a daughter to scold her loving father so. I just wanted to have a look at you. Yer mother, God rest her soul, would be so proud of you this grand night. Why she is, I'm sure, smilin' down on you with those lovely green eyes of hers this very moment. I can feel it. And you, Luke, yer a fine lookin' gentleman if you don't mind me sayin' so. You both make quite a sight. Luke, Flanagan is getting my good carriage ready for you. You young folks be on yer way now and have a splendid time."

Shannon lifted her dress above her ankles and raced up the stairs to kiss her father on the cheek. "Merry Christmas, Papa."

O'Keeffe embraced his daughter and didn't fail to notice the warm, live tears pooling in her eyes. "Are you happy, Shannon?"

"More than I can describe, Papa. More than I ever thought possible."

O'Keeffe squeezed her tightly, kissed her forehead. "Off with you now! Give an old man some peace and quiet in his own home!"

The night was calm and peaceful. Large snowflakes drifted lazily down from the heavens, transforming the world, if only for the briefest of moments, into something pure and good once again.

O'Keeffe's good carriage took the young couple to Dublin Castle where the high and mighty of that city gathers each year to greet the new Christmas. The lovers walked arm-in-arm through the Grecian style portico of Bedford Clock Tower, a redbrick structure with rings of stately windows and topped with a green onion dome, and entered a ballroom filled with people. They danced a little, Ryan not really knowing how to, and laughed a lot. Shannon reveled in the gaiety of the evening and when the well-bred men of Dublin, both old and young, asked her for a turn on the dance floor, Ryan grudgingly gave his consent with a smile.

Envious eyes watched the handsome couple throughout the evening. O'Keeffe's daughter was known by many but her dapper French escort was a mystery and the gossip mills wasted no time churning out their flimsy fabric of speculation and rumor. As midnight approached people said their goodbyes and made their way home or towards the ringing church bells to attend midnight mass.

"Would *Monsieur* accompany me to church?" Shannon asked.

"Oh? Well, ahem. I'm not much of a churchgoer, Shannon. Not sure I even believe in a God. Sorry if this offends you."

She stroked his cheek with the back of her hand. "Never, never apologize for who you are Luke Ryan, certainly not to me. I love you because of who you are - not because of who I want you to be or who I think you should be."

Her words pleased him, he smiled. "Your words have the ring of wisdom. Well, if God in His wisdom will permit a heathen such as myself into His house on this holy night with you on my arm, then so be it! Aye, I'd be honored to escort you to church if that is your pleasure my dear lady."

And so the couple offered their farewells and left Dublin Castle for one of Ireland's most sacred treasures, St. Patrick's Cathedral. Built some 600 years earlier on an island between two branches of the River Puddle where, according to legend, St. Patrick baptized converts from paganism to Christianity. Years later England's Cromwell found the cathedral most useful to stable for his horses while on campaign.

The mariner and the lady found a pew and knelt side-by-side. Both offered up the same prayer to the Father who rules us all, silently giving thanks for the love that was theirs.

For the next few days, the young lovers spent their precious time riding, talking, laughing, flirting and satisfying the cravings of the flesh. They took long walks through snow-covered fields, neither one caring much about the cold, and at night enjoyed reading to one another by the fire with a bottle or two of wine. And then, on the first day of the New Year and wearing his fine, wool jumper, Ryan kissed his *bonny lass* farewell and headed out. She watched him from the porch, a shawl wrapped around her shoulders, as he mounted his horse and started down the road that would take him to the sea.

"I'll see you home soon with the good Lord's blessing, Luke!" she called after him. She did her best to smile, to hide her tears.

The mariner turned in his saddle, blew her a kiss goodbye and disappeared in a heavy snow.

On the first day of 1778, Ryan found his officers waiting for him at the *Royal Oak* in the heart of Rush, a tavern once favored by the infamous Jack the Bachelor and his men. Now his *Shadowmen* claimed the establishment for themselves. Ryan ordered drinks all around. The five mariners toasted the New Year, drained their glasses and then spread out across the town to gather the rest of the crew.

With calm seas and a fair wind to fill their ship's canvas, the long-haired Irishmen, eager for adventure, launched their sleek, black cutter out on the ebbing tide. And once in deep water, they pointed ship's nose southeast, towards France.

Through the winter months the war between Britain and the Colonies raged on and the cost for smuggled goods soared. And while a good number of merchant ships stayed safely in port waiting for spring, the Irishman continued their runs between France and Ireland and morale remained high despite the often dismal conditions at sea. Profits rolled in and there was plenty for all to share.

In Kenure, Shannon assumed more and more of her father's responsibilities as the months wore on and his health did not improve. And when Ryan could manage it, he would steal a few days to visit her and enjoyed traveling with her from town to town as she handled her father's business, including his interests in Ireland's prolific smuggling trade. She hired shore parties and wagons, awarded contracts to distributors, negotiated prices, took care to see that everyone was paid their proper share - including the authorities - and maintained her father's books and records. Ryan loved to watch her work. She was as shrewd as the old man himself and she was *disciplined*. These were heady days for the two entrepreneurs.

And when Spring, gentle and fair, blessed the land with her warm breath, scented with ambrosia, the world changed yet again. Even modern man has not forgotten - not yet - that Spring is the season of life and of renewal. It is Spring's soft hand that stirs the young sapling from winter's deep sleep and once awakened, the sapling's roots stretch down into the good, rich earth to find strength and nourishment. Leaves unfold and flowers bloom. Spring stirs the hearts of men and women in the same way, filling both with new hope and new desire, causing one to reach out for the other. Love's embrace. Often the magic is fleeting, the joy does not last, but, sometimes, sometimes, love's work is eternal. And as Spring tended to her work across the land, the mariner and the lady, hardly immune from Spring's magic, felt the bonds between them grow stronger.

Pacing up and down the length of deck, Ryan found himself dwelling on such matters more and more each day like some silly schoolboy. He had thought he was immune from such foolishness. And so he had been, until Shannon had stepped into his life.

"Great *Gawd!*" thundered Dowlin, storming down the deck towards Ryan. "I swear I'm goin' to skin alive whoever's got the watch!"

It was a pleasant, pretty day with a hint of summer in the air. The Irishmen were close to shore, just south of Churchtown and Carnsore Point, sailing near two small, secluded islands, the Great and Little Saltees, where the Irishmen intended to rendezvous with some of O'Keeffe's men to off-load another cargo. They had sailed from Dunkirk without difficulty, making good time across the Channel, and hearts were light.

Standing at the tiller with Kelly and Morgan at his side, Ryan started laughing at Dowlin's antics. "Why so ornery on such a pretty day, Pat? Weren't you just at the head? What happened? A barracuda jump up and bite you on the rump while answering nature's call?"

"Aye, I was at the head," Dowlin answered gruffly and grabbed a spyglass from Kelly's belt. He extended the telescope and handed it to Ryan. "Your mood won't be so jocular my friend when you see this."

Dowlin pointed towards the larger of the two islands, a spec of land barely more than a large rock covered with grass and clusters of brush.

Ryan followed the length of Dowlin's arm with the glass. "Ah, *Christ...*" he murmured and handed the glass over to Kelly.

"Oh, ho, look'ee there," Kelly said. "You can just make out the masts peaking over the cliff thar and I can see men climbing up the shrouds to drop sails - can they be anything but?"

"Nope," answered Dowlin. "Two revenue cutters lying in wait."

"Sail ho!" the lookout cried down from the masthead. "Two points off your port bow."

"Yer a bit tardy, you great blockhead!" Dowlin angrily shouted up to the man.

Kelly took a second look through the glass before handing it back to Ryan. "Yep. They're makin' ready to sail alrighty, Luke. They chose a damn fine place to hide too."

Ryan took another look. "Aye, so they did. And the commander must be one brazen son of a gun too - the waters around the Saltees can be treacherous. Well, lads, it appears we're about to find out just how fast this ship truly is. Chris, best call all hands on deck, unfurl the canvas - all of it."

"Aye, sir!" Kelly answered smartly and rang the ship's bell. "All hands on deck! Mr. Morgan, stand ready to bring her hard about."

"Aye, sir!" replied Morgan, tightening his grip on the tiller. "Ready to come hard about!"

Kelly turned his attention to the deck, began bellowing out more orders. Men scrambled.

Dowlin reached into his pocket, grabbed his pipe and put it to his lips. "Good thing those bushes and trees are still mostly bare 'cause otherwise I never woulda seen the masts through the foliage."

Ryan patted Dowlin on the back. "I don't know how you saw them at all without a glass."

"I've always suspected," interjected Kelly with a wink, "that Pat did his best work while sittin' on the shitter."

The three men exchanged hardy chuckles. Even the usually staid Morgan stamped his feet and shook with laughter.

"Let's hope," Ryan finally said, "that we can all still find something to laugh about by suppertime. 'Tis only noon on a bright, sunny day. Lots of daylight left. Calm seas too. No place for a ship our size to hide. Wind's been a touch fluky so far to boot."

"You bettin' on the English then, Luke?" asked Dowlin with a mischievous grin.

"Seems to me the odds favor them. Either way, it is goin' to be a long day."

"Aye," Dowlin soberly agreed. "And here they come; they're roundin' the island and heading straight for us. No question about it now! Most probably they had lookouts on the island and they musta known we was comin', Luke. Nothin' except birds come to visit these rocks, so someone went to great pains to set this lovely, little trap just for us."

"My thoughts exactly, Pat. Someone talked."

"You don't think it could have been any of our lads?"

"No. Leastwise not intentionally. Just the same, we best have a chat with the men later and lay down the law about loose lips. I'll speak of it to Mr. O'Keeffe too - should I get the chance."

With two British revenue cutters hot on their stern, the Irishmen drove their racehorse hard and even took the extreme measure of dumping some of their cargo over the side to lighten their load. The British ships were fast, very fast - but not fast enough - and with each passing hour the Irishmen put more and more distance between themselves and their pursuers. And as the sun began to settle on the waves, British gunners opened fire with their bow chasers in a desperate bid to disable the smuggler before she finally slipped away. But the shots fell far short, by several hundred yards, sending up harmless geysers of white spray into the air. And when the night finally wrapped itself around the Irishmen, covering their retreat into the sea's vast realm, British guns fell silent.

Friendship had been baptized by fire. She had proven herself worthy.

Chapter Fourteen
Unhappy Times at Old Mill

elirious and bathed in sweat, Seaman Leonardo Amati cried out in the darkness, prayed for death to take him. Only six months before he had left his family behind in the hills of western Virginia, working a farm as indentured servants, for the Continental Navy. Now he was paying a heavy price for his desire to find adventure. Wracked with pain from a fire in his gut, his shipmates had gingerly placed him on some straw off in a corner. Amati hadn't moved from that spot for two days.

Simmons bent down on one knee to feel Amati's brow with the back of a large, dirty hand. Born in England over forty years ago, Simmons had been raised in the Taconic foothills of New York near Yorktown by an uncle following the death of both his parents. As a boy, he liked to go into Peekskill to watch the boats sail up and down the Hudson and then one day, for no particular reason, he simply signed aboard one and the sea became his home. Despite having the demeanor of an austere schoolmaster, Simmons was, by nature, an easy-going, cheerful fellow with a soft voice. Affectionately known in the yard as 'Old Pappy', he could always be counted on for some bit of kindness or a ready joke, anything to keep spirits from faltering. But beneath his casual ways there was a natural, no-nonsense leader, a capable organizer, and a man who seemed to thrive on hardship. As the senior ranking noncommissioned officer, the officers relied on him to manage the day-to-day affairs of the men. And under his leadership, which he liked to say was nothing more than surrounding himself with real talent and inspiring that talent to succeed, things ran smoothly within Long Prison.

Simmons sighed and looked up at the man standing behind him.

"It's in the Lord's hands now, Capt'n. Nothin' any of us can do for him in this dretful hole. Poor wretch can't keep anythin' down, sir. Not the best time to be gettin' sick after a hard winter and with all these cold rains. Bad luck that is. There's no tellin' how things will go."

Captain Henry Ward Patterson leaned over Simmons's shoulder and looked at the boy's pale, drawn face. He wiped away a tear. His own son, whom he had left safe and well back home, was about the same age as Amati. Patterson, Amati and the rest of his crew had just marched through Old Mill's gate several days before after running their sloop-of-war aground off the west coast of Ireland to deprive the British of a prize.

"Mr. Simmons, could you make the rounds among your people? See if there's any medicine to be had?"

Simmons nodded, pulled Amati's coat collar up around his neck to keep the chill out and gave the boy a gentle pat on the chest. "Aye, sir. I'll see to it directly. I doubt there is any but some of the lads should have something we can use to barter with. The red coats are easily bribed."

"Whatever you can do. Thank you kindly, Mr. Simmons."

Simmons touched his cap and turned to leave. He was not one of the newcomers, who were always quarantined from the general prison population for the first few days. Simmons had only stopped by to see if the new men needed anything.

Patterson looked around the small, damp cell and let his mind wander. His thoughts turned to his family. He pictured them all gathered around their fine, large fireplace in the kitchen preparing for supper. His wife was a fine cook. And she was a strong-willed woman too. *Stronger-willed than I am*, he thought quietly. There were times he had resented her for it but, now, he was grateful for her strength. She could cope and manage things without him for a time and he found comfort in that at least.

He was doing his best to fight off his despair but he knew it was a battle he would lose in time. The depression had tried to drown him before. He could not, must not, dwell on that now. *No, look after the men as best you can...* That was his duty. He shook off all thoughts of home. *Steady now my good man; one day at a time, take one day at a time.*

Not long after Simmons's departure, a small detail of British marines paused outside the cell. One man slid the bolt back on the heavy oak door and opened it.

"Supper time me little oinkers," the sergeant of the guard called out in a gruff voice. The man was small and wiry, had a face hardened by years of service in the king's army - red terror of nations. "Back away I say," he commanded and sent two of his men inside the cell.

The soldiers carried in a large, black kettle filled with a brown broth sloshing back and forth. A small chunk of fat floated on top of the lukewarm mixture. A third soldier carried in several small sacks of bread, dropped them on the dirt floor and went to remove the privy bucket.

Patterson took a step forward. The sergeant lowered his musket at Patterson's chest - not that there was much chance of an escape, not from Old Mill, not from England - but it would have pleased the sergeant to have an excuse to shoot one of the Americans. So far, that pleasure had eluded him. But he was a patient man. The army had given him that virtue and eventually the day would come for a killing and he would be there for it.

Patterson pointed over at Amati. "The lad needs a doctor."

"Is that so?" replied the sergeant, bearing a set of badly crooked teeth. His lips twisted into an unkind smile as he dropped to one knee next to Amati. "Well bless me now, but he don't look none too good. So young too. Always seems like the young ones are the first to go. Cruel world the Lord made. My, my, but aren't we a bit green around the gills my fine, young rebel?"

The sergeant stood and turned to his men. "Did you hear that, Georgie? Seems like these Americans are always needin' somethin', hey?"

"They're a spoiled lot, sergeant," replied a hulking brute of a man with a nose that had been broken more than once.

"At least give us some medicine for his fever," pleaded Patterson.

"Now look'ee here, mate," snarled the sergeant, "Our good King has graciously provided *you* with nearly all the comforts of home. Think how much better off you are here at Old Mill than in that primitive land you calls America. Woods infested with bears and Indians. Air filled with diseases. Swamps infested with snakes and I hear even crocodiles. Or was that alligators? No matter, 'orrible place it is."

"And towns infested with rebels, sergeant!" offered the hulking soldier named Georgie with a grin.

The sergeant smiled back. He liked that.

"Aye, Georgie, just so! Bloody rebels breed like rabbits. Unhealthy climate to boot, always too damn hot or too damn cold. Well I know. I've been there. Much nicer, more civilized here don't you think, Capt'n?"

Patterson didn't care for the sergeant's mocking tone or for his lack of respect.

He straightened his shoulders back and gritted teeth: "Sergeant, I shall remind you - you are addressing a superior officer. Now this boy may die without proper medical attention. I demand medicine at the very least. As prisoners of war, we are entitled to the basic essentials to include shelter, decent food, warm clothing and medicine. If these things are not provided, I shall be forced to make an official complaint to -"

The sergeant's mood, like some gale-force wind suddenly blowing down from nowhere, no warning, turned savage. He pushed his musket into Patterson's chest and cut him off.

"Say what? *You demand? You're entitled?* You'll demand nothin' here yer high and mighty lordship. Now the prisoners across the way there, they're French, frog eatin', stinkin' French. God hows I hate them shitty-pants Frenchies. But they're prisoners-of-war and they've got rights. You Americans aren't prisoners-of-war so you've got no rights. No, sir. You're rebels. Shit suckin' scum. Worse than the cow dung I scraped off me boots this very mornin'. Traitors to the Crown you are and soon you'll be charged with high treason and promptly hanged. By *Christ* if I had me way I'd waste no more time and stretch your scrawny necks at the end of some good English hemp this very day. Now, all you *swine* - get back, get back I say! Get back now or we'll be formin' a burial party in the mornin' for one of you!"

The sergeant jerked his head to one side, giving the signal for his detail to withdraw, and then told the soldier carrying the privy bucket to set it down. He looked at Patterson with raw hate in his eyes. Then he smiled at him and kicked the bucket over, spilling its foul contents over the sacks of bread.

"Oh, how clumsy of me! Dear me, what a pity. Ah well, keep your good cheer there. Eat hardy boys!"

His men laughed. The giant blew Patterson a kiss before bolting the door.

"Jackals, damn your eyes..." Patterson whispered under his breath.

Later that day, Simmons returned with a small bottle of medicine in one hand and an old, tattered blanket tucked under an arm. He had no idea what was in the bottle but it was the only medicine he could find. He gave Amati a spoonful of the green liquid. The boy choked it down.

"That sergeant, Mr. Simmons," Patterson began asking while carefully wrapping the blanket around Amati, "have you had difficulties with him before?"

"Aye, sir, but not to worry, it will be alright," he told Patterson cheerfully. "No need to get your dander up, sir. You've got to go with the currents. Can't fight 'em. Wasted energy that is. Dangerous too. But take heart, they're not all like the sergeant there. He's just one of the ignorant ones."

"Perhaps a complaint to the Commission of Sick & Hurt Seamen might enlighten the sergeant."

Simmons started coughing, trying to suppress a laugh.

"You find something amusing about my threat, Mr. Simmons?"

"Ahem. Oh, please forgive me, sir! You are new. You'll learn. The Commission of Sick & Hurt would indeed normally be the appropriate folks to complain to, assuming you could get your petition past that miserable son-of-a-whore Cowdry, which is most unlikely. But the two commissioners are just as despicable and corrupt as Cowdry. We call them, with no charity in our hearts, 'Mr. Sick' and 'Mr. Hurt' because of the harm they do us."

"Oh?"

"Cheer up, sir. Some of the guards show us a spot of kindness here and there and help us where they can with extra victuals and clothing. Some trade with us and others can be bribed and, on occasion, we even get money from Paris. It could be worse, sir."

Simmons had piqued Patterson's curiosity. "How so, Mr. Simmons?"

"We have lads imprisoned on British barges off New York Harbor and I hear they suffer far worse hardships than we do. Lots die early in them death ships. Miserable places."

Patterson nodded. Every seasoned sailor had heard the horror stories of the New York prison barges. Hell on Earth.

"No, Mr. Simmons, I am well aware there are more evil places than this. I meant, where does the money come from?"

"Why now, sir, it flows in from different sources," Simmons replied cautiously and lowered his voice. "They're many tributaries. But the river's true wellspring is our government's man in France, Ben Franklin."

"Oh?"

"Yes, mostly Franklin but we have some charitable friends right here in England too who occasionally take pity on our lot and see to our safe passage out of England."

"Is that so?" Patterson asked with surprise.

"Aye. But that's a story for another day, sir. All in due time, sir. All in due time..."

Chapter Fifteen
Jones

espite his years and the gout that plagued him from time to time, the old doctor was feeling rather spry. For a few days, Winter had released her cruel grip around Paris and Franklin decided to add an extra city block to his morning stroll to savor the fresh, warm air. He did his best to walk every day and relished the bit of solitude. With advanced age slowly taking its toll on him now, too often he was denied this small pleasure.

He was in a particularly good humor too. Franklin had it on good authority from his friends at Versailles that the king was about to give his blessing to a formal military alliance between France and America. Such an alliance would be tantamount to a declaration of war against England. All of his hard work was about to pay off. The alliance would be his crowning achievement as a diplomat. Saratoga had changed everything. 1778 was shaping up to be a very good year.

He had received word too that, following the recall of Commissioner Deane, Congress was about to appoint him *Minister Plenipotentiary* to the Court of Versailles. But he hardly needed such a lofty title. It hadn't taken the old doctor long to win over the hearts and minds of the French after his arrival to Paris. He was, after all, one of the preeminent scientists of his day. His theory of single-fluid electricity, correctly identifying negative and positive forces within a current, made him the world's foremost authority on electricity. He was considered a fine theoretical scientist too and was well read in the humanities. Franklin enchanted the sophisticated Parisians with his homespun wisdom and legendary charm. He never tired of the attention. And the French, easily bored, never tired of him, never tired of this 72 year old man who had never even finished grade school.

Franklin had used his time in France and considerable guile wisely to make important friends at Versailles. While the French in the beginning had rejected an outright alliance with America, the French responded to Franklin's appeals for money in the French way: with unbounded generosity. A deluge of gold was flowing out of the French treasury and into America.

French generosity was hardly inspired by America's desire for *liberty* or democratic rule though. The French Crown had no interest in liberating the masses. No. France's interest was confined to humiliating Great Britain and the American conflict offered France an opportunity to settle old scores.

From the American perspective, Franklin's mission to France was a stunning success. As a result of Franklin's powers of persuasion and influence, France not only was pouring huge amounts of money into the Colonies but had also started shipping vast quantities of war materials across the Atlantic, including uniforms, muskets, powder, shot and field artillery - saving the Revolution from total collapse during the dark days of 1777.

To many in the king's court it was far less clear whether Franklin's success for America was equivalent to French success. More than a few of the king's advisors had expressed concerns that France was spending herself into financial ruin by bankrolling the American rebels. And even among those at court who supported giving the Americans money, many were adamantly opposed to open war with Great Britain, remembering well France's disastrous losses in the Seven Year's War with her old nemesis. These naysayers, these peddlers of fear, angrily predicted another military fiasco. But the warmongers, the disciples of Machiavelli, eager to avenge old grievances and restore France's former glory at any cost, had the king's ear. *My enemy's enemy is my friend* they whispered to Louis and Louis, in return, gave his warmongers a king's nod.

Even so, the king's generosity at first was not without limits and ended with gifts of money and supplies. The thought of open war with Great Britain made the young king squeamish - and rightfully so. The country-bumpkin Americans seemed totally inept at making war and his generals and admirals could not guarantee an American victory, even with an infusion of French regiments and ships, without American muscle.

And then, a miracle happened. In the fall of 1777, at a place called

Saratoga in upstate New York, a rag-tag army of American regulars and militia, commanded by General Horatio Gates, soundly whipped an entire army of battle-harden British regulars, over 5,000 strong, under the command of General John Burgoyne in pitched battle. The humiliating defeat stunned the world. But Saratoga was only one battle and merely purchased time for the Colonies. Without French soldiers and ships, the best the Colonies could hope for with Britain was a precarious military stalemate.

France's Foreign Minister, the Count Charles Gravier de Vergennes, had been patiently waiting for a Saratoga. Vergennes was the most powerful man in France - and Franklin's staunchest supporter. Like Franklin, he was an extraordinarily shrewd statesman and a man of considerable charm. Some even compared him to the great Cardinal Richelieu. With a round, docile face and double chin, and an exceedingly long nose, Vergennes looked more like a banker than a statesman of great stature. That suited him just fine. Rivals had paid dearly for underestimating him. He was a master of diplomacy, duplicity and power politics. No matters of state were decided without his blessing.

Franklin understood this power behind the throne and had cultivated Vergennes's friendship from the very start. Like many Frenchmen, Vergennes longed to avenge France's humiliation and reclaim her empire but he would not risk plunging France into another pointless war with England unless America could prove that she could actually win. The American victory at Saratoga had made Vergennes a believer and it was Vergennes who then persuaded a reluctant king in early 1778 to enter into a formal alliance with America.

The doctor turned the corner to his small home, located behind the estate of a *Monsieur* Donatien Le Ray de Chaumont in Passy, which, Franklin described to a friend, was a "...neat village on high ground, half mile from Paris with a large garden to walk in." Chaumont, the owner of the magnificent Hotel Valentinoir, and an ardent supporter of the American cause, had provided comfortable quarters for all three American Commissioners, refusing all offers of rent.

As Franklin walked through the front door, he found his grandson waiting for him. The younger Franklin gave his grandfather a cheery smile and followed the old man down a narrow hallway, into a small study with an untidy stack of books sitting on the *escritoire*. The doctor did most of his writing and reading in the study but the room was not his favorite. It was too cold and damp for his liking. He much preferred the pavilion's large parlor with its bright colored wallpaper and cozy fireplace.

Franklin looked at his pocket watch and reflected on the day's prospects. He had a busy schedule ahead of him. That was nothing unusual. Men half is age had difficulty keeping pace with him. Temple locked an arm inside his grandfather's arm, to steady the old man, and guided him towards his desk where the usual bundles of mail and newspapers were waiting for him. Franklin landed in his chair with a great plop.

"This envelope," Temple explained, handing Franklin a package wrapped in oilskin, "was delivered by special courier during your walk, Grandfather."

"Ah, Thornton's report. I've been expecting this. Let's see what we have here."

Franklin continued receiving tales of horror from various sources concerning the cruelties American prisoners suffered at the hands of the British. And the two largest naval detention centers, Forton and Old Mill, were now fully operational with hundreds of Americans being transferred into both facilities.

The British government had flatly denied all charges of barbaric treatment as gross exaggerations. But there were simply too many eyewitness accounts coming across the Channel to ignore. And after Lord Stormont's rude refusal months ago to even discuss the possibility of a prisoner exchange, Franklin had decided to send an emissary over to England to learn the truth of things and chose a Major John Thornton, Arthur Lee's secretary, for the task. He had instructed Thornton to meet with Prime Minister Lord North to address the American government's concerns about the welfare of its soldiers and sailors held in captivity. Thornton was then to personally inspect both Forton and Old Mill, interview prisoners, inspect living conditions and distribute money to as many Americans as he could.

After accepting the mission, Thornton made several attempts to enter England but was denied each time, until the fiasco of Saratoga where British arrogance was first humbled. Thornton was then welcomed and arrived in London just days before Christmas.

Following several meetings with Prime Minister North, which Thornton later described as "tense," he was given permission to visit Forton and Old Mill. But at Forton the British commander denied Thornton entry and so the major did his best to interview American prisoners through a fence under the watchful eyes of British guards. Thornton learned that Forton held 119 Americans and the men complained bitterly to him about the conditions inside. There were beatings, corruption, a lack of food, clothing and medicine and, Thornton was told, several men had died from exposure and starvation in the 'black hole'.

At Old Mill, not only was Thornton prohibited from entering the facility, but he was barred from making any contact of any kind with any of the 289 American prisoners held inside. Disappointed, but satisfied he had accomplished all he could, Thornton had hurried back to Paris in January to submit his findings.

After reading Thornton's report, Franklin removed his spectacles and rubbed the bridge of his nose as he considered matters. Now, with France committed to entering the war, he was free to focus his attention on other issues and saving his fellow patriots held in England from death and torture was foremost on his mind.

"Temple, be a good fellow and find the whereabouts of our good Captain Jones for me. We may have work for that gifted patriot."

Franklin was finished with diplomacy as a means of protecting American lives in English jails. Diplomacy had failed. He reached a decision, a decision he well knew that had risk and one that might produce unintended consequences.

Six weeks earlier or so, on December 2nd, an ambitious, hot-headed young Scot named John Paul Jones had arrived in Nantes with the newly built eighteen-gun sloop *Ranger*, a gift from Congress to Franklin to use however he saw fit. It was Jones who had also brought word of the

American victory at Saratoga to Franklin.

Franklin needed leverage against the British. He needed prisoners. And now, with Thornton's report still resting in his hand, he decided it was time to start his own private war against the English to get them. Jones seemed the perfect soldier for the task.

After reading Thornton's report a second time, Franklin dictated a letter to Temple for Jones. Jones was to put to sea without delay and cruise the waters along the English coast. Jones's primary mission: to capture as many British seamen as he could find.

Jones accepted Franklin's orders with enthusiasm and wasted no time carrying out Franklin's wishes. The moment the *Ranger* had been refitted and reprovisioned he left Brest. Full of swagger, the cocky Scot led his men on a daring raid deep into enemy waters, terrorizing the coasts of both England and Ireland. Jones took several enemy ships in rapid succession and captured 200 prisoners for Franklin. And then, having a flair for the dramatic, Jones boldly landed at Whitehaven for himself, the place where he had learned the art of sailing as a boy. He and his men stormed a small fort there and did not leave until every cannon had been spiked and rendered useless. Not since the Norman invasion some 700 years earlier had an enemy force set foot in England.

The dauntless Jones returned to France a hero with prizes and bearing 200 splendid gifts for Franklin. The old doctor was ecstatic when he learned of Jones's victory at sea. Franklin's private, little war was off to a most promising start. And with 200 British prisoners at his disposal, he finally had leverage...

Chapter Sixteen
Messrs. Sick & Hurt

he First Secretary of the British Admiralty was not a happy man. Sir Philip Stephens's retreat to his country manor had been cut short and now he was back in London sitting at his desk, staring dispassionately at two neatly stacked mountains of paperwork and sipping cold tea. He looked over at a clock sitting on a small credenza against a wall over which hung a dreary oil portrait of the king. The clock, a gaudy Spanish antique - a gift or a bribe, he couldn't remember which - was making the most irritating noise. His head was pounding and it wasn't even 10 yet on a cheerless, rainy morning.

Stephens sighed and forced himself to pick up the first folder in the pile closest to him. Inside the folder he found an official report from the Commission of Sick and Hurt Seamen and the Exchange of Prisoners of War. In theory, this small body, comprised of two undistinguished bureaucrats, commoners, was charged with the administration of naval prisons. But the Commission of Sick & Hurt answered to the Lords of the Admiralty in London, specifically to the First Secretary, the real power, and the task of overseeing the prisons was Stephens's least favorite duty.

Stephens began scanning a cover letter attached to the report and soon concluded that the report was no more than the usual tripe. John Bell, the senior Commissioner, had noted Thornton's uneventful visit to Forton and had enclosed the monthly numbers: guard and prisoner rosters, inventory lists, line item costs and a 30 day financial forecast for each prison. Bell also asked for authority to replace several sentries at Old Mill Prison who had been caught taking bribes from the prisoners and had even been so bold as to offer his own thoughts about how best to discipline the sentries in question. Stephens paused when he heard a familiar knock at the door, a soft but rapid thump-thump, thump-thump, thump-thump.

"And how are we today on this fine spring day, my lord?" his secretary asked as he briskly rushed through the high double-doors on a pair of spindly legs and carrying more folders. No one but Mason ever dared walk into the First Secretary's office without being summoned first.

"Fine spring day did you say? Have you lost your senses, Mason?"

Mason had long ago learned to ignore his master's foul moods and did so now. He touched the side of the teapot and sighed. "Oh, dear me, sir. No. No. This will never do. I'm going to cuff that new servant in the kitchen when I see him. I will get you a pot of fresh-brewed straight away."

Stephens could not resist a bit of fun. He burst out into a hearty laugh and baited Mason. "Haw, haw, haw! You're going to cuff him where?"

"Right in the old kitchen," Mason answered with a straight face and lewdly grabbed his privates. "Where good things are made."

"Haw, haw, haw! Indeed! You're always such a witty rascal, Mason. I say, what is it that you are carrying there? Hm? Something to amuse us or, I fear, more work for the weary?"

"Really, sir, you know you should see me first before diving into these folders!" Mason scolded, half in jest and half in earnest, and ignored the First Secretary's silly question. He looked over Stephens's shoulder to glance at the paper in his hands. "Ah, Commissioner Bell's letter. I have taken the liberty of responding for you - now, my lord, if you will look at the first folder from the left pile..."

Stephens did as he was told and read through a draft reply Mason had prepared earlier for his signature. Stephens smiled. Mason was not only efficient, but knew his mind well. The letter was perfect both in tone and content, had just the right measure of condescension. Bell was instructed to replace all the sentries at Old Mill immediately and leave the matter of discipline to Admiral Shuldham in Portsmouth. Pleased, Stephens dipped his pen in the ink jar and scribbled his name across the bottom.

"So much for Mr. Sick," Stephens said softly. Yes, he knew the nicknames the prisoners had given to his commissioners and rather enjoyed using the insubordinate names himself, though he wasn't quite sure who was 'Sick' and who was 'Hurt.'

"Excellent, sir. Now, if I may. Each folder in the left pile has a proposed draft reply for your review to the corresponding letters contained in the folders in the right pile. These, of course, are all rather mundane matters. The folders I have here in my arm are more urgent and require your personal attention."

"Mason, Mason, Mason. The day is suddenly looking better indeed!"

"I'm glad, sir. Let me fetch that hot tea for you before you go and catch the sniffles again. This folder, with the red ribbon tied around it, well, sir, I fear you shall want to peruse it first."

While Mason disappeared on his hunt for a pot of hot tea, Stephens untied the red ribbon around the new folder and removed a single sheet of paper from it. It was a letter from the Lord Lieutenant in Dublin reporting on the loss of the *H.M.S. Drake* and the capture of all her crew.

"*Christ*," Stephens muttered softly. While the loss of the *Drake* was an insignificant matter, the First Secretary knew her capture would give that old fool Franklin, a man whom he despised and hoped to see hanging from the gallows at Execution Dock someday, fuel for his obnoxious prisoner exchanges. No one within the North government disliked the idea of releasing traitorous rebels more than he. The high lieutenant also informed the First Secretary about another nuisance. One large but very swift smuggler, not the usual sort of small coaster seen meandering up and down the coast like some fat cow, but something altogether different, something very fast, had so far managed to elude capture. She was commanded, or so rumor had it, by a young Irish thug named Ryan, an associate of O'Keeffe. The high lieutenant concluded his report by requesting an additional frigate to hunt the smuggler down.

"Mason, did you see this report?" Stephens asked as Mason walked back into his office holding a silver tray. "The one with the red ribbon?"

"I took the liberty, sir. Yes, indeed I did."

"Don't people understand that there is a damn war going on? The high lieutenant whines like a silly school girl. I can hardly afford to send out a frigate to chase down every damn pirate that eludes one of the king's revenue ships!"

"Indeed not," Mason offered reassuringly as he poured the First Secretary's tea, but ignoring him all the same.

As Mason handed the First Secretary his tea and then, as if by magic, produced a plate of fresh scones and jam and placed the treats on the side of the desk, Stephens thought quietly to himself. Well, this was certainly one of O'Keeffe's ships, not one of his own smugglers, and that meant more competition and fewer profits.

"Then again, Mason... It would be unseemly for us to allow even one Irish punk to insult His Majesty. And as my dear father, God rest his soul, liked to say: always best to step on a cockroach before his ten brothers come to join him. I believe the *Surprise* is in port without assignment. When you have a moment would you be so good as to prepare orders for her commander. Direct him to sail at his earliest convenience. He is to patrol the waters between Waterford to Dublin until otherwise instructed. His primary mission is to intercept and take or destroy any smugglers he finds."

"Certainly, your grace. I shall attend to it straight away."

"Good, good. Perhaps we can send *Messrs.* Sick and Hurt some more business for their prisons, hey?"

"More grist for the mill, sir?"

"Yes, indeed, Mason. Well said, more grist for the mill..."

Chapter Seventeen
A King's Promise

The one luxury they had not stripped from him was his walks. The prison yard afforded him ample space to move about, more space at least than on board the confined area of a ship's quarterdeck. He enjoyed his walks not only for the exercise but because they helped fight the depression constantly tugging at him. To this small extent, his life had improved.

Patterson took in the turquoise sky. The sun was making one of its rare appearances in an otherwise gloomy part of the world. He paused to feel the sun's warmth against his face. It was a fine morning. Still, with less meat on his bones now, the brisk morning air cut right through him. He buttoned up his coat and tightened his belt. With each passing day, his trousers seemed to grow just a little bit wider around the waist.

Patterson resumed his walk, passing by small groups of men scattered across the yard warming themselves by the campfires. Most were playing cards or exchanging idle banter. Here and there he heard bits of laughter. Even in this place, remarkably, there was laughter. *God's blessing*, Patterson thought quietly to himself. *Must be thankful for the Lord's new day. Even in the brutal place, one can find His Glory.*

Patterson then stopped to watch a prisoner, a petty officer named Horace Bragg, haggling with a British guard. Bragg was known as a man who could get things. Cards, dice, clothes, paper, ink, razors, soap, tools, tea, coffee, tobacco, whatever the item needed, Bragg could usually get it. Once, his shipmates had asked him to get them a tub for bathing. They all pitched in some money but no one really thought Bragg could do it. A week later, sitting in the middle of the yard, stood a crude, but serviceable, wooden tub. *There is probably a Horace Bragg in every prison in the world; it must be some kind of universal law*, thought Patterson.

Patterson watched Bragg and the guard with curiosity. The guard was standing against the yard's whitewashed stonewall, his musket slung casually over his left shoulder and, in his right hand, he was holding something up for inspection. Patterson couldn't quite make out the object, but Bragg seemed interested.

"Three pence, have ye lost your wits man?" the American asked with a snooty New England accent. "I reckon you take me for a fool, Smarly. Two pence is the goin' rate and that's for prime - not for this here scrawny little critter. Probably dropped dead of hunger itself it did. One pence is all this pathetic carcass is worth, but I'll give you two. Not a penny more..."

The guard smiled, a smug smile that said: *you Americans need to be taken down a peg or two and herein beginneth the lesson - you treacherous Yankee dog.* "Three pence, Bragg, the price has gone up my good fellow since last time. The Frogs or Dagos will pay if you won't. Supply and demand. 'Tis that simple. As one of me best customers, I naturally came to you first. Now what'll it be? I haven't got all day to just stand around and quibble with the likes of you."

Bragg considered the guard's words, watched him as he swung the dead rat back and forth by its tail. He finally reached into his pocket with a dirty hand and retrieved a three pence and tossed it over. The guard dropped the rat and caught the coin in midair. He smiled arrogantly at Bragg, touched the brim of his shako and left the American with his purchase.

Patterson wasn't sure who had negotiated the better deal. Rat meat didn't offend many at Old Mill. Even on board ship, meager rations were occasionally supplemented with rat. Hunger drove some prisoners to even eat grass or gnaw on old bones discarded in the yard by the guards. But Bragg had drawn the line on that. Eating rat meat was as far as he would stoop. No one saw any stray cats or dogs at Old Mill either. Not for very long. Both disappeared quickly and were served up as delicacies.

Bragg produced a small pocketknife, quickly skinned and cleaned the small animal as best he could, then returned to a nearby fire where his shipmates were gathered. They skewered the meat on a spit and set it over an open fire. Prison etiquette required Bragg to share the small breakfast treat with his friends.

Simmons saw Patterson watching Bragg and walked over to him. "Good morning, sir. How's the good Capt'n today?"

"Fine. Fine, Mr. Simmons. The Lord has seen fit to give us a glorious new day. And you, sir, always looking after the welfare of others, how is our Good Samaritan today?"

"Ah, don't be makin' me no saint, sir. Just doin' my duty as I sees it. But in answer to the Capt'n's question, I'm excellent, splendid as always. No sense in bein' anything but... 'Tis a lovely day."

"Yes. Just so. There is comfort in that at least. How is your patient progressing? I didn't hear him coughing much last night."

"Aye, Capt'n. I didn't have much hope at first but he's a fighter, young and strong. It's better now that he's over in Long House with the rest of us. Maybe he'll make it. Maybe not. Hard tellin' one way or the other yet."

"Hm, we are all so helpless in here," replied Patterson softly.

The sharp sound of a bell suddenly interrupted the serenity of the morning.

Patterson, along with the other newcomers, looked around the yard. "What the devil?"

The old timers all ignored the sound.

"That'll be fat, old Harding and his silly little cow bell," Simmons explained. He could see the name meant nothing to Patterson. "He's, well, I don't rightly know what he is to be perfectly truthful about it, sir. But he comes around here on the first Wednesday of every month tryin' to drum up recruits for the king's ships."

"Is that a fact, Mr. Simmons?"

"Aye, sir. It's sort of amusin' to watch him. The English prefer us Americans you know to the other prisoners because we speak the same language and all - or so the English will tell you if you ask them. The fact of the matter is tho', Americans are the best sailors in the world and those priggish Englishmen know it. Well, if Harding is here, then I reckon this be the first Wednesday of a new month."

"Do any of the men go with him?"

"Aye, Capt'n. On occasion, but seldom, sir, seldom I'm pleased to report. Most of the lads are patriots. Of that much I can assure you. Never understood the bell." And then his lips curled into a smile. "Ha! Lordy be, maybe he's playing the part of the *good shepherd* and is here to gather the flock..."

"Perhaps, Mr. Simmons, perhaps. Only it's not his flock is it now?"

"Indeed not, sir. Indeed not. Tho' he can often times find a stray sheep or two."

A rotund fellow dressed wearing a black long coat, black trousers and a black, wide-brimmed hat, with a bell in one hand and a black bag cradled underneath his arm in the other, entered the yard trailed by two lanky guards carrying a small table and a wooden chair. The modest parade marched slowly past the small groups of prisoners huddled around their campfires until they reached the middle of the yard.

Harding's pace was so labored that Patterson found it actually painful to watch him. *A turtle*, he thought, *moves faster*. Harding's double chin quivered with each agonizing step.

As the guards set their freight down at the lamppost, Harding placed the bell on the table and removed his hat and carefully placed it next to the bell. Long strands of greasy, silver hair cascaded down around his small, round shoulders. Next, he reached into his black bag and removed a stack of papers, ink and a pen and methodically set each item down on his makeshift desk with exaggerated ceremony. The guards, disinterested and bored, unslung their muskets and leaned against the lamppost.

"Attention! Attention all prisoners," Harding commanded in a nasal voice, breathing heavily through a bulbous nose covered in red veins.

Simmons folded his arms and spit on the ground. "Ah, here it comes Capt'n," he whispered. "The dreaded speech. He pretty much gives the same one each month. Never much changes."

"He looks like a tippler," Patterson whispered back, suppressing a laugh.

Harding ran his fingers over his ears to brush back his long strands of hair. "His Royal Britannic Majesty King George the III opens his arms to you in friendship and wishes to embrace you. England is in need of able-bodied seamen and the King has, most graciously, consented to issue a royal pardon to any man here today who agrees to serve in His Majesty's Royal Navy."

In between each sentence, Harding had to pause to gulp down air, to catch his breath. "Comfortable quarters, generous pay, wholesome food and good spirits too awaits any man here who so enlists this day. Enjoy all the privileges and benefits of a British seaman. Ah yes, did I say that a full pardon from high treason will be granted to every man who completes the terms of his service? A most merciful gesture by His most gracious Majesty I am sure you will agree? Come now gentlemen, come now. Who shall be the first? Who among you will add their names to the list of proud and distinguished men of the British navy? Hm? Who will help themselves out from under the misery of these cold, stone walls?"

Men responded to Harding's offer with grumbling and smirks.

Harding gingerly turned his head, his whole body turned with it as if he had no neck, to look around the yard. And, as if he was a minister about to lead his congregation in prayer, he held out his arms, his hands palms up.

"*Pardon* me, your lordship," a face in the crowd called out to the Englishman. "You say good food and spirits? If we accept yer terms, should we be expectin' his most excellent Majesty to be dinnin' with us tonight? I best be puttin' a real good shine on me boots then!"

The whole yard erupted into a hardy burst of laughter.

"Don't be a *royal arse*, Conroy," another prisoner cried out. "His high and mighty Majesty has important matters of state to worry about. He an't got no time for the likes of us - but say there Mr. Governor, sir, perhaps your king could spare one or two of his mistresses tonight, he bein' so busy managin' the empire and all."

Another howl of laughter swept over the prisoner yard followed by jeers and claps.

The Englishman narrowed his eyes at the mob.

"If he does come for supper," said a third prisoner, "he had better bring his own rat - Bragg's three pence barn mouse is hardly big enough to serve us all!"

Even Patterson smiled at that. *God it's good to hear these poor wretches laugh.*

The king's recruiter, his pasty complexion suddenly flushed with red and his patience wearing thin, pounded his fist on the table.

"Order there! Order I say! Insolence will not be tolerated! I'll have order here!"

Then he paused for a moment, as if he had just expended an enormous amount of energy and needed time to summon up more, and took a deep breath while his two guards looked on, their muskets still resting on the ground. One guard yawned and made no attempt to stifle it.

"A fair offer has been extended to all," Harding said slowly, without inspiration. No patriotic fever burned in his gut.

"You are well advised to give thoughtful consideration to this matter. Certainly, you cannot fancy your lot here at Mill? Why continue your suffering? What good purpose is served? To serve a dying rebel cause half the world away? What folly, what a waste of your youth. You could be locked up here forever. Think of your families, your sweethearts - the warm embrace of a lover. Ah, did I not mention: no one need actually serve on a British warship if that offends your conscience. The British whaling fleet is in port and it also has need of good, dependable men. Come now, lads. You Americans are known for your enterprising ways. There is no shame in improving your lot. Only a slow death awaits you here. Or maybe a quick death at the end of the hangman's rope soon - London is abuzz with talk about a new army being assembled to be sent over to the Colonies to crush the rebellion once and for all."

"Our brothers will whip any army England sends over," shouted a faceless voice in the crowd.

Harding ignored the man. "Who can say what the future holds for any man? Certainly for you men here, nothing good. Of that much I can assure each and every one of you." Again he paused to catch his breath and then added, as if to sweeten the deal: "a bonus of five guineas to the first ten men who puts his mark on these papers."

Two men, to a chorus of half-hearted boos and jeers, stood and sheepishly moved towards the table with the brass cowbell. Dirty and stooped with hunger, nothing but filthy rags clinging to their thin frames, neither man looked much like a sailor. They slowly shuffled to the center of the yard, barefoot, towards the brass beacon, towards what they hoped would be salvation.

"'Em two," offered Simmons, "are only one more hard winter away from the hands of the grim reaper. While the crowd may taunt them, no man will truly hold a grudge against these men. Truth is, that bell has tempted each of us at one time or another. We all have our limits, our moments of weakness. These two pour souls have reached theirs."

Patterson nodded. Poor wretches he thought. *Scarecrows.* The two men were probably ten years younger than they looked. Men should not be made to suffer so, not even in the hatred that is war. He bowed his head and silently offered a quick prayer: *dear Lord, I pray I am not here so long as to ever look like those broken, emaciated souls. I don't know if I am strong enough. Please, Lord, give me strength. Always, Your will be done...*

No one tried to stop either man.

"Ha, ha, that's it lads!" Harding exclaimed with a burst of energy, waving the men forward. "Come along now, no need to be shy. That's the spirit lads! You set a good example for all."

After each man made his mark on a sheet of paper, Harding had them stand off to the side, as if they were on display. "Now, who else wants to return to the world as a man today? Hey? Avoid the gallows too!"

But two souls were the only souls the king's good recruiter would get from Old Mill Prison that day. After no one else stirred, Harding shrugged, took his bell, his papers and his ink jar, and placed them in his black bag. Then he slowly retraced his steps out of the prison yard with the two guards, carrying the table and chair, and his two new recruits in tow.

"Yep," Simmons said and shrugged his large shoulders. "Pretty much the same speech as before. Almost word for word. I'll wager those two fellers never sees a guinea of that bonus."

As the men returned to their own matters, Simmons spit on the ground again and then spotted an officer across the yard and pointed. "That gentleman standin' over there, Capt'n Patterson, see him, sir? That's Capt'n Conyngham, Gustavus Conyngham."

"The Dunkirk Pirate?" asked Patterson.

"Aye, the very same. He took sixty ships or more, or so they say, before the British nabbed him on the *Greyhound*. Let me introduce you to him. You'd be meetin' him soon enough bein' an officer and all. He's originally from County Donegal, Ireland, his folks having moved somewheres to Pennsylvania before the war. He was a capt'n in the Continental Navy for a spell and then did some privateering until his capture. Worked out of Dunkirk. He's a good man to know. Not too difficult to figure out that nickname of his is it?"

"No, indeed. Why Dunkirk?"

"Ah, well now Capt'n, the folks of Dunkirk I hear take a liberal view of things. There's a sizable Irish population in Dunkirk too. It's been a safe haven for smugglers for a long time. Lots of skilled Irish seamen there to ship with. Interestin' place Dunkirk. Been there once. An enterprising young man can do some business in Dunkirk. *Any* manner of man, *any* manner of business if..." he paused with a wink and a smile, "you follow my meanin', sir."

"Indeed I do, Mr. Simmons. It all sounds rather *colorful*."

"Aye, that there is a good way of saying it, sir. Now I best warn you, sir, Capt'n Conyngham might come off as being a bit testy. He was recently tried and convicted for treason. His so-called trial was a sham. No need, if I may say so sir, asking him about it. He is waiting for the court to determine his punishment which, we all know, will be death."

"Oh? So the British are serious about hanging all of us?"

"Yep, officers first it appears..." Simmons replied with a grin and then led Patterson over to the man known as the *Dunkirk Pirate*.

Conyngham didn't look like much of a pirate. He was short with pasty skin and oily, black hair that made him look sickly. His 'o' shaped mouth was too small for his face with its long, sharp nose. And he had the sad brown eyes of a puppy.

"Capt'n Conyngham, sir, good day to you," offered Simmons in a friendly tone and saluted.

"Good day to you too, Mr. Simmons," replied Conyngham with a slight Irish brogue, nothing harsh, and returned Simmons's salute. "Lovely day isn't it?"

"True enough, sir. A gem of a day. Too good for English weather. Winds must blowin' in from France. Sir, permit me to introduce Capt'n Samuel Patterson to you."

Patterson extended his hand. Conyngham shook it with his small, almost feminine hand that was cold to the touch.

"The pleasure is mine, Capt'n Patterson. I've seen you about of course. But I prefer to keep my distance from the newcomers for a bit. Sometimes it's hard to know who yer dealin' with inside these walls. I trust you took no offense."

"I understand, sir. Precautions must be observed. No offense taken, Captain Conyngham."

"Beggin' your pardon, sir," Simmons interrupted, "Capt'n Patterson is no spy; we've checked him out carefully."

If Simmons was willing to vouch for Patterson, that was good enough for Conyngham. Simmons was a good man, the best.

Conyngham's sad eyes held their cold stare. "My compliments to you for yer safe arrival to Old Mill."

"Compliments, sir?" Patterson asked, puzzled. "I lost my ship. I'm a prisoner along with all my crew. I'm not certain, sir, compliments are in order."

"Oh? I was informed that you were chased down by three British frigates and then wrecked yer vessel off the coast of Ireland within range of their heavy guns. Is that not so?"

"Well, sounds like one of my boys may have embellished a fact or two. It was one very nimble frigate along with a heavy-armed sloop. But aye, sir, that's the gist of things."

"You saved the lives of yer men?"

"Aye, sir. Though not every man was brought here to Old Mill."

"The English took yer ship?"

"No, sir. We scuttled her, sent her to the bottom."

Conyngham dropped his cold stare and cracked a thin smile. "There you have it then. The hazards of war, Capt'n Patterson. You deprived the enemy of yer ship and you saved the lives of yer crew in the face of overwhelming odds. Compliments *are* indeed in order, sir."

Patterson nodded his appreciation to Conyngham for the kind

gesture.

"Capt'n Conyngham, sir," Simmons interrupted, "Capt'n Patterson might be interested in makin' leg bail, sir."

Conyngham narrowed his eyes at Patterson. "Is that so, Simmons? Leg bail? Indeed. Well now, we'll just have to see about that, won't we?"

Chapter Eighteen

Intrepid Irishmen & Breakout at Poolbeg

⚓

April 1779

hen the Earth gave birth to her four daughters, the Seasons, she handed each child equal powers and equal time, one portion each, to lord it over men. Even mighty Winter - for a time - must yield to the gentle ways of Spring, mistress of new hope, of new beginnings, and cease her rampaging, her cruel lament, against a world she so despises. And so with Spring's soft caresses, at her whispered command, Winter fled back into the snow-peeked mountains, into the mountains where her reign never ends, and released the wild Atlantic from her cold grip, ending her havoc against the wooden ships sailed by mortal men.

And while men and women struggled and sacrificed their lives and property a world away to gain their precious independence - *Friendship's* men continued their smuggling ways. The war seemed as if it might last forever and, with open hearts and full purses, the Irishmen accepted life's pleasures gladly.

At the age of only 25, Ryan was the master of the fastest ship at sea and a prosperous businessman. Now, with two years of success behind him and a pile of cash, he began toying with grander schemes. He began thinking about buying a second, even a third ship.

Still, the carefree Irishmen were not oblivious to the risks. More than one storm had tried to drag them to the bottom and they took note of increasing British interest in their cutter. English revenue vessels, and even a Royal Navy frigate or two, had tried to snare their ghost-like ship on more than one passage between the Continent and Ireland. But each attempt had failed. *Friendship* left each of her pursers behind with the devil's own speed, enhancing her master's reputation for skill and daring in Dublin and Dunkirk and points beyond.

Macatter, standing next to Mulvany at the helm as Mulvany worked the tiller, leaned over the rail to sniff the air and then scanned the coastline with a wary eye. Content, he nodded to the hands at the davits and the men quietly, carefully, lowered the ship's long boat into the water.

Under the cover of darkness Ryan, Dowlin and six stout Irishmen rowed ashore to a deserted stretch of beach near Dun Laoghaire. Ryan left Macatter in command of the ship with orders to land their cargo at a spot of beach north of Rush. The man had proved his competence on more than one occasion. Macatter was to look for a bond fire and two crossed torches, the signal for the 'all clear,' where O'Keeffe's men would be waiting to unload *Friendship's* cargo and put it on the wagons for transport inland. Payment for the goods would be made later, but only after the cargo was safely brought ashore. The risk of loss remained with the smugglers until the cargo was in the hands of O'Keeffe's shore party. This was the time-honored custom. Ryan's Shadowmen had done it all a hundred times before.

Dowlin traveled with Ryan as far as Dublin and there the two men parted company. Dowlin remained in the city to purchase iron fittings and other odds-and-ends for the ship down at the waterfront while Ryan rode on to Kenure to make arrangements with O'Keeffe for the next run where, the mariner hoped, he might find Shannon. The boat's crew whittled the time away at Dun Laoghaire, waiting for Ryan and Dowlin's return.

Shannon heard the sentry at the front gate stop and challenge a rider. She felt her heart flutter. It was late and at that hour the rider could only be one man. She dashed out of the house and ran down the gravel drive.

Ryan dismounted in time to catch her as she tumbled into his arms. The lovers showered each other with hard, fast kisses while the old guard smiled politely and looked away.

Live, warm tears streamed down Shannon's cheeks.

"What's this now, my sweet Shannon, tears?"

"Aye, tears of joy, Luke! Oh, how I have missed you!"

"And I you! Let's have a look at you, my lady. My, my you're a sight for sore eyes! So beautiful! Look at this would you now," he said, pointing to his legs, "you're making my knees quiver."

She held him tightly again for a long moment, savoring the warm, secure feeling of being wrapped inside his strong arms. Then he pulled away to remove a box from his saddlebag and handed it to her.

She passed the horse's reins over to the old man and accepted the box. "Another dress from Paris?"

"Aye. I suppose I'm fairly predictable. That's not good in a lover is it?"

She smiled, locked an arm inside his and led him back to the house. "Well, I suppose that depends on the woman. I love you just the way you are and besides - a woman can never have too many dresses! How you spoil me! Father, I'm afraid, will not be home 'til tomorrow. Though he continues to do remarkably well, the doctors have sent him to some bath near Belfast with waters that have healing powers, or so they say. We're quite alone my gallant, young man... Come, let's get you out of these dirty clothes and scrub the sea out of you. I'll draw you a bath."

"And then?" Ryan asked smiling.

"And then?" she asked returning his smile with a seductive look in her eyes. "Well my good man, if you don't know the answer to that question, you're not half the clever fellow they say you are..."

He slipped his arm around her waist, pulled her into him and, for a long while, the two lovers just stood quietly together in the foyer, holding each other, trading kisses. They slipped away together, if only for a fleeting moment, to a quiet place of serenity and tender joy.

"Business or pleasure first my lady?" Ryan finally asked. "I only have 'til morning."

Shannon ran her hands down the length of his strong arms. "Why there's hardly a choice to be made there - is there? But first that bath..."

Morning's first light touched the foot of the bed, slowly crept up the comforter until finally settling on the pillows. Ryan propped his head up on one elbow to study her face as she lay sleeping, marveling at her exquisite features. As a master painter will deftly add subtle hints of contrast to his masterpiece with the soft strokes of his brush, the sun's golden shafts delicately brushed her skin, enhancing her beauty. He took his index finger, carefully traced the edges of her full lips.

She stirred at his touch, cooed and rolled over to wrap herself around him. She took delight in pressing her naked body tightly against his, in rousing her lover's passion, but when he tried to ease himself on top of her she stopped him, smiled at him seductively, and promised that she would make it worth his while if he saved his strength.

Before breakfast they agreed to go riding. Shannon kicked her heels into her horse's flanks and raced ahead, galloping full speed through waves of golden wheat under a warm but threatening April sky. The air was filled with the sweet smell of honeysuckle, mixed with early morning dew. Woman and horse moved as one in elegant harmony while the mariner struggled, trying clumsily to keep up. But then the graceful rider pulled up on her horse's reins and halted at the top of a hill, one of her favorite spots on her father's property, where one could see for countless miles in all directions.

She turned in her saddle and laughed. In fine clothes or in work clothes, or in no clothes on at all, Ryan always looked divine in her eyes. But on horseback, well, the two paired together simply were not meant to be.

Ryan forced a weak smile as he awkwardly nudged his horse forward, uttering a curse under his breath as he tried to get the stubborn beast to obey his will. When he reached the bottom of the hill, he stopped, just so he could admire her from a distance.

Surrounded by tall blades of wild grass swaying in the breeze, she sat quietly in her saddle, waiting for him. She looked like some heavenly apparition as the sun, peeking in and out of gathering clouds, enveloped her in golden light. Ryan felt his heart stir.

How could this exquisite, intelligent woman be his to love and cherish he wondered? He shook his head in disbelief. His life before Shannon now seemed bland and hollow. No more. Now the world around him seemed a magical place. He savored the air's sweet aroma. He took in the sharp, vibrant colors of the trees, of the earth and the sky.

The world was a pleasure to his senses. He had even caught himself enjoying music where, before, listening to melodies had almost always been a tedious, unpleasant chore. Shannon had breathed new life into his soul.

She rode a little way further, along the ridge of the hill and stopped. She reached down and affectionately caressed her horse's sweaty neck and then waved for him to follow.

His patience clearly spent, Ryan dismounted and started, with his horse in tow, making his way up the hill. His frustration made Shannon giggle. Still, he was a joy to her eyes.

"All in good time, my brave seafarer," she called down to him. "We'll make a horseman out of you yet, Captain Ryan."

"I think not, Miss O'Keeffe," he replied, panting. "Lucky for us we both have other skills in common."

When he finally reached her side, he grabbed her by the collar, gently pulled her face down to his and started to kiss her.

She moaned at first but then playfully kicked him away. "Come Luke, Macpherson's barn is on the other side of the stream below, just beyond the rise over the far bank. That old ruin has been abandoned for years. No one will disturb us. I'll race you there!"

He laughed, looked up at the vaulting skies and offered up his objection. "Lord please spare me - not another race!"

"Oh come now, a little inspiration is all you need Luke," she told him in a low, sultry voice. She flashed her eyes at him, her large, green eyes, and threw him a coy smile. "There'll be," she added, while unfastening the first two buttons on her blouse, "a prize waitin' for the *man* who *finishes* this race. You need not win - second place will do just fine for my purposes!"

She then gave a high-pitched yell and kicked her heels into her horse's flanks again, spurring the animal down the hill and into the stream below, swollen from the heavy spring rains. The water reached the top of her thighs at the deepest part but she continued moving forward and, after clearing the stream and moving up to the crest of a steep embankment, she paused to give Ryan at least a sporting chance to catch up.

Now the master sailor eagerly mounted his horse and chased after his heart's desire. He raced down the hill, recklessly plunged his animal into the stream and guided the beast across as best he could. But midway through, his horse suddenly neighed disagreeably, reared up on its hind legs and rudely flipped its rider backwards. Ryan lost the reins, lost his balance too, and fell backwards, disappearing headfirst into the stream's icy waters.

Shannon burst out laughing when his head finally popped above the surface, the gut-wrenching kind of laugh that brings tears to the eyes. "I pray you aren't hurt my dearest?" she asked.

"No," he replied simply as he waded through the water. He climbed up the muddy bank where his horse stood waiting. The animal eyed him suspiciously when he grabbed the reins and put his foot in the stirrup to remount. "You've had your fun my dear lady! Now I shall have *mine*."

"For a man who can't tame his mount and prances about in wet clothes, you presume a great deal, sir..." she replied playfully. "Well - I suppose you're the catch of the day and you'll simply have to do. I'll be waiting for you!"

She cleared the embankment and stopped to turn in her saddle. "*Don't*, I warn you," she said with mock sternness in her tone, "keep me waiting long! I am a woman with needs, cravings to be satisfied..."

"Oh you're a hard one, Ms. O'Keeffe!"

"*Au contraire, mon amour*, I am soft and supple," she replied. "I am ready for you and on fire - you are the one who best be hard!" Before he could respond she tossed her head back, laughed, and with a flick of her wrist against the reins disappeared into the woods beyond.

His body tingled with anticipation. Her luring words had reinvigorated him. With a gleam in his eye, with new purpose, he spurred his horse on. When he reached the old barn he saw her horse tethered outside to a tree. The barn was nothing more than a ruin, a circle of stone covered over in crumbling thatch. He went inside and found Shannon waiting for him, naked, lying across her horse's blanket spread over a pile of straw. She was seized by a reckless yearning for him, no inhibitions, her green eyes inviting, no, begging him, to take her with all his savage, raw lust. Longing to please her, he frantically stripped off his wet clothes, slid on top of her, and indulged her every craving, holding back nothing. And then, spent and savoring passion's afterglow, the lovers, wrapped as one, rested and dozed - oblivious to the rumblings of distant thunder.

After returning to the house and sitting down to a Frenchman's breakfast of bread, butter and coffee, the lovers passed the time talking about little things and when they had finished, Shannon led Ryan into her father's study. She had him move a bookcase off a rug and then she pulled the corner of the rug back, removed a floor plank and reached down into a secret well to retrieve several books. She sat next to Ryan on a small sofa and started flipping through the pages of one book in particular.

"This ledger keeps track of all your runs, Luke. According to father, at this pace we'll own a whole fleet of smugglers in another year or two. He says you're the finest captain he's ever had the pleasure of doing business with. As you can see by these numbers, you've done exceptionally well. You've done very well indeed. *Friendship's* profits are most exciting."

The book, bound in leather, was more than a ledger. The book included dates, times, places, names, cargo inventory lists, bills of lading as well as monies received and paid. There were even maps attached to the book's back cover marking landing sites up and down the Irish coast. Ryan quickly realized that all the book entries had been meticulously written in Shannon's own hand.

As she continued showing Ryan the ledger, a warm gust of air rushed into the room through an open window, billowing the window's sheer, white curtains like the sails of a ship. Ryan walked over to the window to poke his head outside and saw low clouds swirling around with more intensity now. The air smelled of rain.

"I see you've taken my map making lessons to heart," he told her with his arms clasped behind his back, still looking up at the gray sky. "Ah, a storm's brewin'. Those drawings are beautifully done. I must say, you're certainly well-informed. That is exceptionally fine work, Shannon. My compliments."

She giggled. "You do look and sound so like a ship's captain at times, Luke! Thank you, sir! Father has no son and as he grows older more and more of the responsibility of running his businesses falls to me. I've been keeping the books for a while now and as you know, I often travel in my father's stead to meet with his business associates when he is not quite up to the task."

Her voice then began to rise with excitement. "It was difficult at first. Many of the men I dealt with resented negotiating business terms with a woman. But that has slowly changed. I've been accepted or, well, to say it best perhaps, I've been tolerated by most of my father's associates and they show some modicum measure of respect. I must confess, I do love the business so. It makes me feel, well, useful..."

Ryan turned and caught her watching him. Her eyes sparkled with intelligence. He had no doubt that this young beauty was every bit the *businessman* her father was. He felt a deep sense of pride for her. He returned to the sofa and kissed her on the cheek.

"And what was that for?" she asked, smiling.

"No reason in particular."

"Well, come now, Luke, we'll get you out of these wet clothes and send you on your way. I know it is time and I won't be the one to hold you back from the sea you love so much."

Just as Ryan was about to answer her, they heard the guard, an old but faithful man standing watch down by the wrought iron gate, shout up to the house. A lone rider was coming up the road fast. Ryan and Shannon moved to the window as two burly men, armed with muskets, emerged from the stable and ran into the house to stand at Shannon's side.

"Ah, 'tis only Mr. Dowlin," Ryan said. "Can't imagine what brings him here. Be good for you to finally meet him. He is, well, as I may have mentioned to you, he is a colorful sort. But he's a good man and as a friend, there is none better. You can tell your lads to stand down and go about their business, Shannon. All is well."

Shannon nodded to the men and they returned to their work as the rider dismounted, rather clumsily Shannon noted, at the gate. Ryan's friend was no better a horseman than Ryan.

Dowlin hurried towards the house on foot, panting as he raced up the steps of the front porch where Ryan and Shannon where waiting for him.

"What's your hurry, lad?" Ryan asked cheerfully.

Breathing heavily from a hard ride, his handsome flesh glistening with sweat, Dowlin bent over and rested his hands on his knees to catch his breath before he answered.

"*The cutter!*" he finally blurted out. "Bloody bastards, bloody bastards have taken the cutter!"

Ryan's smile instantly vanished. A sharp pain hit him in the gut like a fist. "What? Slow down man. What do you mean? Who? Who has taken the cutter?"

Despite his urgent need to get his story out, Dowlin took a moment to fill his lungs with air. He took a moment to look at Shannon, his gaze lingering a bit too long, and then smiled appreciatively at her.

She smiled sweetly back. Ryan had told her many stories about Dowlin of course and she at once liked him.

Dowlin straightened up and snapped his head around towards Ryan. "I don't know how - but I seen it with my own eyes. I picked up some parts for the ship and was tryin' to recruit a few more good lads down along the waterfront when I see two ships bringin' *Friendship* in under half sail. Musta been British revenue. They've got her tied up at Poolbeg next to the king's customhouse. Bloody buggers escorted the lads off the ship in chains at bayonet point and marched them down into the city. To the Black Dog most probably."

Ryan clenched his teeth. "The Black Dog?" he asked rhetorically while processing Dowlin's words. He felt his heart sink. His expression turned hard.

In the blink of an eye everything, everything that he had worked so hard to achieve - ruined, finished, gone. At whirlwind speed, his mind began churning out one thought after the other, desperately scrambling to find some plan to turn things around. But the situation seemed utterly hopeless to him.

Shannon saw the blood starting to drain from Ryan's face. She grabbed his arm and squeezed it reassuringly. "It'll be all right, Luke."

"How? How will it be all right?" he asked gruffly.

Ignoring Ryan, Dowlin turned his attention back to Shannon. He removed his hat, exposing his fiery, red hair, braided in a queue and glossy with sweat, and offered her an irresistible, impish smile.

"Beg pardon ma'am," he asked as large drops of rain started pelting the ground. "You must be Shannon. 'Tis my privilege to finally meet you. If you'll forgive my lack of manners, yer a lovely vision to be sure. I'm Patrick James Dowlin, the only fella here on *Gawd's* green earth who is a better man than yer precious Luke. If you ever grow weary of him - I hope you'll allow me the honor of calling upon you promptly soon after. You'd be no worse for the experience, I promise..."

She blushed at his boldness, but smiled too. "I see that you're a charmer just like your friend, Mr. Dowlin. I best be on my guard. I am pleased to finally meet you as well."

Some women might have been offended by Dowlin's direct talk. Not Shannon. Ryan had prepared her for Dowlin's blunt ways and she accepted his words as innocent flattery. The man was just as Ryan had described him: big, strong, exquisitely handsome, and full of himself. But she saw in his eyes the heart of a good man too.

While Ryan was drifting off to some distant place, Dowlin took a moment to study Shannon more closely. Nothing crude, that was just his way.

"Dear lady, truly the good Lord loves Irish women above all others as He favors them most in beauty."

"Not now, Pat," Ryan interjected, rubbing the sides of his forehead with the palms of his hands. Like breakers pounding mercilessly against a rocky shore, he could feel the first waves of tension pounding against the sides of his head. The cruel beast inside him would come now, no stopping it, and try to squeeze his brain until it cracked.

"Woo her later, to your heart's content, if that be your pleasure. This is a disaster. A bloody disaster! We're ruined. *Finished...*"

Dowlin again ignored Ryan's bluster. Ryan's description of Shannon had been true: she was uncommonly beautiful, sensuous without effort and seemed full of fire. Ryan often liked to boast of her strong-will too and Dowlin hoped she had it now because he knew Ryan would need all of her strength.

"Ruined is it?" Dowlin asked him as he kept his eyes fixed on Shannon. "An Irishman ruined? Finished? What nonsense is this slippin' through yer teeth, hey? My *Gawd*, Luke, for such a smart fellow sometimes you talk like a bloody fool."

Dowlin's words had rolled off his tongue more harshly than he had intended. He instantly regretted them. He turned to find Ryan staring down at the ground.

"'Tis a setback to be sure, Luke," Dowlin continued with a softer voice but then quickly added a good measure of confidence in his tone. "But we're alive. You and me are free. We'll get ourselves another ship. True, the lads will do some time, but they won't be locked up all that long and can rejoin us later. You'll see, it'll all work out fine in the end, as smooth as that Chinese silk we sometimes haul over. It always does."

The situation seemed that simple to Dowlin. But for Ryan, things appeared far more complex - and grim.

Dowlin knew there was nothing more he could say or do. Ryan would simply need to stew for a time. He slapped the sides of his stomach and smiled at Shannon again.

"Dear lady," he asked in his easy, casual manner, "forgive my rudeness, but with all the hub-bub goin' on down at the waterfront this mornin' I missed breakfast. Could I trouble you for somethin', nothin' fancy mind you, just some scrap of food to tide me over 'til supper?"

She did not miss Dowlin's cue. "The both of you, come into the house," she commanded. "Let's think this matter through. Every problem has a solution to it. I believe, Mr. Ryan, you told me that once..."

"Aye," Dowlin agreed with a nod, "I've heard him say those very same words myself, dear lady." He looked over at Ryan with a boyish grin. "By the way Luke, have you taken to bathin' in yer clothes or is this some new high fashion? Yer all wet lad, soaked through-and-through."

Ryan ignored him with a grunt.

"Ah, there's a story there, Patrick," Shannon offered with a smile.

"No doubt. No doubt, thar is Shannon. I'd love to hear about it sometime over a good bottle of wine..."

Shannon led the two men into the kitchen and fixed each a plate.

Then she set out three tall glasses on the table and poured a generous measure of whiskey into each as the mariners took seats.

Depressed and angry, Ryan pushed his plate away and ate nothing. He stared out the kitchen window and lost himself in thought. His ship, his cargo, his crew, all in the hands of the hated British. What would he do now?

Dowlin took a long swallow of whiskey and began attacking his food with zeal, nodding his approval as he chewed.

"My God, Pat," Ryan suddenly blurted out, clearly annoyed. "How can you eat at a time like this?"

Dowlin shrugged. "Dunno. Because I'm hungry?"

Ryan shook his head in disgust and looked away. His friend was too carefree, too laid back at times. Dowlin needed to learn that the world was a serious and often cruel place.

Dowlin ignored him and turned his attention back to the food on his plate.

Leaning against a large cabinet for the water pump, Shannon folded her arms and studied Ryan as he sat, motionless, staring out at the empty fields behind the house. He looked like a man broken, defeated.

She felt helpless. She had come to know Ryan's moods, but this was something new. This was something dark and unfathomable. She could sense the despair building up inside of him, with a grip none too gentle, and her heart ached for him. But Ryan, she knew, didn't need her pity now. He needed her strength.

"Luke. *Luke!*" she finally said to break the silence. "What Patrick said is right. This isn't the end of the world."

She reached over and combed an unruly lock of hair off his forehead, then kissed him softly on the cheek when he didn't answer. "'Tis a setback only my love, as Patrick says. Listen well now my darling man. We'll begin anew. We're young and strong and you have a substantial amount of money on account tucked away. Your connections in France and here are all still in place. The organization you've built is intact. Losing a ship was bound to happen someday. Look upon it as the cost of doing business, that's all."

Dowlin chuckled as he bit into a slice of fresh ham. "My *love* is it?"

he asked with a wink towards Shannon and poked Ryan playfully in the ribs. "And just what manner of business have the two of you been up to way out here in the backwoods if I may ask? Country folk always did have their own peculiar ways about doin' things I suppose. Well, once we're back in business, the smugglin' business that is, I think I'll need to keep a closer eye on the two of you."

Lost to his brooding, Ryan said nothing.

Dowlin took another sip of his whiskey. "Humph! I mine as well be talkin' to the wall. How do you suffer him, Shannon? The man is cold Irish through and through…"

"He is a man of many fine qualities and well worth the effort," she offered in a quiet voice, running her fingers through Ryan's long, wavy hair.

"Aye, no doubt he is. And tho' the gods don't hand out their gifts to us poor mortals all at once, this man of yours has many, more than most, and is as sly as the good Lord makes 'em. I'll grant you that much. None more clever than this brigand, I'll tell you plainly."

She smiled sweetly at Dowlin and nodded. "That is what I hear, Mr. Dowlin. I wonder though - idle boastfulness, or is it true what they say about this man, about this man who commands the elusive Shadowmen? Either way, it would appear now that he'll have to prove himself."

"Excuse me," Ryan said crossly, in no mood for playfulness. "I need to walk." He stood and moved towards the kitchen's back door.

Shannon nervously watched him through the window head into the fields, unsure of what to do.

Dowlin set his fork down. "Shannon, go after him. Talk some sense into that thick, Irish skull of his. He'll listen to you."

"I, I don't know, Patrick. I've never seen him like this before."

"I have. Trust me. Go, go and talk to him now. Oh, he'll listen to me eventually, but anythin' I say to him will take longer to sink in than whatever you say."

"Perhaps you…"

"No," Dowlin interrupted, pausing to flash his brilliant smile at her. "You can reach him best. Besides, I haven't finished my meal yet. You've cast a spell over him my darlin' girl. I've seen that magic aura around him well enough these many months. Love I think some call it? Yer both very lucky to have found one another, I'd say."

She turned to him, smiled sweetly. "I'm so happy to finally make your acquaintance, Patrick. When Luke speaks about you, it is as if he is speaking about his own brother. It comforts me to know Luke has you as his friend." She reached down and kissed him on the forehead. "You're a good man, Patrick Dowlin."

Dowlin was beginning to feel the whiskey's magic and the troubles of the world suddenly seemed modest. "Aye, so all the lasses tell me! Now go on with you. He'll be broodin' insufferably for weeks if we don't act quick. After livin' with that man all these years on one small, cramped ship after another, well I know his dark moods. No time to lose, Shannon..."

Shannon ran out into the fields after Ryan and took his arm. They walked arm-in-arm together for a long while without a word between them. Shannon was the first to break their silence.

"Luke... *Luke*," she repeated softly, her tone pleading after he failed to answer her. "I know you are hurting. But this melancholy is no good; it won't accomplish a thing - you must stop, now. You owe that much to Patrick and to your men. They need your strength, your leadership."

Ryan stared down at the ground as they continued walking. He spotted a small anthill, took his foot and kicked the dirt in around it. "Easier said than done, my sweet Shannon. It's finished."

"Finished is it?" she asked in a biting voice. She grabbed his arm, stopped walking and looked at him with eyes filled with fire. She took him by the shoulders and shook him firmly. "I know you, Luke Ryan. I remember when, as a boy, you never let anyone get the better or you! It wasn't so long ago. At the school in Hackettstown, well I remember the day a bullyboy threatened to rob you, a boy a head taller than you. Threatened you with a good beating if you didn't hand over your money to him. He barred your way across the bridge to home. You tricked him - do you recall? You called out to someone behind the boy. You were callin' out to a ghost. There was no one else and as he turned to look, you pushed him over the bridge with all your might. Into the stream below he tumbled! You shamed him in front of all the other lads. That boy never gave you any grief again. If you couldn't win with muscle, you used your wits. The drunkard at Wexford - you didn't run - you fought! A man twice yer size. I've never seen you quit or run from anything. And you always came out all right. I know how proud and clever you are. I know, because that is why I fell in love with you those many years ago. And now the boy is a man, a fine, fine man, smart, shrewd and quick. A man with a good heart. A prince of a man. Yes. You are my Black Prince, noble and kind, but strong and free spirited."

"The Black Prince?"

"Of course. You remember the stories about the king's first knight, a great and fearless champion, when we were children?

"You should take care not to idolize me too much. I have many flaws..."

"Idolize? No. Love? Yes, even with all your flaws. Now my good man, my noble prince, the British have taken something that belongs to you, something precious to you and I say to you - *take it back!*"

Ryan stared at her dumbfounded, struggling to understand her words. He had never seen this side of her before. The sensitive, seductive woman who had ridden across the open fields so elegantly that morning and made tender love to him in the old barn was now a firebrand with an appetite for battle.

"Take it back, Shannon? How? There'll be armed guards on board the ship, the king's own men. If they haven't offloaded the cargo already, they will soon do so, an entire fortune lost. Even with the money I have set aside, I cannot cover such damages. The lads are certainly imprisoned and if they are being held at the *Black Dog* as Patrick suspects, well that place is like a small fortress. It would take an army to break them out of there and then where would we go - what would we do? Shannon, you're a smart, strong-headed woman to be sure. And I love you so. But such talk, while bold, seems foolish."

Her expression, like the sudden, unexpected shift in a sea wind, turned cold and severe. Another look Ryan had never seen from her before.

"Would you leave me in the *Black Dog* so easily? Shush, don't answer. I know that you would not. And I know how much you care about your ship and men."

"But..."

"But," she interrupted, in a voice ringing with power, "*take it back.*" She took his hands into her own. "Take it back with your own two hands if you have to. No good will come from wallowing in self-pity. True, the British have the muscle, so," she paused to tap him on the forehead, "you've got to use this."

"You're a wildcat today my dear Shannon. Fine words. But how can such a feat be done? Dowlin *thinks* he is the equal of ten Englishmen. And perhaps he is. But he and I are no match for a garrison of the king's marines."

A smile, a deliciously wicked smile, touched her lips; her green eyes sparkled with a curious gleam. Shannon preferred speaking in the refined speech of Ireland's upper class. Her father had sent her off at a young age to good schools for ladies in London for a time. But now she spoke more like her father, like Ryan when he wasn't *English*.

"I'll get you the men you need, good dependable lads. And I'll get you the arms and the money too. My father didn't survive this long in his business without having friends, friends who can be bought. I can get you into the *Black Dog*, have no doubts about that my dear man! Now, you start thinkin' of a plan to retake your ship after we have freed your lads out of jail. Then on to Dun Laoghaire you go to gather your other men."

She had piqued his curiosity. Still, Ryan shook his head no.

"Even so, Shannon. Let's suppose for a moment that we can break those good men out of jail and that we are able to retake the ship. That's only the half of it. We'll all be hunted down for our perfidies. 'Tis a hanging offense we're talking about. Don't you see? 'Tis not quite as easy as you imagined."

Shannon thought for a moment. She hadn't considered all the consequences and Ryan was right of course.

"Well," she replied firmly, "let me ask you plainly. Are you willin' to take on these risks for yourself?"

Ryan paused to consider her question and nodded. "Aye. Aye, I am."

"Then," she continued, "why not let your men make that same choice for themselves? My guess is, Captain, they will want to follow you if given the chance."

"It is starting to rain again," he offered, smiling.

"So it is," she replied cheerfully, relieved, confident that she had won him over.

"You're wrong about one thing tho'."

"How so?"

"That bully you spoke of?"

"Yes."

"He still gives me grief."

"Who? No! Pat?"

"Aye, the very same..."

They returned to the house arm-in-arm oblivious to the gentle rain and found Dowlin right where they had left him, leaning back in his chair and sipping whiskey.

He gave them a huge grin. Dowlin knew at once that Ryan's mood had changed and had changed for the better.

"Sweet *Jesus*, yer a sorceress Shannon. What did you do to him? I declare before all the saints in heaven, he looks like a new man! I see tho' that now you've both taken to wearin' wet clothes. You country folks sure keep some peculiar ways..."

"I'm usually a pretty fair judge of character," Shannon replied, smiling sweetly down at the handsome Irishman with the long, red hair, "and I'm goin' to like you very much Patrick Dowlin. This much I know..."

Dowlin laughed. "Feelin's is mutual my lady! Everyone likes old Patrick here!" He turned to Ryan. "And all these years and I thought I had the *gift* when it came to women - but, you've gone and outdone me, Luke. This young tigress of yers is a real prize. A treasure worth holdin' on to at any cost, I'd say."

"We have work to do," Ryan said briskly, "and little time in which to do it."

"Excellent!" Dowlin replied cheerfully. It was his captain speaking to him now and he was a happy man, confident that all would be well with the world again. He looked up at the ceiling. "To You all mighty Father, we pray: thank thee Lord for thy blessings; thank thee Lord for our rugged island and its bounty, for our fair and winsome women and for our plentiful beer and whiskey and, dear Father, might You bless us with the chance of cracking open a few English skulls? They'll not be missed. Hear our prayers oh Lord, grant us our wish - praise be to *Jesus!* Amen!"

"Why Patrick," said Shannon teasingly, "I would not have pegged you for a religious man."

"He's not," Ryan said dryly. "Let's go Pat before the Lord figures out where we are and smites us both!"

Dowlin drained his glass and belched. "Faithful Father Pat is one step behind you…"

It was a night to warm the heart of any thief. No moon cast its pale glow to safely speed the night traveler along his way; no friendly face could be found out on Dublin's streets and alleys. A thick sea mist, rolling in off the bay, moved slowly over the city, covering it like a blanket. And then it began to drizzle, a good piece of luck, keeping all but a few stout Dubliners indoors.

Near the heart of Dublin is a section of the city known as New Hall Market, but there is nothing new or clean about New Hall. It is a dirty, unwholesome place known for its many meat markets and unsavory business establishments where the air is perpetually poisoned by the sickening stink of decay. Cutting through the center of New Hall is Cook Street, with its rows of taverns like the *Old Robin Hood*, the *Sign of the Harp*, *The Sun*, *Baggot's Tavern*, *The Ship Tavern*, *The New Struggler* and, across from *The New Struggler*, its nemesis, the *Struggler*. And just off Cook Street, standing between Wormwood Gate and Newgate, was an unremarkable, stone tower with iron-barred windows known by the locals as the *Black Dog*.

The *Black Dog* was an old building with some history. Legend has it that during the reign of James I, outlaw priests had used a backroom of the castle to secretly celebrate Mass. And after the priests left, the building had come to be known as *Browne's Castle*, named after the building's most famous proprietor, Richard Browne. Browne had been the Lord Mayor of Dublin in 1614 and 1615, and then again in 1620, and had used the castle throughout his mayoralty as offices for his administration. A few years later a man named Barton bought the property and converted the castle into an inn, renaming it the *Black Dog* from the sign of the Talbot or hound. But in 1661, after Barton told some of his customers that "the Earl of Drogheda is a cheating knave," and expressing his opinion that none of the Lords of Ireland were any better, the Lords of Ireland had Barton arrested and incarcerated for his insult. The Sheriff of Dublin then appropriated Barton's inn, turned it into a jail and renamed it Marshalsea Prison. But that name never really took. Dubliners stubbornly continued calling the old castle the *Black Dog*.

With faces covered in black soot, and wearing dark handkerchiefs over their noses, Ryan and Dowlin, together with their six men from Dun Laoghaire and another ten burly O'Keeffe men, crouched low against a brick wall inside a dark alley off Wormwood. And there they waited patiently for the signal. The Irishmen were heavily armed with pistols, knives and swords, all supplied by Shannon.

Wearing a dark hooded cloak, Shannon stood at a side entrance of the *Black Dog* and pounded against a large wooden door until someone cracked it open, just wide enough, to let her and one of her father's men slip inside. A moment later, she reappeared in the alley waving a lantern back and forth, the signal to move. Ryan and his men rushed the door.

Once inside, the Irishmen found a bald man, of immense weight, slumped over a table near the castle's side door. Shannon stood triumphantly over the sleeping giant, her arms akimbo, and tossed a set of keys over to Ryan. The jailer had been paid a handsome sum for taking a bump on the head.

"You lads ought to be able to handle things from here," she

whispered with a proud smile, obviously enjoying herself. "I've had my bit of fun. If you *men* think you can manage the rest by yerselves without a woman's help, I'll be goin' home now to read a good book in a hot tub. And Patrick - I'd be much indebted to you if you could see Luke returned to me whole and unharmed after things quiet down..."

"You have my word on it dear lady. All the whiskey I can drink and p'haps an introduction to one or two of yer lady friends in return?"

"Done."

Still trying hard to shake off the image of Shannon resting in a tub, Ryan kissed her roughly on the lips and sent her home. And then 18 men, with torches and weapons in hand, made their way down the jail's dark corridors, through its stone passageways covered in a slick, brown slime, determined to find their brothers. The putrid stench of sweat and raw sewage hung heavy in the air. The Black Dog was a disagreeable, depressing hole. It was meant to be - such places are good for breaking men's spirits.

Along the way, the Irishmen overpowered, gagged and bound three more guards before they found the rooms holding the king's newest guests down in the jail's cellar. More good luck, Ryan's men were in two adjacent cells.

Dowlin unlocked the door of the first cell, crammed with men and women, mostly thieves and prostitutes, sleeping on the stone floor, and spotted Macatter snoring away in one corner. He woke Macatter up with a poke in the ribs and hearty laugh. "Get yer lazy arse up, Ed! I can see the king's accommodations here are most splendid, but p'haps you would care to favor Luke and me with the pleasure of yer company - outside?"

Startled, Macatter jumped to his feet and smiled once he understood. Dowlin then quickly moved around the cell, shaking and kicking the rest of the crew awake, leaving the civilians to their sleep. Ryan went into the next cell and did the same.

"Lads," Ryan whispered to his men after they had all assembled in the corridor, "gather around. Not much time. We've come to free you. I plan to take back what is ours."

"I don't have to be asked twice," Macatter volunteered wearily, rubbing the sleep out of his eyes. "Let's get crackin' boys and get the devil out of this stinkin' shithole before we catch the gaol fever!"

Everyone started pressing forward until Ryan held up his hands and stopped them.

"Wait, Edward, lads, not so fast. Listen well now. If you stay here, you'll be charged with smugglin' and that carries a short sentence: a month or two, six at the most. Not much to it. A short haul any of you could do standin' on your head, aye, unless you get the fever. Leave with me now and, well, you'll be fugitives. Worse, anyone caught with me most likely will be hanged for treason or piracy because this very night we go to retake the ship. Think on it for a bit lads. Dangerous, uncharted waters ahead - maybe shoals to wreck your lives on. Any man unwilling is free to stay behind, do his time. There'll be no hard feelin's."

As men looked around, searching the faces of friends to see which way they might go, Kelly reached for one of the four pistols tucked inside Dowlin's belt. He didn't need to think anything over. "I'm not wastin' anymore time talkin'," he told Ryan. "The choice is plain enough. With yer permission, sir, John, Tim, let's move! Come what will, we're with ya, Capt'n."

Every man quickly murmured his approval. It was unanimous.

Ryan nodded. "It is settled then. We must move with haste now, my good lords of the ocean..."

The small band of outlaws quickly marched in single file down the jail's grimy corridors and quietly made good their escape into the black night. Ryan was the last to leave the jail but, before he stepped outside, he turned to face a small crowd of prisoners who had been following close behind.

"If you have any friends or family in here," he told them and tossed the ring of keys over to the lead man, "Christmas is early this year!"

Once they were all safely well away from the *Black Dog*, Ryan sent O'Keeffe's men home and then led his Shadowmen on foot down to the coast, south of Dublin Bay, where two good-sized launches loaded down with additional arms and ammunition were waiting for them. More of Shannon's good work.

They only had a few hours to work while men slept peacefully with little care for nightwalkers. Ryan divided his Shadowmen into two teams, with Macatter and Kelly leading one team and Dowlin and Weldin leading the other, and then watched his men pile into the boats and row hard towards Poolbeg.

The first part of his plan was elegantly simple. Ryan figured there would be no more than a dozen soldiers on board *Friendship* with only the night watch, two or three guards, standing on deck. The king's men would never expect a bold assault against the king's property right in front of the king's own customhouse. Surprise was the key to the Irishmen's success.

Ryan rode on to Rush to oversee the new arrangements for landing the ship's cargo and to recruit more hands, men not afraid to mix it up with the king's men. Shannon had already sent word ahead and Ryan knew where to go and whom to see. The master schemer needed the additional muscle for the second part of his plan: *Friendship* would need a much larger crew if she was to sail the waves as a *ship of war*...

There on the River Liffey, in a part of Dublin known as Poolbeg, stood a redbrick, three-story building known simply as the King's Customhouse. At one time, it had been a handsome structure, but now, after suffering from years of neglect, there was talk that the building would soon be demolished in favor of something grander. Still, the street level arcade, with its narrow arched entrances, 15 to a side and made from white cut stone, had retained a certain elegance. And then again, more than one soot-stained window dotting the upper two stories had a missing pane or two patched over with boards and much of the woodwork around the elevated dormers, one for every third window, had rotted away. Overlooking the water on the building's north face, and enclosed in a triangular entablature with projecting cornices, stood a fine clock tower with the empire's ubiquitous red, white and blue Union Jack fluttering in the breeze. Through this portal, according to the law of the land, according to the laws of an English king, all imports and exports to and from Dublin were to pass - with the appropriate taxes collected.

And moored peacefully next to the King's Customhouse stood a fine looking cutter, sleek, black and handsomely built with a rich cargo of contraband on board, waiting to be off-loaded in the morning. Two armed guards from His Majesty's Revenue Service stood on duty on her well-scrubbed decks, one at the bow and the other at the stern. Only two. But at night's darkest hour, neither man could resist sleep's gentle embrace and stood at their posts, dozing, while a dozen of their comrades snored peacefully in their hammocks below deck - oblivious to the history about to descend upon them. None of the king's men in the customhouse, or on board the cutter, heard the muffled oars of two boats drawing near.

Like cats on the prowl, Macatter and his men, silently, nimbly, climbed up the stern barefoot and waited at the aft rail for Dowlin and his assault team to board the cutter at the bow. Dowlin had to suppress a giggle as he watched his men, wearing bandanas and earrings, armed with cutlasses, knives and muskets, shinny up the anchor cable, gingerly step up on the gunwale and fan out along outer bulwark with stealth.

"Damn, if we don't all look like real pirates," Dowlin whispered to Weldin, who was squatting low against the bowsprit next to him.

Weldin rolled his eyes. He did not share Dowlin's enthusiasm for danger. He knew he would only feel better about the day if, by the end of it, they were not all gutted by bayonet or hanging by their necks from a yardarm.

But Dowlin was having too much fun and wasn't about to let anything spoil it. He shrugged off Weldin's indifference and carefully eased himself down on the deck. He was the first to board their cutter, the first to draw his pistol.

With both assault teams in position, Macatter and Dowlin nodded to each other. The Irishmen pounced on their targets simultaneously, clubbing both guards over the head with just enough force to subdue them. The two Englishmen fell with barely a groan and were quickly bound and gagged. Ryan had given strict orders that no one was to be killed or seriously injured. He had no wish to add murder to their list of crimes.

With the upper deck secured, Dowlin and his men quietly began to ready the ship to sail while Macatter took his team below to find the officer-in-charge. They found the man fast asleep in Ryan's cabin. That did not sit too well with the Irishmen and, none too gently, they startled the king's good servant out of his slumber by binding his hands and stuffing a rag into his mouth. The Englishman's eyes bulged with terror as his kidnappers hustled him topside and forced him to sit down next to the two unconscious guards, whom he presumed to be dead.

Macatter left the rest of the king's soldiers sleeping in their hammocks. They could do no harm.

Ryan's men now controlled the ship. But victory was not theirs, not yet. Their cutter was still secured to the king's dock and, to the east, the first sliver of silver light was just beginning to slice open the dark horizon. The dawn of a new day, a promise of new beginnings, yes, but the Irishmen had to hurry. Time was not their friend.

But the plucky Irishmen need not have worried. From the very beginning, Good Fortune, intrigued by Ryan's audacious plan, had smiled on the Irishmen. Owing Good Fortune a favor, the sea unloosed a thin, gray mist to hide the lawless Irishmen from any unfriendly eyes. And then West Wind, wishing to please Good Fortune for her own purposes, sent the small band of fugitives a favorable, hearty breeze, a parting gift, to speed them along their way.

And as the mist thickened, and the winds freshened, Macatter and Dowlin exchanged proud glances - Ryan's plan was going to succeed. Macatter had had his doubts at first but had held his peace, assuming that the old man himself, O'Keeffe, had sanctioned Ryan's risky scheme and Macatter would never do anything to disappoint that good man. Like Weldin, he had expected to be caught and promptly hanged for their treachery. But the English would be deprived of that pleasure on this fine day and his nervous stomach began to settle. Dowlin, on the other hand, had never had any doubts, none whatsoever.

Only a 1,000-pound anchor and several mooring lines held *Friendship* fast to Ireland now and Macatter gave the order to cut the ship's cable, cast off the mooring lines and set the topsails. No one had to be told a second time what to do. Men scrambled, some up into the rigging to drop sail and others to slip the lines. Once freed from her moorings, the Liffey's muddy waters gently grabbed the rogue cutter and pulled her out into the bay.

And as the wind caught her canvas, as the ship began to move under her own power, the English soldiers below deck began to stir. One-by-one they made their way up the companionway ladder to investigate matters topside. As each man stepped out on deck, he was greeted rudely by armed Irishmen, bound, gagged and forced to sit against the bulwarks with their lieutenant.

Macatter then gave the order to drop the mainsail. The cutter responded smartly, lurched forward with increasing speed and quickly closed the distance with the open sea. But no man raised a cheer, not yet. They had one last obstacle to clear.

Anchored at the entrance of Dublin Bay sat a matched pair of floating batteries with heavy cannon. The impressive barges had been towed into place and anchored there a year before in early 1778 to protect Dublin against a possible French invasion following France's declaration of war against England.

Each Irishman held his breath as they drew closer to the king's powerful cannon. And just as their ship began slipping past the nearest barge, Dawn, in glittering saffron robes, wielded her great scepter high, sending shafts of golden light streaking across a steel-gray sky.

Dowlin quietly spread the word: tend to your duties, stay calm, ignore the British.

Bleary-eyed sentries numb from chill saw the dawn and saw the black cutter too. They squinted against the morning light to watch her men spreading out more canvas to catch the sea's hardy wind. They watched the curious vessel sail past their heavy cannon within easy range, close enough to make out the faces of her crew. But the sentries stood idly by, indifferent, and let the handsome cutter pass without challenge - even though the cutter's master failed to give the proper signal. Civilian merchantmen routinely forgot the code. The duty of the king's soldiers was to watch the east, to guard against England's enemies who might come by sea - not by land. And then the cook emerged and started passing around hot tea and warm biscuits with jam for breakfast...

Once the Irishmen were well beyond range of Dublin Harbor's big guns, and they could find no ships coming after them in hot pursuit, they veered northward, sailing around Howth, and made their way to Rush with a good, stiff wind filling the cutter's sails. And at midmorning, with grins all around, the Irishmen forced their English cousins, their prisoners, up on their feet, removed their gags and unbound their hands.

The English officer stared defiantly at Macatter. "You're all damned!" he cried out belligerently in a shrill voice. "I'll have the pleasure of seein' each of you hanged from the gallows for this treasonous offense!"

"And who, pray tell, are you?" Macatter asked softly.

"The name is Draper, Lieutenant Daniel Draper, and you are addressing an officer of the king."

"Oh? And what king might that be? There are so many..."

"You mock me, sir! His most royal majesty King George, of course, as you damn well know!"

Christopher Kelly, who never took kindly to threats of any kind, moved over to Draper's side, towering over him like a mountain overlooking a puny hill.

Draper looked up into the giant's craggy face and swallowed hard.

Kelly forced a smile, and not a friendly smile, in return. "Nothin' pleasant to say, my good man, the king's good servant, on this glorious, spring mornin'?"

The lieutenant said nothing.

Kelly turned to look at his shipmates. "Lads, I think we had best stuff a gag back in this one! He's blabbering gibberish!"

The Irishmen roared and cheered and gave approving nods all around.

Draper's eyes darted nervously back and forth, there was no escape. "This sordid business will come to naught. Do what you will *Irish* - you'll all hang in the end for you insults against the king..."

Macatter took a step closer to the lieutenant. "I you have any wits about you, you'll mind yer tongue, sir. This here is a troubled crew, touched in the head from their time in that filthy Dublin jail of yers. I'd tread lightly now if I was *you*."

The Englishman's left eye began twitching. He swallowed hard again.

"What do you intend to do with us?" Draper demanded, summoning up his last bit of courage, certain he was about to die.

"Do? Why, sir, you and yer men filched our fine ship, took it rudely too I might add," Macatter said playfully. "So I'm guessin' yer all polished, first-rate seamen. Why else would you have need of a splendid vessel like this? Aye, yer all good sailors no doubt and itchin' to do some sailin'! What a fine day it is for sailin' too. But don't you fret none. I know just the thing."

Macatter turned to look at his men. "Let's see how well these English dogs can row! Over the side with them, lads!"

The Irishmen cheered and began muscling the Englishmen towards the rail.

Draper, a soldier, not a sailor, looked apprehensively down at the two launches in tow, the same boats the Irishmen had used to retake *Friendship* earlier that morning. And then he looked towards land. It looked a long way off and the sea seemed a bit angry now with white caps and spray.

"You would be wise not to compound today's skullduggery with murder. I'll risk neither life nor limb in those feeble craft! We're too far out, damn your eyes! You'll put us ashore, or, by God, sir, I'll show -"

With no affection in his heart for any man serving in the king's revenue service - a service that had taken his ship and hunted more than one of his friends down - Macatter, his eyes full of threat, went nose-to-nose with the Englishman. "You can swim back to England for all I care - yer choice..."

Draper tried to hide his shaking hands as he surveyed the Irishmen arrayed against him. They were all smiles, but a rough looking lot just the same, and he was certain their hearts were filled with evil. He glanced over the rail again, stared at the boats bobbing up and down on the briny sea, and considered his options. Finally, he looked at his men, nervous and scared, and gave the order to board the boats.

Among the Englishmen, there were no slackers that day; not one man dawdled. They quickly climbed over the rail and scrambled down the cutter's side and into the boats before the Irishmen had a change of heart.

Draper, the last man to step over the rail, looked back at the Irishmen and shook his fist. He still had his pride. "You're outlaws! You'll all hang, I say! P'haps even drawn and quartered in front of London Tower, a spectacle to please the crowd! There'll be no place for you to hide. No place for you to run. Expect no mercy from the king for this piracy! And rest assured, old Mr. Draper here will be there by God to see it all! To see each one of you brought to justice. Then we'll see - oh, yes, oh, yes - then we'll see, when each of you dances the *Marshal's Dance* at the end of a rope, who's smilin' on that *grim day!*"

Dowlin, who had been sitting against the aft cargo grate with his back to the crowd, having ignored all the lively banter until now, had heard enough. He set aside his whittling knife and block of wood, stood and walked over to Draper.

"I see yer mum bore herself a moron for a son!" he said calmly, looking down at Draper's men in the boats. "Makin' threats against men far stronger than you - blitherin' idiot! It'll take a far better man than you to bring me down. Hang me? Draw and quarter me will you? Ha! Off you go now, you spineless slug. Another word and I'll throw you over. Lad's, perhaps we should run out the guns for some early mornin' target practice! We'll see how well you boast then from the bottom of the sea, Mr. Draper, as the fish feast on yer scrawny flesh!"

Dread seized each and every English heart. The red-maned maniac impressed them all as a very dangerous man, as a man who knew how to kill and who perhaps even enjoyed it. Draper quickly made his way down the ship's side and, after taking his place at the rudder, his men quickly pushed off and pulled hard at the oars. To the relief of Draper's men, their lieutenant said no more.

Chapter Nineteen
Aye, that's the Plan

By late morning the outlaw cutter reached the quiet waters around the small island of Lambey, Old Norse for *lamb island*, just a league or two off Rush. Soon after the cutter's crew furled sail and dropped anchor in Lambey's small harbor, a fishing trawler, flying a large, green flag - the signal for the 'all clear' - came around the island's leeward side to greet the Irishmen.

And standing tall on the trawler's bowsprit was Ryan, holding a jib line with one hand and waving his French cocked hat wildly in the air with the other. His Irishmen lined themselves up along the rails, waved and smiled back at him triumphantly.

As the trawler's crew furled sail, and her master carefully eased his vessel up alongside the cutter, Kelly cried out: "Three cheers lads for our wily Capt'n Ryan!"

The cutter's men answered Kelly with one booming voice. They erupted in unison with a hearty: "*Hip-hip-hooray! Hip-hip-hooray! Hip-hip-hooray!*"

The trawler's men lowered three boats in the water. Ryan took command of the lead boat and was soon alongside the cutter, bolting up the Jacob's ladder in a handsome set of new clothes with twenty new men behind him. His Shadowmen gathered around him and took turns shaking his hand or patting him on the back, every man immensely proud of what they had all accomplished together.

Kelly wrapped his arms around Ryan and gave him a great bear hug. "Damn if you haven't gone and done given us a fine, fine yarn to tell our grandchildren someday! By *Jesus*, well done, sir! Well done!"

Dowlin laughed. "Just so! A story for the kiddies sitting around the fire and the only yarn you'll ever be tellin' yer grandchildren, Christopher Kelly, with any truth to it!"

Men roared. Hearts were light.

Dowlin held up his hands. "Now lads, don't be givin' our good

Capt'n here too much praise. His part in all of this was but a trifle. You see, thar's this certain Irish lass - I won't try to describe her to you 'cause you'll just think I'm exaggerating. But I swear she's like an angel. Luke has her hidden away in Kenure. She helped us greatly and deserves most of the credit for your freedom!"

"Right you are, Patrick!" Ryan readily agreed with a broad smile. "We do indeed have some good friends in high places - and with some interesting resources at their beck and call. And the lady, Mr. Dowlin is referring to, is far prettier to look at than any of your ugly mugs I might add! Why I left her warm affections in peaceful, quaint Kenure, for the likes of any of you, I'll never know…"

He paused for a moment, allowing the laughter to die down, and placed his hands on his hips. "Well now lads, it warms my heart to see each of you safe and sound! My compliments to all of you on a job well done! No one hurt too badly I trust, Mr. Macatter?"

"Nothin' that won't heal in a few days, sir," Macatter answered with a mischievous grin. "A bump or two on the noggin and some wounded, English pride p'haps…"

Ryan nodded, relieved that no one had been killed or seriously injured. That would have complicated matters for the Irishmen. He spun around and did a 360 degree sweep of the deck. It was good to see the men, *his* men, in such high spirits. Barely 24 hours before, he had seen defeat in these same faces in the dark corridors of the Black Dog.

"Gather around, lads; you new men too. Let's weigh things out. Now's the time to think things through with great care, time for each man to set his own course and say his farewells to his brothers, or hold fast and see this journey to the end - whatever that may be."

"Another speech, I fear?" Dowlin asked playfully.

"Aye, Mr. Dowlin, brace yourself," Ryan answered with a grin. "And do try to stay awake this time."

Except for Mulvany, who scrambled up the ratlines and up into the masthead to keep a sharp eye out for intruders, the men formed a circle around Ryan and stood quietly by.

"Hear me now you proud sons of Ireland. Listen to what I have to say, listen well. No doubt the alarm has been sounded at Poolbeg. By now even the king's royal revenue agents will realize that they're missing one ship and a crew!"

Men giggled, hooted and applauded.

Ryan raised his arms high, calling for silence. "Now lads, the past twenty-four hours have been very exciting. You have accomplished no small feat and Good Fortune has smiled broadly down on us all. And I am proud of each man here. I say this to you new men too because you've decided to cast your lot with us even though we're in a bit of a jam here. We can't go back to smuggling. That game is finished, at least for a time. We've kidnapped the king's men, high-jacked his ship and stolen his cargo..."

"Aye!" interrupted Weldin proudly. "And all in the span of only one day! *Jesus*, think what we could do with two or three days if we really put our backs into it, Luke!"

Even Ryan chuckled. But then his eyes went cold, his tone turned sober.

"I shudder to think, Mr. Weldin. But lads, we're wanted men now, criminals on the run, not just petty thieves, but felons, and we'll be hunted down and slaughtered for certain, every one of us, if we ignore the stark truth of our situation. 'Tis a very big sea to be sure, but the British have too many ships and men to count and it's only a matter of time before we bump into something we can't outrun. Death at sea if we fight or swinging from an English gallows with nooses around our necks if we're caught. That's the bitter fact of the matter. So, what to do? What to do indeed?"

"No doubt," offered Dowlin softly, "you have a plan, Luke. You always do."

Ryan patted Dowlin on the shoulder and then walked around the circle to look into every face. "Well, our situation is precarious. I'll tell you how I see things, how I view our choices. As I said, we can't go on smuggling any more. We've insulted British pride and the Royal Navy will scour the oceans looking for this ship and her crew, from sunrise to sunset, from east to west. No place to hide. And there'll probably be bounty money on our pretty heads too, to attract murdering thugs to the fox hunt. We can't look to our friends in Dublin or Rush, we've caused too much of a ruckus. We're trouble. We could try our luck at piracy, which, I'll tell you plainly, is not for me. We could abandon *Friendship*, perhaps sell her, divvy up the proceeds and scatter to the four winds, trust to hope that the British forget about us. 'Tis been my experience tho' that British law has a long memory. We could cross the Atlantic, sail to America. That might be the way for us, but, we'd still be in hostile waters and I haven't a clue what work we might find there..."

He paused for a moment to let his words sink in. "Hm. Or... Or we could stay right where we are and try our hand at - *privateering.*"

Dowlin was the first to take the bait and began scratching his chin, as if that might somehow help him focus better. "Privateering? Privateering for who, Luke?"

All eyes turned to Ryan. He smiled, a confident smile, yes, the kind of smile a man makes when he knows something, some secret, not known by any other. "There's a nice little war goin' on across the ocean, or hadn't you heard about it you big oaf? I've heard talk in Dunkirk that the Americans have been looking to commission a privateer or two. Never paid such talk much mind before. Never had any cause to."

"Fight for the Americans?" Dowlin asked incredulously. "From France?"

Ryan nodded.

"Aye, of course," Dowlin said and slapped his forehead. "We'll sign up with the American Navy and all become patriots of the revolution by thunder! Why think of the enormity of it all. We can plunder English ships, kill Englishmen and be paid handsomely for it! It's inspired Luke. Truly. Well, I've always said that thinkin' is what you do best. That brain of yers never seems to stop. 'Tis an excellent plan, worthy of an Irishman!"

"Beggin' yer pardon, sir," interrupted Macatter. "But how does this solve our problem if we're caught?"

"Ah, don't you see Ed," Ryan answered with a raised eyebrow and a sly smile. "The beauty of it is that with an American commission in our pocket we'll be American subjects and soldiers of the rebellion. If we're caught the English will be forced to treat us as prisoners-of-war. They won't be able to prosecute us as criminals! Well, that's my theory anyway."

Macatter tugged thoughtfully at his beard's black and gray whiskers. "Aye," he mumbled to himself, still deep in thought. "Aye indeed! 'Tis a good plan as Pat said! A good plan indeed! 'Tis a bit of a stretch p'haps, but it just might work."

"Well lads," answered Ryan, "it must work. Nothing is for certain in this world, no guarantees, but unless somebody has a better plan..."

"But if we're caught," asked Kelly, "and the British crush the American rebels, won't we still all hang for treason?"

"That is a very real possibility, Chris," Ryan answered. "But the British would need to execute thousands and I can't see Parliament or the English people having the stomach for that. Maybe the ringleaders, yes, but not all the prisoners of war. This, of course, is only speculation on my part."

"No Englishman is goin' to catch us anyways," Dowlin offered smugly. "This is my absolute word on it: this lovely racehorse of ours can outrun anythin' cuttin' through the ocean's blue waves. Especially with this crew. We have the fastest ship and the best men. The only wild card is lady luck. My thievin' instincts tell me your plan is a fine one. Should we run into some difficulty along the way tho'..."

Ryan had anticipated Dowlin's thoughts. "Quite right, Mr. Dowlin. Quite right. We're going to need something bigger than these four-pounders and the cutlasses tucked inside your belts there. We'll see what we can do about that once we return to France."

"Count me in, Luke," Macatter offered somberly. And then, in a voice punctuated with a bit of drama, added, "I'm with you and I'll see it through, through thick or thin, and to the very finish too by God!"

"And me," Dowlin chimed in, grinning from ear to ear. "Count me in too. I've followed you to every ship, went wherever you went, Luke. Always been good for me. Besides, you'll be needin' a street brawler at your side, someone who's cocksure of himself with proven skills to humble British arrogance!"

The three sons of the Kelly clan nodded their approval next.

"No sense," the eldest Kelly offered, "in lettin' Dowlin have all the fun. Here are three more souls who'll stand tall with you, sir."

Ryan nodded in turn to Macatter, Dowlin and Kelly and looked around. "What say the rest of you lads?" he asked. "Weigh it carefully now. No shame to any man who walks away. I have the trawler standing by to return any man who doesn't have his heart in this back to Rush. I have money with me too and will pay whatever is owed to you right now. If you decide to go back, you can say we forced you to come along with us until you managed to steal a boat and make good your escape."

But not one man budged that day. Not one heart had any desire to return to Ireland. Ryan's plan had inspired them all.

"Very well then. But once we sail, there'll be no turning back. All in favor, say aye."

And the crew roared back with one voice: "AYE!"

"Aye, indeed..." Ryan repeated softly, quietly weighing the consequences of what they had done and what they were about to do. He took a deep breath. "Well then, it seems to me some oath of allegiance, a solemn pledge to bind us, one to the other, and spoken out loud for all to hear, is only fit and proper. Something simple. I thought of this: 'We serve this ship, and one another, faithfully, as brothers-in-arms, whatever the hazards, until we all agree to disband - or until death finds and keeps us.' What say you - do we make this solemn pledge to each other?"

The men of the cutter *Friendship*, every soul, nodded his approval, placed his hand over his heart and repeated Ryan's words out loud for all his brothers to hear. Of course, the fact that large, quick profits could be made from privateering was not lost on any man. A desire to fatten one's purse was common among sailors. Still, there were other ships to sail with, ships that paid well too. And with the war dragging on year after year and the supply of good seaman dwindling, a sailor could pick and choose his vessel. Tens of thousands of seamen around the world were flocking to sail on privateers. No, the Irishmen of the cutter *Friendship* served for more than just the promise of prize money. Each man gave his pledge because it was a privilege to serve with Luke Ryan. If they were going to risk life, limb or liberty for some remote cause being fought half a world away, it would be with someone they believed in, with someone they trusted.

Ryan, a happy man, bowed his head and smiled broadly and then leaned over the rail and waved the trawler off. "Mr. Macatter, I'll have us depart from these hostile waters with haste if you please."

"Aye, sir!" Macatter replied crisply, his deep, gravelly voice betraying just a hint of pride. "What's the Capt'n's pleasure?"

"Head south by south-east, the Welsh coast, Cardigan Bay to be precise. We'll land our cargo there. I've made arrangements with one of our competitors already to recover our freight later and return it to Rush at a better time. Handling the matter this way will cut into our profits some, but I don't want to tarry in these waters any longer. Good Fortune has been most kind to us this day. We should not impose upon her generosity further, lest we seem greedy and ungrateful."

"Cardigan Bay it is, sir. Mr. Weldin, Mr. Kelly, I'll have the reefs shaken out of her tops'ls, the gallants too, if you please. The wind is with us."

Weldin, Dowlin and the Irish giant went about breaking the men down into divisions and set them to work. Every man felt the excitement in the air. Every sailor moved with purpose.

"You there, Thomas," Macatter shouted down the deck after watching Conner for several minutes standing idly near the bow. "Looks like you need somethin' to do. We'll have no loafers on my watch! I'm in the mood for a tune. Sing us a song, man!"

"What kind of song would please the first officer on this fine day?" Conner shouted back.

"Bless me. Hm. How about a pirate shanty? Aye, that would do nicely."

"Very well, sir," Conner replied happily. "A pirate shanty it is then." He took a deep breath and began to sing out loudly:

> "*My boat's by the tower and my bark's on the bay*
> *And both must be gone at the dawn of the day*
> *The moon's in her shroud and to light thee afar*
> *On the deck of the daring's a love-lighted star.*"

And the crew answered him with:

"So wake, lady wake, I am waiting for thee; oh this night or never my bride
thou shalt be!"

And Conner replied:

"Forgive me rough mood unaccustomed to sue
I woo not perhaps as you landlubbers do
My voice is attuned to the sound of the gun
That startles the deep when the combat's begun."

"So wake, lady wake, I am waiting for thee; oh this night or never my bride
thou shalt be!"

"The Frenchman and Don will flee from our path
And the Englishman cower below at our wrath
And our sails shall be gilt in the gold of the day
And the sea robins sing as we roll on our way."

"So wake, lady wake, I am waiting for thee; oh this night or never my bride
thou shalt be!"

"A hundred shall serve - the best of the brave -
And the chief of the thousand shall kneel as thy slave
And thou shalt reign queen and thy empire shall last
'til the black flag by inches is torn form the mast."

"So wake, lady wake, I am waiting for thee; oh this night or never my bride thou
shalt be..."

After clearing Lambey Island and pointing their cutter's nose east,
the fugitives found themselves in Welsh waters before morning and were
soon hauling their valuable cargo onto a desolate stretch of beach
between the Welsh towns of Barmouth and Cardigan. With no barges or
teams of men to help them, the task of transporting hundreds of

hogsheads, crates and boxes ashore using the ship's boats was long and tedious. The Irishmen buried their cargo behind the dunes before nightfall and left behind a crude wooden cross, with green ribbon wrapped around it, to mark the site.

The mariners then weighed anchor and set a course for northern France. They left the past behind them towards, they prayed, a better future - and a chance for high adventure.

Ryan and Dowlin stood side-by-side quietly against the ship's rail, watching the blue waves of a boundless sea roll on and on. Ten days out from Poolbeg found the Irishmen in the middle of the Celtic Sea enjoying fair weather.

Despite their differences, Ryan and Dowlin had come to know the mind and mood of the other well and could stand comfortably together for long hours without a word passing between them. Ryan was the thinker, careful, deliberate, rarely acted in haste. Dowlin more impulsive, sometimes even rash, was always quick to act. Ryan strived to be polished; Dowlin took pleasure in being crass. And where Ryan was ambitious, never losing sight of the horizon that lay ahead, Dowlin contented himself with whatever the day brought him and never worried about tomorrow. Still, the friendship, even kinship, that bound them had grown stronger and richer with each passing year.

Ryan was the first to break their silence. He cleared his throat and glanced askew at Dowlin.

"Luke?"

"Lieutenant Dowlin, I'll have this ship cleared for action if you please."

Startled, Dowlin quickly scanned the horizon in every direction, searching for trouble - but his keen eye saw nothing but open sea. He turned to look at Ryan, puzzled.

"You want the lads to run out the big guns, Luke?" he asked grinning. "You know somethin' the rest of us knuckleheads don't?"

But even before could Ryan answer, Dowlin caught the look in Ryan's eyes, a look Dowlin knew all too well. Ryan wasn't fooling around. Ryan had assumed the role, the aura, of superior officer again and was addressing a subordinate, not a friend. Over the years Dowlin had learned to recognize the difference. His smile vanished.

"Mr. Dowlin, we are wasting time, precious time. I'll have the four-pounders manned and the swivel guns mounted - *now* if you please, now. Every man to his station!"

Dowlin straightened his shoulders, snapped to attention and touched the brim of his hat. The transformation was seamless. He was no longer a civilian. He was a professional soldier once again.

"Aye, aye, sir! Straight away!"

Lieutenant Dowlin gave the order to the boatswains' mate to pipe the ship to quarters. Some men were quick and some were slow. The new men awkwardly stood around with foolish expressions. Even Ryan's Irish veterans, his *Shadowmen*, stumbled about confused. Two years had passed since any man had heard a ship's war cry. The heavy guns were loaded haphazardly - or not at all - and no one thought to bring up the swivels stowed below.

Weldin, bubbling with excitement, hurried over to where Dowlin and Ryan were standing. "Pat, Luke, decks been cleared for action," he reported with a boyish grin. "All hands at quarters!"

"Lieutenant Weldin, you forget yourself, sir." Dowlin chided him, and none too gently. "You are reporting to the lord and master of this ship. This is Captain Ryan and you will address me as Lieutenant Dowlin and you will lose that silly, shit-eating smile, now..."

Confused and a bit hurt, Weldin turned to Ryan for help. But Ryan looked away, ignored him, and that confused him even more.

"Sure thing, Patrick, sorry, I mean Lieutenant Dowlin, *sir*. Capt'n Ryan, ship's ready for action. What are your orders, sir?"

"This ship is ready for action, is that so?" asked Ryan, still avoiding direct eye contact with Weldin. "Ahem. Well, we shall see about that, Mr. Weldin, we shall indeed see about that. In any case, in the future, you'll observe the formality of the proper chain of command when this ship has been cleared for action. *Kindly* make your report to the officer of the watch, not to me... if... you... please, sir. We're losing valuable time here Lieutenant and time is a precious commodity in war and not to be squandered."

Dowlin cringed at Ryan's use of the word *kindly*. Ryan used the word sparingly, to signal his displeasure.

Weldin felt the sting of Ryan's rebuke and winced. He had never seen this side of Ryan before and found it cold and unsettling. Red-faced, he turned to Dowlin and repeated his report all over again, though he knew not why because Dowlin had been standing right next to Ryan the whole time.

"Very well, Mr. Weldin," Dowlin replied evenly and turned to Ryan. "Sir, deck's been cleared for action. All hands at their stations. Yer orders, Capt'n?"

"The time, Mr. Dowlin, the time?"

Now it was Dowlin who turned red-faced, ashamed. Ryan's question was a subtle rebuke directed at *him*. As the officer of the watch it was his responsibility to time the quickness of the gun crews, to measure their efficiency at drill, as they scrambled to their battle stations and to report that time to the captain.

"My apologies, sir. I neglected to have a watch on me."

Ryan's mouth curled into a slight smile. He was having fun. He removed his pocket watch, the one with the gilt metal outer case covered in dark shagreen, the same one that he had given himself when he had first made lieutenant - a lifetime ago - and popped open the cover. He noted the number of minutes that had elapsed and snapped the case shut.

"Never mind. You'd only be embarrassed if you knew. At your pleasure, Mr. Dowlin, I'll have my four-pounders run out and the swivels mounted too. Swivels? Did I say swivels? Bless me, gentlemen. But I see no swivels on my deck. Not a single one. Do either of you? Perhaps my eyes are failing me or worse, I'm going senile. Dear me, but I thought this ship carried swivels..."

Weldin sheepishly looked down at his boots and wisely said no more.

Dowlin rolled his eyes. It was going to be a long day, a very long day.

Ryan sighed. "I blame myself, gentlemen. I blame myself for our laxness, not you. I am the captain of this ship after all. I shall endeavor to do better. My apologies. Mr. Weldin, please see to your gun crews."

Weldin raced down the deck towards the four-pounders with no clue what Ryan had in mind. They were out in the middle of nowhere with no ships in sight. And in his haste and confusion, the young lieutenant, with no military experience and flustered, still didn't think to send anyone below to retrieve the swivels.

Dowlin, on the other hand, understood Ryan's remarks all too well. His head was already spinning. He would set things right. Ryan was making a point for all to see.

The men of the *Friendship* could rightfully boast they were all first-rate sailors, even skilled soldiers, but without organization, without discipline, they were a poor fighting unit. Dowlin was already champing at the bit to remedy the awful deficiency in their training, a weakness that could get them all killed.

As Weldin gave the order to have the guns rolled out, Dowlin looked at Ryan cockeyed, waiting for his orders. But Ryan, rocking back and forth on his heels and looking out at sea, said nothing.

For a time the crew quietly stood by at their stations. And then there was whispering. Something was amiss on the quarterdeck.

Macatter, who had been sleeping below when the alarm sounded, just then scrambled up the companionway ladder, half-dressed, and hurried over to Ryan's side. "Trouble, Luke?"

"Aye," replied Ryan. "*Trouble...*"

Macatter nervously scanned the horizon. Kelly joined Macatter and Dowlin and the three officers followed Ryan as he made his way back to the ship's stern rail.

"Any time, Luke," Dowlin said with feigned impatience. "Any time now you can tell us why we're gettin' the lads all excited here in the middle of nowhere with only empty sea to stare at."

But Dowlin, an old hand at the bloody grind of battle, already knew the answer. His question was rhetorical, asked for both Macatter's and

Weldin's benefit, for the benefit of the inexperienced new men too - as well as for the veterans who had all grown soft.

Ryan took in the faces of his officers one-by-one and broke into a broad smile. "I do believe, Patrick James Dowlin, that all of this smooth and carefree living the past few years has turned your brain to mush."

Dowlin grinned. "Aye, sir. When we put ashore again at Dunkirk remind me to have a drink or two or even three to clear out all 'em cobwebs!"

Ryan, the crew watching him intently, shook his head amused and slapped Dowlin firmly on the back. "Pat, when we are all safely back in Dunkirk, there'll be plenty of drinks all around."

"On your account, of course?"

"Of course," Ryan replied and then raised his voice for all to hear. "Now gentlemen - Mr. Macatter, Mr. Weldin, Mr. Dowlin, Mr. Kelly - this vessel is a merchantman no longer. She's a ship of war. It's hardly too soon to start drilling the men in the art of battle. They're all good sailors. But look there - half of them don't have the slightest notion what they're supposed to be doing. The swivels I see are still stored below along with, I'll wager, most of the muskets and swords too. Almost half our strength! What if a British cutter, or worse, a frigate, came tearing down on us this very moment? What would we do? Spit at her? Surrender? What a fine testimonial to our skills that would be! First things first, gentlemen. Let's find out how many of the lads even know how to fire a heavy gun. Our lives, their lives, may depend upon all our fighting skills someday. But, whether we ever need to draw upon such skills or not, make no mistake gentlemen: I shall have tough, first-rate fighting men crewing this ship, no compromises, no exceptions..."

Dowlin shook his head disapprovingly. "Yer right of course, Capt'n," he said in a low voice. "As a man-o-war this is by far the saddest bucket I've ever put to sea on. But aren't you forgettin' somethin'? There an't no targets out there. P'haps we should wait for a better day. Sea's a trifle rough too don't you think to be lowerin' a boat in the water to tow targets?"

Ryan slapped his thigh and roared with laughter. Down the deck, heads snapped around to watch him. Macatter, Dowlin and Kelly exchanged uneasy glances. No one was sure what the joke was. Ryan glanced down the cutter's long, sleek deck, took in the faces of his men. He caught some staring out at empty sea while others stood watching him and his officers gathered at the ship's stern rail talking. They could see that their captain had found something humorous and was having himself a good, hardy laugh. Always a good sign to see the captain laughing - or was it?

"Targets?" the master tactician asked incredulously after he stopped laughing. "Gentlemen, except for the lads who shipped with Patrick, Chris and me aboard the *Rose*, do you really expect many of these fine fellows to even know how to properly, efficiently, load a four-pounder, let alone hit anything with it? Most of these lads served on merchant ships, or fishing trawlers before signing on with us, not warships. Some I'll wager are landlubbers with very little experience on the water. Anyone care to see to my wager?"

No one answered.

"No? I didn't think so. From now on gentlemen, this is a ship of war I tell you and I expect every sailor aboard to conduct himself accordingly! The crew shall be properly drilled. It is our responsibility, our sacred duty, to see to their training. That is the same as seeing to their welfare. We owe the lads that much at least. And gentlemen - I want warriors - stout men unafraid to mix it up with the British. Our survival, as I say, may depend upon it someday. Perhaps sooner than we know. Now, any questions?"

Macatter, still groggy and paying scant attention to very much of anything after realizing there was no real emergency, stifled a yawn and said nothing. No veteran of cruel, hard combat, Ryan's sense of urgency was lost on him.

But like a thunderbolt out of the blue, the wisdom of Ryan's words had jolted Dowlin out of his stupor and he bellowed out laughing. "Aye, Luke! Yer right, of course. You always was a step or two ahead of the rest of us. This is goin' to be mighty interestin'. Weldin over thar is a good sailor, but I don't even know if he can load, aim or fire a pistol let alone a four-pounder."

"Truth is," offered Macatter in a weary voice and never one to boast falsely, "neither of us has any military trainin'."

"Not to worry there, Mr. Macatter," Ryan replied. "Rest assured, we shall remedy that sad omission in your education straight away. First things first tho'."

Ryan gave a nod to Dowlin and Dowlin grinned. Things would be set right now!

Dowlin used his fingers to comb his wild, red mane back off his forehead, took a deep breath and barked out orders - the way he had when he wore the uniform of an officer of the king - and his words were none too gentle. "Mr. Weldin, you'll check yer guns now to see that they're primed and loaded. And, sir, I'll have my swivels mounted too if you please! *Now!* Times a-wastin', have yer men shake a leg thar. I haven't got all fookin', bloody day!"

Weldin could have taken exception to Dowlin's sharp words just then. He was, after all, the senior officer. No fool was he though. He and Dowlin had become fast friends and Weldin knew that Dowlin far outmatched him in fighting skills. Weldin quickly relayed Dowlin's orders to the gun crew captains and, finally, thought to send a detail down below to retrieve the missing swivels. The gun crews fumbled about, slowly opened gun ports and then pulled on the side tackles to ease the noses of their guns out over the deck. No one worked together. Toes were pinched, some fingers got scraped and more than one knee was bruised. Men cursed at one another and found cause to fume.

Ryan ignored the day's buffoonery, kept his eyes fixed on the boundless sea surrounding them. "Mr. Macatter, you are at liberty to return below. You may as well get your sleep. First, we'll train the men in the intricacies of combat. Then Patrick, Chris and me will teach you and Alexander how to lead them. Mr. Dowlin, sir, the ship is yours. You know what I require."

"Aye, sir, I do and, by *Gawd*, I'll deliver!" Dowlin boasted confidently and then asked with a crooked smile, "All the shot and powder I want?"

Ryan nodded. *God help the raw recruits...* "Whatever you need, Mr. Dowlin, take it. Take all the time you need too. After we reach Dunkirk we'll not set out again - I'll not risk the lives of these good men - until you have satisfied *yourself* that we have a fighting ship and a fighting crew of unmatched quality."

Macatter stifled another yawn and returned to his hammock.

"I understand, sir," Dowlin said. He focused his attention on the work of the gun crews next. Their efforts were pathetic and, his limited patience spent, he stormed down the deck like some tornado.

"Avast there you ham-fisted yokels!" he ordered with a fire in his eyes. "Avast thar I say before you blow yerselves up to kingdom-come and stain my deck with yer sorry guts, or worse, you put a hole in my lovely ship!"

He snatched a flexible rammer out of the hands of a young sailor with a flowing, red beard, one of the new men Ryan had brought on board ten days before. "*Richardson!*" he said, glaring at the new man. "You stupid son-of-a-whore! I thought you was a gunner's mate?"

Richardson hesitated.

With smoldering eyes and nostrils flaring, Dowlin shook his head in disgust. "Isn't that what you told Capt'n Ryan when you signed on aboard this here ship?"

The sailor began to open his mouth but Dowlin cut him off. "Best to keep yer pie-hole shut, lad. No need to offend me ears with any lame excuses, or worse, a lie. That would just make me *truly* - alley-dog angry..."

The men at the guns watched Dowlin nervously as he looked away from Richardson and turned his attention to another. Dowlin stepped nose-to-nose with an older seaman, a man who had claimed to have served with the British navy for many years.

"And you thar *Rowland Perkins!*" he snarled. You don't look to me like you knows much about firin' this here gun! You served in the king's navy didn't ya? Musta been before they invented gunpowder!"

Perkins's face went white and he said nothing. Best to lay low when a storm hurtles lightning bolts over your head.

Dowlin cupped his hand to his ear. "Well? Speak up man! I cannot hear you..."

Perkins shrugged. "I might have exaggerated things just a wee bit, sir."

"Exaggerated is it? What in blazes were you then man? Hey? The *truth* now or I swear by *Gawd* I'll hang you upside down from the masthead by yer toes!"

Perkins meekly stared at his feet. "I was, a, ahem, I was a ship's tailor, sir."

Men chuckled.

"A what?"

"Beg pardon, sir. I, I, I was a ship's tailor, sir."

"A *SHIP's TAILOR!*" thundered Dowlin. "Well piss my pants! Bloody bastard. You damn well coulda gotten us all killed had this drill been for real and not for show. Well, Mr. Perkins, so help me, so help me yer goin' to be a gunner's mate and yer goin' to be a damn fine gunner's mate at that even if it kills the pair of us!"

"All of you," Dowlin continued, pointing an accusing finger at every man. "Listen now. Yer pitiful lives are in my hands and, if I was you, I'd try my very best, my very, very best, to remind old Dowlin here each and every day why yer miserable lives are worth anything…"

But his rage was no more than a bit of drama. Like Ryan, Dowlin was enjoying himself. Only Ryan and the veterans, who looked on with amusement, knew his little secret.

Satisfied the situation was in good hands, Ryan retired to his small cabin to read. He knew his fiery friend didn't need him hovering nearby.

Dowlin slowly took in the faces of his hapless victims, glaring at them, and then sighed. "Damn it all to hell. Sweet *Jesus*, thar's a lot of work to be done here. Alrighty then you brainless baboons, gather around. It's a fine day to play. Time to learn the ropes. We're goin' to learn the art of gunnery right here, right now. We'll start with the basics. Always best to crawl before you try and walk."

While Weldin stood off to the side to watch, Dowlin and Kelly broke the men down into teams, assigning each man a position, four men to a gun. Dowlin began by showing his pupils how to roll the gun out, working as a team with single-minded purpose. Then he picked up a small cloth bag and held it up for all to see.

"This here is a cartridge of gunpowder; they say the Chinese invented the stuff. Don't know much about that. But I do know how adept the British are at using it. Take my word on it, they're damn good. The powder is made from a mixture of saltpeter, sulfur and charcoal. This is French-made and it is the best quality in the world. With a five pound charge, an eighteen-pounder will penetrate two and a half feet of hard wood at four hundred yards or one foot of hard wood at one thousand yards."

Dowlin grabbed a long wood rod in both hands next and held it up for all to see.

"This here's a flexible rammer. Good for rammin' cannon balls down the gun's muzzle and for other various, sundry things." He paused to bob an inattentive seaman lightly over the head with it.

"Ouch, Mister Dolwin!"

"Ouch?" Dowlin asked. "Better a bump on the noggin than a severed head. Now pay close attention thar, Joyce or my next target will that useless purse between yer legs."

Dowlin removed a gunner's knife from his belt, with its copper blade that never sparked, and slit open a paper cartridge, taking care to pour the black powder into the six-foot black muzzle of the gun, and then folded the paper into a wad and rammed the charge home with the flexible rammer. Then he went to a small wooden locker nearby and selected two iron shots. Each ball was three inches in diameter and weighed four pounds, hence the gun's name: *four-pounder*. One ball was smooth and round, a choice shot. The other had slight imperfections. He held both balls up and explained that no two shots were exactly the same. The rounder the shot, the truer its flight he told the men and added that it was best to save the irregularly shaped balls for close up work.

Dowlin set the irregular ball aside and rammed the rounder shot down firmly on the wad and then, with his teeth, ripped open a second cartridge to prime the breech. He ran the gun out by pulling on the tackles, easing it around with an iron handspike until he was satisfied the aim was true. Then he checked his windage and elevation. Next, he took a gunner's pick, slid it through the cannon's touchhole at the breech to clear it and explained that the pick was also used to prick the cartridge inside the muzzle open whenever a full charge was used. Now, with the cannon primed and loaded, he reached for a linstock and blew on the slow match to raise a spark and then stood to the right side of the monster, always the right side, and looked behind him to make sure the gun's path was clear.

Young Tim, a good but inexperienced boy, decided just then to walk around the gun, and stopped directly behind it, to get a better view. Dowlin grabbed the boy firmly by the shoulder and yanked him up off his feet as he touched the base of the ring with the linstock without warning, taking care not to touch the ring itself lest the upward shot of flame and hot gases douse his slow match, and *BOOM!*

Smoke billowed back across the deck and the gun recoiled violently backwards until the breeching rope caught and held it firm. Tim looked at Dowlin with fear in his eyes.

Dowlin released the boy, patted him on the back and gave him a reassuring smile. The boy had learned his lesson, one that he would not forget.

"Standin' where you was boy, we would of had to scrape you up off the deck and buried you at sea if 'em ropes hadn't of held. Well, truth be told young Tim, not much danger of that with this puny four-pounder. But mind you, mind you well boy, someday you might get the chance to fire somethin' bigger, somethin' with a serious mule's kick to it. Best you develop good habits early on when playin' with dangerous toys like these here. Make another mistake like that lad and I won't have the pleasure of disratin' you, 'cause you'll already be stone dead. To all of you, I say remember this: be vigilant always and ever mindful, Doom stalks even the bravest among us."

He winked at Tim's father and ruffled the boy's hair, hoping he had not been too harsh with him. "All of you lads, watch and learn, watch and learn. Pay close attention now. Dangerous business this is. Not for daydreamers."

He paused for a moment, letting his words sink in, and then narrowed his eyes. "Alrighty then you blockheads, schools in and I'm done talkin'. Who wants to go first? We've got a full store of powder and shot to play with and all day to learn. The first lesson is speed. Speed is more important than accuracy in this bloody business and that's what we're goin' to work hardest on. We'll load and reload these here guns over and over again until yer firin' shots off every sixty seconds or so and can keep that pace up even in yer sleep. Remember, mark my words well, the crew that fires off the most shots usually wins. Next lesson will be target practice. Speed isn't much good if you can't hit anythin'. But that's for another day. By the time I'm through with the lot of you, well, we'll see. P'haps I shouldn't be expectin' too much from you knuckleheads. The third lesson, if we're lucky, will be battle and then we'll see who learned lessons number one and two - and who did not..."

Dowlin minced no words with them. He told them plainly how they might need to fight someday with no rest, no water, choking on acrid, thick fumes for hours on end with dead and wounded companions piling up all around their feet. Not an easy thing, war.

"Alrighty then," Dowlin began with a smile. "Here's the long and the short of it: '*silence, man the starboard guns!*' This is the first order you'll get and the strictest silence must be observed. The gun captain will face the gun muzzle; the men on the right and left will stand facing the gun; all will fix their eyes on the captain and wait. Then you'll hear: '*cast loose and provide!*' The gun captain will see his gun cleared and cast loose, the port lid will be unbarred and ready for tricing up, side and train tackles hooked to the side training bolts, and the train-tackle to the eyebolt in the rear of the gun; then you'll place selvage straps and toggles amidships, take off the lock cover. After that the gun captain hands it to the train tackleman, who places it amidships; buckles on his waist belt, provides himself with a vent pricker, puts on his thumb stall and sees that all the gear to service the gun are all in place and ready for action.

"Got it? I didn't think so, but we'll push on... Now, the second gun captain assists in casting loose and middling breeching and he takes off and places the amidships sight covers, selvage straps, and toggles; he handles the quoin; provides thumb-stalls, priming wires, and boring bitt, linstock and equips himself with the first two; clears the lock string, and lays it in a loose coil round the lock and buckles it on his waist belt same as the first captain's. The first loader and the first sponger cast loose the port-lanyard, removes the upper half port and passes it to the men on the left side of the gun, who in turn lay it amidships and let down the half port. On the lower deck, he casts off port-lanyards and mizzen lashings; removes the port bar and passes it to the men at the left side of the gun, who lays it amidships; bears out or opens the port. Handswabs and chocking-quoin are stationed near the ship's sides on the left side of the gun to aid the first Sponger in taking the tampion out of the muzzle of the gun.

"I see eyes glazing over... Stay with me. Now, the second loader aids in casting loose; sees the wads in place, and for rifled cannon places a pot of grease at hand and hooks the outer block of side tackle to the side training bolt, on the left side of the gun. While the second loader is doing this, the first sponger casts loose the port-lanyards and aids the first loader in removing the upper half port and letting down the lower ones, and on lower decks, in removing port bar, bearing out the port and taking off the muzzle lashings. Then he takes out the tampion and passes it to the second sponger, who hangs it amidships and places the chocking quoin on the right side of the gun near the ship's side. The second sponger assists in casting loose and hooks the outer blocks of sidetackle to the side-training bolt on the right side of the gun. The Spongers take down the sponges and rammers, take off the sponge cap and hang it out of the way; then they place the sponges and rammers together on the right side of the gun and head towards the breach. The side tacklemen assist in casting loose; on the lower decks they aid the port-tacklemen, moisten the sponges, being certain that the end of the sponge which touches the bottom of the bore is thoroughly wet. The shellmen assist in casting loose, provide shot and wads, and proceed to the hatchway, ready to pass a shot. The train tacklemen lead out and hook train tackle while the handspikemen take out the handspikes and using a quoin, each standing between his handspike and the side of the ship, place the heel of their handspikes on the steps of the carriage and under the breech of the gun, and raise it so that the quoin may be eased and the lower half port be let down, or when housed the bed and quoin be adjusted. Then, each handspikeman will lay his handspike on deck, on his own side of the gun, parallel with its axis, clear of the trucks and butt to the rear. If we had powder boy, he would stand a little to the left and in rear of the gun with the passing box tucked under his left arm, and the cover closely pressed down with his right hand. In the passing box is the gunpowder cartridge. On a British man-o-war, the crew of a long twelve-pounder has eight men and a boy and the crew of a long six-pounder has six men and a boy. We will make do with less.

"If we are engaged with a single enemy ship we fight eight men to a gun, port or starboard. If we should be so unlucky to be fighting two ships at once, attacking us both starboard and port, then we fight with four men to a gun. The first captain, loader, sponger and handspikeman will man the starboard guns; the second captain, loader, sponger and handspikeman will man the port guns.

"The next order you'll hear in this little death dance of ours will be '*sponge yer guns!*' After the first shot is fired, the first sponger rams the wet sponge down the barrel to the breech wetting the barrel, and the captain places his thumb over the touchhole of the gun while the sponge is removed smartly thus creating a vacuum in the gun, extinguishing any sparks left in the gun from a previous shot. Then it will be '*load cartridge!*' The powder boy passes the powder charge from his passing box to the first loader, who places the powder charge into the gun. The next order is: '*ram cartridge!*' The first rammer rams the charge home to the breech end of the cannon barrel. At the command '*load round ball!*' the first shot and wad man passes the round and wad to the first loader who places the round and wad in the gun barrel between the cartridge and the round. After that, you'll hear the order: '*ram round!*' The first rammer then rams the round and wad against the charge and the gun captain inserts the priming wire into the touchhole, pricking the cartridge bag, and primes the gun by filling the touchhole with priming powder from his priming horn.

"Now then, the ship's Captain will give the command to '*run out the guns!*' The side tacklemen run the guns up to the side of the ship and the gun captain sights the gun. When you hear '*fire as your guns bear!*' the gun captain must warn his crew to '*clear the gun*' meaning to stand clear and the gun is fired. If the ship's capt'n only wishes to disable, he will instruct the gun captains to fire on an uproll at the other ship's rigging using grape or chain shot. If the capt'n wishes to sink the other ship, the guns are loaded with solid shot and you will be told to fire on the down roll at the enemy's hull.

"Easy-breezy, eh?"

Dowlin kicked open a nearby locker and pulled out different types of ammunition.

"This four-pound ball is solid shot and made of cast iron. This other type of ammunition is grape, nine small iron balls on a wooden form wrapped in canvas and when it is fired the canvas disintegrate and the balls scatter. Ouch! Canister is different. It has many more small balls packed in a cloth, leather or tin container with sawdust and is used against flesh. Nasty stuff. Chain shot is usually a bag with an iron ring fastened to five, three-to-four foot lengths of chain, also known as *star shot*. Another type of canister is a split ball, two halves linked together by two heavy links of chain or it can be two cannon balls linked together with a short length of chain. Split chain shot and spider shot are just variations of chain rounds. All of these rounds including grape are used to shred rigging or flesh. The solid shot is used to knock-out enemy guns and penetrate the enemy's hull."

Dowlin paused to let his words sink in, started from the beginning and repeated the lesson. And then, to the amusement of the veterans, the new men began the long, tedious hours of practice drills, firing their guns at the wide open sea over and over and over again. And as they did so Dowlin walked the line parceling out harsh words and reprimands to each man equally but, after a time, when the men began to catch on, his stern demeanor gave way to quiet patience and he worked alongside the gunners like a father teaching his sons the fine intricacies of the family's business. Naked to the waist, streams of sweat rolling off their backs, the men worked their black barrels of death again and again, honing their skills to near perfection under Dowlin's watchful eye.

As battle-scarred veterans have done down the centuries, Dowlin intimidated and insulted his raw recruits at first, he stripped them of their cockiness, disabused them of their sense of individualism. Like a horseman breaking in a new colt, he rode them hard and ground down their spirit, but not too much. Then, as the men improved their skills at gunnery and began learning the knack of working as a team, he doled out his praises, only a little at first, just enough to whet their appetite for more, and with time and patience, Dowlin had himself a company of warriors. *This is how we soldiers prepare for the gruesome work of war*, he told them over and over again.

Ryan from time to time would come up on deck to stretch his legs and check on the progress of the training but he was careful to keep his distance. He had unleashed a whirlwind and knew to stay well clear. Dowlin and Kelly would drill the men relentlessly, new and veteran alike, until flesh and iron had been forged together, until each man functioned like a part in a machine, no emotion, with single-minded purpose and with flawless precision. Any man found wanting would be given his wages and released.

Ryan had meant what he said - he would not sail again without a crew of professionals, not without a crew of unmatched quality. Dowlin and Kelly did not disappoint him.

As the cutter sped across a wine-dark sea towards France, Ryan felt a slight shift in the winds. The change was nearly imperceptible at first. The skies overhead and to the east were clear. But on their stern, to the west, two lines of towering, white thunderheads began rising ominously off the water. Ryan sensed a clash, an ugly clash, between cold and hot in the making.

"Patrick, what do you make of those clouds over yonder?" asked Ryan and pointed astern at the darkening horizon.

Dowlin hadn't noticed the change in the wind yet and looked over the stern rail.

"Dunno, Luke. Maybe nothin', maybe somethin'. Winds are freshenin' tho'. I'll go below and take a look."

Dowlin disappeared down the companionway to Ryan's cabin to check the ship's barometer hanging on the wall. He saw the needle dropping precipitously, a sure sign of approaching severe weather, and hurried back on deck.

"You always did have a good nose for the weather, Luke. Pressure's droppin' fast. Nasty business blowin' our way I suspect. That thar is a squall line buildin' on her stern sure enough."

Ryan nodded. "Right. Clear skies overhead, warm, springtime air but the barometer is plummeting and the temperature is cooling. The seas are starting to turn choppy awfully quick too. I don't like it, Pat. Call all hands on deck. We best brace ourselves for some rough weather. Maybe we can out race whatever's coming our way, but, I doubt it. Closest safe harbor is Brest, but that's over hundred leagues off by my reckoning. Worth a try tho'."

"England's a tad closer," Dowlin wisecracked. "Guess this is an English storm then."

The crew prepared the ship for hard weather. Men scrambled to secure hatches, doused fires and lashed down anything that could be swept overboard or move, double-lashing the heavy guns. And then the sky turned an eerie pale yellow. The winds soon whipped the sea into a boiling cauldron of foam and the ship heeled hard over in the heavy white caps as men hurried to trim sails and raise the storm jib.

Kelly grabbed his son and pointed up at the masthead. "Up you go lad. Time you saw the world from up yonder."

The boy arched his head back, looked up at the towering mast with gray clouds swirling overhead. *It is so very high up*, he thought. The ship was beginning to pitch and roll more violently too and the boy's face turned pale.

Kelly rubbed his son's curly hair affectionately with his great paw. "Thar's nothin' to it lad," Kelly said with a firm, confident tone. "You ever climb up a tree?"

"Aye, sir," the boy replied nervously.

"That's exactly how I've always thought about this here mast, son. It's nothin' but a tree. And climbin' up it is just about the same as climbin' up a tree back home. Goin' out on the yardarm is nothin' more than hangin' off a branch, just easier, 'cause thar's more to hold on to up thar with all 'em lines. Just don't look down. You'll be fine, like a regular little tree monkey. I'll be right behind you. And always, always, remember the Rule of Two."

"The Rule of Two?"

"Aye, God gave you two hands - but the ship takes one. The other is for yourself. The Rule of Two."

Ryan overheard the exchange between father and son, was tempted to suggest that Kelly wait for calmer seas, but then thought better of it. Kelly was always a man of good, clear sense.

Tim swallowed hard and glanced down at his hands tentatively, then grabbed a thick, shroud line, tarred black, and lifted himself up over the deadeyes. He stood on the ship's rail, wrapped one arm around a ratline and gingerly stepped over the ship's side. Below his feet, he saw gray waves slipping by and he could feel the bile rising up in his throat. He choked and heaved his breakfast into the sea.

"*Whoa* there, lad!" cried out his father. "You're turnin' green. Didn't I just warn ya, don't look down! That first step over the side, that's the hardest one. Now up you go. Watch yer step."

"Aye, sir," the boy replied without any enthusiasm, forcing his limbs to move.

Tim began his slow climb up the ratlines followed by his father. He worked his way up to the futtocks, the short out-leaning shrouds, and then through the lubber's hole onto the maintop - the place where the mainmast is joined to the topmast by a wood platform - and paused there on that small island to look around. He had never seen the world through the eyes of a god before and was filled with a sense of exhilaration. White capped waves surrounded the ship in every direction. To the north, he thought he could see land, England, but his father assured him that they were too far out to see any land. What he saw were low clouds or a fog bank hugging the horizon his father explained.

More confident now, Tim scrambled up the second set of ratlines, what his father called the main topmast shrouds, and followed them all the way to the top, to the topgallant mast itself, to the highest point on the ship. His whole body tingled with a curious mixture of fear and joy as he climbed higher. The wind suddenly took his hat. He watched it disappear into the sea but was less scared now. The ship looked tiny and vulnerable. *Amazing* he thought to himself, how remarkable it was that any sane person would venture out across such a huge expanse of cruel emptiness in such a fragile bundle of wood.

Kelly moved up to Tim's side and gave his son a firm hug. "Winds startin' to really blow now," he said. "Proud of you lad. You scurried up 'em lines like an old sea rat. You'll be doin' quite a bit of it from now on, in rougher weather maybe than this. And maybe at night. So get a feel for it Tim. We'll swing out on this here yardarm. Plant yer feet firmly on the stirrups thar, that's the way, take up some of the tops'ls by grabbin' it like so. Good, good. Then we'll work our way back down. Usually best to step out on the windward side first, then cross over to the leeward side."

Tim gingerly balanced himself on the footropes, swaying back and forth with the wind, and again paused to look out over the horizon. He felt like a god. The whole world lay at his feet.

After safely planting his feet back on deck, the crew gathered around Tim and gave the boy a hearty three cheers in honor of his accomplishment. And then someone doused him with a bucket of seawater. It was his baptism. He answered them all with a proud grin from ear-to-ear. He was one of them now.

As if marching out to battle, two mighty armies, massive dark clouds full of threat, one gathering in the north, the other in the west, merged into one giant phalanx and overtook the cutter with frightening speed. Unkind winds and large chunks of hail abused the cutter roughly.

Weldin, the officer of the watch, looked to Ryan and Ryan gave him the nod.

"All hands shorten sail!" Weldin cried out, the crackling in his voice betraying his unease.

Like the pounding of a 1,000 drums, thunder, frightening herald of the god whose shield is storm and thunder, rumbled across the heavens. The angry god let loose his lightning bolts against the Earth like so many spears or arrows, raw power, terrifying to behold. And as a horde of barbarian horsemen, armed with whetted bronze, breasts filled with unholy terror, will charge down a mountainside with reckless speed, hell-bent on destruction with no mercy in their hard hearts for the helpless villagers below, so the fearsome gale swept violently over the small vessel hell-bent on her destruction. And no man could ever rightfully boast he felt no fear that day.

"Lay as close into the wind as she'll carry!" Ryan shouted out anxiously to the helmsman over howling winds. "We're in for some rough going. Keep her nose square into the waves now! That's it. Good. Good."

Dowlin, his hand on his head trying to keep his sou'wester from blowing away, squinted against the stinging rain. "I see that cold bitch winter isn't through with us yet!" he called out to Ryan.

"Aye," responded Ryan. "This is ungodly. Why not get yourself below man? I'll take the watch."

Dowlin shook his head. "You first, Capt'n," he said with a wry smile. But he knew Ryan would stay on deck until the ship was out of harm's way - as would he.

And so the two mariners, standing near the helm side-by-side, braced themselves as best they could against the lashing winds and stinging rains while their hard-wearing racehorse stubbornly plowed through the heavy seas as best she could. Her bow plunged deep into the trough of each huge roller, disappearing in the dark waters, only to again rise up on the peaks as the cutter fought tenaciously for her crew. Towering waves, twenty footers or better, came at her sideways too, cresting over her bulwarks, violently knocking the ship to and fro. Men below deck were thrown from their hammocks or lost their footing and cursed. No one slept.

At midnight the winds, roaring with a ferocious intensity, carried away the main spar. Lines snapped. The mainmast swayed and groaned, threating to crack and topple over the side. Disaster loomed. But no man panicked. Ryan and his Irishmen kept their nerve, coolly secured the mainmast with sturdy rope and cable and kept their ship from floundering. And in the morning, when the angry gale had blown past, the Irishmen saw that the lost spar was their only casualty, along with a broken bone or two - clear proof of the exceptional skill and bravery of the cutter's captain and her crew.

Chapter Twenty
It's About Prisoners

With rough April winds continuing to blow down hard from the north, timid captains crammed their vessels, both large and small, into Dunkirk's fair harbor, waiting for more agreeable weather before putting out to sea again. A whole forest of tall masts had sprouted thick in Dunkirk's waters. But further out in the bay, a new ship, a mysterious, black vessel, a handsome cutter - missing one spar, and one anchor too - sat peacefully in a lonely spot of water and seamen along the waterfront marveled at the sight. Men discussed the cutter over morning coffee, wondering how her crew had survived sailing through the fierce Atlantic gale.

The exhausted Irishmen had dropped anchor far out in the bay, preferring to keep their ship well away from the pack, as they disliked the thought of some fool of a drunk ship's master ramming into their beauty in the dead of night while trying to slip away. Insurers had no appetite for indemnifying smugglers. The Irishmen shouldered all risk of any damage to their ship or cargo.

For a time the two ships could do little more than bob up and down over the rolling swells like two corks in a barrel, making the gunners' work no easy task. But then, with a fresh breeze to fill her sails, the proud *Rose* began lurching forward again, her curved bow slicing through the bubbling brine with ease - and soon she managed to close with her foe. The gusts of wind whipping through her lines and cables played an eerie melody while the long reaching fingers of a greedy sea - always eager to drag men down - spilled over the rails, probing the ship for any weakness. Her wood planks creaked and groaned underneath the strain. But the *Rose* was sound. The relentless cascades of water washing over her decks flowed harmlessly back out through the scuppers. And then, across the boundless waves of a wine-dark sea, puffs of white smoke suddenly pitted the air. The hated enemy had launched a full broadside - hurtling heavy iron at *Rose* - and solid shot came smashing hard against her hull with a dull pop, pop, pop - or shredded sails and flesh. Anxious officers frantically barked out orders to their divisions. Men cursed their luck and braced themselves for pain. Chaos mounting...

He found himself standing alone on the quarterdeck, detached from all the madness raging on below him like some Olympian god. He watched his men slash and hack away against endless waves of enemy sailors climbing over the ship's rail. *Odd*, he thought. He felt no fear. He felt only a remarkable sense of elation - and a need to prove something - but prove what? He didn't know. And then a strong arm shook him roughly on the shoulder and the dream, as real as life, instantly vanished.

"Luke, wake up - Luke!" Dowlin said, shaking Ryan's shoulder.

"Ugh! I'm awake."

"Good, was beginnin' to think you was dead."

"What's your hurry, Patrick James Dowlin?" Ryan asked indifferently. He propped himself up on an elbow and rubbed the sleep from his eyes.

"Boat's in the water and ready to go," Dowlin replied with a cheery smile. "And, if you get yer sorry arse up now, we can be ashore before nightfall. That's my hurry."

"For you and me, the weave was set long ago old friend. The Fates will wait."

The big, fiery Irishman, in looks and build a match for any of the deathless gods, rebuked Ryan with a grand sweep of his arm. "Auck! You and yer book-wise banter. The Fates, ha! To hell with 'em, I say. Let the Fates wait if that be their pleasure. But wait I won't. Stay on board in this cramped, stuffy cabin if you like. But I have an itch that needs scratched. Thar's drinkin' to be done on shore and pretty lasses to bed..."

The American Ambassador to the Court of Versailles sat at his *escritoire*, in the quiet comfort of his quarters at Passy, known as the *Basse Cour*, and massaged the calves of his legs, left numb from the incessant cold showers that had plagued Paris all throughout March and now continued into April. Despite the great matters of state weighing heavily on him, it was the plight of his countrymen languishing in British jails that now monopolized his thoughts. He stared out the window, watching the sheets of rain pelt the cobblestone, where the rue Raynouard and rue Singer intersected, and reflected on the day's events.

In the early years of the rebellion, Lord North's men had arrogantly refused to even discuss the subject of prisoner exchanges. There had been no need. British victory was imminent. British jails had been filling up with traitors by the thousands who had taken up arms against their king, not prisoners of war, who, after the rebellion was crushed, would be executed, not released. Even after the stunning news of Saratoga rocked the world, when it became clear to everyone that the war would no longer be easy or short - and that a British victory was less certain - London still stubbornly rejected Franklin's entreaties to exchange prisoners and Americans continued to suffer terrible atrocities at the hands of their British jailers.

That was when Franklin took it upon himself to be their voice, to be their great champion, determined to use every weapon at his disposal to help ease their burdens as best he could. That was when he had sent Captain Jones out into hostile waters with the newly built sloop-of-war *Ranger* to get him prisoners. And after Jones had returned triumphantly to France with 200 souls for Franklin to do with as he pleased, that was when London, humbled, finally agreed to discuss prisoner exchanges.

The bitter reality of Saratoga, the French alliance, and Jones's brilliant success at sea, had given Franklin the leverage he needed. And, now, a year later, Franklin was rewarded for his efforts.

He looked away from the window and reread the dispatch he had received from the French commander at the port at Nantes dated April 1, 1779. The first British cartel ship had entered Nantes under a flag of truce with a batch of 97 ragged, ailing Americans, previously held in that abomination known as Old Mill Prison, and released them in exchange for Franklin's 200 British prisoners.

The old doctor allowed himself a brief moment of satisfaction and smiled. But scattered throughout England, Scotland and Wales were more American patriots, hundreds of them, no less dear to him. And he continued to receive reports, including eye-witness accounts from escapees, describing the appalling conditions that still existed at the prison camps. Men lacked warm clothing, medicines and suffered from malnutrition. And then there were the random beatings, the deaths and the killings.

Franklin, determined to ease the heart-wrenching sufferings of these men, his countrymen, had continued to send money over to England for food and clothing and had continued to pepper Parliament with petitions demanding an end to the brutality. And with the help of a few British sympathizers, Franklin even managed to finance small prisoner escapes here and there, though most attempts ended in failure.

But Franklin had always understood that the best way to help his countrymen was to buy their freedom through prisoner exchanges. Unfortunately, after releasing Jones's prisoners to the British cartel ship at Nantes, Franklin had only a handful of British prisoners left in his possession who, he let it be known, "were not so comfortably accommodated" on a wretched, French prison barge sitting in Brest.

Franklin simply needed more warm British bodies to use in trade. But snagging British prisoners had always been a tricky business. Across the Atlantic, British forces had invaded the southern Colonies, had taken Savannah and were laying siege to Charleston. The American army was again in retreat. At sea, except for Jones and a few other daring captains like him, the puny American navy was spending most of its time hiding from the overwhelming might of the British naval juggernaut. And rightly so, suicide missions against the colossus of the oceans did not serve the cause.

In a war full of setbacks and heartbreaking disappointments, the extraordinary exploits of Captain John Paul Jones was a source of great pleasure, even pride, to the old doctor. The promising Scotsman never failed to deliver good news and always had an entertaining story or two for Franklin and so now the Ambassador's thoughts turned to Jones again.

He took a clean sheet of paper, dipped his pen into the ink jar, and began scratching out his words.

> *My Dear Captain Jones*
> *Warm Greetings, Sir. I am informed of the first cartel ship arriving in Nantes with nearly 100 American Prisoners. Yet I am uneasy about the terrible Sufferings of our Fellow Countrymen still held in British Prisons and our work remains unfinished. Petitions to the British Government to improve their dredful circumstances are largely ignored. After learning of your exploits last year in the Irish Sea, scarcely any thing was talked about at Versailles but your cool Conduct and persevering Bravery at Sea, I would respectfully implore you Sir to sail your good vessel Ranger out into the Atlantic once again at your earliest opportunity and take into custody as many British Prisoners as you are able. It is Our hope that your Success in these matters will force the British Government into future prisoner exchanges. You and your crew have our Country's Sincerest Gratitude for your recent Victories at sea. May God be at your side in pursuing these Endeavors.*
> *With the highest Esteem, I am, &c.,*
> *Benjamin Franklin*

Satisfied with what he had written, the old scientist, stooped with age but not in mind or spirit, took his feathered pen, signed his name to the letter and then sprinkled sand over the wet ink.

But in the spring of 1779, Jones had relinquished his command of *Ranger* in favor of a gift from the French navy. The French had given Jones a new toy to play with: the *Duc de Durasan*, an old East Indiaman which Jones, in honor of Franklin, promptly renamed the *Bonhomme Richard* after the main character in Franklin's book, *Poor Richard's Almanac*. But there was much work to be done in converting a merchantman into a 50-gun man-of-war and Jones needed time before he could put to sea again. In addition to reconfiguring the *Bonhomme Richard*, Jones was also busy assembling a squadron of smaller ships to support his new battle cruiser.

After receiving Franklin's letter, Jones reluctantly sent word back to Franklin that he would be unable to sail for some time. "Be not discouraged," he wrote, "our Object will not be lost tho' I Should not be able to put to Sea for two Months to come."

Franklin read Jones's reply with little optimism. Despite his admiration for Jones, Franklin had learned that whenever a military man gave an estimate about something, about anything at all - including time - it was usually wise to simply double his numbers at the very least. That meant Jones wouldn't be able to sail for another four months or longer.

While his countrymen suffered the old doctor was in no mood to wait for Jones, to wait that long. But, without Jones, he had no spear, no sword.

Chapter Twenty-One
Duplicity for a Noble Cause

As Franklin read Jones's letter near a fire in the comfort of his parlor, several fugitives from British law pulled at the oars of a small launch, rowing through a cold drizzle, and guided their craft towards the wharfs and jetties stretching out along Dunkirk's waterfront. After securing the launch to a pier and tipping the harbormaster, two Irishmen, dressed like common seamen, made their way south on foot towards the outskirts of the city.

Torris was in his bed when he heard the knocking at his front door. He looked up at a clock sitting on the fireplace mantel and winced. It was well past midnight. He cursed silently to himself, reached for a candle and hurried downstairs dressed only in his nightshirt and nightcap. Because some of his business interests were arguably more illegal than legal, it was not uncommon for late night visitors to stop by his home.

He hoped, as he reached for the door, he would not find one of his drunken captains looking for an advance against his wages. Such visits were not uncommon either and he was in no mood to open his books to do the math.

Even in the dark the Flemish businessman recognized the two Irishmen at once and, relieved, quickly waved them inside. The Irishmen had always been easy to deal with - and they were worth their weight in gold. Before shutting the door though, he took a quick look up and down the narrow street to make certain that no one had followed the Irishmen to his home. Dunkirk was a busy seaport infested with spies working for business competitors, foreign nations and France's own dreaded secret police.

"Quickly, come in, come in, my friends," Torris commanded in his broken English. "Ah, *Monsieurs* Luke Ryan and Patrick Dowlin, it is so very good to see you both!"

"Forgive us my friend for intruding on you at this late hour," Ryan offered apologetically.

"Quite all right, quite all right. Come, please, let's go to my study and sit there shall we? Always a pleasure to see my two favorite Irishmen. Some cognac, gentleman? Mr. Dowlin? I know I can count on you to join me. Something to take the chill out of your bones on this dreary night? Never too late in the evening for cognac!"

He had never known the affable Mr. Dowlin to refuse a drink.

"Don't mind if I do, sir. Mr. Ryan here is a hard capt'n, a cruel master, and runs a dry ship. I could use somethin' indeed to clean out my pipes and wash away all that sea salt. Much obliged."

Torris smiled, led his two guests down a narrow hallway and into a small study. He lit several candles and produced a bottle from a desk drawer along with three glasses. Suspicious of the two Irishmen at first after the young Sartine had introduced them to him, Torris had come to like and trust both men. Ryan was his most reliable and profitable captain and the Irishman had proven time and again to be scrupulously honest. A unique quality among smugglers.

The room, like the rest of the house, was small, but elegantly furnished and very neat. Torris poured a generous measure of cognac into three glasses. And after he assured his wife that all was well when she called down to him from upstairs, and told her to go back to bed, he closed the beveled glass doors to his study and plopped down in a chair behind his desk, a richly ornate mahogany piece polished to a high gloss. He sampled his cognac and smacked his lips approvingly. Short, bald and plump, Torris was physically unimpressive but sitting behind his desk, he exuded power and money.

"Another successful journey, yes?"

Ryan took a sip of his cognac, waited for the burning sensation to pass. It was not his favorite liquor but at least Torris always served them from his best stock. Dowlin downed his drink in one swallow, reached for the bottle and poured himself another, wasting no time waiting for an offer.

"Yes and no."

"Pardon?" asked Torris, perplexed.

"The ship and our cargo were intercepted by the British revenue service in Dublin Bay several weeks ago John and confiscated..."

"Ah? No! No! No! *Friendship* taken? Your men captured? But this is terrible news!"

Torris shook his head in disbelief. While his concern for Ryan's men was sincere enough, his greater concern was for his own losses and he began making some quick calculations on a scratch piece of paper. He frowned and laid his pencil down. The damages were not insignificant.

Ryan understood this and took no offense. Torris was, after all, a businessman who was in the business of making money.

"But you are here, in my house!" Torris said, confused. Then he slapped his forehead. "Ah! Foolish me, obviously you are here! What I mean to say is, well, how is it you escaped, *mon ami?*"

"Ah," interjected Dowlin, smiling broadly. "Now thar's a story, a real gem of a story it is too. One worthy of passing down to the grandchildren!"

"Aye," added Ryan. "You best find another bottle or two of strong spirits for this tale. You still have some live embers in the fire, mind if I add some coal to warm things up?"

"No, by all means, please..."

Ryan and Dowlin then told Torris their story, the Irish way, leaving no detail left unsaid. Ryan began with the seizure of their crew and fine cutter, loaded down to the wale with a fortune in smuggled goods, while he and Dowlin were ashore making new arrangements with O'Keeffe for the next run. He told Torris about the *Black Dog*, the breakout and O'Keeffe's spirited daughter. Dowlin picked up the story from there and Torris listened, spellbound, as Dowlin retraced their steps at Poolbeg to retake their ship and the capture of a dozen or so British marines.

Had anyone but Ryan told him such a tall tale Torris would have dismissed the story out of hand as rubbish and shown the liar to the door. But Ryan had proven his trustworthiness time and again and, unlike many of his peers, the Irishman was never one given to exaggeration or boastfulness. If anything, the cool-headed young man was overly modest, a quality others - in their foolishness - might construe as weakness and underestimate him.

"*Incroiable!* Truly gentlemen, a remarkable story. A mass escape from the high marshal's jail in the heart of Dublin. Stealing a ship under the noses of the king's men and slipping past the harbor defenses. And you managed to sail through that awful gale too. And not one man lost!"

"A damn near thing," Ryan replied. "During the worst of it the foremast threatened to buckle and every man prepared himself to meet his Maker. But the fickle sea was merciful to us that day, contented herself with taking only a spar."

Ryan removed a small leather pouch from his coat and tossed it on the desk. "We sold our cargo to a competitor and unloaded it in Wales before returning to Dunkirk. Good thing we did too because our ship surely would have gone down to the bottom in that ungodly storm with her holds stuffed full as they were. You'll find the profit is slightly less than the usual amount - but it is a profit nonetheless."

Torris couldn't help himself. He smiled down at the leather pouch. Life was good again.

"Luke, you have always had the devil's own luck. This Shannon, O'Keeffe's daughter, quite a resourceful young lady I take it, yes?"

A thin smile touched Ryan's lips. "Aye, that she is..."

Torris caught the smile, its meaning. A Frenchman, even if he is Flemish by birth, can always spot love's gleam. "Ah, perhaps she is more than just a resourceful business associate?"

"She is, I swear," interrupted Dowlin, "the loveliest creature on our fair island. And I never knew Luke here to spend so much time ashore before."

"Hm," replied Torris, "you must bring her to France. I insist you do me the honor of introducing me to her. She would be most welcome to stay in my house as my guest. Perhaps even a trip to Paris would be enjoyable? How the women love Paris, especially the shops! My dear wife is well acquainted with them all! It is, or so I've heard, an enticing city too for young lovers!"

Ryan blushed and drained his glass.

"Well, back to business, what will you do now, Luke? To continue smuggling would be too dangerous now, no?"

"Aye," answered Ryan, "too dangerous. The British will certainly have prices on our heads for this act of piracy and be keeping a sharp vigil out for us."

He looked over to Dowlin and the two men exchanged smiles. "So, we have been, you might say, *inspired* to consider another line of work. Could be as profitable as smuggling, perhaps more so."

Torris smiled broadly and refilled their glasses. "Indeed, Luke," he said intrigued and leaned forward. "I dare say, no one in this room is opposed to making money!"

"Well," Ryan continued and cleared his throat, "the British will certainly hunt us down as outlaws now. And if we're caught, we'll be tried for treason and given a quick trial followed by a quicker hanging. No doubt about that. But what if, what if we turned to soldiering, what if we turned to *privateering?*"

Torris narrowed his eyes, trying to decipher in the darkness whether Ryan was serious. Ryan's suggestion at once made excellent sense to him. He saw that Ryan was indeed serious and slapped his desk to show his approval.

"But of course! How perfect! Why Dunkirk's very own son, Jean Bart, sailed *guerre de course* against the British with tremendous success."

"Jean who?" Dowlin asked.

"Jean Bart," replied Ryan for Torris. "He was a pirate a hundred years or so ago and preyed on British merchant ships. He operated here, out of Dunkirk, and is a hero among the locals."

Torris rubbed his hands together, grinning. "*Pardon*, Luke - a *privateer*, Bart was a *privateer*! But, yes! He led the *Corsairs of Dunkerque* in the War of the Grand Alliance! A true hero. Yes, yes. If I may say, you did well to come to see me about this first. I can be of great assistance to you in this matter. I am certain of it. I have good connections in Paris, including the French Minister of Marine himself. We should be able to obtain a French commission for you with little difficulty!"

He paused and chuckled, considered the financial possibilities within his reach. "I would, of course, be flattered to serve as your agent to dispose of any prizes on your behalf, for a modest fee of course!"

Torris was not slow to see the potential for huge profits with Ryan's plan. It was no secret that privateering could be an immensely profitable enterprise. Fat merchantmen from warring nations plied the waters of the Atlantic and Mediterranean - each one ripe for the plucking. Privateering was nothing new and different nations, including Britain, America, France and Spain, all had made use of them from time to time. Torris could have invested in any one of the privateers sailing in and out of Dunkirk. The problem was, and had always been, that privateering was a high-stakes, high risk business. There were precious few competent captains with any real military skills. And good, reliable crews were hard to assemble with the French navy constantly scouring every port and coastal town in France for able-bodied men to fill the king's levees for his own warships, leaving slim pickings for everyone else.

Privateering required bold men with a warrior's instincts and a good measure of luck. It required uncompromising men, men who could motivate, discipline and hold together a polyglot crew of thieves, drunkards and assorted rogues for long cruises through untold dangers. Torris knew other businessmen who had invested their money in privateers but, almost to a man, they had all come to regret it.

But Torris was quick to recognize that the power of Ryan's plan was Ryan himself. The Irishman was more than a competent master of a speedy merchant ship and he was more than a dependable business partner. Torris had heard the rumors about Ryan's past with the British navy - and hadn't the man just proven his mettle by his daring at Poolbeg? Proof enough for Torris of the Irishman's audacity and cleverness. Ryan was a man worth betting on.

With some plans, trying to force all the pieces to fit can be a tedious, thankless exercise. Such plans too often fail or fall short of expectations despite all the labor and time lavished on them. On rare occasion, a plan will come together almost effortlessly, with pieces crafted to perfection, increasing the odds for success. Torris had a talent for spotting such plans and seized them when opportunity knocked. That was his gift, his talent.

"We can set things in motion tomorrow," Torris said excitedly and rubbed his hands again.

"Not so fast John," Ryan said and waived his arm dismissively. He stood to stretch his legs. "Not a French commission. No. My plan has two purposes you must understand. To make money, certainly. But we must also protect the lives of my lads if any are caught. They're Irish as you know and, save for me and Pat, none can speak much French and Pat and I speak it with Irish accents. If caught, we'll never pass as Frenchmen. No John, we must have an American commission."

Torris batted his eyes, confused. "An American commission, *mon ami?*"

"Aye, an American commission, *mon ami.*"

"But Luke, this may not be possible. The American delegation in Paris is led by a man named Franklin, the famous scientist, and he will only give American commissions to American captains. I am not even certain he has any commissions to give. It has been some time since I have heard of an American privateer operating out of France. The Dunkirk Pirate, Captain Conyngham, was the last and they say he is now sitting in a British prison near Plymouth. It is no secret that Captain Jones is assembling a whole squadron of ships at L'Orient but he is regular American navy."

"Ah, Captain Jones," said Ryan thoughtfully as he rubbed the bridge of his nose. "I've heard of that man. Gifted seaman."

"*Oui*, a great hero."

Ryan plopped back down in his chair. "Well let's think on it. There must be a way. I'll go see this Doctor Franklin myself if I must, but we'll find a way to make my plan work. One way or the other, John, it will work. I feel it in my gut. *Friendship* is the perfect ship for privateering. The plan must work."

"I admire your spirit, Luke," replied Torris truthfully. "Let us sleep on it then? Shall we meet at my warehouse, say after supper tomorrow? I would like time to think on it and discuss this matter with my brother Charles in the morning, see what, if anything, can be done. In my family I am the one who has the head for numbers but it is Charles who has the gift of creativity."

✳

Ryan and Dowlin returned to their ship and spent the following day helping the crew with repairs. The main task was to replace the lost spar and torn rigging. Ryan was annoyed at the loss of the spar as the cost of lumber was exorbitant. A new anchor would cost him a pretty penny too. But, all-in-all, they had been very lucky. Had the spar taken the mast with it in the gale after their escape from Ireland, all their earthly troubles would have come to a quick end.

After supper, Ryan gave the crew liberty and then took Dowlin with him to go and meet Torris and his brother. The Irishmen found the two brothers waiting for them outside a large three story, red-bricked building, outside the Torris' family business warehouse. Charles was an older copy of his brother, short, plump and bald but with a bushy mustache that seemed to sprout out from his nostrils.

"Not waiting long, I trust?" Ryan asked as he shook Torris's hand.

"Not at all, Luke," replied Torris. "We were simply taking in this beautiful *soire* air. An after dinner stretch. This is my brother Charles; Charles, this is Luke Ryan and Patrick Dowlin."

Charles Torris said nothing, simply considered Ryan, trying to get a measure of the man.

"Shall we?" Torris asked and waved them inside to his warehouse.

The warehouse, dimly lit with oil lamps scattered here and there, was filled to capacity. Torris led the Irishmen through a maze of stacked crates, barrels and pallets towards a small office in the back corner of the building. Ryan and Dowlin exchanged glances as they passed a dozen new field cannons destined for America, all smeared with packing grease and with their caissons parked neatly in a line against a far wall. Somewhere inside the warehouse, Ryan knew, was a cargo set aside for *Friendship's* next run too. But that treasure would go to some other smuggler now, along with all the profits.

Bottles of wine, and a platter piled high with cheeses, breads and fruits, had been set out on a small table in the middle of the back office. There was never a lack of good food or drink when Torris was entertaining.

Charles Torris was first to speak. "Gentlemen, please, help

yourselves. Captain Ryan, while we have not met until tonight, I feel I know you well. I have heard many good things about you and your men. I hope you will consider me your friend. I have some questions. I am obliged to warn you first: I do not have my brother's gift of grace or tact, leastwise, not when large sums of money are involved. I am direct. I suppose this is why my brother shamelessly hides me away like some leper! I trust my frankness will not offend you?"

Ryan gave Torris's brother a slight smile, shook his head.

"Very well. First, I have seen your ship in the harbor and at our dock many times. She is a very fine vessel. She is, how do you say - *outfitted - oui*, outfitted for smuggling, no?"

"Aye," replied Ryan simply.

"To carry out your bold plan, you would require a new ship, a warship, yes?"

"No, sir. That would be too expensive. And I expect you won't find many good battle cruisers for sale with a war raging on across the Atlantic, none that a competent master would sail on anyway. With some modest modifications, we can convert *Friendship* to a warship, into a privateer easy enough."

"Ah, ha. Yes, I see. What, may I ask, is required to, convert, your ship from a smuggler to a privateer?"

Ryan had anticipated this question of course. The Torris brothers were after all businessmen with an interest in making money and they knew Ryan would need money, and a fair amount of it, to launch his new scheme.

"May I speak plainly, sir?" asked Ryan.

"*Certainment, mon Capitaine*. Plain talk is *almost* always best."

"I assume your question goes towards the subject of cost. To be sure, sir, it will require a sizable initial investment, more than I can cover from my own funds. We'll need additional armament, heavier caliber guns and more of them, and several hundred muskets and swords. We'll need a larger crew and money for their wages. We'll need provisions for a long cruise, say two to three months' worth. The modifications to the ship will include double planking the bulwarks using harder woods and cutting out additional gun ports for the new guns. We'll need to plank over the cargo holds below deck to increase the living space for the larger crew. The ship's upper deck will need to be reinforced below with large bracing timbers to support the weight of more cannon and she'll need a proper magazine outsized with anti-fire construction materials for storing large amounts of gunpowder. That might prove to be the most expensive cost. Shot lockers will need to be built. Hm, maybe lengthen a spar or two to hold more canvas to compensate for the increased tonnage too. My lads will of course pitch in and do as much of the work as their skills will allow to save us some costs in labor."

"I see. All-in-all, not an inconsequential sum I take it?" Charles Torris asked, trying to visualize the modifications in his mind as he tallied up the cost.

"Charles," Torris interrupted and waved his hand across his face as if brushing away some pesky fly. "Money is always a consideration, of course, but it is not the only consideration. A bold plan requires bold action. Captain Ryan's plan has a reasonable potential for a generous return on investment. We should not narrow our focus on cost only."

"Of course, John, of course. But it is always prudent to weigh the risk against the cost -"

Ryan raised his arms. Two brothers bickering between themselves served no good purpose.

"Gentlemen, gentlemen, please. Permit me to continue. Patrick and I aren't here seeking charity. I am the sole owner of *Friendship*, possibly the fastest, finest cutter in the North Atlantic -"

"She is," interrupted Dowlin boastfully, "the fastest, finest cutter in the North Atlantic."

"Aye, just so," agreed Ryan and patted Dowlin on the shoulder. "I'm sure you would both agree that she is a fine ship - unique even - and she is of considerable worth. I'm prepared to offer your company a half interest in *Friendship*, as security, in exchange for covering the outlay of money I just described. I propose to reimburse your company its initial investment from prizes we take. Think of this money as a loan."

Ryan paused to let his words take effect and then added, smiling, "and of course your firm, gentlemen, would serve as our *exclusive* agent for disposing of all prizes through the French Admiralty Court and be entitled to commissions."

The brothers exchanged glances.

"A most generous offer, Luke," replied Torris and then said, revealing a bit of candor that surprised Ryan, "perhaps it is more generous than it should be. Certainly, it is a plan worthy of serious consideration."

"I don't disagree with you, John," Charles Torris said evenly. "Captain Ryan's proposal has merit. Still, we cannot ignore the risks. The collateral, the commissions, they have no value if the good Captain's ship is caught or sunk. And I mean no offense to our Irish friends but, Captain Ryan, you've lost your ship once already to the British."

"No offense taken, sir," Ryan answered.

Torris vigorously shook his head, clearly annoyed. "All of our investments have risk, Charles! There is never reward without risk. I still say the initial investment is a secondary concern for the moment. We can find other investors to diminish our own exposure if that is your preference - but it will be money straight out of our pockets. First, however, we must obtain a commission for *Friendship*. And this is why we have invited a *Monsieur* Coffyn to join us for dinner."

"Coffyn?" asked Ryan. The name was unfamiliar to him.

"*Oui*, Frances Jean Coffyn," replied Torris. "He is a trusted friend of Doctor Franklin. Franklin is the American Minister Plenipotentiary to the crown and he is the key to getting you an American commission. It is said the good doctor is brilliant in many subjects. But his knowledge about war and maritime affairs I hear is limited. Coffyn may prove invaluable to us in this regard. But first, ahem, but first we must overcome a certain obstacle."

Ryan raised an eyebrow. "Obstacle?"

"Yes," interjected Charles Torris. "You and *Monsieur* Dowlin are both Irish, no?"

"Aye."

"It is true, is it not, the other officers and men on your ship - all Irish?"

"Save for an Englishman or two and a few other nationalities mixed in, quite so."

"No Americans?"

"Not at present. No."

"Yes, well... There you have it. This is the obstacle of which my brother speaks. A French commission is yours for the asking. This can be arranged without difficulty. But, an American commission? I don't know. Franklin, we have been assured, has commissions to give and this is good, but he has been reluctant to do so of late. Some past, unfortunate experiences with the business of privateering have left a bitter taste in his mouth. Then there was Captain Gustavus Conyngham of the American privateer *Revenge*. The *Dunkirk Pirate* as we citizens of Dunkirk fancied calling him. He is an Irishman like yourself, but was living in America when the war began. He and his men were captured off New York earlier this year. Rumor has it that there were some, *difficulties*, between Franklin and Conyngham."

"So John informed us yesterday," Ryan said vaguely. "I've heard of this man."

"One thing, I fear, is certain," Charles Torris continued, "Franklin will not issue an American commission to a foreigner. Certainly not, forgive me, to an Irish fugitive and former smuggler. So, the trick is first to find an *American*, to find you an American who can lend legitimacy to our cause, who can take command of your ship."

Ryan and Dowlin exchanged dubious glances.

"Is that so?" asked Dowlin, suspiciously, not much caring for the idea.

"Yes," answered Charles Torris. "But we think this is not a problem. As it happens, there is an American ship's captain here in Dunkirk as we speak. He calls Boston home. The birthplace of the revolution, no? His name is Stephen Marchant and, at present, he has no employment, no prospects and is borrowing money to pay his room and board. He is in desperate need of a ship. Marchant actually approached Franklin earlier in January seeking a commission for himself but, alas, Franklin sent him away empty-handed."

"Doesn't sound too promisin' so far," Dowlin snickered and reached for a bottle of whiskey. He had been on his good behavior until then.

"Marchant," continued Charles Torris unperturbed, "made the mistake of associating himself with one of our competitors, a disreputable company here in Dunkirk, a company that defrauded Franklin last year in scheme to outfit a privateer. That scheme happened well before Marchant ever associated himself with the company. Marchant had participated in no wrong. He simply was ignorant of the unscrupulous nature of his potential business partners. We took the liberty of interviewing him earlier today."

"I am sorry to say," Torris added with a grin. "That Captain Marchant is, well, to be blunt, not a particularly strong man. Rather he is like soft clay, malleable. But this may be to our advantage as we think you will be able to mold him into whatever you like. He will use us to gain command of a ship and we will use him to obtain a commission."

"I don't like it none," said Dowlin. "I don't fancy risking my neck following orders from someone I don't know."

"A fair point, Patrick," said Torris. "Luke, you would remain on board as owner and as owner, of course, you would have the authority to override any orders given by Marchant you found, shall we say, ill-advised... In truth, you would ultimately still be in command of the cutter."

"A cat's paw?" asked Dowlin as he popped a handful of red grapes into his mouth.

Torris gave Dowlin a blank stare.

"A figurehead, a dupe..." Dowlin explained while chewing on his grapes.

"Ah, *oui*. Precisely Patrick!"

Ryan turned the matter over in his head. An almost imperceptible smile touched his lips. It was a very good solution to their dilemma he had to admit to himself. *Torris is smart.*

"May we meet this Captain Marchant first?" Ryan asked carefully.

Torris rubbed his hands together and giggled excitedly like a schoolboy.

"For once I have anticipated you first, Luke!" Torris replied and joined Dowlin in a drink. "Perhaps I should savor the moment. It may not come again for a very long while..."

"How so?"

"I have him here, waiting outside. Marchant is not our only option but, well, *mon ami*, I should let you judge things for yourself. It is best that Coffyn knows nothing of this arrangement, yes? As long as results are satisfactory, who should care who is captain of the cutter? Franklin, of course, may not see things that way. And, certainly, we do not want to risk compromising Coffyn's position with Franklin. So, we tell him as little as possible. We mentioned Marchant's name to Coffyn earlier today and, as luck would have it, Coffyn knows something of Marchant and holds a good opinion of the American. So this is in our favor."

"Understood," Ryan answered, without committing himself one way or the other.

"I have told Marchant only that we are looking for a captain to command a small privateer. He need not know anything more than that."

Dowlin, having consumed most of the fruit, began attacking the cheese and bread. He gave Ryan a sideways glance and couldn't resist a grin. "Every day just gets more and more interestin' with you Luke," he mumbled, his cheeks stuffed with food. "I think, should anybody be askin' me, we're in for one wild ride..."

"You've never been shy about a wild ride or two before, Patrick!" Ryan said with a chuckle. "Very well, John, let us meet this American of yours."

A big, beefy man with a broad face and a large, hooked nose, a nose that would have been unflattering on most men but gave the American's face a certain symmetry, walked confidently into the small office and took Ryan's hand, squeezing it a bit too firmly. His sheer size and deep voice made him an imposing figure.

"Captain Stephan Marchant," he said, introducing himself, "at your service, sir."

"It is an honor to make your acquaintance, sir," replied Ryan. "And may I introduce Lieutenant Patrick Dowlin to you."

"Lieutenant..." Marchant said and nodded at Dowlin.

"Capt'n," Dowlin replied coolly and stood out of courtesy. But he did not extend his hand. "Always a pleasure meeting an American."

Torris pressed a glass of wine into Marchant's hand and motioned him over to an empty chair.

And then Ryan proceeded to question Marchant at some length about his experiences, trying to gauge the American's grit. Ryan found Marchant gregarious and pleasant enough but quickly concluded that Marchant was not a man he would ever hire as ship's master under normal circumstances. Marchant's nautical skills seemed ordinary at best and he had no military experience of any kind. Ryan found the American to be thick on form and thin on substance. *Useful traits for a cat's paw though*, Ryan concluded. Torris had sized Marchant up well and, Ryan thought, the *plan* was coming together nicely.

"Well, most impressive, Capt'n Marchant," Ryan offered, lying. "I must say, your accomplishments are most impressive..."

Marchant nodded appreciatively. "Thank you, sir. I've done a few good deeds in my day. I possess a lifetime of experiences but, as you can plainly see, I'm still young, still vigorous!"

"Indeed, Captain Marchant. You understand, sir, that if we were to hire you as our ship's captain, I would be sailing with you? And, as one of the principal owners of the ship, I would have *final* authority over any matters of significance?"

"Ah, Mr. Ryan, you fancy yerself a ship's master?" Marchant asked and chuckled.

"Aye, sir. I suppose I do."

"No problem there. Happy to have you along! You seem like a well-bred gentleman to me. Perhaps you'd be interested in a few rounds of whist or chess while we plunder the king's treasures? Cruises can be long and tedious. Be good to whittle some time away with a gentlemen's game or two. Modest wagers of course."

Ryan ignored Marchant's idle banter. If luck favored the Irishmen, there would be no time for gentlemen's games.

"Then you understand and accept my terms should we offer you employment? I mean you no insult. Please understand Capt'n, I do not doubt your abilities but the crew and I have a long history together and we know each other well. It will take time for them to become accustomed to the ways of an American. It will take time to cultivate their trust. And I do, after all, have a substantial financial interest in the ship to protect."

"I understand very well, sir. You're the ship's purser so to speak. I gladly accept your conditions."

A good captain would never have agreed so easily to Ryan's terms. Permitting a meddlesome owner with unknown abilities on board with power to override the captain's decisions was a dangerous prospect.

This man, thought Ryan, *is either a fool or too desperate for employment to care.* Either way suited Ryan's purpose.

"Good. Also, as your own experience with combat is, shall we say, limited, you would be expected to defer to Mr. Dowlin here, or to me, on matters of naval tactics as we have, ahem, some modest skills in that regard. Agreed?"

"Agreed," Marchant replied and tipped his glass at Ryan. "Always ready to rely on the good talents of my junior officers when I can."

Ryan heard the strong ring of truth in Marchant's last remark.

Torris walked Marchant to the door but, before leaving, Marchant turned and flashed Ryan and Dowlin a beaming smile, certain the job was his. And so it was.

"Well?" Ryan asked Dowlin.

"Well what, Luke?"

"Well, what do you think about Marchant? I'm hardly asking you how you like the wine."

Dowlin shrugged, for no good reason he could think of, he had taken an instant dislike to the American. "Weeeeell... the same arrangement worked out fine with Macatter and Weldin. But, truth be told, 'em two turned out to be real sailors and good lads. This braggart seems to know more about parlor games than sailin'. Worst that happens I suppose," Dowlin paused to chuckle, "is we mutiny and throw the bloody bugger overboard. I don't imagine anyone will much miss him."

Ryan and the Torris brothers started laughing.

"Luke?" Torris asked. "What is your opinion?"

Ryan caressed his chin with his fingers. "Hm. I hope our Mr.

Franklin isn't much of a sailor or our goose is cooked. Do you really think Franklin can be persuaded, with Coffyn's aid, to give Marchant a commission?"

Torris shrugged. "Who knows? Let us assume for the moment that he can be so persuaded, what then?"

Ryan looked around the table, stood, and raised his glass. "In that event, gentlemen, if my terms are agreeable to you, we have an accord and I believe we are in business. Yes?"

The brothers exchanged nods, stood and raised their glasses.

Dowlin slowly raised himself out of his chair, cleared his throat, and grabbed a bottle off the table. "A proper toast requires the proper amount of liquor," he explained, flashing his brilliant smile around the room.

"Quite right, Patrick," Torris replied. "Allow me the honor of the first toast: to the American privateer of Dunkirk, may she be a scourge to English shipping and always bring her crew home through hostile waters unscathed!"

In unison, the four men touched their glasses together with a clink and drained them.

"One small matter," Ryan said, setting his empty glass down on the table. "I've been thinking about a new name for the cutter."

"A new name?" Dowlin asked, surprised. Not even he was immune from a sailor's superstition.

"Aye, *Friendship* was a smuggler and that is in her past. Name hardly suits a warship."

"Hm, suppose it's not very warlike," agreed Dowlin, absently scratching the red stubble on his cheek. "I'll be missin' the old girl. So, pray tell, what's her new name to be?"

"I've decided on: *Black Prince*."

"The *Black Prince*?" asked Torris.

"Aye, the *Black Prince*," answered Ryan.

"You mean the English prince who fought at the battle of Crecy, Prince Edward?" Torris asked, perplexed by Ryan's choice of an English hero.

"No, not Edward. I am thinking of the nameless horseman who wore black armor and bore no coat-of-arms. A gallant warrior, a chivalrous knight and a man, if you believe the legends, who fought for noble causes but who was not of noble blood."

"Local folks ought to love that," Dowlin offered softly with a chuckle.

"Why, Patrick," Torris commented, "I believe you are correct. What *petite garcon* hasn't pretended to be the Black Prince with wooden sword and shield in hand? The name stirs the blood! A fine choice, Luke. Gentlemen, shall we call upon *Monsieur* Coffyn? I have already taken the liberty of informing him that we are looking for an American commission for *Friendship*, pardon, for the *Black Prince*, and that she has an American captain. He waits for us."

Ryan laughed, glanced over at Dowlin. "I do believe we've been had, Mr. Dowlin."

"Does sound like we've been set up nicely," Dowlin answered. "Doubt the French ever hoodwinked the old Black Prince himself like that. Not this smoothly anyhows."

As he led his two Irish co-conspirators to a tavern several blocks away, Torris explained that Coffyn was a broker and a royal interpreter by trade, who enjoyed a reputation for intelligence and honesty. Franklin was known to use Coffyn from time to time as his agent to funnel sizable sums of money into England, money used to help American prisoners buy food and clothing and even to fund prison escapes.

When the four men entered the tavern, they found Coffyn already seated at a table waiting for them.

Coffyn stood to greet them. "Ah, John, Charles, wonderful to see you again. I trust you are both well?"

"Very well indeed thank you, Francis," answered Torris.

"And Mr. Bernardson, I am honored to make your acquaintance once again," offered Coffyn with a crooked smile.

The name Peter Bernardson was an alias Ryan sometimes found useful. Ryan instantly recognized Coffyn. He had been introduced to Coffyn once before, but only briefly, and he couldn't remember where.

"*Monsieur* Coffyn, the honor is mine, sir," replied Ryan in French as he shook Coffyn's hand warmly. "Allow me to introduce my associate to you, Mr. Patrick Dowlin."

"Pleasure, sir, I take it from your family name that you are Irish, Mr. Dowlin?" Coffyn asked in excellent English.

Dowlin nodded.

"Many Irish in Dunkirk. Good folk. Please gentlemen, sit. The cuisine here is quite good. I have taken the liberty of ordering a round of whiskey for us. I understand Mr. Bernardson, from *Monsieur* Torris, that you are the owner of a very fine privateer?"

"Quite so, *Monsieur* Coffyn."

"And you desire an American commission for her?"

"Precisely."

"Well, I must be frank with you. Obtaining an American commission may prove difficult."

"Yes. So I have been told."

"May I inquire, who is her captain?"

"Indeed, you may. The ship is ably commanded by a gentleman named Stephen Marchant, an American from Boston. He has many years of experience at sea."

"Hm. And the crew? Irishmen mostly, a few Portuguese and an Englishman or two?"

"Just so. You are well-informed. Fine lads all, none better."

Coffyn was no fool. He knew Ryan was playing a bit of cat and mouse with him but decided not to press Ryan for now. Coffyn had known the Torris brothers for many years and had faith in their overall good business judgment. The three men had profited nicely together in the past and Torris had already vouched for the ship, her captain and her crew. Torris was no fool either.

Coffyn already knew Marchant too. The big American had made a very good impression on him. He had felt sorry for the poor American though when, a few months earlier, Marchant had the misfortune of accepting employment with one Gerrard Poreau, of Poreau, Mackenzie & Co., to command a newly built privateer. Poreau, along with the burgomaster of Dunkirk, had sent Marchant off to see Franklin to ask for a commission but, unbeknownst to Marchant, Franklin had lost a substantial sum to Poreau the year before outfitting another privateer. That ship never sailed and Franklin's money disappeared. Franklin assumed Poreau had swindled him. Once Franklin realized that Marchant was working for the same Poreau who had cheated him earlier, he sent Marchant away empty-handed.

The five men fell silent when a pretty tavern maid appeared to serve them glasses of whiskey with a plate of bread and cheese.

"Excellent, Mr. Bernardson. I can say with certainty that the Americans do have commissions to hand out. Regrettably, the good Captain Marchant already approached his Excellency, Doctor Franklin, this past January for one of them and Franklin turned him away. An unscrupulous man named Poreau had, you see, duped Marchant. No doubt you are aware of this sad story and we need not revisit the details. Poreau is an odious man, a curse to us all."

"Precisely, Francis," Torris offered. "As we discussed earlier, the good doctor's decision, however, was not a reflection on Captain Marchant. Marchant was simply an innocent victim."

"Ah, true enough! Poreau's dishonesty has caused us all some damage. *Maggot*."

"Times," interjected Torris, "and circumstances do change, Francis."

"Agreed. Despite Saratoga, the Americans are losing their war and each day more and more Americans prisoners are marched into British jails. We have all heard the stories of how the Americans are treated. The English can be a cruel people. The great doctor agonizes over their sufferings. He works tirelessly to improve their conditions or to secure their release."

"You see, Francis," Torris quipped, "Franklin may not know it yet, but he needs *Monsieur* Bernardson and his ship and crew. We beseech you - help us make him understand. After the exchange in Nantes, Franklin has no prisoners left. The American Navy is in hiding and

Jones's fleet at L'Orient won't be ready to sail for months. *Monsieur* Bernardson's ship offers Doctor Franklin a wonderful opportunity to go after British ships and British sailors without delay. And remember, unlike the unsavory *Monsieur* Poreau, we do not ask Franklin for money. Not one *sou*. There is little risk to the Americans - even should our venture fail."

"A persuasive argument certainly, John," readily agreed Coffyn. "Assuming for the moment that his American Excellency can even be persuaded to provide you with a commission *Monsieur* Bernardson, how soon could your ship sail?"

"She could sail tomorrow *Monsieur* Coffyn," Ryan proclaimed boldly and drained his whiskey with one swallow. "But we need to make certain modifications to her first to toughen her up some and that will take two, possibly three weeks, at the most."

"Two or three weeks, no longer?"

"No longer," answered Dowlin.

"I am no sailor but that seems, well, a bit ambitious, gentlemen."

Dowlin smiled. "Three weeks maximum. You have my word on it."

Coffyn nodded. "Very well. I am curious, what is the name of this ship of yours?"

"She is," Ryan answered, "the *Black Prince*."

"The *Black Prince*," Coffyn said, repeating the ship's name slowly to himself. "Ah, very good. That name conjures up images does it not? Gentlemen, on occasion Franklin uses me as his representative for certain matters between the Americans and the British. However, allow me to be perfectly clear: I have no special influence with the Americans and I make no false claims to the contrary. If you desire it though, I would be happy to make the necessary introductions for you. Beyond this, there is little assistance I can render."

"*Merci boucoup, mon ami!*" Torris exclaimed happily. "We can ask no more. Allow me to order another round of drinks!"

Coffyn's offer to make introductions was as good as an endorsement from Coffyn and, Torris knew, Coffyn's blessing would carry great weight with Franklin. Torris was confident that Franklin would be more receptive to Marchant this time around. He could already see the headlines: *The American privateer Black Prince, commanded by Stephan Marchant of Boston, captures a fine English vessel of great value!*

"I leave for Paris in the morning, John. We shall see what the mood of the good doctor is then."

"Thank you, *Monsieur* Coffyn," Ryan offered. "Your efforts shall not go unrewarded."

Coffyn smiled politely at Ryan. "Your generosity is well known *Monsieur* Bernardson, or should I say, *Monsieur Luke Ryan?* Yes, I know who you are. Your sterling reputation precedes you, Captain Ryan. I would not have helped you otherwise. But I do not do this for financial gain. I believe in the American rebellion. Their cause is noble and just. We are witnesses to an epic event in the history. Think of it, *liberty* for an entire nation! At birth, every man an equal with all of his countrymen with certain unalienable rights that not even a king can deny! I tell you this, mark my words carefully gentlemen: the *American Revolution* shall roll across the Atlantic and wash over the whole of Europe like some great wave. The old order will be swept away. The genie is out of the bottle and there is no way to stuff him back inside. I only wonder how much blood will be spilt before it is all over. Oceans of it I fear..."

Ryan could only smile. For once, the master tactician had been outmaneuvered. He humbly bowed his head towards Coffyn and said no more.

But as the tavern maid returned with dinner, and the Torris brothers started engaging Coffyn in more mundane matters, Ryan quietly sipped his whiskey and reflected on Coffyn's words about the war, about the revolution, wondering what they meant.

The knocking was persistent. To his annoyance, Franklin had to answer the door himself after pleas to his grandson and his French secretary went unanswered. Franklin hobbled towards the door mumbling to himself. His gout had again flared up and was causing him considerable pain. He could not understand why God had plagued man with old age. It seemed a useless, cruel curse.

"Yes. Yes. Yes. I am coming. Patience. For mercy's sake, give us a moment if you *please!*"

"Doctor Franklin, greetings, sir," offered the late night caller and clasped the old man's hands warmly. "I am sorry for this intrusion without any forewarning. I pray the hour is not too late?"

"Why, *Monsieur le Comte* Clonard," Franklin answered. "How very good to see you! You are always most welcome. Please, please, do come in and out of this chilly night air."

"Ah, *merci.* You are in good health I trust?"

"Fit as a fiddle," replied Franklin, waving his guest inside. *Thank God it is only Clonard,* thought Franklin, *he's a sensible chap, never a makes a nuisance of himself, doesn't overstay his welcome...*

"I must say, you are looking splendid, Doctor Franklin."

"Thank you, *merci,* if only I was a bit younger though," Franklin replied wistfully and winked, "perhaps then the young ladies of Paris would concur with your kind observations and show me favor!"

"Ah, I know better!" Clonard declared and wiggled an index finger at Franklin. "I hear the Parisian ladies are simply mad about you and stumble over one another vying for your attentions. And the talk around town is that you hardly discourage them! Doctor, doctor... Truly, you are a Frenchman at heart, no?"

Franklin chuckled as he led Clonard down a dark, narrow hallway and into the parlor, moving gingerly with the aid of a walking stick. He took a seat near the fire and motioned Clonard over to a chair across from him.

Though Sutton de Clonard was only a minor nobleman, he enjoyed a fair amount of influence at Versailles and had an interest in naval affairs. Louis XV had bestowed the title of count on Clonard's father, an Irishman from Wexford, for his services to France during the Seven Years War and Clonard had inherited the title.

"*Madame la Vicomtesse* Clonard, she is well I trust?" Franklin inquired tactfully. "Such a charming hostess. I find her ability to converse intelligently over a great variety of subjects most stimulating. She is a delight to the mind and to the eye. I so look forward to *Madam's* dinner parties!"

"*Oui*, your Excellency. She is indeed well. Many thanks. We would both be honored, flattered truly, to have you as our guest again. *Madame* Clonard, and I hesitate to reveal this to you, adores your Excellency. Perhaps we shall arrange something for next week? *Madame* Anne-Louise Brillon would be most welcome and I will, of course, ensure the French Court is represented so that the evening is not entirely wasted on small pleasantries..."

The name of Anne-Louise Brillon made Franklin smile. A gifted musician with a harpsichord, an accomplished composer, she had become a dear friend and frequent companion, though there was forty years between them.

"That would indeed be splendid, sir! I can think of nothing better."

Temple had heard his grandfather entertaining an unexpected guest. He rushed to the kitchen, found a plate of *hor d'oeuvres* and a bottle of sherry and entered the parlor with a polite nod to Clonard, and his treats.

"Ah, Temple, there you are my dear boy. My good Count, you know my grandson, Temple."

"But of course. I am delighted to see you again young *Monsieur* Franklin. Your grandfather and I were just discussing the possibility of a dinner engagement for next week. I shall have *Madame* Clonard add your name to the invitation list - together perhaps with the names of several young ladies. Certainly Paris has some *mademoiselle* to offer who strikes your fancy? French women are unsurpassed in beauty and sophistication. A handsome young man such as yourself, approaching your prime as you are, should not be without the companionship of the fairer sex for very long. You cannot remain a bachelor forever. It is, unhealthy!"

Temple blushed as he placed a sterling silver tray on a small table between the two men and excused himself.

"A fine young man," Clonard said as Temple left the parlor. "Handsome. Dignified. The grandson of a great, great man so I am certain he is intelligent too. He must make your Excellency proud."

"Indeed, he does," Franklin answered with affectionate in his voice. "If only I could say the same about his father..."

"Ah, yes. Was he not the governor of New Jersey before the war?"

"Yes. He lives in New York now with his British friends. He is, and will forever be, a grave disappointment to me. We no longer acknowledge the other's existence. He is dead to me."

"Oh, dear. Forgive me for opening up old wounds. I had forgotten that he is a Loyalist, which has caused a rift between you. How goes your valiant war against the English?"

"Ah, it goes," answered Franklin with a trace of weariness in his voice. "It is becoming a very long and tedious affair, a victory here, a defeat there. One step forward, two steps back. I pray God lets me live long enough to see us through this mighty ordeal, to see us victorious in our noble struggle."

"Yes, well, take heart your Excellency," Clonard offered cheerfully and accepted a glass of sherry from Franklin. "Like the tides, the fortunes of war are ever shifting. With France's power and prestige at your disposal, America shall, without doubt, win her independence. It is only a matter of time and of application."

"Application?"

"Yes, the application of brutal, overwhelming force against the vital weak point in your opponent's order of battle. Washington will succeed in this."

"I think you have some knowledge of soldiering my dear friend. I regret that I do not. I pray that you are correct, *Monsieur* Clonard. We shall see. Time is a friend to some and an enemy to others. Of late, too often, I have found myself wondering which side mother time truly favors in this war."

"How true, how true. I understand a British cartel ship arrived in Nantes recently with one hundred Americans on board?"

"Yes, our first successful prisoner exchange."

"Will there be more?"

"Let us hope so."

"Soon?"

"I cannot say. Overcoming British duplicity and arrogance continues to tax my meager skills in the art of negotiating."

Clonard laughed. "Arrogance and duplicity! English politicians have always prized these two qualities above all others! Well, again, I do apologize for coming to your house like this at such a late hour and without invitation. To business then?"

"You are a good friend to America and will always be most welcome in my home. Please, tell me what is on your mind? How may I assist?"

"Allow me to be frank your Excellency. You know me to be a gentleman of good character, a practical man and one who would not squander your time. I come to you with information, information that may, possibly, have some value to you. Information that concerns American prisoners."

"Oh?" Franklin asked with interest, relieved too that Clonard was not making a mere social call. Clonard had always been considerate and sensible in the past.

Clonard held the crystal glass up to the fire and studied the red liquid. "This is a delightful sherry, very good. But I have in my possession some *exceptionally* fine sherry. Tomorrow, I shall have my man bring a few bottles around to you. Your Excellency, if I may, there is an exceptionally fine sloop anchored in Dunkirk Harbor. I have seen this ship myself. One of the ship's principal investors, a man named John Torris, has been a good friend of mine for many years and we have done some business together on occasion. He is shrewd and more honest than most. The vessel I speak of is well-armed with sixteen heavy guns. Her crew is Irish and American. Her captain wishes to try his luck at privateering, possibly for the French but, perhaps, this ship might be more useful, move valuable, to the Americans? This was my thought..."

Franklin had come to know Clonard well. He was a careful, intelligent man who was now speaking to him in the slippery language of French nobility. Franklin had become fluent in the language since arriving in France. Clonard was not asking him for anything. He would never be so *vulgar* as to directly ask Franklin for anything. Rather, Clonard was merely offering his services as an intermediary who could make the necessary introductions.

Franklin sipped his sherry and nibbled on a biscuit, sprinkling bits of biscuit across his blue velvet vest. He absently brushed the crumbs into the palm of his hand and dropped them on his plate.

"And whom may I ask, sir, is the captain of this fine warship that has so impressed you?"

"Ah, your Excellency, an able man, an American from Boston named Stephen Marchant. I would be happy to arrange a meeting between the two of you, at your convenience certainly."

Franklin raised an eyebrow at hearing Marchant's name. *Marchant.* He remembered. The American had come to him several months before looking for a bit of money until he could return to America. *Yes, a big, overly confident fellow.* He had been captured by the British but had been clever enough to escape to France. Franklin had given him enough in coin to get home and sent him away but the big man returned later asking for a commission for a new privateer owned by Poreau, the same man who had cheated him the year before. The sordid business with Poreau was still a fresh wound.

Franklin paused and quietly reflected on Clonard's proposal. While Clonard was not a particularly important nobleman at Versailles, he had influence over others at court who were important and Franklin could not afford to ignore him.

"Do you recall my difficulties with Poreau?" Franklin asked disdainfully.

"Yes your Excellency, I do. I do indeed. A most unfortunate episode. But one does not toss out the whole bushel because of one bad apple?"

"Hm. Now there is some good, old homespun wisdom for you!"

"I believe I learned the phrase from your Excellency."

"It does have the ring of familiarity. Well, right you are of course. If Marchant is not affiliated with Poreau or his toadies, then I shall give the matter careful consideration my good Count. But I make no promises."

"Nor would I ask for any. By the way, *Monsieur* Coffyn also has knowledge of this matter and has a good opinion of Marchant."

"Coffyn?"

"Yes."

"Coffyn is usually a clever, careful man."

"Indeed he is. And, if I may, what news of Captain Jones?"

"It is no secret Jones is in L'Orient."

Clonard knew that Jones was in L'Orient of course, that Jones could not sail for some time, but he had made his point and realized he could push the matter no further. He preferred the game of chess over cards. Little is left to chance in chess. He was a shrewd man of patience and persistence, traits every lesser nobleman at Court needed to survive. He finished his sherry and bid Franklin a good evening.

In the morning, Franklin received a crate of sherry from Clonard and along with the following letter:

> "*Mr. Stephen Marchant of Boston is come from Dunkirk to Solicit your Excellency for an American Commission to Enable him to Command the Cutter of 16 guns which I mentioned to you. I request that you may gratify him therein. This Vessel will have a very good Crew, American & Irish, as She Sails extremely well, She must do considerable Execution.*"

From the beginning of the rebellion in 1776, the American Continental Congress had authorized the use of privateers. John Adams believed using privateers would be, "a short, easy, and infallible method of humbling the English, preventing the effusion of an ocean of blood, and bringing the war to a quick conclusion."

The money was easy at first. With letters of marque in hand, over 10,000 *Yankee* sailors in 136 ships swooped down into the West Indies to ravage English merchant ships. The British navy responded to this threat by sending in its frigates to run the rebel raiders down and suddenly privateering became a very risky business.

Privateers were no match for frigates and throughout the Caribbean, British navy ships began tenaciously pursuing the raiders, sinking or capturing scores of American vessels. And the British kept at it until the privateers had largely been swept from the seas. Some

American privateers switched tactics and tried their luck off the coast of France and England, searching for English prey. But they were a long way from home and not very effective.

Soon after his arrival to Paris in December 1776, Congress instructed Franklin to ask the French government to open its ports to American privateers so they could avoid the long and dangerous voyage home across the Atlantic to refit and resupply. But the French Crown did not receive the request with any fondness as France was then still a neutral power. France had refused at first. But then, for reasons lost in history's murky depths, Franklin eventually prevailed over French reluctance - and British protests - and the French allowed a limited number of American privateers access to French ports.

The British government retaliated by refusing to recognize American privateers as anything more than pirates and threatened to hang every privateer they caught. This did little to discourage the Americans though and before the war's end over 50,000 sailors would put to sea on at least one cruise as a privateer.

But not all Americans were keen about privateers. Officers in the Continental Navy in particular despised privateers for luring experienced seamen away from the navy with promises of riches, leaving them with inadequate and inexperienced crews. And they had contempt for any officer who left the navy to serve with these lowly "licensed robbers." Captain Jones's opinion of privateers was no better. He complained bitterly to friends that privateers were "...motivated by no nobler principle than that of self-interest..." who, because of their greed, "...forced half the American fleet to lie empty and idle in the harbour."

Franklin hastily read Clonard's letter, tossed it aside, annoyed. He had no wish to get himself entangled with complicated business of privateering again and had hoped, foolishly, he knew, that Clonard might graciously drop the matter. Privateering had always been a messy business, attracting the worst sorts. Poreau had cheated him, Conyngham had disappointed him and Jones, a man whose judgment in naval matters he trusted, strongly disapproved of privateers.

But men, even great men, rarely have a say when Destiny chooses to intervene. Shortly after Clonard's visit Coffyn, Franklin's own trusted agent, Coffyn, travelled to Paris to visit him, to try and persuade him to at least meet with Marchant. The owners of Marchant's new cutter, Coffyn explained, were the Torris brothers, reputable Dunkirk merchants with no affiliation to Poreau, MacKenzie & Co. and he assured Franklin that he had already met the officers and crew and that they appeared competent in every way. And the beauty of this scheme, unlike his prior dealings with Poreau, was that no one was asking Franklin for any money. The *Black Prince's* investors only needed a commission. There was, Coffyn told him, not afraid to employ logic against the doctor, nothing to lose.

After listening politely to Coffyn, Franklin sighed and agreed to at least meet with Marchant one more time. Coffyn had always served him well, had always shown good judgment, and now was asking him for very little.

The next day, Marchant and his first officer, a man named Jonathan Arnold from Middletown, Connecticut, arrived at Passy just after breakfast. Marchant squeezed his imposing frame through the narrow doorway and followed Franklin into his small, dark study with Arnold in tow. A warm drizzle began falling across Paris and off in the distance the men could hear the low rumble of thunder. The Americans took seats surrounded by stacks of papers.

"Ah, Doc, Doctor Franklin, your Excellency," began Marchant with a thick Bostonian accent and slight stutter. "Thank you for agreeing to see me again. Permit me to come right to the point. I understand that you are still in the market for a privateer or two but have had no luck finding one. I have found one, one that should suit your purposes very well. She is the *Black Prince*, a very fine cutter. She carries sixteen carriage guns and thirty swivels. She is a burden of one hundred forty tons and is near one hundred feet in length. She'll be fully provisioned before setting out from Dunkirk and we've already recruited the necessary men and officers needed to sail her, that being about seventy in number, sir. All good stock: American and Irish lads, experienced seamen all. I heard of your problems last year with Poreau, sir. Most unfortunate, real shame. When your Excellency granted me an audience in January, I had no knowledge Poreau had done you wrong. Otherwise, rest assured, I would have had no dealings with such a scoundrel. But unlike Poreau, with the Torris company behind me, we don't need money. We aren't asking the United States government for one copper penny. What we need from you is one of those commissions. There's no risk to you, sir. Why, with the right man at the helm, so to speak, it's a golden opportunity if I may say so, your Excellency."

As Franklin listened, Marchant's first officer, an unremarkable man with buckteeth and thin, stringy hair, sat passively in his chair and added nothing to the conversation. Franklin studied the young lieutenant for a moment as Marchant talked. Arnold's sole purpose in life seemed to be to nod approvingly at everything his master said.

Franklin sighed absently. *Marchant's qualifications are suspect; he may even be a buffoon and his lieutenant is nothing more than a sycophant.* He felt a chill and led his guests into the parlor where Temple was already busy stoking a fire. He took the poker from Temple and stabbed the red-hot embers with it as Temple left for the kitchen to brew tea. The logs crackled and hissed at Franklin.

"And you would be that man, the right man to take charge that is?" Franklin asked Marchant with his back still turned to him as he played with the fire.

"Sir?"

Franklin spun around to face Marchant, pointed the poker at him. "You are the man for the job? You have the necessary qualifications is what I mean to ask?"

Marchant looked away, his eyes darted nervously about the room, and that troubled Franklin. Hard to gauge the measure of a man when he won't look you straight in the eye.

Suddenly Marchant's generous belly began shaking. He erupted into a boisterous laugh.

"Cut us loose on the British, and you'll not soon regret it your Excellency! That's Captain Marchant's solemn pledge to you, sir!" Marchant reached over to Arnold and slapped him hard on the back. "Isn't that so, Mr. Arnold?"

"Aye, sir!" Arnold replied with exaggerated enthusiasm.

Franklin could sense the undercurrents. Marchant had the jitters and nervous men always made Franklin nervous and uncomfortable in turn.

The room suddenly turned dark. Large drops of rain began pelting the street, pinging against the windowpanes as thunder rolled over the city.

"The crew of this ship of yours, mostly smugglers, I assume?" asked Franklin as Temple returned with a tray of cups and a pot of tea and started serving his grandfather and their two guests.

"True. But as your Excellency must know, no captain can afford to scrutinize the past of his men too closely. There are no saints aboard a ship. No sir, only sinners. The only thing that matters is that they obey."

"Fair enough, Captain but, if I may ask, where would you begin?" Franklin asked, shamelessly baiting Marchant.

Marchant bit his lip. "Beg pardon, sir?"

"Well, Captain, I most profess that my knowledge of military matters is quite limited. Please forgive my ignorance on the subject. What I mean to ask, sir, as a military man, you have formulated some plan of action?"

"Oh, aye, of course, your Excellency. Aye, well, ahem. Why we'd sail off the coast of England of course and attack anything that got in our way! No need to be too cute about it if you know what I mean, sir. Just sail her in and out, bring back whatever we find out there on the open sea. Not much more to it than fishing."

"I see," Franklin replied disappointed, but not surprised by Marchant's empty answer. Still, he had hoped for something more substantial, something other than a vague boast.

"And what of England's Grand Fleet, Captain Marchant?"

Marchant set his cup down to scratch the bald spot on the back of his scalp. "Ah, well now, sir, we're no match for the Grand Fleet. Perhaps Captain Jones can help you there. We'll be givin' it, and to all other hazards at sea, a wide berth, a wide berth indeed."

"Of course, of course," replied Franklin, his tone turning haughty. Obviously no power on earth could sail against the Grand Fleet, certainly not while stationed in home waters. Franklin could feel his patience wearing thin. "May I inquire, sir, just how long have you sailed with this ship and crew?"

Marchant fidgeted in his chair and coughed. "Ahem, oh, well, now there, sir, I reckon that I haven't actually sailed on this ship or with her crew just yet. I know the ship by reputation you might say. I've seen her though and I've met the owners. Rest easy there, sir. Mr. Arnold here and me, we've sailed together a long, long time. We'll see to it that ship and crew are fit for action. We know our craft and trade well enough."

"I see," Franklin replied in a more friendly tone out of pity. He had heard enough and was just about to show Marchant to the door, just about to send the man away again without a commission. But then he hesitated. Something inside him, a peculiar feeling, tugged at him, urged him to stay his hand. And over the years he had learned to trust his instincts.

"Well, no matter. I am certain, as you say, that you and your lieutenant know your business well enough."

"That we do."

"You both are to be commended for the personal risks you are willing to take to prosecute our cause."

"We are both New England Yankees and true patriots, your Excellency."

"Indeed you are. Anything else?"

"Well, no, sir. I'd just like to say, as foolish as this may sound, that when all is said and done folks will talk about the *Prince* someday. Talk about her with pride. I can feel it in my bones."

And, somehow, Franklin knew Marchant's last words were true. That annoyed the scientist in him, offended his sensibilities as a man of reason and logic.

"Well, Captain Marchant, you have been most persuasive and I shall give the matter the due consideration it deserves."

After some small chitchat about home, and when the tea was gone, Franklin escorted Marchant and Arnold to the door and watched them walk out into a heavy downpour. The sewers were overwhelmed by the volume of water. The streets were quickly flooding. He would not get in his walk today - and that annoyed him too.

The matter of the Dunkirk cutter weighed heavily on his mind for the rest of the day. The crafty, old fox considered things carefully. On one hand, he very much wanted to free more Americans from British jails as quickly as he could. On the other, he feared giving Marchant a commission would ensnare him in future troubles. Except for Captain Jones, naval matters had given him nothing but grief since his arrival to France. But, with Jones's squadron sitting idle at L'Orient, and with his batch of British prisoners gone, he was desperate to do something, anything, to capture more British sailors and soldiers.

And Franklin knew he had to act fast. Clonard, Coffyn, Marchant, they had all hinted that *Prince's* owners would apply for a French commission if he refused Marchant. Then any prizes caught, any prisoners taken, would be the property of the French Crown. The risks seemed small enough. What, he wondered, could go wrong - except perhaps for the loss of one, inconsequential ship with a mostly Irish crew?

The next morning Franklin sat at his *escritoire* and considered the blank commissions in his hand. He only had three commissions left and wasn't even sure if they were still legal. John Hancock had signed them back in the fall of 1777 as President of the Continental Congress. But Hancock was retired now and living in Massachusetts.

Franklin rarely allowed such petty details to distract him. "Temple!" he called out in a loud voice. "Be a good lad and find me the bond and allegiance that are to accompany these damn commissions. I dare say I've misplaced them again. I'll need some more writing paper too."

Temple hurried to his grandfather's study. "You are going to do it Grandfather?" Temple asked excitedly. "You're going to give the Dunkirk smugglers a commission?"

On more than one occasion, Temple had approached Franklin, asking his grandfather for his blessing to serve in a soldier's uniform. The old man could see Temple's thoughts now. Peering over his bifocals, he wagged a finger at his grandson.

"You can set any notions about going to sea rolling around in that empty head of yours aside young man!" But he instantly regretted his harsh tone and added, more softly, "I need you here, Temple. You are indispensable to me. I'd be lost without you."

Temple knew not to pursue the matter further, nodded sheepishly and disappeared to find the bonds and the allegiance.

Franklin dipped his pen in the ink jar, dated the commission May 19, 1779 and signed his name to the document. As the *Prince* weighed over 100 tons, Franklin set the bond amount at $10,000 American dollars but left the ship's owner's name blank. Congress required the owners of vessels weighing 100 tons or more to pay a $10,000 bond while requiring only a $5,000 bond from the owners of smaller ships. The bond money was used to guarantee the crew's full compliance with the rules, a code of conduct, printed on the face of the bond. If the rules were broken the owner forfeited the entire bond amount and the commission was revoked. The commission was good for three months, after which it automatically expired, unless Franklin saw fit to renew it.

Franklin sent the commission and the ancillary papers on to Coffyn in Dunkirk with instructions that Coffyn was to collect the bond amount and have the owner sign the documents before the cutter sailed. Franklin also sent written orders to Marchant, instructing him to bring back as many prisoners as he could because "... they serve to relieve so many of our Countrymen from their Captivity in England."

By this simple act, by commissioning *Black Prince* to sail as a privateer, Franklin had set into motion a series of events he could not have foreseen. He had unleashed a force far greater than he could have every expected, a force that would make history.

It was an unusually cool day for June. Swirling, dark clouds threatened Dunkirk on all sides. But the raw weather did nothing to dampen the spirits of the Americans and Irishmen gathering at the Torris warehouse. There was purpose in each man's step. Every face radiated confidence. The Torris brothers greeted the seven mariners with broad smiles and hardy handshakes and then led them to the warehouse's back office. Coffyn arrived for the ceremonies punctually at 10.

With every one present, and observing formal military protocol, the *Prince's* officers drew themselves up into two, neat parallel lines and snapped to attention. Front and center was the American Marchant - the honor was his as captain - and to his right stood his number two, the gangly, awkward Mr. Arnold from Connecticut.

Ryan's officers fell in behind the Americans. Macatter, the feisty, black-bearded Bostonian with a heavy, Irish accent that said County Cork, was first in line and standing at his side was his number two, the quiet and competent Weldin. Next to Weldin - a father to the crew and towering over all of them - was the Irish giant Kelly. And next to Kelly, a match for any of the deathless gods in build and beauty, stood Dowlin with a casual, easy grace. Ryan, just a spectator now, leaned against a wall off to the side in the shadows, alone.

With the Torris family Bible, a French Bible, tucked under his arm, Coffyn moved in front of Marchant and held the Good Book out. "Captain Stephan Marchant of the American privateer *Black Prince*," Coffyn began solemnly. "Are you prepared, sir, before these good witnesses - and before God - to take the Oath of Allegiance?"

Marchant cleared his throat and placed his meaty hand on top of the holy book. "Aye, I am," he boomed, his great voice carrying across the warehouse like an echo across a canyon.

"Then," continued Coffyn and handed Marchant a piece of paper, "with the powers invested in me by the Continental Congress of the United States to administer the oath, with your right hand on the Bible, I ask you to swear your undivided fidelity to the United States of America."

Marchant held the document out in front of him, the Oath of Allegiance, and cleared his throat again. "I, Stephen Marchant, do swear allegiance to the United States of America and each of its thirteen member states and vow that I owe no obedience to King George and swear that I will, to the utmost of my power, support, maintain and defend the said United States against the said King and his heirs and successors and his and their abettors, assistants and adherents... *so help me God!*"

Coffyn smiled and shook Marchant's hand. "Congratulations, Captain. Now, if you will, please sign the bond here."

After Marchant scribbled out his signature, Coffyn countersigned the bond as an authorized agent of the United States and then had Charles Torris and Ryan both sign too as the ship's lawful owners. Ryan used his alias, Peter Bernardson.

Coffyn administered the oath to Arnold next and then approached Ryan's plucky, swarthy Irishmen and did the same. One-by-one, Macatter, Weldin, Kelly and Dowlin all stepped forward, placed his hand on Torris's family Bible and gladly swore his allegiance to his new country, a nation some 3,000 miles away, that none of them had ever seen.

With formalities completed, Torris stepped outside his office briefly and soon returned with four musicians and a platoon of caterers for a proper celebration. As the musicians unpacked their instruments and began to ply their trade, playing lively, uplifting tunes, the caterers set up tables and brought in large quantities of the best food and drink Dunkirk had to offer. The Torris brothers spared no expense and everyone settled into a mellow, buoyant mood. Everyone, that is, except Ryan.

While savoring his coup, and with only a twinge of guilt over his bit of trickery with Franklin, uncertainty gnawed at Ryan too. The mariner quietly slipped out of the warehouse, walked across the street and continued walking until he reached the end of an empty pier where he stood, alone, to brood.

Staring out into the cold, gray waters of the North Atlantic, and deep in thought, he wondered: had he just saved his men or condemned them all to die? He tried to shake off his uneasiness, to set aside his doubts. Today was a joyous day he told himself.

After all, he had thrown the dice and he was winning. His plan, so far, had worked. His men were free. He had his cutter and he had his commission too. *Black Prince* was an American warship and his Shadowmen were American subjects. They were all sons of the *Revolution* now. As for all the rest, as Ryan well knew, the Fates claim sole dominion...

Epilogue
A New Day for a New Tale

As the first shafts of light of a new day peeked through the tavern's small windows, the nor'easter having finally quit its cruel siege against the small sea town called Newport, the young reporter looked down at his hands, smudged with black ink, and set his quill pen aside. He considered the large stack of disorganized papers sitting in the center of the table, with his notes scribbled on the front and back of each page, and smiled. The old man had talked straight through the night with barely a pause. Crook had in his possession a fine story, told the *Irish way*, leaving no point unsaid.

"Remarkable. Truly a remarkable story, Mr. Trevett."

"Glad you find it so."

"But the war?" Crook asked impatiently as he massaged his aching fingers. "You only hinted at events during the war. There is much more yet to tell. There is so much more I would hear if you are agreeable."

"Mr. Crook, you've been an attentive listener and a most gracious host. I thank you for that. Now, I've given you enough thar to fill a book. I need to sleep. You need to sleep. I don't ship out for a few weeks yet. Come back on Friday night, if you have a mind to. Same table."

"But..."

Trevett rubbed his eyes and stood to leave. "But... You young pups, always in a hurry. Friday. Friday I'll be here and no doubt in a mood to talk. Well, I'll be in a mood to drink anyhows. And don't forget to bring yer purse..."

Trevett made his way up the tavern's rickety staircase and to the door. But before leaving he paused, turned to look back at Crook and saw the reporter still sitting at the table, still writing. The old mariner smiled to himself, pleased that the young reporter had found him interesting. He wrapped his old, tattered scarf tightly around his neck, the one with the blue crescent moon at the tip, and braced himself for the cold.

Separating Fact from Fiction

This book is a composite of both fact and fiction. Because we have been left with only a thin historical record, the author has taken artistic license to 'fill-in-the-gaps,' to romanticize true events to both entertain and educate.

So what do we really know about Benjamin Franklin's audacious Irish mariners? Well, precious little (Franklin's letters, reproduced in a number of books, offer some color and for pure history there is William Bell Clark's excellent book *Ben Franklin's Privateers* (Baton Rouge: Louisiana State University Press, 1956)).

Ryan and his officers, Macatter, Weldin and Dowlin, together with Ryan's original crew of smugglers (his *Shadowmen*), were all real people.

Captain Luke Ryan (February 14, 1750? - June 18, 1789?)
Hibernian Magazine, May 1782

The O'Keeffes are fictional characters, although certainly Ryan must have had both good business contacts, and good political connections, in Ireland and France. In France, his connection was a real Flemish businessman named John Torris. David Sartine is a fictional but the Count Antoine de Sartine was real enough. And Philip Stephens was indeed the First Secretary of the Admiralty and, of course, we all know something about the great Doctor Benjamin Franklin.

Sartine served as the King's Minister of Marine from 1774 to 1780 (prior to this he was Lieutenant General of Police of Paris and had control of France's internationally respected secret police) and commissioned several of France's own privateers (Sartine launched one of his ships, *Le Cerf*, in the evening of March 7, 1779, entrusting command to one of his protégés, Ensign Varages, who had a short and uneventful history). To Sartine and Stephens (and others) I have ascribed (or embellished on) certain uncharitable characteristics for fun for which there is little evidence or is fiction (though as events unfold in the second book, *Prince of the Atlantic* (shamelessly promotes the author), Ryan there is evidence to support that Ryan may have been betrayed by the French which, presumably, would have been approved by Sartine or by his successor in 1780, Charles Eugène Gabriel de La Croix de Castries). There was no intent to disparage the memory of either Sartine or Castries or anyone else.

And Count Charles Gravier de Vergennes was indeed France's gifted Secretary of State for Foreign Affairs at Versailles during the war. An interesting exchange of letters from Sartine, Vergennes and Franklin, regarding American privateers, are reproduced below.

Antoine de Sartine (painted after his retirement in 1787)
Artist: Joseph Boze (1746 - 1827)

Ryan never served aboard the *Rose*. In fact, there is no evidence Ryan ever served in the British Navy at all.

But Ryan's phenomenal successes against the British navy, successes as we shall learn about in more detail later, cannot be easily explained without the benefit of some sort of formal military training. At Ryan's piracy trial in 1782 (covered in *Napoleon's Gold*), the king's prosecutor introduced evidence that Ryan, as a young boy, had been employed first as a stable hand in Hackettstown in 1760 and then as an apprentice two years later to a man named John Grimes, a shipwright of Skerries. Then, in 1766, again according to the king's prosecutor, Ryan was indentured to an Edward King as a ship's carpenter at King's boatyard in Ringsend until Ryan turned to smuggling. This evidence may or may not have been true, but it hardly explains Ryan's extraordinary gifts as a brilliant soldier and cunning mariner - uncommon gifts indeed for a common carpenter and thief.

Some say that Ryan did serve in the military, that he was lieutenant in the Irish Dillon Regiment (or Irish Brigade of France) before he turned to smuggling. But I suspect these folks have confused Luke Ryan with his father, Joseph Ryan, who did in fact serve as a lieutenant in the Dillon Regiment.

Old Mill and Forton were the two major naval prisons in England during the war and the conditions at both facilities for the Americans were horrendous (for a pure historical account of these two prisons, you might try Sheldon Samuel Cohen's excellent book: *Yankee Prisoners in British Gaols: Prisoners of War at Forton and Mill, 1777 - 1783* (University of Delaware Press 1995)). As for the characters described at Old Mill, Cowdry and Conyngham were real people, the rest are fictional persons invented by the author to represent true historical events.

Except for *Le Toulon*, all other vessels described in this book were real, including the *Rose*, although Captain Hughes is a fictional character and, again, neither Ryan nor his men served aboard her. As the *Toulon* is fictional, the engagement between the *Rose* and *Toulon* is, of course, fictional too.

We have detailed pictures and descriptions, and in some cases complete reproductions, of many of these wonderful ships. The *Rose*, for example, was built in Hull, England in 1757 (the ship used to film the movie *Master & Commander* is a reproduction of the *Rose*). She was a Seaford class frigate with the following specifications: 179' overall length, 135' deck length, 13' draft; 500-ton weight, and 13,000 square feet of sail area.

Naval ships were divided by "rates" back then, a first rate being the largest of these vessels, carrying 100 to 110 guns on three separate gun decks. The *Rose* was a sixth rate ship, the smallest class of ship that would have been commanded by someone holding the rank of captain. She was the modern day equivalent of a destroyer and would not have participated in major fleet engagements except perhaps to relay messages. The primary job of the frigate was to operate as a scout for the fleet or to patrol the waters of belligerent countries. That is primarily what the *Rose* did during the American Revolution. The *Rose* was built for the Seven Years War (or the French & Indian War) when Americans were still happily subjects of Great Britain (including one George Washington who served as a colonel in the British Army during that war).

During the course of that war, the *Rose* fought along the coast of France and in the Caribbean. In 1768, she was sent to America where things were beginning to heat up due to the imposition of new British taxes that were intended to recover some of the costs of defending North America during the recently concluded war with France. She patrolled the Northeast coast of America, her crew impressing or conscripting sailors from American merchant vessels whenever the opportunity arose and they sought out provisions for the British garrison at Boston.

In 1774, the *Rose*, under the command of James Wallace, was dispatched to Narragansett Bay in Rhode Island to put an end to the lucrative smuggling trade there that had made Newport the fourth wealthiest city in America. Rhode Island enjoyed a very liberal charter of self-government dating back to the time of King Charles, a charter so liberal that Rhode Island was the only colony permitted to appoint its own customs agents. The combination of this lax customs arrangement and the natural protection of Narragansett Bay allowed Rhode Island merchants to broker the best trade deals in the Colonies. Even during the French & Indian War, products from the French West Indies flowed freely through Newport.

Since the *Rose* was much larger than any American vessel of the time, and with the extraordinarily competent Wallace in command (the Rhode Islanders considered him to be a brutal pirate), Rhode Island's robust smuggling trade nearly evaporated. This so decimated the economy of Newport that four-fifths of the population fled inland. Rhode Island's powerful merchants petitioned their colonial legislature (which had relocated from Newport to Providence) to create a navy to deal with Wallace and backed up their petitions with money to refit a merchant vessel, the square tops'l sloop *Katy*, for naval service. The *Katy* was armed and recommissioned the *Providence*. A young rising star named John Paul Jones was given command, his first, of Rhode Island's new sloop-of-war, and Rhode Island then declared its independence from Great Britain on May 4, 1776 - two months before the rest of the Colonies. Rhode Islanders later also petitioned Congress to build a Continental Navy to rid Narragansett Bay of the *Rose*.

In July of 1776, the *Rose* played a significant part in the British invasion of New York, shelling the land-based fortification and making forays far up the Hudson. Wallace was later knighted for his actions in helping to drive Washington and his troops from the city. *Rose* finally met her end in 1779 in Savannah, Georgia. The British had occupied the city and the French, who were now fighting on the side of the Americans, sent a fleet up the Savannah River to attack the British from the riverfront while Americans, aided by Poles and other allies, continued an assault from land. The British scuttled the *Rose* in a narrow part of the channel, effectively blocking it, and the French fleet was unable to reach Savannah. The city remained in British hands until the end of the war. After the war, the *Rose* was destroyed to clear the channel and today only a few artifacts from her remain.

Captain Gustavus Conyngham, the "Dunkirk Pirate," was in command of the *Revenge* when he was captured by the British frigate

Galatea on April 27, 1779 off the coast of New York. *Revenge*, a cutter similar to the *Black Prince*, had a complement of 106 officers and men and carried 14 six pounders and 22 swivels.

Revenge in action in the English Channel
(Painting commissioned by the U.S. Department of the Navy)
Artist: John P. Benson (1865 - 1947)

Conyngham's other command, the *Greyhound*, has been described several ways. We have two letters that simply described her as a cutter painted in black and yellow. But the following detail in a third letter gives us a little more insight:

> *"[She was] 150 Tons, clinker built, Tarred Sides and black bottom, one yellow moulding all along the Gunnel, nine ports on a side, and a row port between each, Stanchions on the top of the Gunnel all round, supposed to be for supporting a Network, Stern with a round Tafferail painted black and yellow mouldings at the main boom is a driver boom... at the bow-sprit end is an Iron for a flying-Jib-boom occasionally A very lofty Top-Mast with a Royal Mast; the top Mast irons in the fore part of the Mast... small mizzen Mast which ships in the quarter occasionally... [and carried] 14-4 pounders."*

(Excerpt taken from a two part article by David Engen: *The Appearance of the Eighteenth Century Ship* in the Nautical Research Journal, Vol. 37 No.

3, pages 161-168, and Vol. 37 No. 4, pages 222-231, 1992)

We know that Captain Lambert Wickes's brig *Reprisal* was built in Philadelphia. Her "Stern [was] Painted Black & Yellow, the Mouldings upon her Quarters painted White, a Black side [with] No Quarter Galleries" and she had "brightsides." Mounted on *Reprisal's* prow was the figurehead of a woman. Her armament included 18 nine-pounders (the aftermost main deck gun being "as far forward as the after part of the Main Chains"), swivels mounted on her quarters and forecastle and, in her tops, she carried eight coehorns (a small howitzer of about 4 2/3 inches in caliber, named after the Baron van Coe'horn of Holland).

After delivering Franklin safely to St. Nazaire, Captain Wickes headed out for the Irish Sea and *Reprisal* became one of the first American raiders to operate in European waters. During a return voyage to France, *Reprisal* encountered a British 74-gun warship in the Bay of Biscay and her crew was only able to outrun the battle cruiser by jettisoning all their guns overboard to lighten their ship. In 1778, *Reprisal* foundered in a gale off Newfoundland in the Grand Banks and, except for the cook, went down with all hands. About Wickes, Franklin wrote, "He was a gallant officer, and a very worthy man."

Reprisal's men raised black and white striped colors to declare themselves American privateers but, for reasons perhaps lost to antiquity, many American privateers flew black and yellow striped colors.

Although in mid-1779, where the beginning of our story ends, France and the fledgling United States of America were allies, it was not always a harmonious relationship. American privateering in European waters in particular was a source of constant irritation, if not outright strain at times, between the two countries. Even before Ryan and his men fled Ireland for France to join the American cause as privateers in the spring of 1779, the French Court was trying to rein in what it perceived to be American lawlessness on the high seas.

The following letter, dated May 15, 1778, from Count de Vergennes to Benjamin Franklin, Arthur Lee and John Adams (the three American Commissioners), expressing his displeasure over the "reprehensible" conduct of the American privateer *John Warren*, provides a glimpse of this discord:

> "*I have the honour, Gentlemen, to send you the Copy of a Letter, written to Mr. De Sartine, by the Consul of France at Madeira. You will see, in it, all the Circumstances of the Conduct, which an American Privateer, named John Warren has held, towards a French Snow or Brigantine, Captain Rochell, which he seized, near enough to the Land and in Sight of the City of Madeira. Procedures so reprehensible, cannot remain unpunished, and I doubt not Gentlemen, that you will make to Congress such representations, as will produce the most efficacious measures, not only that the Captain John Warren may receive the punishment his conduct merits but also to procure for the French Vessell, the Satisfaction and indemnification which are due to her. I rely, in this respect, on the Necessity, of which you must undoubtedly be convinced, of restraining such Excesses, the Consequences of which will not be less felt by the Congress, than they are by Us.*
> *I have the honour to be, most perfectly, Gentlemen your most humble and most obedient Servant*
> *De Vergennes*
> *Messrs. les Deputes des Etats Unis*"

Vergennes enclosed the following letter, from Mr. De La Ruilliere,

Consul at Madeira and dated February 15, 1778 to Mr. De Sartine, with his letter:

> "*I have the honour to inform you, that on the fourth of this month, a French Snow or Brigantine, which is believed to be the Prudent Captain Rochell of about one hundred and fifty tons, coming from London with a Cargo of Commodities, and some flour, for this Island, was met, visited and captured, near enough to the Land and in Sight of this City by an American Privateer, which is said to be from Boston and is named the Lyon Captain John Warren, and finally sent to Boston, under the protest that the Cargo belonged to Englishmen. The Circumstances which accompanied this Capture, render the Action of this Cruiser not only extremely blameable but they characterize him rather as a Pirate, than as a Privateer authorized by any Government. Following the directions of a Portuguese Fisherman, whom the said Vessell had taken for a guide to conduct her into the Road, the Privateer entered into this Vessell as into a Prize, taking immediate possession, and even ill treating the People, and after having transported them by violence on board the Privateer, taken and kept all the Papers, which could prove to whom the Vessell belonged, and of what Nation he was, she put on board an American Crew with whom she sent her to America, naturally in the Intention of selling there, the Cargo, and perhaps the Vessell, with the Ventures of the French Captain and Seamen, and all that might belong to Merchants of Neutral Nations, with the Insurgents in some of our American Islands, where the said Cargo of Commodities, ou bien de Pipes en bote, would sell to great Advantage whereas they would be of very little Value, if sold in the English Colonies of the Insurgents, which abound in such Merchandizes. I have made haste, my Lord to inform you of*

this fact, persuaded, that after having reflected upon its importance, you will condescend to take all the measures necessary, to obtain restitution of so irregular a Capture, to cause the Captain of the Privateer to be punished for his Crime, and to prevent in future all similar Outrages, so prejudicial to our navigation and commerce, and so inconsistent with the Safety, and the respect, which all nations preserve, for our flagg, in the present Circumstances."

Franklin forwarded Vergennes's complaint on to the President of Congress with this cover letter, dated May 19, 1778:

"Sir

"We have the Honor to inclose a Copy of a Letter received from Monsieur the Count De Vergennes, the Secretary of State for foreign Affairs, with a Copy of a Letter inclosed in it, for the Consideration of Congress, not doubting that Congress will give it all the Attention, that an Affair of so much importance demands.

We have the Honor to be &c.

B. Franklin, Arthur Lee, John Adams."

And finally, here is Franklin's response to Vergennes:

"Sir

We have had the Honor of your Excellencys Letter of the fifteenth instant, inclosing a Copy of a Letter from Mr. De La Rouilliere, Consul at Madeira of the 15th. of March 1778.

We have inclosed to Congress a Copy of your Excellencys Letter with a Copy of its Inclosures, and have recommended to Congress, the earliest attention to the Subject, and have no doubt that justice will be speedily done.

We have the Honor to be &c.

B. Franklin, Arthur Lee, John Adams."

From this exchange of correspondence, it would appear that Franklin was able to retain his diplomatic composure. After all, the captain of the *John Warren* was not the only one being chastised by Vergennes, of being accused of committing a crime, as it was Franklin, as Vergennes well knew, who was ultimately responsible for American ships operating in and out of French ports. Nevertheless, Franklin, as we shall soon learn in *Prince of the Atlantic*, would, unfazed by French concerns, continue his quiet search for dependable privateers. And so it would seem that Franklin's letter to Vergennes was little more than polite lip service.

Franklin remained steadfast in his determination to do everything in his power to save as many of his fellow Americans, his fellow patriots, from the horrors of the British prison camps - but he needed leverage, he needed his own prisoners to bargain with and, to get prisoners, he needed ships and men willing to set out against a Goliath. And so the stage is set for Luke Ryan, and his band of renegade Irishmen, to make a bit of history - and embrace the chance they would, most eagerly.